MW01273220

The Hidden World
Of
Terrafirma

Book Three

Insight

Author
Tina M Engel

Book Cover Artist
Sarah Bangs

Paperback book
ISBN 13: 978-1718131453
BISAC: Fiction / Fantasy / General

Amazon Kindle Direct Publishing

Dedication

I want to give thanks and so much more to my mom, for without her love, support and devotion to my family and community, this book would never have happened.

You are a very special woman, Kay Leslie Engel and have given so much of yourself to so many young people as they struggled to find themselves, in a world that constantly changes. Your nonjudgmental attitude as well as your ability to listen and understand others thoughts, feelings and beliefs, instilled in me the understanding and acceptance of all people and to respect their beliefs. Your faith in me, gave me the strength to face and conquer the challenges that have created, the me of today. I strive every day to be as good a woman, mother, daughter and friend that you have been.

I love you mom!

Tina M. Engel

The wind blows

Leaves fall

The waters flow

The end is never the end.

The sun rises

The earth turns

The sun sets

The end is never the end.

There is always death

The stars shine

There is always life.

The end is never the end.

Justin Stroup

Tina M. Engel

Table of contents

Tina M. Engel

Tina M. Engel

Prologue

Have you ever wondered what was out there, just beyond your sight? You can see it but just not quite. You see a movement just out of the corner of your eye, but when you turn to look, it's gone.

I was back in the wheat field, all golden, with the sun shining brightly. The tree stood tall, as the leaves rustled gently in the breeze. The ocean waves crashed against the cliffs, greeting me in a rambunctious manner.

"Think Emilee." I said softly. "Why are you here again?"

I went to the edge of the cliff, looked out towards the ocean so wide, and a dark presence seemed to hover over the horizon, grey, eerie clouds pushed into the blue of the sky, trying so desperately to reach me.

I sat on a large boulder and recalled the past months. I was home, in Pineville Washington, a quaint town on the East side of the Cascade Mountain Range. I lived in a small house, worked in a small grocery store and lived a low key, unexciting life, but it was okay with me. After getting my heart broken, it was better to play it safe and simple, and boring was the safest way to exist.

It was too good to last though, slow and boring, that can only last for so long before your destiny finds you again. Funny thing, you don't know how strong you are, until you're faced with challenges you never knew existed.

It started with faces in the trees, dreams of water, noises in the bathroom sink, (Yes, really), and then a tree fey tried to abduct me. I didn't know however, at the time, that fey even existed, and it wasn't long before my beautiful boring life was turned upside down, and I was thrown into a world that I thought only existed in books.

Fey; beings that live in a dimension on this planet, that I called home, they called Terrafirma. Yes, they exist and I am one of them. A fey princess to be exact, but a princess from where, the water, land or sky?

It was Brett McNight, the one who saved me from what I thought was a tree fey. The fey turned out to be Brett's brother, Stephan DeMill, who was the one who broke my heart so long ago.

Brett took me on an adventure against my will, I might add, through the underworld where I met many different types of fey.

Kimberlite, was a lava rock fey (best friends with Brett) large, and strong but his looks could frighten the toughest person or fey. He was really just a teddy bear, kind and gentle, but when it came to me and my protection, he would do anything, even die for me, I believed.

Queen Anahita; a water fey, was the queen over the hidden springs in the Northern and Southern Americas as humans would call it. She had some kind of relationship with Brett a long time ago and still had feelings for him but didn't keep them hidden very well.

Douglas; a tree fey elder was a mentor to Brett. He and Brett had a very special relationship, almost like a grandfather and grandson bond even though they weren't related that way. Douglas knew things and helped guide us when he could. He was never far away.

Eagle; (another friend of Brett's) is a shifter, who can turn into an eagle that humans see, or his fey self, still resembling an eagle but with human parts.

Tobias and Tilly were the elders of a troll clan, a large family and they welcomed me with open arms. Their home was deep within the mountains.

I met Captain Adam Banks and his partner Jordan Davis on a fishing boat on Lake Erie as we traveled eastward, as we continued this very strange adventure. I discovered an incredible world under the waters, fought a mega octopus and escaped Stephan once more. I learned that Jordan Davis, who had a negative energy surrounding him, was connected to me in a way I would never have believed.

And of course, I can't forget Rose and Lily, two very special fey. The bond I had with them, I believed was unbreakable. Rose was a pixie, the one who gave me part of what I needed to survive, her blood. No, I was not a vampire, but exactly what kind of fey I am, was yet to be determined.

Lily, a cat, was a shape shifter like Eagle. She could change into a domesticated cat as humans see them, and her cat fey shape. She was a moody, trouble making fey but I think it was just an act, covering up who she really was and why she was with me.

There was also Ragnar and Eliza; members of a goblin clan who helped us, and Queen Widow, (a very large black widow spider) and her family, many hundreds of her babies.

There were many others who helped along the way, and I considered them family and missed them so. They all came together to protect me.

Proteus, I was told in the beginning of this journey, was my father. He lived and ruled in the Atlantic Ocean, the City of Bermuda. I was thought to be in danger after I was born, so Proteus had me hidden as a human, but the Dark One found where I was hidden, and Proteus wanted me back with him. He was not my father, I learned, but he played a part in this crazy adventure I was on and I had to learn what it was, to continue.

Kimberlite, Queen Anahita and Douglas all gave me special gifts. These gifts all had the power to help keep me safe.

Kimberlite's gift was a diamond necklace, filled with baby lava pebbles who kept me company, allowing me to handle heat and kept me connected to Kimberlite when he wasn't with me.

Queen Anahita's gift was pearl earrings. When put into my ears, they attached themselves to my cheeks and neck, forming a shells of sorts. It was a rainbow color, like the inside of an abalone shell, that became a shield that surrounds me for protection, if need be.

Douglas gave me a barrette that turned into a very sharp dagger, which attached to my hand when I released the barrette from my hair in a certain way. It had taken time to learn how to use these gifts but as time went on I got better with them.

Brett...as I sat starring out at the ocean, the greyness coming closer, the breeze changing to a wind, cold and icy, Brett was in my mind. We were connected in a way that was comforting and scary at the same time. I loved this fey, and I knew he loved me, but he kept a barrier up most of the time. I could break through once in a while, but then he put it up again.

Why was I here in this place again, my dream world or vision? I thought it might be both. As I remember back to when this adventure or nightmare started, I found myself here, remembering everything but ...my mother. We were trying to get to my mother. We were on a ship, my mother was there, she saw Jordan and ...

Brett was in my mind again. "Come back Emilee, Come back to us."

Tina M. Engel

Chapter one

When the past is revealed,
Then the present
Makes sense.

When I opened my eyes, there was Brett, the only face I saw, with a look of concern and relief. I felt his hand holding mine and as he ran his other hand across my cheek, brushing a strand of hair from my face and tucking it gently behind my ear, that warm safe vibration I felt when he touched me sent a shiver down my spine and a hunger again. I couldn't understand...a hunger for what?

The room I was in became clear and as I looked around I saw all the worried faces, and as I came to my mother's face, I remembered. The ship, we had been on the ship. I met my mother, and she and Jordan knew each other. Jordan had called her Lena.

As I started to sit, Brett said, "Take it slow Emilee." He helped me to sit and then stand, never letting go of my hand.

My mother, Angelina, took my other hand and they led me over to a couch. As I sat down, I looked at my mother's face. She was looking up, and I followed her gaze. She was looking at Jordan and he had a look of confusion mixed with worry in his eyes.

The room was quiet, no one spoke, not knowing what to say. As Jordan and Angelina gazed at each other, they were speechless for a moment.

"You died, they told me you died." Jordan said, softly.

Angelina let go of my hand and went up to him, touched his cheek softly as if afraid he would disintegrate if touched too hard, and said, "It was as if I had."

Her smile was sweet and eyes full of sadness as she removed her hand and walked back over to me, sat down and took my hand again. The silence in the room was painful as we waited for someone to speak.

Angelina looked towards the porthole as if looking at something far, far away, and then spoke. "I was told, after they finally healed me, certain I would live, I was placed in a deep sleep, deep in the darkest depths of the castle. I slept in a trance-like state, for years.

"When I was awakened, they told me I was with child and the baby within me slept too, not growing, but was alive and well.

"I was brought up into the castle but in a part that no one entered, and only two elders knew I was even alive. I was given food and clothing and was told to rest for the night and all would be revealed as to my future soon."

Angelina looked towards Douglas as she commented on the two elders who knew she was alive. I assumed with the tilt of Douglas's head, that he was one of them.

Angelina continued, "I woke in the night to a woman standing next to me, a beautiful woman, whom I felt I should know but couldn't remember. It was time to leave. She gave me specific directions on where I was to go, and said someone would meet me there.

"I got out of bed, and as I turned to look in her direction, she was gone. There were clothes at the end of my bed and I dressed quickly. There was a knock at the door and as I opened it, there stood one of the elders who had brought me here." Angelina said, as she looked towards Douglas again.

She then continued. "He guided me out of the castle, to an area I had never seen before. I was on my own then in the dark night, with only the stars to light my way.

"I was heading to the sea, walking a path through a forested area, barely a path beneath my feet. As I approached the sandy beach, I wondered where I was to meet this person and when. I walked to the water's edge, just far enough away that when the waves crashed on shore, they would leave me be.

"There at the edge of the sea was a water fey and he informed me that he was here to help. He handed me a necklace and told me it would hide my appearance. He was going to take me somewhere, to live a different life, where my child would be safe. I didn't know what else to do and had no idea exactly what he meant. I felt that he was truthful and I could trust him.

"I put on the necklace and before I knew it I was a water fey. I understood as long as I had the necklace on, I would remain in this form.

"As we swam to the great city of Bermuda where Proteus ruled, this water fey shared with me a story, the story of my new life. I was his daughter who had lived in a small village throughout my childhood, but on my 18ᵗʰ birthday, it was time to come home, wed and have a family."

Angelina turned to me then and continued, "When you were born, the woman came to me again and told me you were in danger and that I had to convince Proteus to send you away somewhere safe.

"He was against it, at first, but with my persistence I convinced him to share my concerns with his land allies. They seemed to agree and convinced Proteus that the safest place to hide you was with the humans, and they changed your body, as much as they could, to resemble a human.

"I didn't understand why I was brought here only to lose you but I trusted this woman, I felt that I knew her somehow. I was told to stay with Proteus, continue to play the role I was to play and one day I would be reunited with you.

"The woman came to me several times in dreams, when I was most frantic to be with you. She reassured me that you were fine and I needed to play out this role, to continue to keep you safe as well as myself.

"I was also given a task, to find something that would be important to us all in the future. As I waited until the day I would see you again, I searched and found it, just before you were to come home.

"When I was told that you were being brought back home, I was so happy, until rumors of you not being a total water fey started spreading. Rumors of me not being a pure water fey was causing turmoil and Proteus was starting to doubt me.

Tina M. Engel

"Proteus came to me, asking again if I was a true water fey and was I being honest with him. He touched my necklace and asked about it. Why had I never taken it off, all the years that we had been wed, even though he had given me more beautiful jewelry? When he touched it, Proteus saw the real me for a moment.

"Proteus knew then, that something was not right and told me not to leave my room, as he closed and locked the door behind him. I was frightened and didn't know what to do.

"That night, again in my dreams, the woman came and showed me the way out. Upon waking, I realized I had to do what she said, and going to the door, I saw that it was unlocked. I left the palace, following her instructions, and there at the entrance to the palace grounds, was the fey who had pretended to be my father years earlier.

"He told me he was here to take me someplace safe. I ended up here on Captain Adam's ship, waiting, not knowing why I was here at first.

"The woman came to me the first night I was here and told me I would be meeting my daughter again and all would be revealed soon, as to why you were sent away and who we were protecting you from.

"I had no idea that Jordan was alive. I was told he was dead and I had no reason not to believe it."

Angelina looked at Jordan then with such sadness in her eyes as she said softly, "I didn't know."

Jordan came over to the couch, and kneeling down in front of us, took my hand from Brett, (Brett didn't seem willing to let go, I might add), and looked at me with such affection and said, "My daughter."

I looked from Angelina to Jordan, my true mother and father. Tears of joy and loss, staining their cheeks. Joy of finding me and each other and the loss of the years we could have been together as a family.

I took both their hands and placed his on hers with my hands surrounding them. I had started to cry also and all of our tears were falling onto our joined hands, mixing together. My hand on the top, onto which the tears were landing was tingling just a bit. I looked down and saw a strange discoloration start to appear on the back of my hand.

I looked up to see Jordan looking down with a curious expression on his face and a slight grin. Angelina let out a soft gasp as she removed her hand from between mine as Jordan took both my hands in his.

We watch the backs of both my hands take on the appearance of the shield on my cheeks, a rainbow effect. I touched the back of one hand and it felt like scales. Tiny circular ridges framed the area, covering the backs of my hands.

Brett pushed Jordan's hands away, taking my hands in his, and said in a protective and urgent voice, "Let her go, you're both hurting her!"

Jordan stood and grabbed hold of Brett's shirt, lifting him up off the couch and turned him away from me. This action forced Brett's hands from mine, and it sent a shockwave through my body.

Angelina put her arm around my shoulders leaning me into her chest as I saw Brett remove his knife from his pocket. Just as Brett was about to swing the knife in Jordan's direction, Lily appeared in the doorway.

"Calm down, everyone!" Lily shouted.

Until that moment, the entire room was filled with chaos, and then all was silent except for the sound of the waves outside, hitting the sides of the ship and sea gulls singing a song that only I could understand, telling each other where food was and who they wanted to share it with.

Lily entered the room, and as she walked towards me she said in her matter of fact way, "Jordan, let him go, and Brett put that knife away. We don't need any more liquids flowing right now. There is enough going on at the moment."

I found that comment a bit perplexing but was glad to see the angry look in Brett and Jordan's eyes lessen as Jordan let go of Brett and Brett put the knife away. They both still had overly protective looks on their faces as they tried to stare each other down.

As Lily knelt down in front of me, she waved her hand in their direction and said, "Enough, both of you! Emily needs both of you, so get over yourselves."

Well, this made Rose giggle and as Lily looked at me, she had a small smirk on her face. Brett and Jordan looked embarrassed, but then Jordan put his hand on Brett's back in a gesture of apology and the air around them calmed.

Tina M. Engel

Lily took my hands in hers and she suddenly seemed to have a strange glow about her as she said, "This is the next step, Emilee. Don't be afraid. Tears of love from the ones who made you will start the next phase of your transformation.

"Remember, you are more than one type of fey, you are many, and they all must develop at their own speed when the conditions are right."

I looked down at my hands and as the discoloration disappeared, the tingling continued to spread as it reached my shoulders and then to my back. As my back started to spasm, I felt a panic inside and I stood uncontrollably, pushing Lily back.

Lily caught herself before hitting the floor, chuckled softly and stood, taking my hands in hers again, she said, "Don't fight it Princess. Let it take control. It wants to be a part of you, it is a part of you, awakening, after all these years."

Lily then said in her matter of fact way, "It would be nice to be shown to our rooms. I am assuming this is where we will be staying for a while. Princess Emilee needs a quiet place to let this part of her transformation complete itself. Rose and Angelina, please join us. The rest of you go find something to do."

At that, Lily, still holding my hand, headed towards the door. She looked at Adam and held out her hand towards the door, insinuating he lead the way to our cabin.

Brett said, "Emilee?", as if not sure what to do.

I turned to him and with a smile of acceptance and reassured him that it was alright and that I was okay. I turned back towards the door, and as Lily led me out, Rose and my mother followed.

We were led down another set of stairs, down a short hallway and into a room. It was a simple room with two beds and when Angelina entered, Lily asked her to shut the door, leaving Adam outside.

Rose giggled again and Lily turned to her, with a slight smile, but then said with that cat attitude, "Rose, she needs you now."

Rose, with a look of pride, knew what Lily meant. Lily pointed to the bed and Rose obeyed without giving any attitude. This was definitely a different role we were all playing.

As Lily gave orders she continued to shimmer and I could see something behind the shimmer. She was veiled, but why? She was covering herself and I could almost see through this shimmer, but then it stopped. The shimmering glow, which had been surrounding her was gone, and it was just the Lily I knew and loved.

She was still, however, bossy and told Angelina to help get my shirt off so my back could be free. Now I thought this instruction, a very strange one, but Rose gave me her wrist and Lily instructed me to eat, so I said nothing and ate.

As I drank from Rose, the irony taste soothed my nerves. Suddenly, an intense pain in my upper back just over my shoulder blades, caused a shock wave that vibrated throughout my entire body. As I removed Rose's wrist from my mouth, I dragged my fangs across her skin creating a large gash.

Rose let out a yell and grasped the open wound with her other hand.

I stood then as something started to protrude from my back. There was a mirror on the wall across from where I stood and I watched as something spread up and out. Wings! I had wings. The same color that had appeared on my hands earlier, a rainbow shimmery color.

"Your father's side of the family." Was all that Lily said as she got up and headed to the door. As she opened it to leave she said, "It would be a good thing Princess, if you would heal Rose before she makes a mess on the floor, and Angelina, please insist that the princess rests. She can practice with her new additions later." And she left the room, shutting the door behind her.

I looked at Rose then, and the expression on her face wasn't that of fear but excitement as she looked at my wings.

"Princess, you have wings! We can fly together now. I can teach you!" Was all she could seem to spit out as she held her wrist out for me to heal.

I wrapped her wrist in my hands and after a few minutes I removed them; her wrist was healed, with just a fine, pink line, where I had cut her.

I went closer to the mirror and Angelina followed, standing next to me. "They are beautiful." She said as she touched them gently.

I could feel her touch. These wings were a part of me. They were beautiful and as I turned to take a better look at my back, my wings hit a lamp and knocked it to the floor. We all laughed an uncomfortable laugh and my mother suggested I put them away for the time being.

I looked at her with confusion, not sure how, but then just thinking about it, they seemed to disappear into my back, leaving two lines where they entered.

She smiled as she led me to a bed. I was so tired. As I laid down, Angelina told me to rest and that she and Rose would be here when I woke.

My thoughts were racing though. How could I sleep? What had just happened and who is Lily, really? I opened my mouth to speak but all that came out was, "Lily?"

My mother put a finger to my lips and said, "Sleep. All will be revealed when it is time."

Chapter two

Remember,
Your destiny is yours,
And yours alone.
Others have their destiny,
And it is just as real,
And challenging as yours.

He was standing there in front of a grand throne, arms crossed over his bare chest. His glare was intense but there was affection in his blue eyes; a light, shimmering blue. It was him, Proteus. The one I thought was my father and he believed it too, but did he still? How did I know this was Proteus? I had never seen him before, but I knew, somehow, I knew.

As I looked around the grand room I was in, I was in awe of the beauty that I saw. There were large tapestries, pictures of beautiful water fey, great battles, and places I had never seen before; on land and beneath the waters.

I found it odd, though, I was sure we were in the underwater palace, but the room had no water. All was dry and we were breathing air. Proteus had legs, not a fish tail, like the other water fey that I had seen in Andean's lake. So this was his true fey form. Was he able to walk on dry land I wondered?

It was just he and I in the room, and I wondered where everyone else was and why I was here. I knew I was in my dream world again but I was sure that I would be here in this real place, in the near future.

Tina M. Engel

We stood staring at each other and I was starting to feel uneasy and childlike, (not a feeling I was wanting to show).

He put his arms down at his sides then and his expression changed to relief and pleasure, as he descended the steps that separated his throne from the rest of the room. His arms reached out and as he approached me, he took me in his arms in a loving embrace.

I wrapped my arms around him also in an uncomfortable fashion, knowing that I should be hiding my displeasure about being here, better than I was.

When he released me, Proteus took my hand and led me over to a bench, where we sat. Again I looked around, confused regarding the dry room and his appearance.

Proteus reached out and softly touched my cheeks, touched the shell that would create a shield around me if need be. His smile was genuine, he knew what it was, who gave it to me and was proud and almost in awe, that this gift was given to me.

He said then, "Not many receive this gift. It is special and they must believe you are special too. The longer they kept you from me, the more I realized that you were truly the one and I knew you would come back to me on your own."

Proteus then put his hand on my back in a fatherly manner and I was ready for his reaction but it was not the reaction I was expecting. He touched the area where the wings had been and would protrude again when the time was right.

Proteus smiled then, a smile of pleasure as he stood and stepped away from me. I expected

Tina M. Engel

shock or confusion but it was as if he was aware of my wings.

I stood up then as my wings were released, large, shimmery and colorful. I wasn't afraid, I felt strong and confident.

"I came here of my own free will, not to stand beside you as my father, you are not my father, but to find out what this place has to do with me and what part you are to play in discovering my true self, and where I belong." I said, assertively.

His eyes turned red as his shape started to change, and the room filled with sea water. As Proteus's legs transformed into a large fish tail, like all the water fey I had met, I became the fey that I was in Andean's great lake, with one exception, my wings were still outstretched. I understood then, why they were covered in tiny scales, not feathers.

Proteus smiled eerily then, as he said, "You are the one. He told me you were but I was skeptical until now. She should have protected you better. I know now, seeing your wings, you are not my daughter but you will stand beside me."

I opened my eyes to a room, the cabin that I had been in with my mother and Rose, on the ship. As I looked around the room, sitting on the other bed was Rose, tending to her arm, the arm I practically bit off earlier in the day. (Okay, exaggerating a bit!) Standing next to a porthole looking out was my mother, Angelina, seemingly lost in thought.

I sat up, and the rustling of the blanket beneath me brought her back to this place and

Tina M. Engel

Angelina turned around. She smiled a loving smile as she came to stand next to my bed.

Rose on the other hand, jumped off of the bed she was sitting on, and landed on my bed next to me with a thump. The mattress was a bit springier than she realized and I bounced, almost falling off the bed. Angelina was there to stop me from falling and she gave Rose a look of displeasure.

Angelina asked me, "How are you feeling after your nap? I heard you talking in your sleep on and off and mentioned Proteus several times." She had a grave look on her face, as she held her body tight with nerves.

I had so many questions, but suspected my mother wasn't the one who had the answers, she probably had just as many questions as I. We had both been living a lie and I felt strongly, that now was the time for answers for both of us. I was to meet this fey, Proteus, but he was powerful and I needed to know as much as I could before I faced him.

I shared with Angelina and Rose my dream, or vision more likely, and Angelina had a look of sorrow and embarrassment when I was done. I knew she had played a role that was difficult for her, to say the least, and the pain and fear she experienced during the time that I was portraying a human, not knowing the truth, must have been unbearable at times.

I leaned forward and as I wrapped my arms around Angelina, I whispered in her ear, "We will find the answers together and I understand that you did what you had to, to protect us both."

Then I felt it, that vibration that was so calming for me. It was Brett, and then a knock came at the door. As it opened, there he stood with that loving smile and twinkle in his eyes as our eyes met.

My mother let me go as she turned to see who had come in, and as she looked from my face to Brett's, I could tell she disapproved. I felt hurt somehow, that my mother would feel this way.

Brett was there, in my mind again, of course, and his smile turned to a bewildered frown as his eyes fell on Angelina. "Is there a problem?" He asked, as he looked at her.

She realized that her thoughts were escaping through her looks and as Angelina stood, she said, "There are things that you don't understand and things I don't either, but tread lightly with your feelings, for they could cause your future decisions to be even more painful and difficult."

I remembered then, that she had special powers too, the sight of the future, even though they might be just fragments or pieces of what is to be.

She stood then, as Brett suggested we go to the mess hall to eat. Douglas was wanting us all together to discuss what was to happen next, now that we had been at sea for a few hours.

I reached out, taking Angelina's hand in mine to stop her from moving away from the bed. I had to ask a question and wanted to ask now before we were with Jordan.

"You're not water fey yet you portrayed one for years. You let me go, not knowing where I was, yet stayed with Proteus, pretending. You became his wife even though you knew I wasn't his child. What kind of fey are you? I know you can see into the future, bits and pieces, yet you didn't know that Jordan was alive?"

I wished I hadn't said anything, as that last question left my lips. The look of hurt on my mother's face was painful to see. She recovered quickly but not before the look of hurt turned to anger for just a moment.

Her expression softened then as she said, "I saw Jordan often, in my dreams, but I thought because I missed him so, that they were only that, dreams. I believed that my longing for him was so great that it wasn't a vision, couldn't be a vision, I couldn't hope and be crushed once more...my deep sadness caused the dreams...only dreams."

As Angelina said the last few words, a tear escaped from her eye, one tear. She wiped it away quickly, changed her expression from despair to determination and said quietly but firmly, "We do what we must to survive and I knew I must survive for you. I do not and will not regret anything that I have had to do and endure, to keep you safe."

She removed her hand from mine, turned and walked to the door where Brett still stood. She turned again and looking at me, said with a hardness in her voice, "Love, a silly emotion, can get in the way and blind you from what you were destined to do!"

At that, Angelina walked past Brett and disappeared into the hallway. I looked at Rose, still sitting next to me and her head was hanging down, eyes looking at her hands. I could see the uneasiness she was feeling, in her body language.

Tina M. Engel

Brett, still standing in the doorway, but eyes looking down the hall where my mother had just disappeared, said in a whisper without looking at me, "She may be right."

I couldn't believe what I just heard, did I hear him correctly? I wondered.

"What did you say, Brett?" I asked, as I got up off the bed and walked over to him.

Brett turned towards me then as I reached him and as I tried to search his mind, he shut me out, saying, "Nothing important. We need to see what it is Douglas wants to talk about.

"Your mother has been through a lot and is trying to grasp the knowledge that Jordan has been alive and suffering all these years and the fact that you are with her now.

"She has questions too. Her life has been as much a falsehood as yours has been, but even though it had to be this way, it wasn't easy for either of you. You however, didn't know until recently, but she lived through it."

Brett took my arm as Rose reached the doorway, and he gently nudged me in the direction down the hall, first letting Rose go ahead of us. As he shut the door he again said in a whisper, "She may be right."

As we walked down the hall I wondered again, what kind of fey was she, my mother?

Chapter Three

If you wait patiently,
It will all make sense.
But it is the waiting
Patiently part,
That is difficult.

As we entered the mess hall, the atmosphere was peaceful with quiet voices all around. Douglas was sitting at a table discussing something with Adam, Adam seeming to be intently listening as Douglas spoke.

Rose was over in a corner talking with a large man, whose back was to us, and as he turned around, I saw that it was the pixie who had been on Adam's fishing boat. The one that Rose was so smitten with back on Lake Erie. Rose gave me a slight thumbs up, as this pixie was turned my way and her smile was sweet.

Jordan was sitting at another smaller table with Angelina, holding her hand in his on the table top. They were deep in conversation, not realizing that we, Brett and I, had entered the room.

The doors to the kitchen swung open and out came Eagle carrying a tray of something and Trevor following behind carrying a pot of coffee. Trevor; my favorite leprechaun fey, short and stocky with tattoos everywhere, where I could see anyway, was Captain Adam Banks' cook and became a special friend when we were on the fishing boat, on Lake Erie.

When Trevor spotted me, he immediately put down the coffee and hurried over to me. Our embrace was that of affection and joy, I hadn't known if I would ever see him again. As we parted, he took my hand and did the traditional fey greeting, forehead to the back of my hand thing and then he gazed at the ring on my finger, the one he gave me before we parted ways in the past.

"Princess Emilee, the ring fits perfectly." He said, a glimmer of pride crossing his face. "Has it helped you on your travels?"

I shared with him briefly about the storm we were in, how Stephan DeMill tried desperately to get us and the injuries we sustained. I also shared how I believed the ring helped me to heal Brett's illness, after our bloods mixed from our injuries.

Douglas then cleared his throat rather loudly, letting us all know that he was ready for silence so he could speak. Douglas did have a way to get everyone's attention.

As we all gathered around Douglas, Angelina came over to where I was sitting. She sat down next to me and took my hand in hers, squeezing it slightly, and as I looked at her face she had a heartfelt smile. I was sure, it was to let me know, she was sorry for being so gruff earlier.

Brett was standing across from me, next to Eagle, and they were being a bit rowdy. Douglas gave them both a stern look, asked if they had something to share with the rest of us, and if not to please shut up. (Yes, he said, shut up). They both had looks of shame on their faces, as if getting in trouble by the teacher. I chuckled, Rose giggled and over in the doorway, a voice said, "Boys will be boys!"

Tina M. Engel

We all looked over to see Lily, meandering in like a cat who couldn't care less. Douglas stood up as if she were someone special and as soon as he did this, a look of uncertainty crossed his face, momentarily, and then it was gone. His authoritarian presence was back, and he sat down. I think I was the only one who caught this and Douglas gave me a look, as if to say, not now Emilee, and then he looked away.

Lily went over to a corner away from the rest of us and sat down on the floor. She turned into her domesticated cat form and proceeded to clean herself. She looked up at me once and I swear she winked and then went back to her bath.

Douglas took a sip of water and then said, "There are many here who have questions, lots of questions, and it is time for some to be answered. I will share with you all what I can at this time and then I expect everyone to let the rest be, for the time being."

I opened my mouth to speak but before I could say anything, Douglas put up his hand to stop me. I stood then, not wanting to be silenced. (I was tired of being treated like a child.)

"Go ahead Emilee." Was all Douglas said with a sigh, looking a bit weary. (I think I exhaust these fey, at times).

"You're an elder, a member of the council and have been for a long time, isn't that true?" I asked in a respectful tone.

"Yes, Princess Emilee, I am."

"Then you must have known all along who I am, and that Jordan was alive and who he is, and that Angelina is my mother, and you could have fixed all of this a long time ago, couldn't you?" (Yes, I was babbling again. Okay, I felt like a child).

Douglas got up from the table, glanced at Lily and then walked over to a porthole and gazed out. All was quiet, as we waited for him to speak. I looked over at Angelina and then Jordan, and they both had looks of anxiousness on their faces. The pain they both had endured all these years would be explained, I hoped, but would the answers to these question make any difference now, one way or the other.

Douglas turned, went back to where he had been sitting, and started, "Emilee, there is a lot that I know and have known for a very long time. We all have a destiny of sorts but some of us need a little help along the way, to ensure that we get there.

"Every living creature has many roads that are set before them on their journey of life. We all have free will and can choose which road we want to take. Every road gives us a different route on our journey, to our finale destination.

"Some take the road that looks the easiest, from what they can see, but this road is usually filled with more obstacles and challenges than they realize. Some roads lead to dead ends and then you must go back, start over and pick another road.

"I was given the task to ensure that a certain fey's destiny was not interrupted or destroyed. In doing so, I had to make sure that several fey were set on the proper road in the beginning. There was no time to sit back, wait and hope that these fey chose wisely."

Tina M. Engel

Douglas had been staring off into space as he was talking but then turned his head to look at Angelina as he said, "Yours was one of them."

He looked to Jordan, saying, "And yours was another."

Angelina and Jordan looked at each other and then Angelina turned to Douglas and asked, "What do you mean?"

"Your destinies were written for you both, long before you were born. Angelina, I was given the task of taking you to the fey couple who would raise you as their own, to keep you safe until the time came for you to begin your role in Emilee's future."

Angelina let out a soft gasp as she opened her mouth to speak but Douglas put up a hand to stop her, turned to look at Jordan and said, "And I was the one who took you to the Orphanage so many years ago. You, Jordan, were not a fey who had broken laws and had your memories erased, becoming a baby again to start your life over. You were brought there to be protected until the time came for you to begin your role, to meet Angelina and, well, you know the rest."

Jordan's face had a look of horror and then anger as he stood in a rage. It was Adam who quickly stood, went to Jordan and putting both hands on his shoulders, suggested he stay calm and let Douglas continue.

Adam had a way with Jordan, they were more brothers than friends, because of the years they spent together, with Adam always stopping Jordan from finding someone to kill him, and

Jordan helping Adam with his many adventures, be it on land or waters.

As Jordan sat back down, Adam turned and asked in a slightly humorous tone, "I suppose my journey has been tampered with a bit too then, me being around to stop Jordan from getting himself killed?"

Douglas chuckled softly and this eased some of the tension that was filling the room.

"Yes, all in this room were guided down paths that they may have not taken, at the proper time, when it was needed. Some of you made decisions however, that did change things slightly, but that is for another time."

Jordan, with a calmer attitude asked then, "Why did we need to be protected and from who or what?"

"The Dark One!" Was all that Douglas said as he stood up and walked back over to the porthole and again gazed out as if looking for something.

Douglas turned towards Lily then as if waiting for her to do or say something. She looked up at him after a moment or two as the silence was getting uncomfortable for all.

Lily transformed into her fey form and said in a patient but authoritarian manner, "You are doing fine Douglas. So far you haven't shared anything that I would have to fix, so please continue."

I looked at Lily confused about what she had just said, and as she looked directly at me, our eyes met and I was transported to my dream world; *the wheat field, the large tree, the raging ocean behind*

*me and my grandmother's voice saying, "Emilee,
listen and learn."*

Then I was back in the room, on the ship,
with my friends and family around me. Lily gave
me a sly smile, went over to a chair, away from
everyone, and sat. She had a slight shimmery glow
around her, and as I looked around at everyone,
they didn't seem bothered in the least. Did they
see what I was seeing, I wondered?

"Sit, everyone." Lily said, "and please
continue, Douglas, you're doing fine."

Douglas continued in a gruff voice, seeming
to be a bit annoyed, "There's not much more to tell
at this time. Angelina and Jordan, you both know
now that you are Emilee's parents. You were
brought to the places in which you were raised, by
me, and we are all here to help Princess Emilee
reach her full potential and complete her destiny.
Without her, this planet, and all that live in the
many dimensions which share this planet, will
perish."

Brett asked, with a scowl on his face. "Have
I been just a pawn in this game you seem to be
playing with this strange woman, who is calling
Emilee home, and who Angelina said she kept
seeing? I'm guessing it is the same woman, is it
Emilee's grandmother?"

Brett and Douglas both stood then as
Douglas bellowed, "Don't you give me attitude
youngster. You play a role in the survival of this
world and you should be grateful for it."

"Grateful!" Brett yelled, "Grateful for what?
Almost getting myself and my friends killed
numerous times, lives lost who have helped us

along the way, finding out that my brother is alive and is working for the Dark One? I would rather think him dead. And falling in love with someone who I may not be permitted to be with, when this is all over?! Grateful?!"

Brett's eyes were full of anger as they widened when he said the last part. He looked at me with flushed cheeks.

I felt embarrassment, desire and fury as his eyes pierced mine, our thoughts were connected for a moment, and then he shut me out, closed his eyes and turned away.

As I took a step towards him, my mother grasped my hand to stop me. I looked down at her as she sat on the edge of the chair, as if getting ready to stand and hold me back, if need be.

Douglas said, gently but firmly, "Brett, that is enough. Sit and I will explain more."

Brett turned his head, looking at Douglas with hate in his eyes and then turned back towards the door and stormed out, slamming it behind him.

I looked around the quiet room at everyone, and no one knew what to say. Everyone's eyes were down, looking at the floor, uncomfortable with what had just happened, it seemed. Douglas was still staring at the door where Brett had stormed out and Lily was looking at Douglas with a look of frustration on her face.

Lily broke the silence then, saying, "Well that went well!" And she got up from her chair, and left the room.

I stood then and headed in the direction of the door, as I moved away from Angelina, her hand slipped from mine, she had no intention of holding me there. I wouldn't have let her if she had tried. I left the room quietly, leaving the remaining fey to discuss whatever they wanted, it made no difference to me. (He loved me, Brett loved me), was all that was in my mind.

Chapter four

Different,
It's all different now.
It will never be the same.
Sometimes knowledge
Isn't what you want,
But you must take it
Anyway.

I didn't know where I was going as I headed down the hall and up the stairs to the top of the ship. It was a large ship and it took me a while to find the doorway out to the fresh sea air. I wasn't looking for Brett or Lily and didn't want to talk with anyone. I needed to be alone, to try to make some sense of what I had just learned. I knew that everyone was struggling in their own way, with the knowledge they had just received, but I didn't care at the time. I just needed to get away.

As I opened the door to the sea, I saw Brett and Lily talking quietly. I walked in the opposite direction and headed to the front of the ship, to see where we were heading. It didn't really matter, but I wanted to see the direction in which Proteus's home was. The walkway was along the edge of the ship, with just a steel railing that kept me from the waters far below.

I stopped walking just a short distance from the front of the ship, went over to the railing and grabbed hold as I looked down. I thought about what Brett had said, he loved me but we may not be together at the end of this journey. It was all I could think of. It filled my entire being.

I had to get away, somewhere, where I could grasp all that I had learned. I had to get away. Then, I did just that. I stepped up onto the lower bar of the railing and swung a leg over the top one, to sit there on the top bar. I leaned forward and gracefully (I might add) let myself go, down to meet the sea.

I made a slight splash in the great waves and I let myself sink down, not afraid, not excited, feeling nothing really. Sometimes feelings complicate things, make it more difficult to see reason, to see the logic in what is going on. So I allowed myself to feel nothing as I drifted down, deeper into the magnificent sea, with my eyes closed.

I could feel my body tingling slightly and as I brought water into my lungs, I could feel the pleasure, my entire body was singing as the water touched every cell, nerve, every part of me.

As I opened my eyes, I saw the underwater world of Terrafirma with colors so vivid. Everything had a life form in it and I saw them all, from the smallest larvae and plankton, to the largest grey whale, several of them, coming towards me.

I was nowhere near the bottom, it was deep and dark down below. I looked up, saw the sun shining in the world above, causing the water to sparkle, showing every tiny bit of life all around me.

As the whales approached me, they were talking to each other, questioning what they were seeing (me of course) but they didn't know who I was, could I be the one? I felt a presence behind

Tina M. Engel

me, and as I turned to look, I saw sharks, Hammerhead sharks, menacing in looks and all talking at the same time.

"Who is she? What is she? Dinner? Snack? Play toy?" So many voices coming from the school of sharks.

As the biggest shark approached me, I held out my hand, not in protection, but in an offering of kindness. I wasn't afraid. I knew somehow, I could protect myself and didn't want to hurt these animals. The shark changed then, into its fey self, large, muscular and striking.

From behind me, one of the grey whales, said, "She is the princess, the one. No harm shall come to her."

I turned to look at them, and from behind one of the whales, came a smaller one. Not small at all, compared to me. It was a baby and it came right up to me and let me touch it.

As I was petting this sweet creature I could still hear the ramblings from the sharks, "Just a taste? How do we know she is the one? Dinner?"

I turned back in the direction of the sharks just in time, as one of the smaller sharks passed the one who had turned into a fey, swimming at me in a frenzy. I put my hand up in front of me, the hand with the ring that Trevor had given me, and a flash came from the ring, a bolt of light that struck the shark. It was still, laying over on its side and then started to float down, down to the cold, dark depths.

All the other sharks turned into their fey bodies, and had looks of horror, anger and fear on

Tina M. Engel

their faces. I knew it was dead. I had killed a living creature, not meaning to, but I did.

The grey whales were there, one on each side of me then, not turning into fey, but staying in their large, whale bodies.

One of them said, "She is the one, not to be trifled with. Go now before anyone else gets hurt."

The largest shark, the leader and elder of the bunch (I knew somehow) came up to me, took my hand, did the fey greeting and said, "My apologies, princess. We didn't know you were here yet. That was a young pup, inexperienced and hungry."

This fey had a strange look in his eyes. It was a deceitful look and I didn't trust him at all. I was polite though, not wanting to let on how I was feeling. I shared with him my sorrow for killing the young shark, but this fey didn't seem to care that it was dead. At that, he turned back into his shark shape, the rest did the same, and they swam away.

I watched them go down to the darkness and disappear. One of the whales told me that these waters were not safe for me to be alone in, and I should call on them when I wanted to enter. They would be following the ship and would be here to help as long as I needed them.

From above came movement, and as I looked up, there was Brett, swimming down to reach me. Brett had a look of panic and anger in his eyes, panic for my safety and anger, that I was being irresponsible, I assumed.

"Emilee!" Brett spouted, in my mind, of course. "What do you think you're doing? Can I not leave you for an instant without you getting into trouble?"

Tina M. Engel

Brett had a look of impatience on his face and I became immediately angry. But angry at what, I wondered; Brett for storming out of the room, for saying what he said, the predicament that we were in, the uncertainty of my future? Maybe it was all of it, but I just knew I was angry. I had just killed a creature, a living being, and I felt sick about it.

"Trouble?!" I yelled, "I can't seem to get into trouble these days. Trouble seems to find me without my help. Maybe these so called gifts that I have been given, are a magnet for trouble.

"I just killed an innocent creature! Okay, so it wanted to eat me, but that is beside the point. I didn't even mean to, or want to. I didn't think about killing it, but I did. It just happened.

"How can I trust myself with anyone around me with these gifts, or curses, since they seem to have a mind of their own?

"Trouble! Trouble, you say?"

And at that, I turned and started to swim down to the darkness. Maybe that was where I belonged. Maybe I was a dark fey after all.

Then, as I reached the boarder of the darkness and light, Brett said, "Emilee, please stop. You're not a dark fey and you don't belong there. Please!"

I stopped and turned to look up. Brett hadn't moved from the spot where I had left him. The grey whales were where they were moments before. No one moved. I stared at them and then back down to the darkness. I felt such despair and loneliness.

Tina M. Engel

My thoughts went back to what Brett had said. He loved me but we couldn't be together in the end. Why? I wondered.

"Emilee, please come back, it will be okay. I shouldn't have left the way I did." Brett pleaded. Then I heard, "or I will come down there and drag you back, if I must!"

As I looked at Brett in astonishment for what he was thinking, he started to grin, giving me that silly smirk that always seemed to calm me somehow.

"Please, Emilee, if I don't bring you back willingly, when I do get you back to the ship, Douglas will take me apart bit by bit, and slowly. Then Lily will finish the job. Don't put me through that!" Brett said, and the smile turned to a sober pout.

I shut my eyes, took in a large breath of water, blew it out and as I opened my eyes, Brett had that silly smirk on his face again. I gave him a smile, not sure if I really meant it, but decided I really didn't want to go down into the darkness, and found that I wasn't really angry with him anyway. I was just angry with everything, it was all out of control.

I started up, but only moved a few feet before something grabbed my ankle and yanked me down. Whatever it was, cut into my skin, and I let out a yell, (if you can yell in the water), and was pulled down so quickly that as I looked to Brett for help, he disappeared as I entered the darkness.

I looked down, trying to see what had a hold of me, but could see nothing, it was so dark. My diamond started to glow a dark orange color, danger, and gave enough light for me to see my ankle. There wrapped around it, was a tentacle of sorts.

Then looking in front of me as dark as it was, I saw a face, Queen Anahita's to be exact. Behind her was a shape, another fey, but I couldn't make out who or what, female or male. I was shocked and as I reached out for Queen Anahita to help, she disappeared into the darkness, as it seemed that she was dragging the other fey with her.

I felt him then, Brett next to me, fear in his eyes, and shock; he was in my mind and saw Queen Anahita too.

My shield then took over, and as it surrounded Brett and I, it severed the tentacle from the beast that was trying to drag me down.

I looked to Brett and I was sure I had the same surprised look on my face as he had on his. Brett grabbed my arm and we started to swim up as the Grey whales came into view. They swam past us, heading down to the darkness, and I heard the one say, "Watch our young one", as they disappeared.

We headed to the young whale and then headed up to the surface of the water. Brett wanted me out as soon as possible but I stood firm, or swam firm I should say. I wasn't going to leave the baby whale alone.

Brett knew that I would be stubborn about this so he gave me an accepting but frustrated look as he said, "Could you put your shield around the baby too then?"

I smiled a triumphant smile and did just that, we were all in my shield and we waited, wondering what was happening and hoping that the two Grey whales were okay.

My ankle was throbbing and I knew that a piece of the creature was still wrapped around it, with its sharp spikes imbedded in my skin. As I looked down, I could feel Brett's eyes looking down too and as our minds joined again, he was overtaken with anxiety, fearing poison.

I jerked my head up to look at Brett and saw the fear in his eyes. Just then a rush of water came out of the sea, just feet from us, the two whales. They were safe but one had several gashes across its back.

I released my shield and the baby whale left my side, swimming over to its family. I headed over to them too but Brett took hold of my arm saying, "We need to get your ankle taken care of, Emilee."

"I need to tend to the injured whale first." I said in haste, sensing that the gashes were filled with the same fluid or poison that I now knew was seeping into my blood stream.

Brett came with me, never letting go of my arm. As we reached the great beast, Brett helped me to get on top of it, where the gashes were.

Looking at my hand with the ring on it, that I thought was supposed to heal, not kill, I hesitated for a moment. I wondered why it killed the shark.

I put my hand in the largest crease, into the oozing bloody wound, and as the ring started to glow, the entire gash, started to glow. I removed my hand as it closed up. I did the same to the other wounds and then laid down on the whale's back, exhausted from what I had just done. He was healed but I was in bad shape.

The whale sank into the water just a bit to allow Brett to get on top and then the whale swam over to the ship. Brett picked me up and walked to the whale's head, just above his mouth and the whale raised his head up to meet the deck of the ship. Brett was able to hand me over to Adam and then he climbed over the railing onto the ship.

I thanked the whales for their help and apologized for my ignorance in the water. They reassured me that they would be close by, throughout our journey in the seas and would help us as much as they could.

I asked then, "What happened down there, and what was that creature?" but before they spoke, (or maybe they did but I didn't hear it), I was in the wheat field again.

Chapter 5

Dreams,
The safety in our own mind.
Dreams,
Are they visions of what may be?
Or
Hopes for what we want?

The wheat was dead, dried and broken. It crunched beneath my feet as I turned to look at the tree, the beautiful tree. It was destroyed, the trunk split in half, the top of the tree, branches and leaves, dead and dry, laying all about. The sky was dark, grey and gloomy. A gust of wind came and blew me backwards, but I caught myself before I fell.

There was a dense fog behind what was left of the tree. It moved and slithered as if alive. There was something there, a silhouette of something large, a building?

The fog moved, swirling, moving as if someone was telling it exactly where to go. It moved, some to the left and some to the right until I could see what was in front of me. It was a large palace-like structure, in shambles.

This had never been here before in my dreams, I thought. Why now and what has happened here? I wondered.

Then from behind what was left of the large trunk of the tree came a figure; a large strangely grotesque, deformed shape. I took a step back, and as I inspected this creature more intently, I

Tina M. Engel

realized that it looked like an insect, but not one that I had ever seen before.

Its head was small, too small for its tall, muscular body, rounded at the top with a very narrow, pointy chin and two very large, egg shaped eyes on both sides of its face. Its arms, two of them were long and muscular from the shoulders down to the elbows, if you could call them elbows, they moved as if double jointed, but his lower arms were skinny with what looked like pinchers for fingers.

He smiled at me, (yes, I was sure it was male), and said, "Welcome home Emilee, I have been waiting so long for this reunion."

Before I could say anything, another movement came from the other side, Stephan DeMill.

My ankle started to burn, and as I took a step back, I gasped in horror, seeing Stephan here with this creature. I put the foot down that was paining me, and I fell as it gave way.

As I looked towards my foot, my ankle was swollen, double in size with what looked like teeth marks all around it. Blood was oozing from the marks but there was also a white foamy substance.

I felt ill, dizzy as I looked up and saw Stephan walking towards me and the creature walking back towards the crumbled structure.

I tried to stand, but couldn't endure the sizzling pain in my lower leg, now so intense. I scooted back as Stephan got closer. He bent down to grab me, and I yelled as I fell back on the ground, the dried wheat crumbling at my back, and cutting into the skin on my neck as I lay there trying to get away from him.

Tina M. Engel

I tried then, to put up my shield for protection and reached behind my head for my barrette, but it wasn't there and the shield didn't appear. I looked on my hand for the ring but it was gone too. I was helpless, there was no one around to help me and I couldn't seem to help myself.

As Stephan bent down with a smile so evil, he touched my arm, and I screamed, "Don't touch me!" as I kicked and struck out with my hands.

He said then with calmness in his voice, "It's alright Emilee, I'm here, and you will be alright. We can heal you. It's me Emilee, Brett." And then as I looked at Stephan's face, it started to change.

It was Brett, my Brett, holding my hands in a guarded way and I realized that Jordan was holding my legs down. Angelina was at my other side, opposite Brett, and I could see Rose over in a corner, crying. I was back on the ship, in a room, not in my dream world.

"It's dead, everything is dead!" I said, as I started to sob. I tipped my head back, looking away from Brett's face and up to the ceiling. I knew somehow that this was a vision of what was to be, if I didn't stop it, but how? How could I be so powerful, to save the planet and all who call it home.

I sat up then, and looking into Brett's face, the fear and confused look I saw there was frightening. No one knew what I had seen and seeing me in this condition caused them all to be full of anxiety. I could feel the uneasiness that filled the air.

I felt it then, a strange sensation, not painful but like hundreds of ants, just under my skin, rushing up the leg that the creature had taken hold of, spreading to the other leg, and up my torso to my chest. My face felt cold, and then the sensation went down my arms to my hands. I looked down to see my hands, white, silvery white, for just a moment and then they were my normal color again. I looked back up into Brett's face and he was looking at me but he had a strange blank stare, as if he was not with us anymore.

We were there then, he and I, the field was golden, the smell of wheat ready to be harvested. The ocean behind us, crashing against the rock wall below, sea gulls crying out, looking for an easy meal. The sun was warm against my skin and Brett was standing next to me, holding my hand, looking around in awe.

He turned his head to look at me, with a questioning expression across his face.

"It was all dead, everything was dead and he was here, Stephan was here, but not alone, a creature, a hideous creature was with him." I said, quietly.

As I turned to face the tree, it stood tall and healthy but things were different now. There behind the tree in the distance, was a castle, a majestic palace with tall columns on all four corners, a large gate in the front, but what was truly magical was what was behind it. It was a mountain, a large rocky mountain that sparkled as the sunbeams hit it. The castle seemed to have been carved out of the mountain, it was a part of it, glistening in the sunshine as well.

"But the mountain wasn't there, it was just a pile of rubble, the castle was in ruins." I said, as I

Tina M. Engel

let go of Brett's hand and started to walk towards it.

Brett walked up next to me and taking my hand back in his, stopped me from continuing. He turned me towards him, and asked what I had seen before.

I looked down at our hands and mine were white again, but not cold, only my face felt cold again. The same feeling of something just under my skin, racing up my body, and my hands tingled, like pinpricks as I held Brett's hands.

I suddenly had a hunger, a hunger deep down. I knew what it was for, I knew I needed him. I looked up into Brett's eyes, and he knew it too.

I looked away quickly, feeling embarrassed at the need I had, knowing that he understood. I removed my hands from his and hid them, crossing my arms over my chest.

Looking towards the castle, I told him of the dream I had just had, the death all around, darkness, and the castle in ruins. I told him in detail about the creature that was there and what he had said. "Welcome home Emilee, I have been waiting so long for this reunion."

I looked back up at Brett and said, "Home? Could this be my home?"

Brett looked over towards the castle and then back down to me and said with a look of guardedness and questioning in his voice, "I don't know, I've only been here with you when you have let me."

The wind started to blow and as I took Brett's hands again, there was a voice in the wind,

Tina M. Engel

calling softly at first, in a whisper, "Emilee, Brett, come back." It became more forceful, each time this voice spoke, "Emilee, Brett, come back!"

We were suddenly back on the ship, in the room where we had been. I was still sitting on the bed with Brett sitting next to me, our hands still joined and my hands were white again. The hunger that I was feeling in that dream world was still with me, only more intense now.

I looked around the room and there stood Angelina, Jordan, Rose, Adam and Eagle, all staring at us.

Lily knelt down next to us and said, "It's not time to be there, not yet."

Brett was looking at our hands, and I knew that he saw the change in color but said nothing as he looked back up into my eyes and I saw that same strange blank stare.

Lily looked down at our hands, placed hers on ours as she separated Brett's from mine and as she did so, Brett's eyes became clear, he was with us again.

The white coloring that was covering my hands, seemed to slither and swirl, up onto Lily's hands. The crawly feeling in my body, calmed some but was still there, as if hiding.

Lily stood and staggered slightly and everyone took a step or two away from her as she shut her eyes and just stood there perfectly still. She let out a strange moaning sound and then as the discoloration on her hands dissolved, she opened her eyes.

"Well now, that was fun, wasn't it?" Lily said in a sarcastic tone. She then came back over to me, told Brett to move, in a not very patient manner and knelt back down next to me.

Lily took my ankle, which was still oozing a white foamy substance, in her hands and asked me to please put my hands over hers. I did so without questioning, I somehow knew that questioning or arguing would get me nowhere.

Lily then said impatiently, "It wasn't the appropriate time for this. I don't think you are strong enough to handle it yet. I can't remove it, but let's get this healed, shall we, so we can move on to the next part of this journey, as you call it."

I wasn't sure why I needed Lily to help me to heal my leg, but as I put my hands on hers, I could feel a tingling in my ankle. (Which wasn't a good feeling at all, let me just say) My ring started to glow as did my diamond necklace, and suddenly there was a flash of light that seemed to come from Lily herself, that blinded me for a moment or two.

As my vision came back, I looked around and believed that everyone else had lost sight for just a moment and all had a perplexed expression on their faces.

I looked over at Lily then as she removed her hands, stood, and stumbled just a bit before centering herself. As I looked down at my ankle, it was healed, just pink dots where the wounds had been.

I looked up into Lily's face and she had a weary expression as she said, "It wasn't time yet, Emilee. He shouldn't have done what he did. The skin is healed, but it is done. I tried, and I can't change it now, I only slowed the process down."

Tina M. Engel

She turned to Brett and said in a very kind and caring voice, (not typical of Lily), "Brett, you are sensitive to Emilee's touch. You cannot let things be rushed. Her needs have changed and intensified, thanks to him. You must get her there safely and we are running out of time."

Lily looked over at Adam and said then, "How much longer, until we reach the Island of Bermuda? The next part of Emilee's transformation was supposed to happen there, not here."

Adam told her that it would take another day or so but he would get us there as soon as he could, weather permitting, to reach our destination. He also told us that not only were the grey whales following us but also other creatures from the deep, to help keep us safe.

The whales who had helped save me, had told Adam the creature that had tried to take me was from deep in the darkest parts of the waters, a mysterious creature, which not many had ever seen before. It didn't seem to be following us and Adam suggested, we should all get some rest.

Lily remarked, "Mysterious indeed, but he knows it very well."

Adam looked at me then and said in a matter of fact way, "Emilee, you will not go back in the water. If I need to put a guard on you 24 hours a day, I will."

Lily chuckled at this statement and said in a sly cat like way, "Don't you worry your pretty little head over this, Adam. She will be guarded quite closely." And Lily looked over to Rose and said, "Won't she, Rose?"

Rose, who had been very quiet through all of this, which was very unusual, spoke now with firmness in her voice, "Not to worry, I won't let her out of my sight." And Rose had a very strange, almost wicked grin across her face. (When I say wicked, I don't mean that Rose was evil in anyway. It's just an expression, to be clear.)

I looked back to Adam and asked, "The animal that had tried to take me, I cut the end of its limb off. It was still attached to my ankle. Where is it? Did you keep it?"

Adam looked to Brett and then said, "We have it in the mess hall, in a sealed container in the cooler."

"Why there?" I asked feeling confused.

Brett then spoke, "It's still alive, moving as if it has a life of its own. It's trying desperately to get out but the container is a non-breakable container, we hope, and we will keep it there until we can figure out what to do with it."

"Why?" I asked. "If it is a living thing, we should set it free. Let it go back to where it came from. Send a message that we are stronger than it is."

I looked to Lily, and she said in a very odd tone, "I don't think it is trying to get out to go home. It's trying to get to you, to finish what it started."

I looked at Lily in disbelief and asked, "Why?" Again. That seemed to be all I could ask.

Lily said, almost to herself but we all heard her, "Maybe you should go and see it, maybe it is time."

Tina M. Engel

At that comment, Brett piped in, "Over my dead body! We will keep it away from Emilee."

Well when Lily heard Brett say (over his dead body) she got a sad look on her face and said, "Not now Brett, it isn't time."

Brett gave her a scolding look and continued, "The cold water that its in, seems to be keeping it calm, but if it sees Emilee, we don't know what it will do."

I was feeling a bit miffed at the fact that everyone seemed to think they knew what was best for me and I was feeling sick to my stomach, I assumed from whatever it was that the animal put into my body. I looked at Rose and she knew immediately what I wanted.

"Okay everyone, let's let the princess rest, and she needs some nourishment, so leave!" Rose said with a sharpness in her voice.

Lily started to chuckle softly as she headed towards the door. "Well, as I said before, I don't think we have to worry about Princess Emilee getting into any more trouble."

I started to stand as I spouted off, "Wait just a minute, I can take care of myself and further more..." before I could finish my sentence, the nauseous feeling I had, took over and I felt faint. The craving that I had wasn't for Rose, but Brett and that hunger was growing rapidly.

I sat back down and saw everyone staring at me; their faces were all distorted as if I was seeing them through a carnival mirror. My eyes were burning, and the hunger grew more intense.

Brett came over to me but Lily hollered before he reached me, "Brett, don't touch her. Let her feed on Rose. Everyone, leave!"

They all left one by one but Brett stood nearby. Rose sat down on the bed next to me, but it wasn't Rose's blood that I wanted; I wanted Brett's, and Lily knew this. I had no desire for Rose's blood anymore. Lily had a look of sadness on her face.

Rose lifted her arm to my face and the scent of her skin, caused my stomach to rumble, so I guessed Rose's blood would do.

Lily said with a slight chuckle, "Brett you too, out of here so she can eat in peace."

I heard Brett in my mind, asking if I was okay, and should he leave. It was such a safe feeling having him there, with me, never far away.

I reassured him that I was fine but he then commented gruffly, "And no, you are not going to see the creature. Not without me anyway!"

I smiled, knowing that I had won yet another small battle, he couldn't go back now. He said not without him. I was going to go, as soon as this nausea passed.

I took Rose's wrist and placed it in my mouth and biting down gently, I sucked. As the liquid entered my mouth, my taste buds, happy to have nourishment, seemed to tingle. Rose's blood tasted funny though, but my body was hungry, so hungry, that I got a bit rough with her. I couldn't get it in fast enough. Rose's blood wasn't satisfying my hunger, at all.

Rose let out a cry of pain and fear as Lily came to me, put her hand on my forehead, and said quietly, "Emilee, slow down and be gentle."

I looked from Rose to Lily, and saw the fear in Rose's eyes and the concern on Lily's face. My eyes were no longer burning and I could see clearly again.

Brett was still standing in the door way, and as we joined again, he said with a smirk on his lips, "Emilee, she is your meal ticket, don't drain her, not a good thing to do." As he shook his head and chuckled.

I removed Rose's wrist and looking down, saw a few small gashes that I had caused, and put my hand over it, to heal her.

"Rose," I said humbly, "I am so sorry, I was so hungry for..." I stopped suddenly, looking at Brett, and Brett and I both sighed, at the same time, as he walked out of the room.

I didn't finish my sentence, there was no need. I could feel the vibration that was always there from Brett, we were always connected but his mind was closed off. Or was it mine? I couldn't hear his thoughts.

Lily, still looking unhappy, suggested that I lay down and rest, let Rose's blood work its magic, so to speak, and Rose was to stay with me. She headed to the door, mumbling something about the timing being off, and I thought she said something about Rose and her blood, as she looked back at us both, shook her head side to side slightly, and seemed then to just be staring off into space, not seeing us at all.

I did as she suggested and Rose, sweet Rose, covered me with a blanket, saying that she would be here if I needed more. I wondered what Lily was mumbling about, what about the timing, and what did this have to do with Rose?

As I shut my eyes and I started to drift off, I heard Lily say to Rose, "Don't let her drink from you while you are both alone. She can't control the hunger. It's not for you, that her body hungers for, but it isn't time yet."

Rose must have had a pouty look, not that I could see it but I know Rose so well, and Lily said, kindly, not like the typical Lily, "She still needs you but she won't for long in this manner and I'm not sure..." And she stopped her thought in mid-sentence and I heard the door close.

I drifted then, not going to my dream world, the wheat field, but just drifted, in the darkness, a greyness, but soft and warm, sounds of a soft humming, a wind blowing far away. The smell of salt water, sea weed, pine trees, a spring rain, as I drifted through these fragrances, feeling nothing around me, as if I was floating in the greyness.

Tina M. Engel

Chapter 6

> *Hunger,*
> *Not for food!*
> *Hunger,*
> *It pushes you to the limits,*
> *Hunger,*
> *You need it to*
> *Survive!*

I heard voices, it was Brett and Rose, talking softly, close by. I lay there with my eyes closed, listening as they spoke, Brett insisting that he stay until I wake, just in case, and Rose not really wanting to co-operate with this.

"Just in case, what?" I asked, still with my eyes closed. I smiled slightly as I waited for an answer.

I opened my eyes and sat up slowly, leaning my back against the head board of the bed.

"Well Emilee," Brett started, "I don't want you to..." and he looked over to Rose, "over indulge." And he came over and sat down next to me on the bed, with a silly grin on his face.

Rose wasn't at all happy with what he had said or the fact that he was here, in my room.

Brett asked me if I needed to feed on Rose again, and if not he would like to be alone with me for a bit.

Well Rose wasn't going to go along with that. She huffed and puffed and stormed around the room, letting us know that she would go talk to Lily if need be.

At some point on this journey it seemed, Lily had taken charge, and I was a bit perplexed and amused, by this.

Brett and I both laughed slightly and I assured them both that I was not hungry for Rose, and I wanted to get up and take a walk.

Brett and Rose looked at each other, and Brett informed me that I was not going to go see the creature that was locked up in the mess hall.

"Who said anything about that?" I asked innocently, but yes, that was exactly where I was planning on going, with or without them.

I brushed Brett aside as I uncovered my legs and turned them out over the side of the bed to stand. Brett stood and reached down, took my hand, and helped me to my feet. I felt very strong and rested but let Brett think he was helping me. I wanted him on my side, to go see the piece of the creature, so if I had to act a little needy, then so be it.

Rose interrupted my acting, by clearing her throat loudly, and asked if I needed to eat more. I reassured her I was feeling fine and just wanted some fresh air and to go see Trevor, the cook, whom I so enjoyed visiting with, in the mess hall, of course.

Brett, scowling, grumbled, "You're not going to see that thing, Emilee. I forbid it."

"Excuse me?" I said, with an attitude. "I will do what I want, when I want, and how I want. This is my quest and I need to see it." I turned and walked out the door, letting it slam behind me.

I hurried down the hall and up a small flight of stairs, as I heard Brett yelling behind me, to slow down. I had no intention of doing this. I wanted to get to the kitchen and see the piece of the creature that had tried to drag me down to the deepest part of the waters that we were sailing in.

Brett was there, in my mind, not happy at all and saying a few words that I had never heard him say before. Now I, on the other hand, had no problem saying them, back when I was a human.

As I reached out to grab the handle of the door to the mess hall, a hand clasped over mine and looking up I saw Brett, a very upset Brett, with eyes glowing red and his mouth twisted in an unpleasant way.

"Emilee!" He fumed, "This is no way to act. You're behaving like a spoiled child and I'm here to protect you and keep you safe, no matter how I do it."

At that, he removed my hand from the door and scooped me up in his arms. What could I do, but laugh. I laughed as I looked at his furious but concerned face, then put my arms around his neck and kissed him on the lips. (Yes I really did)

At first the kiss was all one sided, I shocked Brett, but it was only moments before the kiss was reciprocated. This kiss was different from the other few we had, this was a deep, intense kiss. My entire body tingled, a strange sensation swept over me, I became warm, but not warm as if I was in the sun, a warmth that came from within, deep within me.

Our lips parted, but our faces were still close, and I could see his eyes, green with need and I could see myself in his eyes, as if they were a mirror. It wasn't me, I saw. Not the me, I was used to.

Behind Brett, was the door with a window in it. I could see my reflection and it was someone else in Brett's arms. Oh, I knew it was me but I had a glow that radiated from my body. My eyes were green, the same as Brett's but my skin was not the tan color anymore, but silvery white.

I looked back at Brett, his eyes still green with hunger and he placed his lips on mine again. I felt my fangs protrude as our kiss deepened and I bit down on Brett's lower lip, breaking the skin.

My tongue glided over the puncture as we released the kiss and I wanted more, so much more. Brett just stared at me as if in a trance, not moving his face from mine, eyes still green. I leaned my head just a bit, to his neck, and somehow knew that I wanted to drink from him.

It was Rose who stopped me. She let out a squeal that sounded like a cat in a trap, and Brett dropped my legs, placing me on the ground. If I hadn't still had my arms around Brett's neck, I would have fallen.

I turned towards Rose as I let go of Brett and he turned away from me, in Rose's direction too. Rose had a look of panic on her face and she was pale, as if she had seen something that frightened her. I was sure it was us, me and Brett who frightened her, and it frightened me a bit also.

"What are you two doing?!" Rose shrieked, as she came over to me, grabbed my arm rather roughly (I might add), and tried to pull me away from Brett.

Tina M. Engel

I went with her willingly because I wanted to calm the situation down that we seemed to be in.

The mess hall door opened then with a crash, bumping Brett and sending him flying a few feet but he caught himself before he tumbled to the ground.

It was Trevor, with Jordan following. I must have still had a strange look about me, all silvery white, I assumed, because when the two of them looked at me they had a concerned look on their faces too.

Jordan came over to me, placed a hand on my cheek and said, "Emilee, what happened, are you alright?" and he then glanced in Brett's direction.

I did too and Brett's eyes were still green, with a faraway stare. Brett then inhaled deeply and looked up at me. His eyes where back to normal and he seemed focused again.

"What are you all looking at?" Brett inquired rather gruffly. "Emilee, are you okay?" He came towards me, but Rose still holding my arm, yanked me behind her and away from Jordan, in a rough manner and stood in front with a stance that let everyone know she meant business.

I looked down at my arms and they were still silvery white and the taste of Brett's blood was still on my lips. I wanted to shove Rose out of the way and be back in Brett's arms, but before I was able to make a fool of myself and do that, Lily came walking down the hall towards us.

"Back away, everyone please. Can I not get away from you all for just a bit, to find a nice tasty snack down below?" Lily said in an annoyed voice, that if a cat could talk, is how they would sound.

Brett stepped aside slightly, not moving far from me while Jordan moved to stand next to me. Neither of them had any intention of moving away too far. Rose didn't budge but as Lily approached her, she placed a hand on Rose's arm and with a kind smile she gently removed Rose from in front of me.

"Princess, now what have you done to yourself?" Lily asked.

Lily looked over at Brett and with raised eyebrows said, "Brett?"

Brett gave her a confused look and shrugged his shoulders.

She looked back at me and took both my hands in hers and said, "Talk to me Emilee, tell me what you need?"

"I need to go see that thing in the kitchen. Brett tried to stop me and ..." I looked over to Brett, our minds were one and he remembered, as I did, what had just happened.

"Emilee," I heard him say, but no one else did, "Be patient, we will do this together."

Lily looked over at Brett and then back to me and whispered, so only I could hear, "He's right."

I looked at Lily, and she grinned slightly, then looked down at my hands. I followed her gaze and saw that my hands were my normal color again.

"What do you need, Princess?" Lily asked again, calmly, as if I would tell her something different.

Tina M. Engel

"I need to see the creature's limb. I feel it inside of me, please." I said.

Rose was still out of sorts with what she had witnessed, so of course she had to express her disagreement in a way only Rose could. She threw up her arms, and in a frenzied tone, said, "Are you all crazy, did you see what she looked like? Did you see his eyes and hers, for that matter? Am I the only one who is rational right now?"

As I watched Rose carry on, our eyes locked for a moment, and in that moment I knew there was something else going on. Rose was afraid of that thing in the cooler, not afraid for me, but for her?

When Rose was done with her rant, she looked at me and she knew, I knew. Why she was afraid, I didn't know but as she realized this, she turned her gaze towards Lily. As they looked at each other, I knew something was about to happen and they both knew it.

Lily nodded her head and Rose put her head down slightly, looking away from Lily. Rose headed towards the door to the mess hall, pushed the door open and went in.

Lily, being the old Lily that I knew and loved, said, "Well, that was very entertaining, now wasn't it? Shall we follow her inside and see what other form of entertainment she can provide?"

Lily chuckled as she headed for the mess hall, still holding one of my hands. Even with the chuckle, which I felt was faked, I felt there was something going on.

Brett followed closely behind as the others, Jordan and Trevor came in last.

Rose was mumbling and flinging her hands about as she headed into the kitchen. "Let's just get this over with, why not just do it, let them see each other, it is supposed to happen eventually, anyway. She has to learn it all, so why not now?"

I was so confused by what Rose was saying, she was make no sense at all. When we entered the kitchen, Rose was at the cooler door and as Lily released my hand, I went to Rose before she could open the door and asked, "Rose, what are you mumbling about? You're not making any sense."

I put my hands on her shoulders and she looked up into my face. There was such sadness in her eyes. "What is it Rose? You're not afraid for me, but for you, Why?"

"It doesn't matter Princess Emilee, but I think you should eat one more time before you go in to see that thing." Rose said, and when she said, that thing, she said it with acceptance in her voice.

I told Rose that I didn't need her right then but maybe later. That was the wrong way to put it, for Rose looked at me with pain in her eyes, as if I had rejected her. I immediately realized how it sounded and corrected myself, saying that I just wasn't needing her blood right then, as I was remembering the odd taste that it had the last time I drank from her.

"You won't need it at all, soon, Princess, so take from me now, to gain any strength you will need, before seeing that piece of meat in there." Rose said, as she looked towards the door of the cooler.

Tina M. Engel

I informed Rose that I would always need her and want her by my side. I took her in my arms then and hugged her lovingly.

Rose's body was trembling slightly, and as I released her and reached down, I took her hands in mine, and said, "Rose, it can't hurt anyone as long as we are all together. We are all strong, as one."

Rose had such a sad expression and said, "Princess, we are here, all of us, for you. We each have a different reason for being here, but you won't need me, in this manner, soon."

I was dumfounded by this statement and looked around the room at everyone. I saw that Adam and Angelina had joined us. I had no idea when they came into the mess hall, but as they all stood there looking at Rose and I, I realized that Rose was right. They all had a purpose on my journey and I would always need them all.

It was Douglas, who spoke as he entered the room, in his usual take charge voice, "Rose is right..." and he walked over to us, smiling down at Rose as she removed her hands from mine and stepped away from me, so that Douglas could open the cooler door. "...we are all here bringing different pieces of your journey, to help you reach your destination."

I thought about Queen Anahita then, down in the water, wondering if Douglas knew something about her being there. Was she really there? And who was the other water fey?

I looked at Brett then, realizing he knew what I was thinking. He was confused by what I had seen too. If it really had been Queen Anahita, he knew nothing about it.

Tina M. Engel

Brett's thoughts seemed protective as he said, "Let it be for now. We can ask questions of Ana, later."

Was Brett being protective of me or her, I wondered? And with a look of embarrassment and frustration, he shut me out of his thoughts.

With the cooler door open, Douglas reached out his hand in a gesture for me to enter. Brett, of course, was not extremely excited about this and said sharply, "Douglas!"

Douglas turned his head in Brett's direction, gave him an almost scolding look that quickly changed to understanding of Brett's fears, but turned then, looked at me and told me to go in.

I looked at Brett, and he was there with me again. He let me back in. I felt him in my thoughts, saw his fear, but with us joined, his fear lessoned some and my strength increased. We both let go of the issue of Queen Anahita, for now.

I went in and over in a corner, was a table with something sitting on it that was covered with a cloth. Douglas stopped everyone else from coming in, but Lily said in a tone of authority, "Brett, you can come in too," as she glanced at Rose, and then walked in after Douglas.

After Brett entered, Lily asked him to shut the door which, I wasn't too sure of. I hated being in a confined area but I wasn't alone, so I turned to the table, walked over to it and reached out to remove the covering.

Brett, being there in my thoughts, said, "You're strong with us, don't show fear."

I turned and looked at Brett and saw the love and confidence in his eyes. There was a bit of sadness too. He knew something that he was keeping from me. It was hidden deep inside of his thoughts. So deep that I couldn't reach it. Whatever it was, it caused a sadness that he tried to keep hidden but I could feel it.

I turned from Brett and took hold of the cloth and removed it. There in a clear box filled with water, was the piece of the creature that had been wrapped around my ankle. It was about a foot in length. It was silvery white, and it was still, as if dead, floating in the middle of the box.

I put my hand on the box. It was glass, cold and smooth, and as I did this, the creature quivered a bit, and then moved towards my hand.

Brett was suddenly behind me and put both hands on my waist. He didn't pull me away and no one stopped him from doing this. I felt a deeper strength, with Brett's touch and knew somehow that he was supposed to be with me.

As the part of the creature in the box touched the glass too, my hand tingled, and then turned the same color as the creature. The color spread up my arm and I knew that my entire body was the same color, the way it was when I kissed Brett.

Somehow I knew that I needed to hold the creature, and reached up to open the box. Brett started to object but Lily suggested he keep quiet, in a not so kind voice.

As I reached my hand into the water, the creature came to me and let me pick it up. I held it as if holding a small animal, gentle and caring. I felt something sharp then, as if many needles entered my hand.

Deep inside my body, I felt a sensation, the tingling went from mild to that same sharp pain, which my ankle felt when the creature grabbed me and put its fluid in my body.

Brett felt it too, I knew, for his hands held tighter, and I could feel his body behind me stiffen a bit, but he didn't let go. I was one with this animal, the entire animal, even though it was deep in the waters somewhere. The creature that did this to me, was still attached to its appendage and I became aware of it.

It wasn't an octopus, as I had thought. I couldn't make out exactly what it was, but somehow I knew that I would see it again.

I felt the creature let go of me then, and I put it back into the water. The creature moved away from my hand, shivered in a convulsive way, and sunk to the bottom, Lifeless.

I looked down at my hands, still stinging. I saw several dozen small egg-like things on the spots where the needles had pierced my skin. They suddenly moved, and sunk into my hands. The pain increased, and then the small puncture wounds closed as I could feel these things, whatever they were, creep up my arms and spread through my body, spacing themselves out as if knowing exactly where they were supposed to be.

My hands and arms turned back to my normal color and the pain deep down, ceased. I felt a new sensation, as if something had awakened inside of me, a part of me that had been dormant but now was awake, aware, and caused the need I had, that different type of nourishment, to be even stronger.

Tina M. Engel

The door to the cooler flew open and suddenly there were voices, commotion and chaos, coming from the kitchen. As I turned towards the door, my mother, Angelina came rushing in.

"It's Rose!" She said. "Something is happening, she started trembling and then crumbled to the floor." Angelina said in a panic.

Douglas glanced at Lily and then was the first out the door. I followed, with Brett still having one hand on my waist. Lily was last and shut the door behind after taking one last look at the box.

I dropped to the ground next to Rose on one side and Douglas on the other. Lily touched Douglas's shoulder and as he looked up at her, he moved away, letting Lily get down next to Rose.

Rose looked up at me and reaching up, put her hand on my cheek. She said weakly, "Its okay Princess, you will be okay, I will always be with you. I am inside of you. We will always be together."

I put one hand on Rose's hand that was still on my cheek. It was cold, like death. I put a finger in my mouth and bit down, intending to put it in Rose's mouth. I had to heal her, save her.

Lily touched my hand as I was reaching down to Rose's lips. "No" she said firmly but kindly. "It won't help."

I looked up at Lily's face and saw it filled with anger. I was beside myself with fear and anguish and told her that we had to do something. Rose was dying.

Lily's anger grew as she said calmly but more forceful, "It isn't time, and he knew this. His meddling has got to stop. I don't think you were supposed to feed on Rose after this new element was placed in your body, but I wasn't told this. For some reason, I didn't see this. You still needed her blood for strength until the time was right. Why did I not see this?"

Lily then looked at me and said, "She is not dying, not yet anyway. Emilee, put your cameo on her left side, just above her breast, put your ring on her right hand, on the finger that it fits the tightest and put your diamond necklace around her neck."

I looked at Lily stunned, confused as to why she would want me to give Rose my gifts, the gifts that gave me such strength and protection.

"Now!" bellowed Lily. "There isn't much time!"

I did as I was told, first the cameo, then the ring, which fit tightly on her right middle finger and then the necklace.

Rose's skin coloring had been changing as the minutes had passed, turning deathly white, but when I put the necklace around her neck and laid the diamond on her chest, her color came back just a bit, not the vibrant tan, still pale, but not death white. I could see Kimberlite's face in the diamond, and acceptance was what I felt coming from him.

Rose looked at me with a sweet smile, touched my cheek again, and then as her hand dropped, she stopped breathing.

I looked to Lily in anguish, as my tears started to flow. "She isn't dead, Emilee, but it wasn't supposed to happen this way and at this time."

Tina M. Engel

Lily stood then, as Douglas turned towards Trevor and said, "Come with me. We'll take Rose, and place her where she will be safe for now."

Lily shouted with anger in her eyes, "Douglas, find the fey on the ship who is working as his eyes. They must be closed!"

I was so confused by her statement "His eyes." Whose eyes? I thought, and looked to Douglas as he acknowledge what she said, in an understanding manner.

Lily then said to Eagle, in a calmer tone but still agitated, "Come with me, we must stop him before it's too late. It isn't time yet. If he continues to interfere, he will ruin everything and destroy us all. Damn him anyway!" And she headed towards the door, with Eagle following.

My head was spinning. Trevor reached down and picked up Rose in a gentle manner, with deep sadness on his face. Angelina and Jordan were standing next to each other looking at me, and Captain Adam was talking to Douglas but I couldn't hear anything, my mind was so full of my own thoughts.

As Lily and Eagle ran from the room, I followed, with Brett behind me, insisting I stop. I felt his hand on my arm and it slid down to my hand, which jerked me to a standstill.

I turned with venom in my eyes and told Brett to let go or come with me, but I was following them, I wanted to know what was happening.

I turned back and headed out the door and up the stairs, with Brett right behind me, as he tried to get into my thoughts. I could feel him, but he wasn't able to enter. Was I stopping him or was something else?

All I could hear were my thoughts, confused, who is he? What did Lily mean? There was no way I was letting Rose die.

As I reached the deck, I saw Lily point towards the sun, saying, "Take me there.", and turned into her domestic cat shape.

Eagle scooped her up in his talons and soared into the sky. As he flew away from the ship, he yelled back down to me, "Don't worry Princess, I won't drop her, I know how cats hate water." He chuckled and then let out a yelp, as Lily reached up and scratched him slightly with a claw, not finding what he had just said a bit humorous at all, at the moment.

They heading towards the sun. I had to put my hand up, to shade my eyes from the glare, to be able to see them and then they just disappeared. They were gone, just gone.

Chapter 7

Sadness,
Fear,
Emotions we need to
Survive.

I gazed up, looking directly into the sun,
wondering where they were, what place they
entered, for I knew somehow they had left
Terrafirma. Did they go to the humans' dimension,
Earth or another place?

I felt a hand on my shoulder and turned my
head to see who it was. There stood, Angelina my
mother, my mom. She was my mom and I hadn't
even called her that yet, my mom.

I suddenly had such a need for her, my
mother. She stood there with love in her eyes, and
I turned and crumpled up into her arms. The tears
started to flow as my knees buckled and my legs
gave way. I let them go, let it all go and as I wilted
to the ground, Angelina came down with me, as if
in slow motion. She kept me safe in her arms and
we rested gently on the ground. I laid my head in
her lap and sobbed quietly.

My hair was plastered to my face by my
tears and Angelina carefully and lovingly, brushed
the hair away. She wiped the tears and soothed me
by whispering over and over again, "I'm with you
now, you're okay, its going to be okay."

I could feel Brett close by, that vibration, the
safe feeling I had, the connection we shared. He
stayed some distance from us though, not wanting
to intrude, he knew what I needed then, not him

but her. He wasn't offended but relieved, I could tell, our thoughts were one again. He was there, but not intrusive.

I sat up finally, and Angelina removed the hair from my other cheek with a kind smile across her lips. I looked at her face, so beautiful and warm and said in a whisper, "Mom", and she just smiled.

We stood and Brett came over then, knowing that I was okay. I said, in a rather babbling manner, "I need to see Rose, I need to talk to Douglas, I need to know what is going on, and who was Lily talking about, where did they go?

Brett tenderly put a finger to my lips to quiet me for a moment. His touch sent a slight zing to my lips but it didn't hurt.

"Emilee, Rose is in a safe place and Douglas is trying to figure out who is on this ship that shouldn't be. We will get more answers soon and will tell you as soon as we know, I promise."

I smiled up at him, knowing that he was being truthful and Brett continued, "You need your rest now Emilee."

I opened my mouth to object, but before anything could come out, Angelina spoke quickly and firmly, "I agree with Brett completely and I will be with you while you rest. Brett will have someone outside the cabin door to make sure no one comes in except Douglas, Adam, Trevor or Brett.

I realized then just how tired I was and I wanted Rose, but then remembered she wasn't with me. I couldn't feed from her and the sadness overwhelmed me all over again.

Tina M. Engel

We went down to my cabin and as we entered, I thought of Rose, she should be here with me too.

"Why?" Was all I could say, as Angelina led me over to the bed. I kicked off my shoes, and crawling under the blankets, I felt suddenly cold.

Angelina sat down on the edge of the bed, kissed me on my forehead and told me to shut my eyes and rest. She would be here when I woke.

I shut my eyes and heard, as if someone was calling from far away, "Emilee, it's time to come home."

I heard Rose calling me, "Princess Emilee, wake up, Princess Emilee!"

I opened my eyes, and was blinded momentarily. The sun was shining brightly in my eyes, as it seeped between the branches of the tree that I was lying under. I put my hand up to shade my eyes and turned my head to see that I was in the wheat field.

I heard voices, happy, squealing voices, a child and Brett. As I sat up, again I heard Rose, up above me, "Princess, nap time is over!", as she giggled.

I looked up to see Rose and Lily, sitting on a big branch. Lily was laying lazily in cat form, grooming herself, acting irritated as Rose stroked her.

I turned back to the wheat field and saw Brett and Katie running through the field, with Katie holding a string. As my eyes followed the string up into the air, there at the end was a kite; a dragon, large and red, with golden eyes that seemed to be looking down at me.

Tina M. Engel

Brett stopped and turned, and our eyes locked in a loving gaze and his smile, as always, made my hearts skip a beat and that tingling sensation swept over my body.

He turned back again to Katie and the kite, and continued to back up towards the cliff and ocean below, causing the kite to soar even higher.

I stood up and turned away from them, looking behind the tree, and there stood the castle, large and grand, as it sparkled in the sunlight. This was my home and Brett's, with Katie our daughter, I knew it. I felt such happiness and peace within.

I could hear Katie giggling again, and Rose and Lily up above fussing with each other and I smiled contently. I was home, finally, and Rose was alive and well.

I turned back to Brett and Katie, as Katie pointed up and laughed, saying, "Look Daddy, look!"

I looked up to see, flying around the dragon, an eagle. It was Eagle, and he was here too.

I heard a noise behind me and as I turned, there in the distance was Kimberlite, standing in front of the castle. He had an odd look on his face, and a strange slight glow around him.

Suddenly, from behind the mountain that the castle was protruding from, came a cloud, dark grey, as it swirled and churned, engulfing the castle and Kimberlite.

The wind started to blow and I turned around to look at Brett and Katie. They were looking up in horror. I looked in the direction they were staring and saw the kite turn into a real *dragon, and it consumed Eagle with one bite. The string to the kite fell as the dragon flew towards the greyness that seemed to ooze towards us and then the dragon disappeared.*

I ran to Brett and Katie as they rushed to me. As I turned back, I saw the greyness overtake the tree, with Lily and Rose still up in the branches, and heard Rose yelling, "It can all be different, don't quit."

I looked up into Brett's eyes and knew there was nowhere to run, and as I wrapped my one arm around Katie and the other around Brett, with Brett's arms holding us both, I shut my eyes as the greyness engulfed us.

I opened my eyes as I sat up, gasping for air. My hearts were pounding as I looked around and saw I was in the cabin on the ship, with my mother sitting there in a chair, reading. She looked up with concern and rushed over to me, dropping the book on the floor.

She was there in a moment, sitting next to me and as she wrapped her arms around me, and as I looked over her shoulder, the book lifted from the floor and set itself down on the table.

Suddenly, there was a shadow. Maybe my eyes were playing tricks on me, but I saw a shadow. It cleared just enough that I saw her there, she had picked up the book, it was Rose. As quickly as I saw her, she was gone, but not before she smiled, put a finger to her lips as if to shush me, keeping a secret of sorts.

"She's alive?" I said in a whisper, as Angelina pulled away just a bit, still holding onto my arms. Her look was that of worry but she said nothing.

"Rose," I said, "I want to go see Rose."

Angelina smiled a faint smile, and said, "Let's wait for Brett. He went to talk with Douglas and then we will know better what this is all about."

I agreed, with a nod of my head, and told her that I needed water. Angelina got up and told me she would get me a glass of water. That wasn't what I wanted, I needed water, to be in water and told her so.

I stood up and headed to the door, letting her know that I was okay, but needed to be in the ocean, for just a while. I needed water, I was so thirsty. I opened my wings, and they seemed dry, irritated, they needed water.

Angelina started to argue, out of concern I knew, but I turned to look at her feeling angry for some reason. She had a look of uncertainty on her face for a moment, and then composed herself, as she came to me.

I lowered my wings as she put her arms around me, kissed my cheek, and said, "I love you and will be with you to the end, but I don't think going into the waters below is a good idea at the moment. Go do what you must in the bathroom, and I'll be out here waiting. Please."

Looking into a mirror behind Angelina, I saw my reflection again, it didn't look like me, I was silvery white, with eyes emerald green. Then as I pushed gently away from her, I was back, my tan color with blue eyes.

Tina M. Engel

Angelina smiled and kissed me once more before releasing me as I turned and entered the bathroom. As I shut the door, I could feel Brett then, that vibration, tingling throughout my body as he entered the room.

He was there in my mind, calm and kind, as he said in a joking way, "Remember, if I need to, I will come in so don't get any mischievous ideas about taking a swim in the ocean. That's not going to happen."

I smiled slightly, happy that he could still be silly, as it calmed me some and I took off my clothes and stepped into the warm shower. As the water fell on my body, I could feel it entering every pore as my body drank the liquid that I needed so badly. I released my wings partly, letting them lay down my back, as the tips touched the shower floor. They were what needed the water.

It wasn't the only liquid I needed though, and I wondered why I wasn't craving Rose's blood. Why did her blood taste so odd? I knew that I didn't need her anymore and that terrified me. Why, I wondered, and then reflected on the dream. In my mind, I kept hearing Rose say, something about it could be different and don't quit.

I didn't know how long I had been in the shower, I kept reliving the dream over and over, trying to make sense of it. I knew then, the dream was my home and it was my future, or could be, I hoped.

The door opening brought me back to the bathroom and shower, as a voice said, "Emilee, are you okay?" It was Angelina's voice, soft and eager.

Tina M. Engel

I shut off the water and grabbing a towel, wrapped it around myself as I opened the curtain to see her standing there. Her smile was full of love, as I told her I was fine and would be out in a bit. I told her I had a dream and needed to share it with everyone, especially Douglas, and wanted her to collect everyone in the mess hall.

She gave me a questioning look and I knew she was unsure about leaving me. I chuckled and told her to leave Brett in the room. He would make sure I behaved. Of course she also knew my heart, my feelings for Brett and the need to be alone with him. That concerned her too, a bit, she is my mother after all.

Angelina's quick response to that was, "Is it safe to leave the two of you alone?", as she lifted her eyebrows, tilted her head slightly and smiled. She nodded then in agreement and turned, leaving the bathroom and closing the door.

I spread my wings out fully, waving them in the air to shake off the excess water before letting them shrink back into my back. I dressed quickly, feeling Brett's anxiousness and as I entered my room, his look of relief quickly turned to desire. I felt it too, such a need, but it was different than before. I felt such a hunger deep down, it scared me.

Brett suggested we head to the mess hall then, not waiting around, and I knew he felt it too, and he knew we shouldn't be alone together.

I went up to him and took his hands in mine. I wanted to be alone with him, it had been too long since we were together, enjoying each other's

Tina M. Engel

company, but this feeling was so different and I wanted the old feelings back.

"This is the way it is and must be for now, Princess." Brett said, with sadness.

He called me Princess, not Emilee? I thought, and in my mind, he was there, and said, "Emilee, it has to be this way for now. I am no longer stronger than you. I can't stop you. You must stay in control, be strong. It isn't time."

I looked into his eyes, they were green with need but I felt fear in his body as I held his hands. Brett bent down and placed a soft kiss on my lips, our thoughts linked and he thought, "Fear will not stop me from letting you..." And the door opened.

Brett and I both turned towards the door, letting go of each other's hands, and the strange connection that I felt was gone. It was our touch, which was different now, but why?

It was Adam, at the door, and his look was that of relief, as he said, "Well just in the nick of time, I guess. Everyone is in the mess hall waiting for you both. We are just hours from our destination, near Proteus's city." And he stepped aside from the door, extending his hand in the direction of the hallway, insinuating we leave the room.

I left, with Brett following and Adam in the rear, closing the door as he left. We headed down the hall, up the stairs and into the mess hall, but as we passed crewmen, they looked at me queerly, as if they were slightly afraid.

Chapter 8

> *Fear creates anger,*
> *Anger clouds the mind.*
> *We must stay focused*
> *To fix the damage that we create*
> *Or that others created.*
> *Believe in those around you,*
> *Forgive if you must to continue*
> *Forward.*

We entered the mess hall and it was Jordan who came to me, and his look of relief concerned me. He hugged me tightly, a bit too tight, I thought, and as he released me, he had a look of embarrassment on his face.

Jordan took my hand and led me over to a table where Douglas was sitting and I sat down across from him. Brett started to sit next to me but Douglas stopped him, suggesting he sit next to him, with a look of caution.

It was Angelina who sat down next to me and took my hand in hers, holding it softly. I looked up at her smiling face but could see that she was feeling unsure about something.

I looked to Douglas then, feeling angry again and said rather rudely, "What in the hell is going on? You all look like you are just waiting for me to turn into a monster and devour you."

This caused some chuckling and Trevor said, "Don't be silly Princess Emilee, not all monsters are evil."

Everyone in the room had a look of horror, and Adam, who standing next to Trevor, smacked him on the back in a supposedly comical gesture and commented, that he didn't mean it that way.

When Trevor realized that what he had said, didn't come out the way he had meant it to, he said, "What? It's the truth, but Princess, I didn't mean to say you are a monster, or will be soon."

Adam gave Trevor a look of displeasure and I started to laugh. Everyone was on pins and needles, so to speak, and I found it so entertaining, they were all a bit intimidated by me. Little old me, and my laughter calmed everyone a bit.

I looked to Douglas then and asked more seriously, "Douglas, what is going on? Where are Lily and Eagle, and who is this person that Lily was talking about?" I had more to ask, but Douglas put up a hand to stop me and with a stern expression asked everyone to sit down.

"Princess, things have moved faster than they were supposed to. We are trying to slow it down but we had to find the fey on the ship that is working for..." Douglas stopped then for a few seconds, looking around the room and then back to me.

"Who?" I asked, frustrated.

"Princess, the creature who came up from the deepest part of these seas, was sent not to bring you to him, but to put the venom in you, to stop you from needing Rose's blood. It sped up your transformation, changing what your body needs, to reach your full potential. This was supposed to happen, but just not yet.

"He is in a panic, thinking that maybe we are too late to change things, fix things and stop the greyness from spreading." Douglas said.

Tina M. Engel

"I saw the greyness." I said.

Douglas, with a curious look on his face, asked me, "What do you mean?"

I then told them all about my dream, the place that I have gone to, since this journey began. I told them about the castle, which was never there before, and about the greyness that swept over the castle and us, Brett, myself and Katie.

When I said the name Katie, I looked at Brett and he knew who I was talking about but said nothing. He was there, with me, feeling my fear, helping me to continue.

Douglas asked, "Katie?"

I replied, "My daughter...and Brett's."

Douglas's eyes widened just a bit, this was something unknown to him and that caused a panic in me. Douglas had seemed to know so much of what was going on in this crazy journey.

"What else was in your dream, or better yet, who?" Douglas asked with a bit of anxiety in his tone.

"Rose and Lily were in the tree and they were swallowed up by the greyness, and Eagle was eaten by the dragon, a kite that turned into a real dragon, and Kimberlite..." I stopped then and felt where my necklace usually hung, but it was around Rose's neck now.

With confusion in my voice, I looked firmly into Douglas's eyes and said, "Kimberlite was there, standing in front of the castle. His look was strange and he had a slight glow around him. The greyness engulfed him, too."

"Kimberlite?" I whispered.

Tina M. Engel

It was quiet for a moment and then Brett broke the silence by saying gruffly but with questioning in his voice, "Kimberlite is on our side, has been all along! He has been my friend for ages!"

Douglas, turned and put a hand on Brett's shoulder but Brett jerked away and stood. "NO!" He yelled, "Kimberlite is not working for him!"

"Maybe he was trapped." I said, as I looked at Brett, but he wouldn't look at me.

I continued then, questioning with a tremble in my voice, "Where is Lily and who is this fey that you are all afraid of? Is it Proteus? Where is this place I keep seeing and what is the greyness?"

A voice came from the doorway, "So many questions Princess, but are you really ready to hear the answers?" Lily, it was Lily, with Eagle standing behind her.

I got up and rushed to her, throwing my arms around her and hugging her as if she was a long lost friend. Lily wrapped her arms around me also and hugged me kindly, and as she gently pushed me away, she kissed my cheek.

"Okay Princess, you are messing up my fur." She said, as she fussed a bit, smoothing it down.

She took my hand then and led me back to the table where she insisted I sit, and she took the seat next to Douglas, where Brett had been sitting. Brett went over to a window and sat down on a small table.

No one spoke, the silence was excruciating. I could see in everyone's faces, as I looked around the room, that they all were feeling the same as I, except for Douglas. He seemed to know so much more than everyone else.

I looked back at Lily, and saw she had that strange glow around her again, and I could see that the cat fey she portrayed, was just that, a disguise. She was something else, someone else, but what? Who?

Lily looked at me and smiled, that smile that a cat would do, when they knew they were caught doing something that they shouldn't be doing, but did it anyway.

I looked around the room at everyone, wondering if they saw this too, but no one seemed disturbed or questioned anything, just waited for answers.

When I looked back at Lily, it was Lily, the cat fey that I knew, (or did I know her at all?) Lily said then, "So, tell me about this last dream. I walked in at the end, Brett all up in arms about Kimberlite?"

I looked at Brett and he had a strange perplexed look, and as I tried to read his thoughts, I was blocked, he was stopping me from being one with him.

I looked at him with shock and dismay and then I was angry. Fine, I thought, be that way. And I turned away.

I told Lily from start to finish all about the dream and when I was done, no one spoke but Lily got up and paced the floor for a bit.

She came back to the table, sat down and began, "The greyness are all the dark fey spirits, joined together, trying to spread confusion, fear, jealousy, sadness and evil throughout Earth. He

Tina M. Engel

has been gathering them over time, patiently creating his own dark army."

When Lily paused, Brett spoke, feeling my lack of understanding of the grey spirits. "Remember Emilee when we got off the fishing boat in New York, you saw the wisps of color, a rainbow of sorts? I told you what all the colors meant, they all had different personalities.

"I told you about the grey wisps, dark fey who visit the realm of Nirvana and the white wisps who are the ancient fey who keep the peace there. Humans see the colors as a rainbow, the greyness are the clouds before a storm and the white spirits are the white clouds in the blue sky that try to push the greyones away, when they get too disorderly.

When the white spirits of the ancient ones and the greys collide, that causes the great storms in the humans' world. It is all about balance. The grey spirits are tolerated, as long as balance is maintained."

I looked back at Lily and asked, "Who is he, the one gathering the grey spirits, or wisps? Is it Proteus?

"No child." Lily said.

Child? I thought. She has never called me that before. But someone did, a long time ago. Before I could question this, Lily continued.

"Don't interrupt, please, Princess, I will tell you what you need to know before you go down to Proteus's city of Bermuda." Lily said, with a bit of frustration in her voice. "We don't have much time, we must close the door quickly."

Tina M. Engel

I looked at her and felt anger. She was treating me like a child, and after all that I had been through, with all the secrets and danger that these fey, all of them, had put me in, now to be treated like a mere child, to be put in my place, so to speak. I had had enough, and started to rise as I felt my body tingle all over again, as if the ants just under my skin were on the move.

Douglas, reached out and took my hands quietly, and asked me to sit back down. I saw that my hands where white and assumed my entire body was again so I took a deep breath, and looked over at Brett.

Brett was deep in thought, looking out the window and I slowly took my hands from Douglas, released my wings from my back, needing to ease my anger and tension, and walked over to him.

I reached up and touched Brett's face. He was so deep in thought, he didn't even know I had come over to him. As my hand touched his skin, he jerked just a bit, and then looking at me, our eyes connected, and he let me in.

We would be going down there together, he knew this, and he was anxious to get going, but also anxious for this to be over, not just going down to Bermuda, but this entire journey.

Was he wanting to get rid of me? I wondered.

When Brett realized what I was thinking, he took my hands in his and reassured me that he didn't want it to ever end. (Of course, this was in my thoughts, not spoken out loud for all to hear.)

When he touched me though, that feeling of need, longing and hunger was there, just under my

Tina M. Engel

skin, and Brett's eyes had the green of hunger, look. We both let go of each other, knowing now wasn't the time.

"Princess", Lily said, "please come back and sit, there is much to tell you, before you both go down to the city. We don't have much time. I don't believe that Proteus is aware of our arrival yet, and I would really like it if you got down there and did what you must, before he realizes that you are there.

I looked at Brett, he nodded for me to go sit and he walked back to the table with me. He touched my shoulder lightly and said, "Listen to her, and hear what she says."

Brett walked back over to the window and sat down on the small table next to the window. I folded my wings into my back, as I sat back down, and Lily continued.

"You have so many questions, but let me tell you what you need to know first, then if I haven't answered all of your questions and I think it important for you to know, I will tell you."

"But you're just a cat?" I questioned. "Why are you telling me this, and not Douglas?"

Lily smiled, and looking at Douglas, he smiled too as if they had been friends for a very long time, or maybe more than friends.

"Emilee, as you know, there are many dimensions that share the humans' Earth. Terrafirma is just one of them, and all from Terrafirma can get to Earth just by thinking it. The worlds, Earth and Terrafirma, are so closely linked that there are no doors that keep them apart. It is the young minds of humans that keep them out of Terrafirma.

"Nirvana is the dimension, which fey from Terrafirma go to when they need to rest and rebuild their inner peace, but it is also the place they go when it is time to leave their fey bodies for good. You have been told this?"

I nodded my head and responded, "Yes."

"The grey colors that are seen in Nirvana are the fey who caused trouble in their fey lives. I don't like to use the word evil, because fey are usually not bad, they do what they must to survive and follow the few rules set down by the elders. Some are predators and some are prey. That is the way of life everywhere, but there are rules.

"The grey spirits are not allowed to live in Nirvana when they leave their fey bodies, for they have broken too many rules. There is another place they go, to roam for all eternity, unless they are able to mend their negative ways before their bodies die."

"You mean evil ways!" I said, with a bit of hostility in my voice.

Lily smiled and tilted her head slightly, as if to agree without saying it. She continued, "These fey, while still alive, can go to Nirvana as they want, like the rest of us, but their essence is dark so they have a grey hue to their bodies. They are tolerated as I said, because we hope they will change their ways.

"They are now getting unruly and we are, from time to time, finding a grey spirit, one who died as you say, and has been found hiding in

Tina M. Engel

Nirvana and stirring up trouble, and gathering the grey fey and taking them to him.

"It is all about balance, Princess, we need the grey along with all the other colors to survive. We must stop him from taking any more fey, though. He is the one causing the split between the dark fey and light, it is not the land fey versus the water fey, as some think.

"The Dark One does feel that the humans are a plague on this world, which we share with so many others, in dimensions you know nothing about yet." Lily shuddered just slightly when she said, "Dark One".

I think I was the only one who saw this and it disturbed me. I kept quiet though, Lily was sharing what I needed to know and I didn't want to upset her and have her stop.

"The storms in the humans' world," I said and paused, "that's him, wanting to destroy all humans?"

Lily smiled a grave smile, and said, "I'm afraid so." and then continued. "When the humans' Earth started to show signs of viciousness, we, the fey of Terrafirma became concerned. Yes, humans are a very young race, and must find their way through the dark times, as well as the light, but this was different. The darkness became more evil, more and more humans began to show signs of darkness; anger, hatred, greed, jealousy and selfishness, not seen before where light couldn't bring them back.

"We have been trying for centuries now, to stop it, put light in the way of darkness, give some humans the knowledge and goodness, to fight this disease of cruelty, but we are losing this battle. If he can get enough grey spirits, dark fey, to follow him, they will be able to destroy the humans' earth, and Terrafirma will be destroyed too. Only evil and darkness will thrive."

"Who is he, the Dark One that you all keep talking about? I've been led to believe all along that no one knew who he was, but you know, don't you?" I asked with frustration. "If it isn't Stephan, then is it the creature that I saw in my dream?"

Douglas replied, "The Dark One has been hiding his identity for centuries, Emilee. We have suspected different fey, from time to time, but were always wrong, finding out that they were just following another, and we were never able to discover his true identity."

It was quiet for a few moments as Lily and Douglas looked at each other. I was starting to think that maybe I didn't really want to know who this Dark One was, but maybe I had already met this fey.

As I looked around the room, everyone was waiting but it was Eagle who seemed to be a bit fidgety, pacing, going from the window to the door as if wanting to go somewhere. When he caught me watching him, Eagle went over to where Brett was sitting and leaned against the wall.

Lily looked around the room at everyone waiting and it was Brett then, who had had enough of the silence and spouted, "Could you please just tell us if you know or not and if you do, who!? We have a right to know!"

"Emilee, you have met him, in your dream but the appearance that you saw was just a façade.

He is still keeping his identity hidden, to all but a few." Lily paused and then said, "Stephan is one, who knows him." As she looked to Brett.

Brett took a deep breath before speaking. I could feel the anger that was covering his pain. "Where do I find my brother, so I can beat the information out of him? Brett said, with such calmness in his voice that it frightened me just a bit.

Douglas chuckled, he actually chuckled, and told Brett that it wasn't for him to go off halfcocked and get himself into trouble, just to get the chance to beat up his brother. It wouldn't help anything and he might get himself killed.

Lily mumbled under her breath, "And that would change everything."

Brett started to speak again, but this time with bitterness in his eyes and Douglas stood up and bellowed louder than I had heard before, "Brett you will sit down and shut up! You have a role to play, but so does he. If you interfere with this, then all will be lost. Keep your cool and do your duty, by Emilee. That is your job and your responsibility, only to get her to a certain place and then she must go alone."

Douglas had a look of sadness then and Brett sat down, but had a look of hate on his face. Douglas said then in a compassionate tone, "Your job is important, but Stephan is a part of this too, it was written a long time ago. This is all I'm going to say now about this."

I could feel Brett's pain and anger, still seething deep down. He didn't hide it from me, didn't shut me out. He looked up at me and I saw the fear in his eyes, and heard his thoughts, "I don't want to lose you."

I got up, went over to him and touching his cheek, I said, out loud for all to hear "You won't, I won't let it happen."

I went back to my chair, as everyone watched and wondered, I was sure, what that was all about, but looking at Lily, she knew. Lily knew and understood much more than she let on.

"Lily, please tell me who you were talking about, when you said that he was interfering again? And Rose, what is all of this about Rose?" I questioned.

"You don't need to worry about him, interfering again, anyway. If he does, he will feel the full power of my wrath, not just my annoyance next time. As for Rose, let her sleep for now. Know that she isn't in pain and she wants you to focus on your quest. It will all make sense in the end, but we must make it there in time." Lily said.

I didn't want to let it go, about Rose, I was so worried and wanted her by my side. Her strength and sassiness was so comforting to me, but I let it go because I had yet another important question to ask and wasn't sure if they would answer it or if they even could.

"Who am I or better yet, what am I?" I asked. "How am I supposed to fix this?"

"You, Emilee, are not just human or fey, and you know this, deep down inside, so I can tell you without you freaking out." Lily said with a chuckle and I had to smile. She was right, I did know this, somehow, somewhere along the way, I knew.

Tina M. Engel

I nodded my head, agreeing, and looking at Brett, he had known it too. I wasn't upset with him, he had to let me discover this on my own.

"What am I then, and how can I fix this?" I asked, and Angelina, took my hand in hers, squeezing it softly and said, "With our help."

"Yes..." Lily said, "To a point, and then you must finish alone."

"But, what am I?" I asked again.

I knew that I could turn fire red, and now a silver white. With my shield I could protect myself and those around me, and with the ring, given to me by Trevor, I could heal others. The diamond let me stay in contact with the underworld, rocks and lava, and I now had wings. I had needed pixie blood for a while but those cravings were gone, and I only wanted Brett's.

Lily smiled and said simply, "You are you." And at that she continued with the information I needed.

"That place you dream of, the things you have seen there, are possibilities of the future, but everything must fall into place just right, in order for that to happen. You have seen many different versions of your future, both dark and light and everything depends on your choices, the path you choose to take.

"I can tell you only so much, but you, Emilee, will be the one to make the decisions and face the consequences, and so must we, with the choices you make."

"Where is this place I see in my dreams?" I asked.

Tina M. Engel

Lily just smiled and told me that I would find it when the time was right.

It was Douglas who spoke then, before I could question Lily any further concerning my dream world.

"Emilee and Brett, it is time." Douglas said as he looked towards Brett.

Brett turned away from the window and came over to us, and pulling a chair next to me, sat down. When Brett got up, Eagle went over to the window and gazed out, seemingly more interested in what was out there than what Douglas had to say.

I had an odd feeling about Eagle. Something was wrong, I could feel it, ever since he rejoined us after his injuries when we battled with Stephan and his band, in the goblins' village. I could not get distracted with this now, though, or should I?

Douglas continued, "The city of Bermuda is large, with many places that haven't been inhabited in years. Proteus has kept these places locked, forbidding anyone from entering.

"Yes, Emilee, he still thinks you are his daughter, well he wants to believe it anyway, and wants you back to rule beside him. He suspects you are the one and wants you there to help him protect his city and people, when the Dark One succeeds.

"Proteus believes there is no stopping the Dark One, and will make as many deals with him as he can to keep his little piece of Terrafirma safe. With you by his side, he feels that he can do this.

"He knows that the Dark One wants you, but believes with your powers and his, you both together can keep him out of Bermuda, anyway.

"We, the council, have strung Proteus along with the belief that we were bringing you to him, but he now knows that we have all along known his plans and kept you from him, long enough for you to acquire your strength and abilities.

"Angelina was our way into his city and into Proteus's life from the beginning, when she was sent by the elders, being with child." Douglas said, as he looked to Angelina.

I looked to her also and she had a look of sadness, and acceptance and I realized she had known this for some time.

I asked her, "Did you know from the beginning, when you first left the elders and the lady led you to Bermuda? Did you let them take me away from you, did you do this on purpose? I don't understand."

Angelina, brought my hand to her lips, kissed it softly and told me that she was told the night I was born why she had been brought there, to Proteus. The lady had come to her again, explaining her role in this deception, to keep Proteus thinking that he had the council fooled. All the while, Angelina could search the city until she found the doorway that must be closed.

"Proteus knew of the doorway, had it hidden from all, for centuries. It was his father, Poseidon, who first discovered the doorway, deep under the sea, in the humans' world, and working with the elders' consent, had the city of Bermuda built and

Tina M. Engel

put his son, Proteus, there to protect the doorway and keep it closed.

"At some point, Proteus became poisoned by the Dark One, no one knows exactly when or how, but the council learned of Proteus's joining with him, and his work to cause destruction and chaos in the humans' world.

"Angelina found it." Douglas said, "Just before Proteus suspected she wasn't who he thought she was, and we knew that we had to get her out of there."

Angelina, still holding my hand said, "Emilee, we had to keep you safe, that much I knew, but it was the hardest thing I have ever done, letting you go. Your safety though, was all I cared about. I willingly helped the council, played the role I was destined for, I am a member of the council after all, even though they kept secrets from me as well."

She looked at Jordan then with sadness and longing in her eyes and said, "I was told you were dead, they lied to me too. I have forgiven the deception and I understand the elders' worries. If we each knew the other was alive, would we still cooperate and be able to pretend, in order to carry out this scheme, to find the hidden doorway and close it? Would we be able to keep hidden the fact that we knew that Emilee was our child and that she was the one to save us all from him? It was too much to risk."

Angelina turned away from Jordan, his anger apparent, and looking at Douglas, she said, "Is this lady who has visited me so many times, my true mother? And if so, why has this been so

Tina M. Engel

secretive? Wouldn't it have been easier if I had known all along?"

Douglas answered, "No Angelina, knowledge can sometimes get in the way. We needed you to believe completely until the night Emilee was born. We couldn't take any chances, we needed this plan to work. We have tried many other ways, but lost in the end."

Douglas looked to Brett then and said, "We had to make this as real as possible. That's why all of your lives have worked out the way they have, and why certain fey and humans have come into your lives. It was all planned a long time ago. There could be no errors this time."

Lily continued, "The Dark One has been right there every step of the way, knowing things, that we thought were kept secret, but we have been able to distract him, so to speak, at times.

"The Dark One somehow found you, Emilee, and sent Stephan to evaluate your growth process. For those years you were with Stephan, we the council were in the dark as to what was really going on with you. We could get glimpses of you as we told you, so we knew you were still where you needed to be. But until Stephan left you alone, we had no idea that the Dark One was so close to our every move.

"We still didn't know it was Stephan who was with you for those years, until that night when Brett saved you from him, and then all the pieces fell into place and we discovered just how close the Dark One was and is. He seemed to have blocked our view somehow, keeping Stephan's role a secret.

Tina M. Engel

Oh, we did know that Stephan had a role to play, but we didn't know about this time frame."

Brett then began to talk, but more to himself than to the rest of us. "Stephan's father died, but Stephan always blamed my father and me." He then looked directly at Douglas and asked, "Did he really die?"

"Brett, this isn't the time or place for this. You and Emilee must go down to the city and close the doorway." Douglas said quietly.

"This is the time, Douglas, I want to know, was my role planned for me all along?" Brett spouted.

Douglas had a look of frustration but calmly answered, "Brett I don't really think you need to know, but fine, Stephan's father was working for the Dark One, long ago. No he didn't die, he disappeared when the elders found out. Your father…"

Douglas paused and Brett bellowed, "What about my father?"

"He was sent to your village to try and find out where Stephan's father might have gone, hoping that we could figure out exactly who the Dark One was. Your father was then given the task of courting your mother. Your task of helping Emilee was set forth before you were born."

Douglas looked at Lily and continued. "It was all written in the stars, I guess you could say."

He looked back at Brett and grumbled, "Now you know and we can discuss it more later, but for now, put that anger that you are feeling to good use, get Emilee down to the city, find the doorway and help her close it. Then, when this is all over, you can strike me, since I know that is what you want to do!"

I looked at Lily and asked before Brett could spout off again and get us side tracked, "Is Stephan's father the Dark One?"

Lily smiled with sadness in her eyes, and said, "No child, the Dark One has been around a long time."

When Lily called me (child) again, I knew, I knew who she was and as our eyes connected, she knew that I knew, and I then understood.

"Who sent the creature to poison me? I asked.

Douglas stood up in a huff, tired of the questions, I was guessing, but I was going to stand my ground. I stood too, wings out stretched again, staring at him with my arms crossed over my chest.

"If you want me to go down and shut some stupid doorway, I have a right to know where it opens into, what place? And I deserve to know who is after me, trying to stop me from closing the doorway and taking me for their own?" I said calmly, but with a harsh tone.

Lily reached out and took Douglas's hand pulling him back down to sit at the table.

Lily continued then, "There is a place I can go to see everything below, a quiet place to view all paths. I suspected who it was, but I had to know for sure who sent the creature too soon, who was wanting to rush your transformation.

"The one who sent the creature to put the venom in you, to speed up your transformation, can go to this place also. There are only a few who can go there, and I dealt with him."

Tina M. Engel

"Who?!" I asked more aggressively than I planned.

"It isn't necessary for you to know this, it makes no difference in your quest, but if you must know so we can move on, it was Poseidon. Since the doorway is in his seas and he has been responsible for protecting it and keeping those who dwell on the other side, out, he feels that he has the right to interfere just a bit. But he must not."

Lily looked at Douglas then and changed the subject, saying, "You found the one who has been his eyes, here on the ship?"

With a sadness on his face, Douglas said, "I believe we have it figured out, but let's discuss it later."

Douglas bent down and kissed Lily on the cheek and I saw her differently, for a moment, and then it was Lily, my Lily, who put a hand up to Douglas's face, touched his cheek saying, "Now, now, let's have none of that. You will ruffle my fur."

"Who?" I demanded. "Who is on this ship and working for Poseidon?

Before they could answer this, I stood up and said, "It doesn't matter, I want to see Rose. I need to see her before I go down to Bermuda. I saw her in my room when I woke from my dream."

Well that brought a shocked look to everyone's faces, except for Lily's.

"She isn't dead and I need to see her." I pleaded, looking from Lily to Douglas.

Douglas looked at me with a strange expression on his face and I knew then, that Rose was the one they suspected, the one working with Poseidon.

"No." I whispered. "She wouldn't."

Brett came over to me as I stood, knocking my chair over behind me. I turned as he grabbed hold of my shoulders, and a strange dizziness took over. He was there in my mind and knew what I was thinking.

Brett looked over my shoulders at Douglas and asked if it was true, had Rose been working for Poseidon all along?

Douglas explained that they were still not sure, but she may have been, unintentionally. The pixie that Rose became close to on Captain Adam's boat, on Lake Erie, they believed to be working for Poseidon, and Rose, not knowing and trusting him, may have given information to him. This fey now, was nowhere to be found.

I told them I had to see her at once, and turned, jerked out of Brett's arms and headed to the door. I stopped then and turned, realizing that I had no idea where she was.

Lily came to me, took my hand and led me out the door, down to the very bottom of the ship. Behind a locked door in the very back, was Rose. She was in a glass box, filled with what looked like smoke or fog. I went to the box and touched it. It was cold as ice.

I looked at Lily as she came to me, and she told me that this box was the only thing, along with my special gifts, that was keeping her here with us and stopped the deterioration of her physical body.

As I looked back down at Rose, she turned her head towards me, opening her eyes, and reached up to put her hand on the glass against my hand. She smiled and I heard her say, in a whisper, that everything would be okay.

I looked around at everyone and they didn't see it. Was I seeing things? I was the only one who saw Rose looking at me with her hand against mine. When I looked back, she was as she had been, laying still with her hands down at her side, eyes closed in the cold box.

"Don't I need my gifts to succeed in closing the doorway?" I asked as I looked at the diamond resting on Rose's chest.

"We think it's best to keep the diamond there with Rose. If Kimberlite..." and Lily let the silence take over the rest of her sentence as she looked at Brett.

Brett finished her sentence with a strange calmness, "is under the spell of the Dark One, he is better left there with Rose. He and the lava pebbles are helping to keep her here with us, so let's let him do something good. We will figure the rest out later."

I looked back down at Rose and at the cameo and said, "But I need the cameo and the ring. I can't close the doorway for good, without them." And I looked up then at Lily. "I don't know why, but I know I need them. Please Lily." I pleaded.

Lily put a hand to my cheek and smiling, told us all to leave the room. She would meet us up on deck; that it was time to get this done.

Chapter 9

> *Believe,*
> *Go forward,*
> *Don't let the*
> *Fear*
> *Stop you.*

Standing outside on deck, the sky was clear, so blue, with the sun shining down on us as if it was a part of our team, helping us to complete this part of our journey.

I looked up at the sun, the same sun that Lily and Eagle had disappeared into just hours ago and I suddenly could see, I was in the room with Lily and Rose.

The room was filled with glowing light, like the sun. Lily put her hands on the glass of the case, which Rose was resting in, and then her hand went through the glass as she retrieved my cameo and ring. When Lily removed her hand from inside the box, the room became the way it had been, no sunny glow.

Lily looked right at me, she knew I was with her, and she smiled a very proud smile, she knew that I was almost there, almost complete.

Then as quickly as I saw this, a cloud covered the sun and my vision was gone. I felt a hand on my shoulder and turning to look, it was Lily, beaming as she pinned the cameo on my dress.

She took my hand then and placed the ring back on my finger and bent down and kissed it. As she stood, I saw the stone glowing brightly and I felt a warmth on my finger beneath the band. It was one with me, even more so than it had been before.

I asked Lily, "I know I need these to close the doorway forever, but will Rose be safe without them? Or does it even matter? If the doorway isn't destroyed, everything will be in vain anyway."

"Rose is in a safe and stable place, for now. She needed those gifts to get there but now, with Kimberlite and the lava pebbles with her, and a little help from up above, she is still with us." Lily said, with a curious smile on her face.

Just then I saw something out of the corner of my eye. Out in the waters, so deep and dark, there came a light rising from the depths. The closer to the surface it came, it looked like a sheet, a bed sheet drifting up to the surface as if dancing to music only it could hear.

I realized as it reached the surface of the ocean, that it was a jelly fish, an enormous jelly fish. Then there were two. They were beautiful, clear on the outside like a window, so I could see everything inside. The colors were pulsating with reds and oranges that moved, so graceful, as they held their place in the water against the waves that tried to push them against the ship. Their glow was like a large flash light shining up to the heavens.

These creatures were here for a reason, to help or hurt, that was the question. As soon as this thought came to my mind, I knew they were here to help.

Brett came to my side and started to pull his knife out from his pocket. I put my hand on his shoulder and looking into his eyes, I smiled and shook my head.

"They're here to help." I said calmly.

It was Adam who spoke next, "So what do we do now? How can they help?"

Angelina came over to me and gave me a folded piece of paper. When I opened it, I saw a map of the City and surrounding area.

Brett came over to us and Angelina showed us the safest way to get to the doorway. She explained that this part of the city was full of dangers. There were creatures from the other side, small but vicious, that were able to enter, from a very small hole in the door, which the Dark One had created somehow. It was too small however for his army or himself to enter through.

I wondered then, if the Dark One couldn't enter, then how was he able to communicate with Proteus and Stephan, and how was I going to destroy this doorway before he could open it?

Lily came over and held out her hand to me with something in it. She placed it in my hand and as I looked down, I saw a small bug-like creature, the size of a dime. It was quite spectacular in looks, a beetle of sorts. Its color was a deep purple with emerald green horns on its head and a tail that looked like a scorpion's, with a very sharp point at the end, which was the same green color.

"This is a creature from the other side of the doorway." Lily said. "You must find the small opening, so this creature can go through. It will then destroy the doorway, from the other side." Lily said.

Tina M. Engel

I looked from the creature in my hand back to Lily and said, "How do you know it will do this and how do I find the hole? And what is the place that is on the other side of the door? "

The creature in my hand then, made a strange screeching noise and as I looked down at it, it stabbed the palm of my hand with its tail. The pointed end of the tail went completely through my hand, and as it did this, the beetle flattened across my palm, wrapped around the back of my hand and attached itself to the tip of the tail.

I swayed, as the pain was excruciating, but I never made a sound. Brett caught me as he let out a shriek of pain, for he was there with me in my mind and he felt it also.

The pain left within seconds and I stood up on my own and knew then, that this creature was on the side of good, and it would show me how to get it through the doorway, to the place it belongs.

I looked at Lily, and asked again, "What's on the other side?"

Lily had a look of sorrow as she said, "It is the place where the dark fey go, their spirits go, when they leave their bodies. Instead of Nirvana, as I said, they go elsewhere to spend all of eternity.

"This place is called Hades and deep within Hades lies Gehenna. The doorway that must be closed, is an entrance to Gehenna. If this door is opened fully, humans' earth will be destroyed and the evil will then enter Terrafirma and dark will rule over light."

"You said that Poseidon was not supposed to be influencing me, but he is, why? What does he have to do with this place, Gehenna? You said that the city of Bermuda was built where it is, to guard the doorway, but is Poseidon good or evil like his son?" I said, in frustration.

"Poseidon is good as I am but he is a bit impatient, not a good characteristic for one with such power." Lily said, with a slight smile, as she shook her head.

Lily continued then, "Poseidon has eyes everywhere, it seems, wanting to keep an eye on things, me, I guess. He sometimes doesn't think I am doing things in the correct time frame.

I was so confused then, and said, "But you are interfering, aren't you, by helping me? You are telling me what to do and what to think and I just want to go home, to Emilee's home in Pineville and let this all be just a dream."

"Emilee," Lily said, "these fey around you are here to help and give you tools to assist you, but you are the one leading them all, this is your story. You could have chosen at any time to take a different path, but you have trusted them and yourself as you have journeyed to this point. You are in control, not them.

"As for me, I am not allowed to interfere either." Lily said, as she winked at me and said with a little chuckle in her voice, "but I do bend things just a bit. He and I...well let's just say that we have different ideas as to how we get to the end, or beginning, whichever way you look at it.

"As for the fey on board, the deck hand, some are calling him a spy, he isn't bad either, just doing what Poseidon wants, keeping an eye on you when he can, getting information about your abilities and getting the information back to Poseidon.

"I want Poseidon to come to me when he wants information. I don't need others snooping and putting their spin on things, getting Poseidon all riled up. He jumps then, as he did with the creature, rushing things."

I saw movement behind Lily and saw Rose, standing at the side of the ship where the jellyfish were, down below, waiting. She was smiling and I walked over to her. I knew that no one else could see her, but I did.

When I got to her, she reached out and took my hand. I felt it, she was real. She placed her forehead to the back of my hand in the gesture of greeting and said, "I will be with you always," but only I could hear, and then she was gone.

I looked back at everyone, staring at me, and realized that right now, it didn't matter what I had just learned or that I still didn't understand much of what Lily had just told me. The only way this was going to be over was if I continued forward, and that meant taking a leap of faith.

At that, I stood up on the side of the ship, and stepping off, I fell as if in slow motion, landing in the water next to one of the beautiful beasts. As I went under the water, I could see just how large they were and even more beautiful now that I could see them in their entirety.

As I emerged on the surface, Brett was in my thoughts, freaking out a bit, asking me what the heck I was doing.

"They're here to take us to the palace safely. You and me." I said.

And at that I went under the water, just under one of the jellyfish. It opened its body and lowered itself, covering me completely as if swallowing me whole.

I looked up at the ship, the body of this creature being transparent, and saw all the horrified faces of the crew. I communicated to Brett that this was safe, and the fact that they would be able to get us down to the palace without any harm; no other creature would dare challenge these two.

I was in his mind and knew that he was sharing this with the others on the ship, but I was more interested in what these two jellyfish had to say.

"Princess Emilee, we are here to take you to the forest, just outside the palace. There you will have to find a way in on your own. Poseidon sent us and we will stay until you return, so we can get you back to the ship safely."

As I listened to the creature that surrounded me, I was looking out into the depth of the waters and could see more jelly fish coming from the darkness. There were so many that I couldn't count, and didn't need to. They were here to protect my friends.

The great creature continued, "Proteus is putting together a small army to come and destroy the ship and all your friends. We are here to stop that. You don't have to worry, they will all be safe, but you and your companion need to hurry so we can get you down to the forest and back again, before the army is gathered and ready."

Brett was in my mind and heard every word. He was explaining it to the others as he was hearing it. When Brett was done, there was a splash in the water, and I watched Brett being swallowed up by the second Jelly fish.

I looked back up at the ship one more time, and as my eyes fell on Lily, she winked and nodded, as if knowing that this was to happen, that Poseidon was helping.

As we descended, the beauty all around was breathtaking. The underwater world of Terrafirma was so vivid with color, the creatures, so many, all different sizes, colors, shapes and the sounds they all made, so strange and beautiful, as if a song with hundreds of voices, all different but saying the same thing. It was all about life, living, sharing the waters, being respectful, but survival was there, at the front of it all.

It wasn't a greed for survival but a love that filled the waters. A love for each other, every life form loved each other and even though, some were predators and some were prey, the deep respect and love for each other was overwhelming.

The jellyfish kept us safe, hidden in their centers, but we were not harmed by their poisonous tendrils. They were cautious with us.

As we got closer to the ocean floor, I could see the great City of Bermuda and the great kelp forests surrounding it. We were in the middle of the Bermuda Triangle, as humans called it, the great City was in the center and no humans had any idea what was really down here.

My feet hit the sandy bottom and the jellyfish lifted themselves gracefully over us and went just inside the kelp forest, and stopped. They told us that they would be hiding there until we returned.

Tina M. Engel

I looked over at Brett and saw that he was having no problems in the water, he was able to let the water fill his lungs, as I could, we still had legs, no fish tails, and I giggled at this thought. Brett gave me a strange look and then laughed too as he pointed towards the forest and we both entered.

The forest was magnificent, the kelp, tall with thick bases. It reminded me of the old growth forests in the humans' dimension. They were massive and home to so many creatures great and small. The colors around me were different shades of yellows and pinks, purples and blues, greens and oranges, so vivid, and I was in awe.

Brett took my hand and we started swimming deeper into the kelp forest, heading in the direction of the city, the part of the city where no one had supposedly lived for years, and Proteus had guards, keeping all away.

We knew that this part of the city was in the back, up against a great underwater mountain. The City of Bermuda was tucked down in a great valley in the bottom of the Bermuda triangle. We would have to make our way along the edge of the city, between the city and rocky cliffs, to get to the back side of the city, unless we wanted to wander right down the middle and get noticed. Not something I really wanted to do.

We got to the edge of the forest with very little problems. There were a few sea creatures lurking in the forest, well they did live there, but they didn't seem too concerned about us. A few even approached us with glee, happy to see us and guided us for a short time, keeping us out of sight of those who would turn us in.

Tina M. Engel

At one point, an enormous white shark came gliding through the kelp, on guard and very menacing looking, and before we could look around to find a safe place to hide, several large tentacles wrapped themselves around us and pulled us into a shallow cave.

Brett's sword was out at once, and there in front of us was a creature I had never seen before. She looked like a woman, with a human body and head, but she had many tentacles instead of arms and legs. She reassured us that she was there to help and then suddenly there was movement all around as her babies came scrambling out from hiding places behind rocks.

As she wrapped her arms around her babies, I noticed one of her arms was missing the tip. I looked up into her face and she knew that I realized who she was. The one who had filled my body with her venom.

Brett knew instantly, when I realized, and his sword was out in front of him as he took his other arm, and wrapping it around my waist, pulled me to him and told me to surround us with my shield.

She said then, "Princess, there is no need to fear. I am not here to hurt you and I wasn't sent to hurt you before. It was my job to further your progress, before you entered the palace.

"Right now was the time that it was supposed to happen, but he was in a hurry. He was afraid there wasn't going to be enough time for my venom to mix with your blood, to make you strong enough. He wanted your body to have my liquid in you for as long as possible before you entered

Proteus's city. I do as I am told, he is the one I follow."

I looked at Brett and then back to this creature and felt safe in what she was saying. She came over to me then and asked if she could touch me. Brett held me tighter for a moment, but I let him know that it was okay, I felt safe here with her.

Brett had a look of uncertainty but I moved away from him as his arm dropped from my waist. I held out my hands and she wrapped a tentacle around them and I felt her attach to my arms. It didn't hurt, but I felt that same crawly feel, under my skin.

"Your body has accepted my essence well, Princess. It was meant for you and you alone. My blood, my essence would kill any other. You are now a part of my world. You truly are the one. I am so honored to be able to be a part of you." She said as she let go, and went back over to her babies.

When she let me go, the strange crawly feeling was gone, but I could still feel that my body was different, my blood was different.

"Rose?" Was all I could say, as I looked to Brett.

I looked back at this creature and asked, "I wasn't supposed to feed on Rose after your venom was placed in me, was I?"

The creature, with sorrow in her eyes, just replied, "I am not the one to ask. They all know what my venom will do to any living being, outside of my home, my realm."

"Will she die then?" I asked.

Tina M. Engel

"It is all written in the stars, I am told." The creature said as she looked at her babies. "We all have a part to play on the journey that all living things call life. It is not for me to decide if your Rose will live or die, or if you were meant to drink from her."

"Your realm? Where are you from, if not here in Terrafirma?" I asked feeling a bit confused.

"I live in Terrafirma." And she turned, pointing to the wall behind us.

The wall started to shimmer and suddenly a doorway appeared and I could see the other side, as if it were a window. It was water, like what we were in, and creatures were swimming in the distance, creatures that were foreign to me.

The doorway closed then as she said, "Terrafirma is much larger than you know, with many doorways that lead to other parts. Poseidon rules all the water worlds in Terrafirma but he keeps most of the doorways to each realm closed to each other, for safety reasons.

"My world, the waters that I live in, is different from the waters of this realm. My waters would be poisonous to your water creatures here, for now."

She looked at Brett and continued, "There is so much more to Terrafirma than you know or have seen."

I looked from Brett to this creature and opened my mouth to question more, but she said before I could speak, "This was all he wanted me to share with you, I can say no more."

The doorway opened again and this creature and her babies entered. She turned and looking at us, smiled, and said, "Good luck Princess, we will meet again one day, I am told." And the doorway closed.

We waited for a while after the creature had left us, to make sure the shark had gone, before we left the cave. I wasn't really sure though, if the shark was a menace to us or not.

When we got to the long, narrow area between city and cliffs, we realized that we would be entering the edge of the city, the only way to get to our destination.

I put my shield around us again, feeling that it was important to do so, and we were able to walk. The water seemed to stay out of the city, like there was an invisible barrier between the kelp forest, the ocean water and the city. The fey that lived here were not water fey that I had seen before, they were fey, similar to Brett, in looks anyway.

We stayed hidden though, weaving around buildings, and staying as close to the rocky cliffs as possible. We hadn't gotten far when we saw a male fey, standing and looking around, as if waiting for someone. We waited and waited for him to leave, but he wasn't budging.

Brett told me that he didn't want to hurt anyone, but we had to remove this fey so we could go on. He told me to release him from my shield but keep myself surrounded, and if I had to, go on without him. (Well, you know how that went over, I don't think so.) I did let down my shield for Brett to exit and I put it back up around myself, but there was no way I was going on without him.

As Brett approached the fey, instead of having a look of fear or aggression, he had a look of relief and joy. He came to Brett with hand out in greeting, and they started to talk. Brett put his sword away and motioned for me to come.

This fey's name was Zale, and he was here to get us through this part of the city. He explained that he was told, years ago, he would meet someone here, on this day, at this time, and to take them to the forbidden part of the city.

I asked him, who had told him to do this, and he informed us that it was Angelina, and that she had others here in the city who obeyed only her.

This group of fey had been contacted by a woman many years ago. Some of them were now so old, that it was their children who were now here to follow Angelina. It was Zale though, who was to guide us to the forbidden part of the city.

I started to ask more questions, but Zale put a hand up and said quite sternly, "Please, ask no more questions. I'm here to guide you only, not share with you what I know. Not that I know much, but I am not supposed to converse. I can't take a chance on changing the future."

Well that was very interesting. Visiting could possibly change the future, but then as I thought about it, knowledge does give one ideas and thoughts that we would not have, if not for knowledge that we are given, at any given time.

I let it go then and he started to move through the city, as we followed him. At times, I would see just a blur of movement, and soon realized that it was other fey, keeping watch, but not wanting to be seen.

Tina M. Engel

After what seemed like hours of walking, hiding behind buildings and structures and crawling, at times, through large pipes that linked one section of town to another, we followed Zale into a basement of a home, where there was a circular stone.

Zale pushed open the stone and there below was a tunnel, several yards down. He threw a long piece of rope down it and informed us that we had to climb down and go the rest of the way, without him. He couldn't chance getting caught with us. Zale told us to follow the tunnel and it would take us to another stone covering to enter the forbidden part of the city.

Suddenly, there was commotion upstairs, and down the stairs stumbled another fey. He informed us that a group of Proteus's guards were in the area and he had to get back upstairs and close off the area where the basement was hidden.

I went up to Zale, gave him a warm hug, (to his surprise I might add), and I went back to the opening, grabbed hold of the rope and climbed down. Brett followed and when he was at the bottom with me, the cover was placed back over the opening and then it disappeared, as if never there.

I looked towards Brett but it being so dark, I could hardly see him or my surroundings. Not having my diamond necklace to give us a little light, I didn't quite know what to do. Suddenly the walls started to softly glow, and it gave us just enough light to see where the tunnel led.

I went over to the wall and inspecting it closer, I could see tiny rocks in the dirt wall and they were glowing. I thought of the lava pebbles in

Tina M. Engel

my diamond and realized just how much I missed them.

I put my hand on the wall as Brett came to stand by me and he reached out to grab my hand, but I gave him a stern look and he thought better of it. As I rested my hand on the wall, I could hear them talking to each other, millions of them all in sync with each other. They were there to help.

I then felt another presence, a sad, angry one, and the small rocks, told me to hurry, they couldn't stay lit for long. It would find us and give our whereabouts away, if we didn't hurry.

Brett was there with me, heard everything, and he grabbed my other hand and we started to run. As we ran the lights disappeared behind us. This urged us on quicker, our running became more panicked and suddenly the tunnel ended and the lights went out completely.

It was totally dark, and I was glad to have Brett's hand in mine. I don't like the dark, never have and never will, (just so you know).

Suddenly, there at the end of the tunnel, on the dirt wall, came a speck of light, and then another, and more, creating a large circular door and I assumed it was the opening to the city. Brett let go of my hand and walked over to it, with me following close behind. It was still, after all, very dark.

Brett ran his hand around the circle and it seemed to move inwards, towards us, and Brett was able to push it to the side. There on the other side was the city, the Forbidden City.

Brett went first after taking my hand back in his and we entered the opening. When we were through, it closed back up and the lighted circle disappeared, and the wall appeared solid, with no way in or out.

As I looked around, the city was in ruins; the buildings crumbling, great fountains that once had grand spouts of water, now were just trickles spilling into the streets that were overgrown with sea weed. There was a strange black ooze that I couldn't identify, and didn't really want to.

The smell was that of decay and sadness, if sadness had a smell. Everything was gray and cold. There were strange lights here and there on the walls of the crumbling buildings.

"Now what?" I said in a whisper, not wanting anything to hear me. I remembered what we were told, that small creatures from Gehenna, the dimension where the greyness lived, were here as guards to keep all out of this area, at all cost, waiting for the doorway to open.

Brett took the map out of his pocket and opened it, resting it on a large slab of stone. It took some time to agree exactly where we were in this part of the city, and what direction we had to take to get to the doorway that I was supposed to close, in the Earths realm.

I was a bit perplexed as to how I was to close a doorway between Earth and Gehenna, if I was in Terrafirma.

The realization came to me then, there are no doorways between Earth and Terrafirma. Closing the doorway to Gehenna in the dimension of Terrafirma would close it in the humans' world too.

I knew where it was. I looked towards the far side of the city, and saw a large mountain that the city seemed to come out of. I turned to look in the opposite direction, and in the distance, I could see the beautiful city of Bermuda, in all its glowing splendor.

Proteus was there, somewhere, and did he know that I was here, in this part of his great city, about to close the doorway? Did he want me to, or did he want the doorway open, letting evil in? Did he really think that he and I could contain such evil and be a part of it, in some way?

I could feel him then, he wasn't close to me, but I could feel him, and I knew he was aware of me at that moment. I would be face to face with him soon. Was this a part of the plan, me seeing him? Was Lily aware, that I would be facing this fey? I thought she probably was.

Brett, still holding my hand, tugged it slightly to get my attention, and as I turned to look at him, he was looking over to his right.

I looked in the same direction and could see movement, as if a cloud of emerald green, was drifting towards us. There was a strange buzzing noise coming from that direction too, and suddenly my other hand where the beetle type creature, was attached, started to hum, but a different sound than the sound coming from afar. As I looked down at my hand, I saw that the creature was glowing and there was blood oozing from where it had attached.

We knew that we had to hurry, before the cloud of green reached us. We knew that it was the creatures Lily had told us about, the ones here to stop us from reaching the doorway.

We headed in the direction of the great mountain, going around destruction, climbing over crumbled stones that were once glorious buildings, I was sure. As we ran, my hand throbbed and I felt like the creature was trying to release itself from my hand, which was why I was bleeding.

I put my shield around both of us, so I thought that the creatures chasing us couldn't get to us, but then, I wasn't 100 percent sure. I didn't know exactly what they could do.

The wave of green got closer and closer as we ran, and soon I could see that it wasn't one massive being, but thousands of creatures, like the one on my hand. I thought of my shield and visualized it pushing out, away from Brett and me. I wanted it to spread as far as it could reach, to keep these creatures away from us.

As we reached the large mountain, there in front of us was a wall that was covered with vines, dried sea weed and thorns. My shield was a good 20 feet away from us and connected to the wall. As the creatures descended upon it, they couldn't break through. They did, however, surround the shield, covering it entirely and trying desperately to get in. The buzzing sound was deafening and my hand was so painful that I crumpled to the ground.

Brett, knelt down next to me, and asked with a panic in his voice, "What can I do to help you?"

"We need to clear the wall, find the doorway." I replied trying to stay calm.

Brett got up, and with his sword, he started to chop away what was attached to the wall and as

Tina M. Engel

he did, I could see that there was a smooth golden surface underneath. It was made of solid gold. When Brett was done, he had uncovered what looked like a sun carving, and I could feel warmth radiating from it.

The creature that was attached to my hand was suddenly free, but did not leave my hand. I stood up and walked over to the wall. I didn't know what to do. I looked around and with my other hand, I started to feel the stone. It was warm and pulsed as if whatever was on the other side was desperate to get through. The creatures surrounding us were screaming, shrieking and I feared that they would break through soon.

Suddenly my hand brushed across an indentation of some kind. It was small and oval shaped and as I looked closer, it was an indentation of a cameo.

I looked up at Brett and he had a look of shock, as I must have had too. The creature that I was holding, wiggled out of my hand and jumped up onto the wall just above the indentation and just stayed there, waiting.

I removed my cameo and placed it into the indentation and it fit perfectly. Suddenly the ring on my finger started to glow and a beam of light came out of it and struck the cameo. Suddenly all was quiet. The creatures stopped, as if frozen.

The cameo then fell out, and Brett reached out and caught it. I kept the beam of light on the hole and it grew to the size of the bug that was just above it. Suddenly the wall started to rumble and I feared that I had done something wrong.

Tina M. Engel

The creature then disappeared into the hole as the beam continued to penetrate the hole. The creatures all around started to buzz again but it was almost calming, this time.

I somehow knew that the creatures surrounding us, weren't after us; they wanted back on the other side of the door. They were chasing us to get back to where they belonged. I shrunk my shield so that the creatures could get to the opening on the wall. They entered one by one, as my ring continued to shine on it, as if holding the small hole open.

It didn't take long, for the bugs seemed to become one flowing movement, and as the last one disappeared into the hole, it closed up and the beam of light was gone. The wall was just a dirt wall, nothing was on it, as if it never was. The door to Gehenna was closed.

I looked up at Brett and as he looked down at me and our eyes met, the relief we both felt washed over us like a wave. Brett took me in his arms and I wrapped my arms around his waist and we just stood there for some time.

My hand, that the creature had been on, was tingling and as I pulled away from Brett, looking at it, it was healing right there in front of me. Within moments, it was healed.

Suddenly around me, the surroundings started to lighten up. As I looked around, the city, all crumbled and destroyed, was putting itself back together. Within minutes, the city was beautiful, golden buildings, magnificent fountains, cobblestone streets, but all empty of people.

This part of the city was different though, from the city where fey lived. This city was like a picture from the past. Was it the ancient city, where the ancestors of these fey once lived? I wondered, and somehow I knew it was.

Chapter 10

> *The past touches the present,*
> *It is all around us.*
> *Look around, see it,*
> *Feel it,*
> *Do not be afraid.*
> *It is a part of you.*

I could see them then, living their lives here in this beautiful place, they were the guardians of the wall. They were different than the fey of today that live in the City of Bermuda. They looked similar to Brett from the waist up but had a large fish tail from waist down. The color of their skin, however, was different too, matching their lower extremities, slightly.

The city was in water, there was no barrier between water and city. I was standing there, in the middle of this great city with fey all around, and they could see me, they would look at me as they swam by, smiling as if I had always been there.

I felt a touch on my elbow and looking over, there was Brett standing with me. He could see it all too, he could see what I was seeing, as he touched me.

This city and these fey were here so long ago, but their spirits never left, they were the guardians of the doorway, not the creatures from the other side. Something happened long ago. The creatures from Gehenna escaped, came here and destroyed the city.

The true guardians never left. They were waiting for me to free the city from evil and now that the doorway was closed for good, they were free to continue to live, even if in spirit only. I wasn't here, looking into the past, this was now, but in a different dimension from the city of the present. The past, present and future were just different dimensions too. These fey, who were here so long ago, were still here, just waiting.

I felt him then, he was close. It wasn't Proteus, it was the other, the true king of all the waters on this planet. I knew him then, as Lily did. He was the one who interfered, to push me, rush my transformation and had angered Lily.

I looked up at Brett and then down at his hand holding onto my arm. He knew what I was thinking. He had to let go of me and go back to the City of todays' fey, where we had been standing moments ago. I knew that Brett just had to let go of me, and he would be there.

Brett shook his head no, but I took my other hand, and placed it on his. I smiled and reassured him that I had to do this alone, and with that, I brushed his hand away from my arm and let him go.

I was alone then, and as I looked around, the fey that had been there just moments ago, now were gone.

I felt him close by and as I turned, there he was, he was the great white shark, which we had seen in the kelp forest. He was a magnificent, grand being, as large as the great grey whale I had seen days before.

He swam towards me slowly, as if just meandering, not in any rush to get anywhere. I went to take a step back, but instead I tilted backwards just a bit and a fish tail came up into my sight. I didn't have legs, but a fish tail. I was like the ancient fey, my tail a silvery white.

I looked back up as the great white shark transformed into a fey, male fey above, but fish below. He was tall and muscular, dark in color with long white hair and a beard that made me think of Douglas. His facial features were like all the fey that resembled humans, but his eyes were piercing, green in color, like emeralds, and they sparkled as the lights from around us hit his face.

He smiled and his intimidating appearance changed slightly, and I relaxed a bit. I didn't realize that I was anxious, but I was. (Sharks, like spiders, are not my favorite creatures, just saying.)

It was him, Poseidon, I knew before he introduced himself to me. I thought he had died long ago. As this thought came to me, I realized that those all around me, had died long ago, but still lived on, in yet another place, dimension, or time.

"I've been waiting a long time to meet you Child." He said.

Poseidon bowed his head slightly in a respectful gesture and as he lifted his head, he continued, "I'm sorry for trying to rush things earlier. My son seems eager to let evil reign. Yes, even we can be impatient at times, but she put me in my place. Only she could do that." And he chuckled as he said the last part.

Tina M. Engel

Poseidon approached me then, and taking my hand in his, did the fey traditional greeting. I wasn't frightened, but in awe of this great fey, but didn't quite know why he was here, or why I was here with him.

I asked then, "If you are the one who had the beast put its venom in me and changed my make up to not need Rose, but now have a need for …" I stopped then, feeling embarrassed to admit that I needed Brett's blood, but then continued, "and Lily said you both have different ideas on how to save us all."

"We have the same agenda my child, just different ways to get there. Lily, as you call her, well, let us just say, has a responsibility and it is all consuming. She believes we should go in the order that she sees fit, proceed at a snail's pace, at times, to ensure things turn out the way she wants.

"I, on the other hand, think that we can skip some of the middle ground, so to speak, and get things done quicker. She never gets tired of letting me know, though, that she is in charge, even though this situation is in my ocean.

"The poison was to push you along, the need for Rose was a temporary thing, to strengthen you to a point. I rushed things a bit, but it was still to happen.

"I did it without her permission though, which I don't feel I need to get, but I will humor her, for now. You are stronger than she realizes, or wants to believe at this time. You are more important to her than she lets on." Poseidon said, with a twinkle in his eyes.

Tina M. Engel

When Poseidon paused, I was able to question, "What do you mean, Lily, as I call her? She is a cat, a fey yes, but a cat."

Poseidon laughed then, and said, "You know better than that."

I wasn't perplexed by his response, but somehow I knew that Lily was something else. I also figured that I wouldn't get more information from him on this matter, so I changed the subject to keep him talking.

"Is Stephan, working for you, as is the fey on the ship who got close to Rose? Will the venom that was put in me, end up killing Rose? She was an innocent pixie."

Poseidon laughed, a hearty laugh, before he spoke. "There is no living creature on this planet or anywhere in the universe, as humans call it, which is totally innocent. It will be what it was meant to be, I just sped things up a bit."

"But Stephan" I continued, "he is working for the Dark One, but I think you are interfering with him as well, are you not?"

I swallowed hard and continued, "Stephan is evil and vile, so does that make you evil? Lily doesn't think so, but I am starting to have my doubts. You seem to be playing God."

Poseidon started to laugh then, and shaking his head, he said, "No child, I am as good as Lily is."

I asked then, "What do you know about Stephan and aren't you interfering and helping him to get me? Why does Stephan want to take me to the Dark One, and then have me for his own?"

Poseidon replied in a matter of fact tone, "Stephan has a very special role to play, be it good or evil, it remains to be seen, and it is up to each individual, in the end.

"Knowing that Stephan was working for the Dark One, I became curious, was it because he believed in what the Dark One wanted, to be all powerful, destroy those who tried to destroy him so many years back, or was he just trying to gain his father's respect and ... well, love?

"Even the strongest of animals have a weakness, deep down and that can save them or destroy them."

"But why Stephan, he isn't a water fey, like you. How can you even be in contact with him?" I asked, feeling angry now, not understanding the significance of his interference.

"Child," Poseidon said, "He is more than what you see and plays a much larger part than anyone realizes."

Poseidon paused then, took my hand in his, the one with the ring, and as he touched the stone, its color changed to the emerald green of his eyes.

He then looked into my face and continued, "Stephan and Brett are bound together. Good and evil go hand in hand, happy and sad, beginnings and endings, the sun and the moon, and the humans' god and their devil. You can't understand one completely, without the other, now can you?

"Lily brought Brett into this situation, shall we call it, a long time ago, to even the playing field so to speak, when the future showed Stephan's role in the success or failure of all life. I am not helping

Stephan, I never have, but I am watching him closely.

"She is overseeing it all, but I have been around a long time and my opinion is important, and is heard, even when she doesn't want to hear it. My opinions matter. This is my home, not hers."

I started to open my mouth to speak, but he put his hand up to stop me. He had a look of concern then and said, "Enough Princess, our time is up. I may have said too much, but it has been a real pleasure.

"The ring now, will strengthen your perception of what is the right thing to do, even if others tell you differently or the human, emotional part of you, gets in the way.

"The substance that my creature injected into you has increased your strength to do what you must, when the time comes. The desire for another's blood, will only strengthen. Don't run away from what you know is right. You are not a child anymore, it's time you took your place, even though she wants to think of you as a child."

I said then, "I see Rose, but no one else seems to. Well I do believe that Lily does. And then I change into someone else, something else, white, silvery white, like I am right now." as I lifted my lower body, the fish tail. "The substance that the creature put into me, is that helping me to see what is real in this world of confusion and chaos too?"

Poseidon let go of my hand as he smiled, and with a twinkle in his eyes, as if he knew that I was starting to see things and understand, he turned and swam away, towards the back of the city, but before he turned into the great white shark, he said, "You must go see Proteus, now."

Poseidon and the city disintegrated before my eyes, my fish tail disappeared and I was standing in the ruins again, with legs.

Brett was sitting on a crumpled pile of rocks, not far from where I was standing. I walked over and sat down next to him. He said nothing, looking at me, waiting calmly for me to explain. I realized that while I was there with Poseidon, Brett and I were not connected, he couldn't see what I had seen.

We were both perplexed by this and I realized that I wasn't just seeing that other world in my mind, but that I actually had been there, and Brett was still in this world. We had been separated in two different dimensions and we could not feel each other during that time.

I shared with Brett what Poseidon had said and held out my hand to show him the ring. I was starting to understand what exactly he was meaning when he said that the ring would help me to see things differently, show me the things that I wasn't ready, or refused to see.

I chose not to share with Brett the part about Brett and Stephan being bound together. I didn't think he would like it much, and I didn't need a distraction right then.

Brett suggested we get out of there, find our way out of the city and back to the ship, but as he stood up, taking my hand in his, I told him he must go back alone.

Brett's eyes widened with surprise as he shook his head and spouted with firmness, in his voice, that I would be accompanying him back to the ship, if he had to drag me there.

I laughed at his display of being my protector, but I knew that I still had another agenda down here. I knew my dream wasn't just a dream, but a vision and it was time to meet Proteus, the fey who believed for so many years, that I was his daughter. Was the vision actually how it would happen, or just a possibility? I didn't know, but I was ready to face him. I had to.

"Brett," I said, "I must meet with Proteus." But before I could continue, Brett bellowed, "No!"

I just gave him a quirky smile, took his hand up to my mouth, and kissing it softly, I said, "Brett, you can't always be near, to protect me. I know it is your job, as you say, to keep me safe but I have a job to do also, and I must meet with him, alone."

Brett started to open his mouth to argue again, his eyes were turning red, really red, and as I put a finger to his lips, a tingling sensation pulsed through my body and I was sure it did his too. We both inhaled deeply, and the need I had for him was painful.

We were connected, I could see his thoughts, not just hear them, and he was in just as much pain as I, his need for me to drink from him. His desire was great, his need for me, but in a way that I didn't understand. *I saw him then, on the ground, in my arms, our pain combined.*

Brett moved back, letting go of my hand, letting my finger drop from his lips, and the connection was gone. I could only hear his thoughts, not see them.

"Emilee," Brett said calmly now, "he wants you and if you go to him, he will hold you and I may not be able to save you. I can't let you go, especially not alone. I was given the task to keep you safe, and I must do that until the end."

When he said, "the end", Brett had a strange sadness in his eyes, and I felt a stabbing in my hearts, as if this wasn't going to end well.

Before I could respond to Brett, I heard him, and so did Brett, a voice that said, "Emilee, I'm waiting!"

It was Proteus, I was sure, and he knew we were here.

"Brett, I can do this and must. I am stronger now and will not be fooled by Proteus or anyone. Go back to the kelp forest and wait for me. I will be okay and I have no intention of being his prisoner, or accomplice in allowing evil to enter the humans' realm or Terrafirma. Please believe in me."

Brett reached up and stroked my cheek, and as he did, the wonderful vibration was there, we were connected and I felt even stronger. I was ready to face this fey, with Brett's strength and support, behind me.

"I do believe in you Princess." Brett said with a sad smile, "and I always will."

He kissed my hand, turned, and headed over to the edge of the crumpled city, hoping to find a safe passage along the mountain which the city was built up against, and find his way back to the kelp forest to wait for me.

Tina M. Engel

I knew somehow that he would be fine. Proteus had no intention of harming him or the rest of the crew up on Adam's ship, at this moment. He was ready, however, to do so if he felt the need. How I knew this was perplexing to me, but I did, my thoughts were different now, stronger and much clearer. This was to be a meeting to size up both of our strengths. He knew I wasn't going to work with him. He knew.

Chapter 11

We meet at last
The road has been long,
We have rules to follow
In peace and war.

I watched Brett until I could see him no more and when I turned around to face the direction of the city, there stood a fey, a male guard. He said nothing but turned and headed back to the city, and I knew I was to follow.

I wasn't afraid, I walked with my head held high, as we walked down the middle of a stone road, with fey on both sides watching, pointing and I heard several saying, "It's her.", or "She's come.", and one female said to another, "She is just as majestic as her mother."

He was standing there in front of a grand throne, arms crossed over his bare chest, just as in my dream. His glare was intense but there was affection in his blue eyes; a light shimmering blue. It was him, Proteus, the one I thought was my father and he had believed it too, but did he still?

As I looked around this grand room, I was in awe of the beauty that I saw. There were large tapestries, the pictures of beautiful water fey, great battles, and places I had never seen before, on land and beneath the waters. It was exactly like my dream.

We were in the underwater palace but the room had no water. All was dry and we were breathing air. Proteus had legs, not a fish tail. So this was his true fey form. Was he able to walk on dry land? I wondered.

It was just he and I in the room, just like my dream, I was here at last.

We stood staring at each other for I don't know how long, and I was starting to feel uneasy and childlike, but unlike in my dream, I stood taller and released the anxiety that was starting to creep into my mind and the uneasiness disappeared. I could feel the ring on my finger, it was giving me a sense of ease. I knew that I was safe, that Proteus would not, or could not, harm me.

He put his arms down at his sides then and his expression changed to relief and pleasure as he descended the steps that separated his throne from the rest of the room. His arms reached out as he approached me, and held me in a loving embrace. I wrapped my arms around him also in an uncomfortable fashion, knowing that I should be hiding my displeasure about being here, better than I was.

When he released me, Proteus took my hand and led me over to a bench, where we sat. Again I looked around and was in awe of the beauty surrounding me and the fact that this room and the city was dry, a barrier between water and city.

Proteus reached out and softly touched my cheeks, the shell that would create a shield around me, if I felt the need for protection. His smile was genuine, he knew what it was, and who gave it to me.

He said then, "Not many receive this gift. It is special and he must believe you are special too. The longer they kept you from me, the more I realized that you could truly be the one and I knew you would come back to me, on your own."

Proteus then put his hand on my back in a fatherly manner and I was ready for his reaction but it was not the reaction I was expecting. He touched the area where the wings had been and would protrude again when the time was right.

Proteus smiled then, a smile of pleasure as he stood and stepped away from me. I expected shock or confusion but it was as if he was aware of my wings.

I stood up then, as my wings were released, large, shimmery and colorful. I wasn't afraid, I felt strong and confident.

"I came here of my own free will, not to stand beside you as your daughter. You are not my father. But I need to find out what this place has to do with me and what part you are to play in my discovering my true self, and where I belong." I said, confidently.

His eyes turned red as his shape started to change, and the room filled with sea water. As Proteus's legs transformed into a large fish tail, I became the fey that I was in Andean's great lake, with one exception, my wings were still outstretched. I understood now, why they were covered in tiny scales, not feathers. My skin changed to silver white, but my fish tail had a slight rainbow shimmer, like my wings.

Proteus, smiled then, an eerie grin as he said, "You are the one. He told me you were but I remained skeptical, until now. The wings were the last sign, you are a part of both of them. She

Tina M. Engel

should have protected you better. Why she let you come down here alone is beyond me."

At that, Proteus turned into a great white shark, but not as large and grand as his father, Poseidon. He came towards me with great speed, but instinct took over and my wings came forward with such force that they pushed me backwards as they forced Proteus away.

Proteus turned back into his fey self with frustration across his face. He said, as he waved his hand, that held a long staff with a golden ball at the top, which I hadn't seen before, "You think you closed the door, but really you destroyed it. The creature that she gave you which attached itself to your hand, and all the others of its kind, she believed were working for her. She had put them there to protect her side of the door, keeping everyone away, guarding it.

"She created those tiny beings knowing that when the time was right, they would go to the other side, cling in one mass to the door and become one, solid, a material that nothing could penetrate. The doorway would be closed for good.

"But he found out, so long ago, and with my help and the help of another… water fey…" and Proteus smiled a wicked smile and chuckled.

He continued then, "We changed their body configuration, their internal fluids that allowed it to melt the metal that the door was made of when the creatures joined and became one.

"That water fey…she has connections to others, familiar with minerals, metals and such…what luck it was to find her in a very vulnerable time in her life." And Proteus grinned

Tina M. Engel

and raised his eye brows in a way that led me to believe that I knew who this water fey was.

"She tried to stop the beast from wrapping its tentacle around your ankle, my blasted father always getting in the way. But it doesn't matter. Even with the substance that flows in your body and those wings, you will not succeed.

"Now the door is just a simple rock wall that can be crushed, blown open for him to come and extinguish these pitiful humans, along with all in Terrafirma who try to stop him. Fools, all of them and you, just a child, they thought you could be their savior.

"He will take over, opening each doorway, one at a time, to all the worlds, and dimensions, in which life exists, and those that have no life as yet, and conquer them all. This speck of dirt that you call earth is really just a doorway to all that is out there.

"You will be alongside him, willingly or not, to help. I will see to that, as will Stephan. After all, Stephan will stop at nothing to have you for his own and only when he has what he wants, will Stephan be granted the prize he most desires, you."

I held up my hand with the ring, as the stone, now emerald green, shone brightly. Proteus gasped at the sight and said with a tremble in his voice, "What? My father will pay for his interference."

I realized that my meeting with Poseidon was not planed, therefore not foreseen by the evil forces. He was afraid of this ring and what it could do.

"No bother, dear Princess. Daughter by blood you may not be, but you will serve him, I swear, if by the death of me."

Proteus laughed then, waved the staff and a flash of light blinded me for a moment and he disappeared.

Suddenly the water receded, all was dry again and I transformed back into my more human or fey self, with legs. The ground began to tremble. My wings, still spread out, with strength and agility, lifted me into the air as a pillar tumbled towards me and crashed to the ground, shattering into pieces, where I had been standing.

The large chandeliers that hung from the ceiling swayed gracefully, as if positioned in just the right places to do little damage to them. A few of the tapestries came loose in a corner here and there, and the sound of falling rocks from afar filled my ears. Then all was still.

I lowered myself back to the ground and my wings slowly disappeared into my back, but now I knew, could feel, that they were there whenever I needed. I thought of them coming out again, and there they were, spread wide and glorious, shimmering as the lights that were surrounding me touched them.

I felt him then, not Poseidon or Proteus but him, the Dark One who everyone was afraid of. He was in my mind, searching for something, a memory or thought, I wasn't sure. Then I heard from afar, "Emilee, be strong, hold tight to your beliefs."

I looked around, thinking someone had entered the great room without me realizing, but it was empty, only I was there. It was a woman's voice, not a man's, and when the voice spoke, he left my mind, as if afraid.

There was movement along the wall to the left of the great throne. A tapestry that had partially fallen during the disturbance, drooped a little more, bringing my attention to it. Behind the tapestry was a circular area that was all aglow and shimmering, moving in streaks as if being stirred with a large spoon.

I walked over, and moving the rest of the cloth, could see the entire area. The shimmering light died out and it was replaced with an opening to a tunnel.

Again I heard, "Emilee, continue. Its time to come home." The voice wasn't urgent or aggressive, but I knew that whoever it was wanted me to come into the tunnel. It was a woman's voice, not a man's so I was relatively sure it wasn't him, the Dark One. But could it be a trick.

I had heard rocks falling from far away. Was it the wall where the door that I thought I had closed for good, had been? Has it been opened, the door separating the Dark One's world into ours? I wondered.

Suddenly, I felt him, Brett, and I turned around as he came rushing into the room with panic across his face. Then it was replaced with relief as we met each other in the middle of the room holding each other in an embrace that had the feeling of safety and calm. Soon it turned to passion and we separated just enough so I could see his face, his eyes staring at me, a dark green, showing his need.

Tina M. Engel

Our lips touched softly at first but then more aggressively, Brett's arms tightened around me as if he couldn't get close enough to me. I didn't want him to let go though, I needed him and knew he needed me.

My wings, which had retreated into their proper place earlier when I had approached the tunnel, now spread out wide and then came around Brett, wrapping us both in a type of cocoon. I wanted him, his blood, his essence, everything he had, body, mind and soul. He did too, I could read him, our minds connected.

Then I heard her, and Brett did too, "Not yet. Come home."

Our lips parted, but we still were in an embrace, my wings holding us captive, as we heard her say again, very calmly with a bit of amusement in her voice, "Not yet."

My wings released us and disappeared into my back as Brett's eyes changed from the green of passion, to the calm blue that I so enjoyed getting lost in. "You heard it too, didn't you?" I said, as I tried to compose myself, still feeling the desire to sink my teeth into his skin, anywhere on his body, and drink.

"Yes, I did." Brett said with a look of longing which then changed to understanding. "We can't let that happen again. No matter what, we must stay strong, he is close."

I looked up into his eyes as he said this and realized the fear he had experienced, when the earth shook. I was in his mind and the fear was so strong, all consuming.

Tina M. Engel

Brett took my hands in his and said, "Are you alright? When the ground started to shake, I heard her voice telling me to find you. From a short distance away, I saw a great white shark looking at me. Then it turned, and somehow I knew I was to follow it. It led me here to this room and then disappeared along with the water."

I smiled and reassured him that I was shaken a bit but not hurt and then Brett said, "He will not have you, I will die before that happens!" His tone was full of bitterness.

I realized that when our minds were connected, he saw my meeting with Proteus and heard our conversation. He wasn't talking about the Dark One either, but Stephan.

I smiled, squeezed his hands slightly and told him that I trusted in our strength and was confident we would be triumphant in our task at hand. I had no intentions of him dying to save me.

Brett had a strange look then, which crossed his face briefly, a sadness. He smiled then, brought my hands up to his mouth, and kissed them delicately before releasing them.

"What is it?" I asked. "What's wrong?"

I tried to connect with his mind, but he shut me out. I was shocked and I realized, frustrated, not hurt this time. He was keeping something hidden, down deep inside, and didn't want me to see it. The ring should have let me see what it was that he was hiding, but I couldn't see.

Brett ran a finger across my cheek and the tingling sensation that I got was a calming one, but I still had a look of impatience on my face, wanting to know what he was hiding.

"Let's just go see what's in this tunnel," He said as he pointed in the direction of the opening, "Since I know that you are intent on doing so." Brett said with a bit of a smirk on his face, trying to change the subject.

"I know something is wrong, you are worried about something but don't want me to be worried too but…" I said, as Brett put a finger to my lips, cutting me off, and just shook his head from side to side. With his lips pursed shut, I knew I would get no more information from him, at this time.

Chapter 12

Deception is all around,
We can't escape it.
They don't play fair,
But we will adjust,
We will prevail.

The tunnel was dark and damp; green algae clung to the walls. It was not a part of the city, built with brick and stone, gems and gold. There were shimmering specks in the solid dirt walls that glowed just enough to allow us to go forward, guiding us to wherever the tunnel led.

Soon the walls started to change, gradually, from earth to stone. The stones were all symmetrical, placed side by side, creating a wall. The stones were different colors; gold, blue, purple and orange. They were laid out in patterns, as if an artist created these abstract, beautiful pictures.

There were indents in the stone wall, where lights were glowing softly. The lights were round balls floating in the indents, not attached to anything, just floating and glowing a soft white light.

I saw it then, at the end of the tunnel, a golden door, with a silver border. As we approached the door, there in the center, was a symbol, a star, and in the middle of the star, was an indentation and I knew what it was.

I reached out my hand to place my finger in it, but Brett took my hand to stop me. "We don't know what this is." He said. "I don't think you should touch it."

I took my hand from his, giving him a slight look of annoyance. Reaching up with both of my hands, I removed my cameo pin from my dress. Brett's eyes, showed understanding then and he didn't object as I reached out to place the cameo into the middle of the star. It fit just like it did in the doorway to Gehenna.

Brett had his knife out the entire time we were walking in the tunnel, but now he extended it to be his sword. He looked around to make sure no one was there, and then focused on the cameo as I slid it into the space.

As I brought my hand back away from the door, we waited for something to happen. Suddenly, on both sides of the star, indents started to appear. When they were done, they resembled hand prints, small, like a woman's hands.

I looked to Brett as he turned his head to look at me, and letting out a deep breath, as if holding it, he whispered, "Be careful."

I touched his shoulder in an affectionate way, and approached the wall again. I felt Brett behind me, close enough to feel the warmth of his body. I realized that I was chilled all of a sudden, maybe a bit frightened. I reached up and placed my hands into the handprints. They fit perfectly.

The area under my hands started to glow, as did the cameo, then suddenly, a strange pulsing sound started. The sound seemed to be coming from the star symbol. My hands tingled and I felt Brett's hands go onto my waist, just above my hips. He didn't pull me away, but was ready to if need be.

I knew somehow it was time to remove my hands. As I did, the cameo fell, and without thinking, I reached out to catch it before it hit the ground. As I stood and backed away just a bit, Brett stayed firmly behind me, hands gripping a bit firmer, as a split appeared down the middle of the door, and it swung open, as if someone on both sides was opening it slowly.

I turned my head to look up at Brett and he had a look of curiosity, but also wariness on his face. I turned back to face the open doorway. It was dimly lit but looked like a large room of sorts, from what I could see.

I turned towards Brett and in doing so, removed his hands from my waist. I said in a somewhat silly way, "Do you want to go first or shall I?"

Brett of course, saying nothing, stepped forward towards the door. I didn't move, just watched as he approached the opening, but when he attempted to enter, it appeared that he ran into something. He was stopped abruptly and a vibrating sound came from the entrance.

Brett turned towards me with a perplexed expression and then turning back, put his hand up in the doorway. His hand stopped and the strange vibrating sound happened again.

"Well it looks like I'm not welcome inside." Brett said.

I came up beside him, and asked if it hurt and he informed me that it didn't. Whatever it was that had stopped him, didn't want to hurt him. I reached my hand up, assuming that I would be blocked too, by the invisible barrier, but my hand went right through. I took a step forward, intending to enter but Brett stopped me.

Tina M. Engel

"We don't know what's in there and you are not going in alone." He said adamantly.

I took his hand in mine and reached up, interlocking our fingers. We put our hands in front of us and they went right through the doorway. I gave Brett a triumphant look and walked forward, through the doorway, bringing him with me.

As we crossed the threshold of the doorway, the room brightened to where I was blinded for a few seconds and I felt behind me a rush of wind, and then stillness.

My eyes adjusted and I turned around to see what had caused the feeling of air movement. I could see through the door, but as I put my hand up, I couldn't go through it. The barrier was stopping me from leaving. Brett had turned his head to see. He put his hand up and was also unable to leave. The door suddenly closed behind us.

"Well now, I guess, we are here for a while." I said, with as much humor as I could muster, feeling a bit leery now, of my former confidence, that this was what I was supposed to do.

I turned back, looking around the room and Brett did the same. He took my hand in his, the one closest to him and was holding his sword out in front of him in the other. The room was white, and I do mean white, sterile, as if in an operating room just before a surgery.

The room was empty except for a strange circular table with what looked like chairs around it, and in the middle of the table was a sphere, a half rounded object protruding up from the table about a foot high. It was humming and the color was that of clouds, white with wisps of grey swirling inside.

Suddenly a voice came from somewhere in the room, but I couldn't tell what direction, "We don't need that." And Brett's sword turned into the knife, on its own, as Brett sucked in a large breath, shocked at what had just happened.

From the right side of the room, closest to me, came a figure. I say figure because I couldn't tell if it was male or female, person or animal. It was a shape, shifting and changing, iridescent, but at times I could see through it.

"There is nothing in this room that will require that piece of weaponry, I assure you," the voice said, as it continued to move to the middle of the room, towards the table.

The closer to the table it got, the more solid it became and suddenly it stopped changing. It was a male, similar to the type of fey that Brett was, but his skin was white, albino white. His hair was white with streaks of silver and when he turned his head to look at us, his eyes were the color of silver.

He was dressed in a robe, similar to what a monk might wear, but it was a shimmery aquamarine color. His facial features where somewhat feminine but his voice was definitely masculine.

He smiled a very kind and genuine smile but I could tell he was serious and business like as he continued, "I have been waiting a long time for this meeting. I wondered if you would make it this far. They reassured me that you would, and she was very confident, but then, there are so many paths one can choose and so many obstacles that can distract one, I was not as optimistic as she."

I realized that as he spoke, his mouth wasn't moving, he was thinking, and we could hear him. My puzzled look caused him to smile again as he said, with his mouth this time, "It is not necessary to verbalize with the mouth, that is such an ancient way to communicate, but if you are more comfortable with speaking from the mouth, then that is what we will do."

He held his hand out towards the table in a gesture for us to sit as he settled himself in one of the chairs. The chair he sat in was different from the others. His was larger, and had strange symbols on the arm rests, and an indent in the back of the seat. As he sat, the back came up and seemed to connect to his body and head

The chairs that Brett and I took had shorter backs and the arm rests were just smooth and cold. As I sat though, I felt as if the chair was attempting to link with me. I could feel its pulse, searching, winding its way through my body and finally to my mind. It was a strange sensation but not threatening in the least. When it connected completely, there was just calm.

I looked over at Brett and could see he was not having the same experience as I. He was not finding this union, if you could call it that, a pleasant experience and I decided to join his mind, become one with him. I saw that he definitely wasn't cooperating and the chair was getting a bit more forceful with him.

Tina M. Engel

"Brett" I said, "look at me." He did so and I reassured him that it was safe, they were not here to harm us.

"They?" Brett questioned out loud and I realized that I felt that she was in the room, too, whoever she was, and maybe others.

As Brett and I were with one mind, he relaxed and when the connection was complete, calmness came over his face.

As I turned to look at our host, if you could call him that, I said, "She, you said she? Who is she and for that matter who are you? What does this room have to do with the Dark One and who is he? Do you know?"

"So many questions and so little time." He said with a slight hint of humor in his voice.

"I don't find any of this funny!" I fumed, slightly.

"No it is not, but I find it difficult to not find humor in humans and fey, for that matter, such young species."

I looked at Brett, thinking, fey, young species? And Brett, understanding my thoughts, looked at this individual and commented, "Fey are not a young species." In a very defensive tone. I could sense that Brett didn't like this being very much.

Our host held up his hand in a truce fashion and reassured us that he meant no disrespect. He shared with us the fact that there are many other species from many different worlds, as well as dimensions on this planet, much older than our kind and he informed us that his name was Biton.

He continued then, "She is in charge of overseeing the dimensions on this small speck of land the humans call earth, and that fey call Terrafirma. There are other dimensions, one of them is where certain water creatures call home, Atlantis.

"The doorway to that dimension, and yes a doorway, was near the Island of Goza. The lost city of Atlantis as the humans called it, was a great city, the gateway to the Atlantians home, another part of Terrafirma.

"Terrafirma is much larger than what you know of. There are doorways one must find to enter these mysterious sections of Terrafirma. Some are much older than the Terrafirma that you know, Brett, and others are much younger, earth being one of them.

"Unfortunately when humans appeared on the planet, the Atlantians became too curious, wanting to take them in as pets, so to speak, and she couldn't let that happen. So the great city was destroyed, closing the doorway between dimensions until the time that humans could understand the vast expanse around them without fear.

"There are some Atlantians still in the part of Terrafirma that you come from," as he looked to Brett, "who can travel between earth and Terrafirma but stay hidden, deep in the darkest waters. They became stuck when the city was destroyed, not heeding her warning to go home."

"This isn't the dimension that I am to learn about though, is it?" I interrupted, when Biton took a moment to gather his next thoughts.

"No my child, it isn't. I just wanted you to understand that there are many living creatures who are depending on you to close the doorway to his prison for good." Biton said with a determined look in his eyes.

"Was the creature that put its venom in my leg, from this place, Atlantis?" I asked, even though I was certain I already knew the answer.

"Yes, she is, and has now gone back to her home, her job here being completed." Biton answered.

"Why are you here in this place and why you, to tell me about that world?" I continued. "Why is she not here, whoever she is?" I paused then and continued, "My Grandmother?"

Biton smiled and then with a look of longing in his silver eyes, told us that he was chosen from many, to watch over and guard this area, until the day that I would come. He told me that she would come when the time was right. Before I could ask again about my grandmother, he continued with the information he felt we needed to know.

"Gehenna is a realm, the Dark One's land, full of greyness, in the dimension of Hades. This dimension, and so many others, share this planet. This planet is also the spot in this vast universe where doorways to other planets exist. This is the one spot where all can meet and travel to other worlds.

"She keeps it safe, watches for trouble but the greyness, those who are sent to Hades when they die, he is recruiting. He brings them to his realm, Gehenna, to be a part of his army of sorts, to take over all that is. For some reason the one who truly rules Hades, is allowing this.

"She sent him there a long time ago not realizing that his strength would join the creatures there, becoming a stronger mass of life. She didn't know until recently that he was the Dark One.

"The balance is now in jeopardy and if he is able to take Earth and your Terrafirma, he will have no problem opening the doorway to Atlantis and then he will take them all, one at a time, the other realms of Terrafirma as well as the other worlds, until he has control of all the doorways to this part of the universe.

"There are doorways out there that she keeps closed, locked and protected from all, keeping their whereabouts secret from all but a few. The hostile and violent beings there, have not evolved enough to travel and learn from others.

"The Dark One wants those doorways open, to take over and create a larger more evil army. His anger is great due to the treachery and betrayal that he believes happened to him.

"Would you please put your hands on the sphere now, so we can get started? There is much to discuss before you leave here."

Biton was quiet then, and so were we as I put my hands on the sphere. As I looked towards Brett, he seemed to be deep in thought as he stared at Biton while putting his hands on the sphere also. It seemed that they were having a stare down. Were they communicating to each other without speaking? I tried to penetrate Brett's thoughts but was blocked, whether by Brett or Biton, I didn't know.

Tina M. Engel

Feeling frustrated with them both, unable to connect with Brett, I removed my hands from the sphere, stood up, and pushed my chair back, which brought their attention to me. As I stood though, I broke the connection from the sphere and chair, and a shockwave went through my body like a lightning bolt.

A flash of light blinded me, as I bent over in pain. I felt him there in the room, in my mind, searching for something. When the pain subsided and I stood, I was no longer in the room, but there in my dream world.

The wheat was golden and tall, the tree branches waved slowly in the breeze and the grand castle was there, standing tall in the distance behind the great tree. I could hear the ocean behind me and the sound of birds high above. What I was doing here and how I got here, I didn't know, but figured I would soon find out.

Then I saw movement from behind the castle, behind the mountain that the castle was carved from. It was small at first, just a speck coming towards me. Then I saw it, a dragon, emerald green, and getting larger as it came towards me. This wasn't the same dragon that consumed Eagle in one of my other dreams but still large and menacing looking, the closer it got.

I looked around, wondering where I should go to seek shelter and realized there was nowhere to hide so I stood firmly planted, placing my shield around myself. I took the barrette out of my hair, released my weapon and allowed it to attach to my hand, turning into the simple, but sharp dagger.

Tina M. Engel

I was ready as the great beast landed just feet from me, its wings causing a large gust of wind as it landed, almost knocking me over. I regained my composure quickly and stood still but firm, trying to hide my fear.

"There is no need for that feeble weapon." It said. "I am not here to hurt you, for I belong to you. But then you do not know this, for you are not with me yet. We will meet soon, do not fear. Look for me. If you do not find me, everything will change. He knows this and has hid me well.

And at that, the pain came back, deep inside and I bent over trying to steady myself, for I was certain I was going to pass out. Just before I laid down on the ground, letting the wheat field swallow me up, I saw her, Rose, not clearly, ghostlike, but I saw her, where the dragon had been. I laid still then, trying to calm my quivering body.

Then the pain stopped and as I opened my eyes, I was back in the room, sterile and gleaming, so white, with faces looking at me.

"What happened?" I asked. "I was there, in the wheat field, but with a dragon?" and I attempted to stand.

Brett reached out to take my hand and helping me up, said, "Dragon?" As he looked to Biton.

"Come sit back down, reconnect with your surroundings quickly!" Biton said. "He has seen what you saw. It wasn't supposed to happen this way. You were to see your dragon in the protected field. Interesting though. Tell me everything you remember." Biton ordered.

As I turned to go back to the table, standing next to it, with her hands on the sphere, was Rose, for just a moment. I said nothing but sat down and allowed the chair to reconnect.

Brett didn't leave my side until Biton ordered him to do so. Brett, looking at him with murder in his eyes, started to speak and I knew what he was about to say, being connected with him, his hands on my shoulders.

"The hell with you and this craziness" was what Brett was about to say, so I quickly reached up and placed both my hands on his.

"Brett, its fine, I am fine. Please sit down and let's finish this so we can get back to the ship. I need to tell Lily what happened." I said, with a pleading expression. "And Rose."

Biton spoke then, in a more diplomatic fashion with urgency in his voice, "My time is running short, and we must finish this. This place has been hidden from him for so long. He knew it was here, that I was here, but now that you have broken the barrier, by removing your hands, he has found me. Please sit Brett, so the barrier can be solid again."

Brett was frustrated and I could feel his fear. He lifted his hands from my shoulders, walked to his chair and sat down. He didn't fight the connection this time. He knew it was no use and we needed to finish this quickly.

When the connection for all of us was complete, Biton spoke, but not with his mouth, we were all connected in our minds and we could hear each other's thoughts.

"Tell me what you saw or better yet, show me. Show me all of your dreams, please." He said. "Put your hands back onto the sphere, both of you."

We did as we were directed, and there in the sphere were my dreams, one at a time until this last one was complete. What was different though was that both Biton and Brett were there standing close by, watching, as were others but I couldn't make out who or what they were.

When the last dream was complete, the sphere went back to the cloudy swirls but we kept our hands on it.

Brett commented, "Rose?"

Before Brett could say anything else, Biton started, "The dragon knew this was going to happen, that you would break the barrier and find out about her, before you were supposed to. I don't quite understand why this was supposed to happen but it has. The past, present and future are all so fragile."

Biton continued, "I was to show you this." Suddenly the sphere cleared and I could see, like watching a movie.

I saw myself in a place that I knew but couldn't remember where it was, and I was picking up a large, egg shaped object. It looked like a large emerald, but I knew it was an egg, a dragon's egg to be exact. Douglas, was there as was Lily, no, it wasn't Lily. Who was it? Then the sphere turned back, to its cloudy mass again.

I looked to Biton and spoke, "I was supposed to find the egg with the help of Douglas and Lily, or who? Or is this how I find it now?"

Tina M. Engel

Then I knew where that place was. I should have remembered when I saw it but I didn't, I had forgotten, but why? I had been there so many times, played there with my imaginary friends. The dragon's egg was hidden at home, in Pineville.

"That was where it was hidden, and now, the future is unclear to me as to where the egg is. He was here trying to listen, but as long as we were connected to the sphere he couldn't hear or see. He has left, choosing to retrieve the egg and hide it, not destroy it." Biton said with a tone of confusion in his voice. "Instead of waiting for us to be done and destroying this place and us." As he looked to Brett. I knew he was implying the two of them.

He wants me, I thought.

Biton removed his hands then and Brett and I did the same. "He is gone, we can talk without fear. The dragon is an important part of you, Princess Emilee, given to you by them, those who exist in your special place. It was hidden there in Pineville, protected by you friends, your forest friends, but now all is in jeopardy. I fear it is too late to retrieve the egg before he does.

"Your vision proves it, your dragon sent you a message, to find her. Once he has the egg, she will hatch in captivity. He will try to break her, turn her to his ways. He believes if he has your dragon, then you will go to him and join him more easily."

"But my friends in Pineville, my family?" and I paused, standing. "What..."

"Sadly, Princess, there is nothing..." Biton started to say but then the rumbling started again.

Tina M. Engel

Chapter 13

Questions,
So many to ask.
But deep down inside,
You know the answers.

"The doorway to Gehenna, it must not be opened." Biton thundered. "This didn't go as planned. How didn't she see this, know what the Dark One had done with the help of others, or maybe she did?"

I cut him off. "The others who helped him, Proteus and a water fey. Who is she?"

Brett stood then with a look of contemplation, as he was in my thoughts again, remembering what I saw in the water as the creature injected her venom into my leg. He then mumbled, so I knew that he had searched my thoughts, "Water Fey?"

Brett's face turned a sickly pale color and his eyes widened as his thoughts went to the same as mine...Queen Anahita? "She wouldn't." Brett said in a whisper.

We both looked to Biton for answers. "All I know is that it is a female water fey who has been working for the Dark One, for a long time. We had no idea why or what they were doing. I only know what I saw in your mind, Princess Emilee, Queen Anahita, but is she the water fey helping the Dark One, I don't know. She and they, now know too since this sphere connects us all together."

Tina M. Engel

Biton paused then and said more to himself than to us, "Maybe she has always known, she does know most things, sees most things."

I put up a hand to stop him from talking and I shouted, "She, who the hell is she?", "and then a bit calmer (okay, not calmer at all), I continued, "and who is connected to this sphere. You keep saying, she and they, as if these people, fey or whatever monsters, are up above playing a game of good versus evil, and this is no game!"

Brett then seemed to come back to the conversation, after letting the idea that maybe Queen Anahita was the spy all along, soak in, and came over to me to calm me. I was surprised at his behavior since she had been his very good friend, and maybe more, for a long time. How could he be so calm? I thought.

Brett, with a sober expression, took my hand in his and the zing and humming that I felt was safe and calming. I took a deep breath as Brett turned to look at Biton and spoke so calmly that it was a bit creepy. "What are we supposed to do now? Obviously things are not going as whomever the hell they are, planned, I assume."

Biton looked a bit sheepish, if that is possible, but composed himself quickly and went over to the sphere, sat down and placed his hands on it.

"Brett", I said.

"Not now Princess. There is no time to get sentimental or assume anything at the moment. Things seem to be going haywire and we must figure out what to do to get back on track. Why was Rose there?" Brett said, with calmness but confusion in his voice.

I was one with him, in his mind, and his thoughts. Where Queen Anahita was concerned, his thoughts of her were buried so deep, I couldn't find them. Brett looked down at me, shook his head from side to side as if to say, not now, and then put his attention back to Biton.

"Princess Emilee, come and sit, let us see what it says." Biton requested, but Brett had other ideas.

Brett took my arm in his and as he turned towards the doorway, he demanded that Biton open it so we could leave. He practically had to drag me, since I had other ideas, like going back to the table.

Biton, with firmness and authority in his voice, bellowed for Brett to cease and for me to put my hands on the sphere. Brett continued to try to physically pull me to the doorway and as I looked back towards Biton, his look changed. His eyes, once silver were now black as coal. As he removed one of his hands from the sphere, a blue light came streaking out from it, hitting Brett in the chest and sending him flying into the wall.

"Enough of this childish behavior. Why she puts up with all of you is beyond my comprehension. Princess, we don't have much time. Come!" Biton demanded.

I went over to Brett, bent down and placing my hands on his chest, I could tell that he was going to be fine. He just had the wind knocked out of him, and a few slight burns on his chest.

I placed my hand with the ring, under Brett's shirt, in the area that had the slight scorched spot on it. I could feel the skin was hot and I looked towards Biton, feeling my skin start to warm (okay, really hot). The last thing I needed to do was hurt this being that was supposed to be helping, but I wanted to at that moment.

I turned back to Brett, and looking down I saw that my arms were that silvery white color. I calmed myself and let the ring do its magic to heal his slight wound.

Brett was still slightly dazed but fine, so I got up, but before I could walk over to the table, Brett reached out and took my hand, stabilizing himself as he stood. He was a bit shaky so I pushed him gently up against the wall and told him to stay put. I didn't need to fix a head wound, if he fell again.

I walked over to the table but could feel Brett right behind me. Before I had a chance to sit down, the room started to shake again. Wasting no more time, and not allowing me to sit, Biton grabbed my hand with the ring on it and forced it onto the sphere.

I saw it then, the doorway, blown apart, and me standing in the middle of it, I was silvery white but the bubble I was in was red. I was standing in a bubble filled with lava.

Brett had his hand on my back, and saw it too, and gasped as he said, "No, Emilee."

I removed my hand from the sphere, as did Biton, and he stood and spouted, "There isn't much time, you must go and close this doorway for good. This entrance connects his world, Gehenna to the humans' earth. We can deal with the other entrances that he can still open, later."

I didn't like what he had just said about other entrances, but there was no time to ask. I did ask though out of fear and concern, "What are you going to do?"

Biton chuckled, more than I thought was possible for him to do and said, "You don't need to worry about me Princess, I will be fine. You must hurry though. I need to seal this room and destroy the passageway, for no one can touch this sphere unless they have the blood running through their veins. Go now and don't fail."

As we reached the door, it opened and I knew somehow we could leave, and we passed through the archway with no problem. I stopped to look behind and said loudly, "What about Rose? She was there!" And the golden doors swung shut, disappeared and suddenly bricks were falling from the walls.

We turned and started to run in the direction that we had come, as Brett was saying, to himself more than to me, but out loud, "The same blood?"

I knew what it meant but didn't have time to explain, and suddenly he was in my mind, of course. (Not the right time, but then, when does he do things at the right time.)

I knew that I had the blood of these beings flowing through my veins and Brett had just enough, after our blood mixed during our fight against Stephan and the trees. I thought at the time, it was going to kill him, but instead it probably kept him alive. What would have happened in that room, touching the sphere, if he only had his fey blood?

Things happen the way they are supposed to. Brett was supposed to get injured and I was given the ring at the appropriate time, so as to heal him as my blood joined with his.

I wondered then, even though Biton said that things didn't go as planned, maybe they had. Maybe all of this was supposed to happen.

I looked back at Brett, seeing he knew my thoughts and looked a bit perplexed. I turned away, putting only the thoughts of what was at hand, what I had to do, in my mind and ran, with the thought of Rose, lingering there also.

I could see the beginning of the tunnel and the rocky walls all around were crumbling. I didn't think we were going to make it in time, and was about to put my shield up to protect us from the falling rocks, when suddenly, the rocks froze in midair as if someone was holding them back for us to escape. I said in a whisper, "Thanks Biton," and I heard a voice quietly say, "You're welcome, Princess."

As we emerged from the tunnel, it closed, leaving only a wall covering, as if it had never been there. We were alone in the grand room and no more damage had occurred since I had been there earlier. It seemed the rumbling had stopped for now.

"Now what? How do we get to the doorway without being seen or stopped?" I said, looking at Brett, who had a look of curiosity on his face.

Brett came up to me and took my hands in his and lifted them slightly. As I looked at my hands, I realized that I was still the silvery white color, I hadn't changed back. I wondered why I had turned this color again anyway, what was going on in my body?

Suddenly the floor started to rumble, but not the same as minutes before. Then, not far from us, a hole opened up and guess who should appear but Kimberlite. I was stunned, shocked that he could be down here so deep.

Kimberlite's smile was large, the pride spread over his face as he said in a boisterous manner, unable to keep his enthusiasm at bay, "Well someone had to come give you a hand, and here I am!"

I asked him how he was able to get down here and know exactly where we were, as I walked over to him, and gave him a hug as he crawled out of the hole.

As Kimberlite shook Brett's hand and gave him a slap on the back in a gesture of true friendship, he said, "Queen Anahita told me that you needed help and led me to the underwater city. The lava pebbles in your necklace led me the rest of the way here."

Kimberlite reached out as he said the last part, and took the necklace in his hand. "Okay, I know how to get you to the doorway, so follow me. We'll go under the city, where there are no eyes to see us. No eyes that are interested in us, anyway." He said, with amusement in his voice.

Kimberlite jumped down into the hole he had come out of, and reaching up, helped me down.

Brett commented grouchily, as he jumped into the hole, "Just what do you find amusing about all of this, and how did Ana know where to find us?"

Tina M. Engel

Kimberlite's face, still beaming with pride, said as he looked at Brett, "Well it is always nice to be needed, and when I can help out when you are struggling to keep the princess safe..."

Before Kimberlite could continue, Brett cut him off as anger took over and his eyes turned red, "I am doing just fine without anyone's help..."

"Oh, you didn't need the shark's help to get back to the princess?" Kimberlite spouted."

"Enough!" I yelled, as I stepped in between them. "I think we have a doorway to close and this is wasting time."

I turned to Kimberlite then and asked, "How did Queen Anahita know where to find us and that we needed help."

"You will have to ask her." Kimberlite commented. "I had been at the beach, where you left on Adam's boat, and she came to me, telling me that you needed my help. It took some time tunneling under the sea but, I managed." And he gave me a slight grin.

"We can discuss Ana later, if you don't mind." Brett said, gruffly, "but we do seem to have a world, or many worlds to save right now."

He was right, I knew, and Queen Anahita wasn't or shouldn't have been a concern, but she was, and Brett knew it, as did I. We had seen her in the water, just after the creature from the other dimension injected me with her fluid.

It was Poseidon who sent the creature, but was Queen Anahita trying to stop it, working for the Dark One, or was she helping Poseidon. Which side was she on? Biton had talked about a female water fey working for the Dark One, was it Queen

Tina M. Engel

Anahita or the other fey that I saw with her? Or was it someone else?

Kimberlite turned and headed down the tunnel and we followed. My mind wondered, as we went, how was I supposed to close the doorway? What did I, standing in the middle of it, surrounded by lava, have to do with anything?

As we hurried along, the ground and surrounding walls started to rumble again and things started to crumble all around. Kimberlite yelled, "We need to hurry before we are buried. I can survive but I'm not sure about the two of you and we don't have time for me to dig you out, if we are buried."

I put my shield up around us, and the falling rocks and sand from all around rolled off, keeping us safe for the moment. I knew that if the tunnel completely caved in, we would be in the shield but still stuck and would have no air to breathe. I thought then, silly as it was, how were we getting air down here, anyway.

I heard Brett chuckle, and knew he was in my mind and found my thoughts funny. I turned to look at him and started to laugh, as he did the same. "Well", I said, "I think odd things when I'm stressed. How is the air getting down here to breathe?"

Brett, smiled that silly smile that I so loved and hadn't seen for so long, and said, "Let's just be happy we are, and not worry about it."

I turned my head forward, just in time, to keep me from running into the wall in front of me. Brett grabbed my arm at the same time to stop me.

I looked up above and there was Kimberlite, looking down.

"Give me your hand Princess." He requested.

I did so and he lifted me up out of the hole, and as Brett jumped out, the tunnel collapsed and the hole was gone. Everything around us was shaking and as I looked around, I saw we were in the old part of the city, the crumbled buildings, crumbling more as the earth seemed to move.

We were there, where we had closed the doorway earlier, but it was there again, not earth as we had left it. The golden door turned a deep red color suddenly and I could feel heat radiating from it.

I knew it was going to explode and pieces of hot metal would fly everywhere. I suggested, calmly, that we should take cover. Kimberlite and Brett looked at me strangely at first and then looking back at the door, they understood and we ran to the nearest pile of rocks and got behind it just in time.

My shield was still around us for protection but I wasn't sure how well it would protect against hot, flying metal. An explosion broke the silence, and red hot metal came flying over our heads. Kimberlite stood then, bending over me and pulling Brett up under him too, protecting us from the falling fire balls, just in case my shield failed, not that I thought it would, but he wasn't too sure.

Soon, the sound of the falling metal stopped and Kimberlite stood up and said, "Well it looks like you didn't need me this time, Princess. That shield of yours is pretty handy."

Tina M. Engel

Brett and I stood then and looking over to where the doorway had been, there was an enormous hole. Suddenly, things started to come out, creatures, not like the small beetle type that had entered earlier, but grey wisps. Then I could see what was inside the greyness. They were people, fey and creatures that looked like him, the bug like creature in my dream, ghostly grey in color, scowling and angry, as they entered our side of the door.

I knew what I had to do. I had to close off the entrance to Gehenna, and there was only one way. I turned to the boys and told them to keep the enemy busy while I closed the door.

Brett grabbed my arm, swinging me to him, to stop me. I reached up, put my arms around his neck and kissed him hard and passionately. When I pulled away, just enough to look into his eyes, I saw fear and pride in them.

Brett bent down, and placing his lips on mine, he gently kissed me, and pulling away said, "Be careful, we are not done yet." And he let me go.

I dropped the shield that surrounded us and I ran around the rock wall that had been our protection. Brett and Kimberlite came around the other side, yelling and carrying on to get the attention of the Dark One's army. I ran to the doorway, as I put up my shield around myself.

I stood in the middle of the doorway, my shield grew to the size of the opening, and no creature could get out, or in, for that matter.

I watched as Brett and Kimberlite were destroying the few creatures that had come out of the doorway. They were not difficult to destroy. I found this curious, Kimberlite just had to strike out and they disintegrated and Brett did the same, one swing of his sword and they disappeared.

I didn't have time to contemplate this, for as I looked into Gehenna, on the other side of the doorway, I saw them, thousands of creatures, like the one I had seen in my dream, like overgrown insects. I saw him then, larger than the others, with a smile so evil that I felt instantly nauseous.

I knew what I had to do then. I released my wings, and as they extended out, they touched the sides and top of the doorway. I took my necklace in my hand, and held it tight, thought of the lava babies inside and spoke to them. I told them that I needed their help, we had to close the doorway.

My wings became stiff as stone, vibrating as if sending waves of energy into the walls. As I looked at my arms, still white, I knew that my entire body was the same color.

Suddenly, I was surrounded with glowing, red hot lava. The lava seemed to be coming from me. I shut my eyes and focused on the lava, pushed it out, spread it up towards my wings, away from my body, until it filled my shield, touching the rim of the opening of the doorway.

As the lava touched the rock wall, my wings withdrew into my back, and the lava started to cool and harden. My wings had softened the rocks around the opening so that the lava could attach to it, mold into it. I waited until the lava was rock hard all around the outer edge before I shrunk my shield, so it was just around my body.

I was still standing in the middle, in the center where the lava was still liquid and wondered how I was going to get out. Maybe I wasn't supposed to. Maybe this was my mission, to close the door and then somehow I would be taken home. Home, where was it, how I longed for it, right then.

I heard then, "Emilee, it's time to come home. Come." And a hand reached into the lava still surrounding me, and pulled me through an opening that appeared, and I was outside the lava rock.

There was Brett, pale in color and panic on his face. When he saw me, the panic quickly changed to relief and I realized that it was Kimberlite who had pulled me to safety, his hand still holding onto my arm. I turned around to see the opening he had pulled me through, close up.

Where the doorway had been, was a hard lava rock, solid, and attached to the wall that the doorway had been in. It was closed, we had done it.

"She is calling me home, I heard her, I felt her. I thought that was the end of me and she was coming for me." I said, with a faint sadness in my voice. "I'm tired, I want this to be over." I said, as I watched my arms go back to the nice tan color that they usually were.

Brett came to me then as Kimberlite released me, looking wearier than Brett. As Kimberlite sat down on a pile of rocks, Brett took me in his arms and held me tightly, so tight that I had to push him away, just a bit, to breathe. We both chuckled and he kissed me on my forehead as he said, "I thought I lost you. It isn't time yet." And he took me in his arms, gently this time, and held me. I didn't ever want him to let me go, I wanted

Tina M. Engel

this feeling of protectiveness to stay, always, but I knew it couldn't be.

"It isn't time, yet?" I asked then, as he released me.

Brett gave me a peck on the lips and said with a strange tone in his voice, "Questions, always questions."

It was Kimberlite who interrupted us so I couldn't be persistent in pushing Brett to explain. Kimberlite suggested we get out of there before anything or anyone came to stop us from getting back to the ship. He assumed that the doorway was what we came here to close and the longer we hung around, the more danger there might be.

I asked him how he was going to get back to the surface, and when would I see him again and he gave me an enormous grin, got up and gave me a sweet hug, and said, "So you need me, huh?"

He looked at Brett then, and slapping him on the back, said, "See, she needs me, you both do!" And he laughed a hearty laugh and disappeared into a hole that just appeared out of nowhere. I heard him say before the hole closed up, "If you need me, just call. Otherwise I will see you on dry land."

Chapter 14

When past and present
Collide,
Emotions run wild.

I looked towards Brett, and saw that he was
staring off into space and I saw what he was
thinking. I didn't hear his thoughts, I could see
them, like a movie. We were in the water again,
just after the creature clamped onto my foot, and
there was Queen Anahita. Brett held onto that
memory, holding her there, frozen in that moment.
Suddenly it ended, Brett let the memory go
and was looking at me with concern and confusion
in his eyes. I went up to him and brushed my hand
across his forehead, brushing away a strand of hair
that was dangling lazily in front of one of his eyes.
He smiled then and placing his hands softly on my
hips, pulled me to him.
The instant his hand touched me, I wanted
to be in his arms. I willingly and eagerly let him
lead me to him, pressing his body to mine. Brett
looked down at me, our faces only inches apart,
smiled and all I could do was stare back into his
eyes. The need I felt then was so overwhelming,
the need for his blood. Oh, I wanted more, but the
blood was overpowering.
I stood up on my tippy toes and placed a soft
kiss on his lips. I whispered that he should let me
go and we should get out of there quickly, but with
a smirk across his lips, he kissed me again but with
more force than I had, and with such passion that I
couldn't stop him, even if I wanted to.

Tina M. Engel

I finally found a small amount of will power, deep down inside, and said in my mind, knowing that he was listening, that he needed to let go. I couldn't, I had such a need, that if he didn't stop, I wouldn't be able to control myself and I was frightened by what I wanted to do. I wanted to drink from him, drain him completely.

Brett pulled back then, his lips from mine, but didn't let go of me, our bodies still touching. He said, "Don't be frightened, I won't let you do anything that you are not supposed to do, at this time."

I looked up into his eyes, the dark green color of need, such desire, and I knew that my eyes where the same. But what he wanted was different than my need. Why did I want his blood so desperately?

Before I could ask him and before he kissed me again, which I knew was going to happen and I could do nothing to stop him, a gust of wind came at us and at the same time water started to fill up the area of the old city that we were in.

The cool water swallowed us up, engulfing everything. I wasn't worried about drowning, we both could breathe under water but I looked around, wondering why the water filled the city now, when it had been dry.

I spotted them then, two sharks, great whites, one bigger than the other. Brett still had one arm around my waist, as I put up the shield around us. The two sharks came face to face with each other, and then transformed into Poseidon and Proteus. They were half man and half fish, face to face, staring each other down. Proteus was holding the same staff I had seen him with earlier, before he disappeared.

Poseidon, reached out towards Proteus, a lightning bolt protruding from his hand, brought the staff to him. Proteus, let out a groan as if in pain as the staff was removed from his hand.

The water around us started to bubble, as Poseidon swirled the staff over his head and I heard him say, "This staff belongs to me, and me alone as long as I am alive."

At that, Proteus struck out, throwing a lightning bolt in Poseidon's direction, as he raged "I can arrange to end your life, father!" But Poseidon swung the staff forward, towards the lightning bolt, blocking it before it reached him.

Proteus looked towards us and threw a bolt of lightning our way, but with my shield up, it bounced off, sending it back towards him. As Proteus dodged the bolt, it struck a nearby structure, still somewhat standing, and it crumbled into a pile of sand.

Poseidon laughed a robust laugh and said, "You are not welcome in these waters anymore. You have failed in your work for the Dark One, and if I lay eyes on you again, it will be the last thing you will ever see!" Poseidon's eyes, turned black, and he started to glow and a force came out from around his body that knocked Proteus back and caused my shield to vibrate.

Proteus composed himself and looking at me with conviction in his face, said, "You will be his, you can run but you can't hide. He will have you and when he is done, you will belong to Stephan.

He has seen the future, he knows all the tricks that she plays."

Proteus then turned his gaze back to his father, Poseidon, and as he chuckled, his face twisted in hate, as he said, "It will be your death at my feet and the staff will be mine. I will be the ruler over all the waters, it has been promised to me. He will succeed, take over and rule all. She will be his slave, for what she did to him. It is written in the stars." And at that, he spun in a circle, creating a water funnel, and disappeared.

Poseidon, not looking at Brett and I, allowed his shoulders to droop a bit as the water started to subside. Exactly where it went, I couldn't tell you, but it slowly disappeared.

Poseidon looked over at us, his fish tail turning back into legs, and motioned for us to come to him. He went over to a golden bench that had not been destroyed and sat down.

Brett and I went over to him. Brett was wary and tense but I felt strong and safe. When we reached him, and I stood in front of him, Poseidon took my hands in his and placed his forehead on them in greeting. As he looked up at me, I could see the sorrow in his eyes, the exhaustion he was feeling.

Poseidon then looked at Brett and his posture changed, he sat upright, showing a more demanding attitude and said, "Things have changed, Emilee is stronger now, and has almost everything she needs to face him, but he knew things that we thought were kept from most. You, Brett must keep her safe." He said, as he looked towards me for a moment.

Poseidon then looking back to Brett, continued, "Her need is getting stronger, but she must wait, it isn't time yet, she must not..." and he stopped talking, looked up into my face again and smiled wearily.

"Don't let the desire and need interfere with your mission, Princess. We can beat him, stop him from succeeding, but not without you. We have waited too long now and we cannot wait for another to come. It must be you. Home, she is calling you home, follow her voice, it will lead you to where you must go next. Proteus is still out there, and will stop at nothing to get to you, to help the Dark One win."

Looking at Brett, Poseidon continued in a gruff tone, "Be vigilant, and do not trust your surroundings. Don't let Emilee's needs and desires take over. You must keep her in line, and you must keep your..." and he paused for a moment, looking at both of us, one to the other, and then looking back at Brett, said "Your feelings are not important, remember that. Keep it in check."

I asked when he paused, "Queen Anahita, what does she have to do with this? She was there, in the water. I saw her as did Brett. Why? Is she working for you, helping you to get the beast to me or working for the Dark One, trying to stop it from happening?"

I paused for a moment and then added, "But there was another water fey there, I could only see its silhouette, but it was there. Who was that?"

As I tried to continue with my questions, Poseidon put his hand up to stop me, and smiling said, "You do ask so many questions but you know the answers to most." And he looked to Brett for a moment before walking a short distance away from us.

I started to feel like a child again, frightened and frustrated that I could get no answers from him, so I put up my shield around myself and Poseidon. Of course, that sent Brett through the roof, so to speak.

All Brett could get out of his mouth before I told him to shut up, was, "Emilee!" And after I told him to shut up, Poseidon laughed, a simple, innocent laugh, but it did make Brett angry. (I did find a bit of humor in it, I will admit)

"She can tell you what you want to know." Poseidon said.

I released my shield then and said in a tone that was firm but respectful, "Please, you are a water fey, supposed to be the God of all the waters, so the stories go, in the human world. Queen Anahita is a water fey. I want to hear this from you and I'm not leaving until I get some answers."

I then said in a more sarcastic tone, "I don't even know who "She" is, or where "She" is! All I know is that you all, everyone keeps talking about "Her or She", as if "She" is a goddess or something!"

Poseidon turned away from us for a moment as if he were waiting for something to happen, or for someone to appear, and then turned back to us and spoke, "Very well Child."

Well, you know how I don't like being call a child, but before I could get all riled up again, Brett took my elbow in his hand, pulled me gently to him and whispered softly, "Let's get some answers from him, before you piss him off and he disappears." He then gave me that stupid, smirky smile that I so loved.

I pursed my lips to silence myself, looked at Poseidon and waited. He gave Brett a smile of approval and commented that was how Brett must keep me in control.

Brett tightened his grip on my arm just a bit, as I tensed in anger at what Poseidon had said, but before I could spout off and maybe ruin the opportunity for answers, out from the darkness came Queen Anahita.

"It's my turn to talk." Poseidon said in a demanding manner. "If you want answers, then listen."

I looked to Brett as he looked at Queen Anahita. His look was that of suspicion and loss. I tried to get into his thoughts, but he stopped me so I turned back to Poseidon, not wanting to look at her at the moment.

"Yes, Princess Emilee, I am the leader of all the water fey in Terrafirma, Earth and elsewhere, God, well, as much as we all liked the way the humans treated us as such, so many years ago, God, I'm not. Older than most, knowledgeable and one of the chosen ones to help her when she asks, is who I am.

"The look on your faces, when Anahita came out, leads me to believe that your trust in her has been broken. She was only following orders, orders from me. When I give them, it doesn't matter who you are, you listen and obey." Poseidon said with authority in his voice and Queen Anahita looked down at the ground.

As I watched her then, she seemed small and frail, not like the strong willed fey that I knew in the past. She looked up at me then for only a moment. I saw irritation and annoyance in her eyes, as she glanced at Brett and then back to me before she lowered her head again to look at the ground.

"Queen Anahita was asked by me, to keep an eye on you and guide you through areas as needed. I felt the need to keep an eye on you. Queen Anahita may not have been thrilled at this mission that I gave her, with the past she and Brett share," and Poseidon looked at Brett for a moment, causing Brett to squirm just a bit. "But I knew I could trust her to keep me informed, as did Andean, by the way.

"I can't be everywhere but want to stay informed so I have my eyes in places too, even though she doesn't necessarily approve of my ways, at times.

"It was I who gave Queen Anahita the earrings to give to you. And yes, not many receive this gift, and" Poseidon looked at Queen Anahita as he raised his eye brows and said, "She was not too happy to give it to you."

Queen Anahita looked up with fury in her eyes, as she swung her body around to face him and spouted, "We didn't know if she was the one or not, back then, and those earrings are very special. They are ancient relics that shouldn't be thrown around like they are costume jewelry, as humans would say."

I was shocked at the venom in her voice, and was worried for a moment that Poseidon would strike out at her disrespectful behavior, but instead he actually found it humorous, which made her even angrier.

Poseidon then composed himself, and continued, "Those of us who stand beside her, are the ones who gave you your gifts."

Before he could continue, I mumbled, "Douglas, Kimberlite, and Trevor?"

Poseidon let out a boisterous laugh and said," No Princess, Kimberlite and Trevor were given the gifts to give you, as Brett was given the gift from Douglas. We were told, under no circumstance, not to get personally involved. Well I figured if Douglas went against her wishes, which he did by allowing you to stay at his home and providing extra guidance to you at times, then it wouldn't hurt if I got involved. So here we are."

I questioned then, "So if the shield is from you and the barrette that turns into a weapon was from Douglas, then who gave Kimberlite the diamond necklace and Trevor the ring? And the wings, they appeared when my tears mixed with my mother and father's. Is that a gift from them?

"You sent the creature to put the substance into me to speed up my growth, changing my body again, stopping me from needing Rose. My skin turned white after the creature did what it did, why? And the ring, you gave my ring more power. You said it will strengthen my perception of what is the right thing to do."

"Questions upon questions, I give you answers, and I get more questions." Poseidon said.

Before Poseidon could say any more, we heard a voice say, "Enough Poseidon! Emilee, it's time to come home!" In a very irritated tone. We all heard it, not just me.

"She needs to be explaining this, to you, and she will soon." Poseidon said. "I have said too much already. Queen Anahita is not the enemy, though, Princess, I think you would like her to be. But the two of you need to put your silly emotions aside, for now, anyway, and work together."

As I looked to Queen Anahita, she was looking at Brett as he at her and I could feel the jealousy bubbling inside of me. Then I felt Brett's hand wrap around mine and he squeezed it firmly as Queen Anahita looked at me and then down to our hands, with fingers intertwined.

Queen Anahita's demeanor changed then, back to the professional fey that I remembered, put together, self-confident and distant. She said then, "I will continue to help in any way that I can. The wellbeing of all life depends on it, and that means that we must first save the humans from the Dark One."

She then looked at me and said in a sarcastic manner, "They say, without the humans, all will be lost, but I still wonder about this."

I was irritated with her and this entire situation but remembering what Biton said about a water fey, I asked, as I looked at Poseidon, "Biton said it was a female water fey that was working for the Dark One. You know Biton and I assume you were in the room with us. Biton said there were others, and I felt others present, even though I couldn't see them.

"Are you sure that Queen Anahita is really working for you, or is she pretending?"

Queen Anahita, with fury in her eyes, started to speak, but only got a few words out, " How dare you, you pathetic..." before I thrust my hand out towards her, and thinking of my shield put her in a bubble, so as not to hear her voice.

Queen Anahita was still spewing words but we couldn't hear her, so I continued, feeling triumphant at what I had just done, "If she isn't working for the Dark One, which I am questioning, then do you know who this mysterious female water fey is?"

Poseidon looked at Queen Anahita, lifting his eyebrows in a questioning fashion, looked back at me and answered, "I stay out of that room, with all those strange contraptions, that odd sphere is from out of this world.

"As for Biton, he is a strange character and not someone I, as humans say, hang around with. He has been hiding in that room for so many millennia, keeping it hidden, that I at times forgot it and he was there.

"It was only when she invited me to participate with the others, to discuss changes in the future due to choices made by some that I remembered about that strange being.

"I had hear rumors of a female water fey who was causing problems, but ... well, I don't bother with trivial matters."

Poseidon turned back to Queen Anahita and looking at her with uncertainty on his face, said quietly, "Princess, you have the power of perception, the ring. You should be able to sense if she is with you or against you." And he turned back and gazed at me with a look of amusement.

Tina M. Engel

I looked down at my ring, and back to Queen Anahita. I saw the anger, but also fear on her face. I wondered if I could tell if it was her, and whether I wanted to know. I liked the idea of her being intertwined with the Dark One. It would make this part of my life a bit easier, if she was working for him. Get rid of this jealousy that haunts me at times.

But then I thought, if I found out that she wasn't working for him, how easy it would be to ignore what I learned. Let them all believe that she is evil. That was the fear that I saw on her face. She didn't trust that I would be honest.

I had the answer that I needed to find, deep down inside of me. I, no, we all needed to know for sure. If I could see that she was with us or against us, I must try and tell the others the truth.

I walked over to Queen Anahita and lowered the shield. I held out my hand with the ring towards her and asked her, nicely, (I might add) to put her hand in mine.

Queen Anahita looked up at Poseidon with a pleading stare and he just nodded his head, telling her to do so. She turned towards me and with a look of loathing, she put her hand in mine.

My body turned again, that strange silvery color and looking in her eyes, as she tried to stare me down, I saw. The love that she had and still did, for Brett was painful. There was such fury that she felt, when she was ordered to help us. But there was nothing to insinuate that she was, at this time or ever had been in contact with the Dark One. I only felt disgust, along with fear for him, radiating from her.

I also saw Queen Anahita dragging another fey away from me, when I was injected with the water creature's venom. As this fey turned and looked at me, she looked just like Queen Anahita.

I let go of Queen Anahita's hand with a jerk, as I saw in her eyes, that she knew what I saw. I was shocked and confused at what I had just seen.

I told the others that she had never been working for him. I didn't go into detail, about her feelings for Brett. It was no one's business but hers, what her feeling were, and I felt sad somehow, that I had intruded in her inner most feelings. The anger and hatred that she had, changed to embarrassment and shame.

I shared with them then, what I saw regarding the other water fey as I looked to Poseidon for answers.

"You handled this, correct?" Poseidon said to Queen Anahita as he looked down at her.

As I stared at Queen Anahita and our eyes met each other's, I was back in her thoughts, there were two of them, a twin, and it had been the twin who ended the relationship between Queen Anahita and Brett. Brett never knew that there were two of them, one full of light that he loved so, and the other, dark, filled with envy and jealousy over the relationship of her sister with Brett.

I left her thoughts, as the look of anger filled her face, knowing that I had intruded again. She looked then at Brett and I turned to look up to his face and saw the shock as I realized that he was there with me, in my mind and saw it all.

"She has been taken care of, Poseidon. She will never cause trouble again. I have personally seen to it." Queen Anahita said with conviction, but also sorrow in her voice.

She turned towards Poseidon then, and taking one of his hands, did the fey parting, and told him that she would guide us out of the city and get us safely to the ship, if that was his wish. He said nothing but nodded his head.

Queen Anahita glanced at Brett with sorrow in her eyes and then walked away, back towards the darkness from which she had come.

Queen Anahita stopped then, turned towards us and said, "I suggest you both follow me, if you want a safe passage out."

I turned back to look at Poseidon, but he was gone. Queen Anahita turned and disappeared into the darkness and Brett followed.

As we entered the darkness and my eyes adjusted to the dimly lit surroundings, I realized that we were in yet another part of the city. It was still the ancient city but it wasn't destroyed, the grand buildings still stood. All was quiet, still, nothing moved.

The city was lit only with strange orbs floating over the pillars that were scattered sparsely around. Looking closer, I realized that the orbs were actually bubbles filled with water, with a small sea creature in the center, all aglow.

I stopped then, feeling a strange sensation, as if someone was watching us from a short distance away. I heard then, "Emilee, it's time to come home."

Queen Anahita stopped and turned and Brett held my hand a bit tighter. I said out loud, with frustration in my voice, for whomever was to hear, "I'm trying to, but you are not helping me much! Where is home?"

There was movement in a building not far away, and as I faced it, I saw a slight glow in the windows, dim but visible. It hadn't been there a moment ago.

"Well," I said with acceptance, "let's go see what or who is there."

Queen Anahita shrugged her shoulders, as Brett looking towards her, asked if she knew what was there and if it was a good idea.

Queen Anahita answered, "There are dangers down here, and this part of the city has been untouched by all for so long. I would suggest that we continue out of here but then, what do I know. The princess here seems to have all the answers, or she pretends to."

I was stunned by her attitude and answer and suggested that if she would prefer not being here, she could leave and we would be just fine without her. (Yes, I was feeling pissy, and was a bit sassy, in how I spoke)

Brett, removing his hand from mine, put them both up, one towards each of us, and suggested we stay calm and civil, that we needed each other. Queen Anahita lifted an eyebrow and scoffed a bit, stood still, not moving towards the building or continuing to guide us out.

I heard it again then, but it was a voice I recognized this time, "Emilee, we are waiting."

"Lily?" I said, and headed towards the building as Brett followed close behind. Approaching the door, I pushed it open slowly and

Brett then stepped to my side, squeezing into the room before me.

There in the middle of the room, was a circular glowing area that was a milky color but was swirling and pulsing. As I approached this thing, I turned to see Queen Anahita enter the room.

"What do you think?" Brett asked her before I could. "It's a doorway, I know, but to where?"

"There are doorways, hidden from eyes that can't see, and are available only to those in need. They can be anywhere, and appear at any time. You know this.

"It appears to me, someone has opened this for you. Do you trust that it is your friends, or the Dark One? It is your decision to make. Go through it or follow me." Queen Anahita said and stood still, just looking at me.

I realized then that she wasn't connected to a water source, and hadn't been since she appeared. I must have had a stunned and confused look as I searched around her, trying to see anything that would resemble a bit of water that she was connected to and she smiled as she said, "I am in the water, my dear, it is all around me. Shall I show you?"

As her hands rose up from her sides, up over her head, the water started to come up out of the ground rising slowly, but rising.

When it reached my knees, Brett hollered, "Stop this ridiculous behavior, both of you! Can we please act like mature, grown fey for a change and get the hell out of here? Then you can both have at it, fight any way you choose, but I am sick and tired of this stupid competition!"

Brett looked at Queen Anahita and said then, more exasperated, "Ana, stop this. It was over a long time ago. You made the choice, you." And he got a sudden look of confusion and anger as he was remembering what he saw in my mind, a twin.

"I'll request you be relieved of this duty, if I must, but we do need you, for now." Brett said as he shook his head slightly from side to side, with a look of sorrow in his eyes.

As I looked at Queen Anahita, her expression changed to regret as she lowered her arms and the water disappeared, seeping back into the ground.

"Go then", she said, "It looks like they want you quicker than it would take for me to get you there. Yes, it is safe, I knew it was there but wanted you to take the long way. Go, before I close it myself, and I can, just so you know.

She looked at Brett then, and said, "I will see you both when you are back on dry land. I am not needed here anymore, unless you decide to stay and explore more, and get yourselves into trouble."

Suddenly, from the darkness we had just left, came what looked like a very large bubble, elongated, and it swallowed her. It was filled with water and as it disappeared back into the darkness, it took her with it.

I turned and looked at Brett and saw sorrow in his face. As he looked at me he was frowning slightly, and I could feel sadness radiating from him, as he held out his hand towards what Queen Anahita had said was a doorway.

Tina M. Engel

I opened my mouth to speak, but before I could say anything, Brett put a hand up, and said, "Not now Emilee, please, not now. It is safe, and we need to go." Brett took hold of my elbow, and led me towards the glowing, swirling area and we walked into it.

I was blinded for only a moment and then realized that I was in the water, standing just outside the kelp forest, and the great jellyfish were there waiting for us. I looked to Brett and his expression was still sorrowful, but I also saw relief. We were where we needed to be.

As they communicated to us that they were there to take us back to the ship, wanting to get us there safely, I felt a bit irritated that everyone and every creature, thought I couldn't take care of myself.

As I looked around and up into the great waters of the ocean, the beauty all around was stunning. I realized, that I had been so busy trying to stay one step ahead of the Dark One and stay alive, I should say, that I forgot just how beautiful the fey's realm was. The colors all around, plants and animals were so vivid, the movement of plants and animals so graceful, like a dance, and I decided that I didn't need the jellyfish at this moment.

The jellyfish were a bit concerned, since they had been given orders from someone, and I assumed it was Poseidon, to bring us up to the ship safely, but I reassured them that no trouble would come to them for disobeying.

Brett, on the other hand, was very calm about this and I found that a bit disturbing. I figured the fight would come from him. As I looked

Tina M. Engel

to Brett, waiting for the argument to begin, his look was that of acceptance. He turned towards the jellyfish, and thanked them for their help and they lifted themselves up into the waters above, gracefully drifting away.

Brett then turned to face me and said with a sigh, "Let's go, they're waiting." And he held his hand up as if to insist that I go first.

I smiled smugly, feeling as if I had won a small battle, but really, I knew that if there had been danger around us, Brett would have insisted we accept a ride with the jellyfish.

As we swam up towards the surface, the beauty took my breath away, the closer we got, the more sunlight filtered down, and created rainbows all around us. The sea life sparkled as they danced through the water.

I felt sad as I saw the bottom of the ship, knowing I would have to get out of the water, and realized that the water was still where I wanted to be at this moment.

Before we surfaced, I released my wings, and spread them out as far as they could go. Being covered by tiny scales, I was able to move them gracefully through the water and did a few circles, as the wings could push me through the water quickly. I found this delightful and swam down a ways, only to come back up quickly, but with grace. I felt amazing and then really didn't want to leave this peaceful place.

When we arrived at the surface, I saw faces looking down at us. Most seemed relieved, but Lily was impatient.

Over to my right I saw movement and up from the water came a whale, one of the whales from earlier, who helped me. She came up to me, with her baby at her side.

The whale came over and as the baby swam around, excited to see me again, the mother whale lowered its head so we could get on top of her. I knew that she was going to lift us to the safety of the ship. I ran my hand over the baby's side as it glided through the water in front of me.

Brett was already on the large whale as I came over to her, and Brett reached down to help, but as he reached for my hand to help me get on the whale, I took flight.

As I lifted myself up out of the water and flew past Brett, his expression was that of exasperation. He shook his head as the whale lifted him up to the deck of the ship. I landed on the ship as Brett was helped by Adam, and the whale made a sound so soft and sweet, as it said its goodbye.

Chapter 15

The road of life
Has twists and turns
Of many,
Decisions create new
Forks in the road,
Which one do you
Take now.

They were all there, Adam, Jordan, Angelina, Trevor, Eagle and Lily, all but Douglas and Rose. My heart sank just a bit, as I had hoped that Rose was better and would be there waiting to give me a piece of her mind, believing that I hadn't been behaving, and that she should have been with me. I smiled at the thought, but despair still filled me. I had seen her twice down there, once with the dragon and once standing next to the sphere. Why, I wondered.

I cleared my head of these thoughts; there was another matter more pressing at the moment. Pineville, my home, or Emilee's home. The Dark One was going there to get the dragon's egg and my family, or her family, the real Emilee's, was there. Would he hurt them in order to find the egg? I wondered.

I rushed over to Lily, as she was saying in a casual tone, "Well now, we were starting to wonder if you would ever join us back here, after you closed the doorway to his domain."

Before she could continue, I cut her off, saying a bit anxiously, "Pineville, he is going to

Pineville to get the egg, my family, I mean, her family, they may be in danger!"

Lily put out her arms as I reached her and she wrapped me in a warm embrace before saying, "Let's all go down below and you tell us everything that happened. Then we will decide what to do about your Pineville."

I pulled back slightly, to look into her face, stunned at her lack of concern regarding what I had just said. I continued with a bit of annoyance in my voice, I was sure, "You know what went on down there, don't act like you don't."

I pulled away from Lily, took a few steps away from her and continued, "You somehow opened that doorway in the city for us to get out sooner than if Queen Anahita had lead us out. Biton, you know who he is and he was communicating with you, wasn't he?"

I saw movement behind Lily then, and that stopped me from continuing with my rant. Stepping around Lily, was Rose. I swear my hearts skipped a beat as I let out a gasp, saying in a whisper, "Rose."

I rushed to her, and grabbing her into my arms held her tight, (a little too tight I might add) and she had to push me slightly away so she could breathe. Rose smiled her sweet smile, and bending closer to me, placed a kiss on my cheek. I hugged her again, this time not quite so tight, but I didn't want to let her go. If this was a dream, I didn't want to wake from it.

Rose suggested then, as she stepped away, but reaching out and taking hand, "I think we should do as Lily asked, go down into the mess hall, hear what happened down in the city, and she can tell you what has been going on up here."

I looked around at all the faces staring at me, smiles of relief on their faces, and it was Angelina who approached me then, took me in her arms and gave me a wonderful motherly hug.

"Well, I think we can all continue with the hugs later." Lily said in her whatever tone, which she gives, as only a cat can. But I knew she wasn't a cat at all. Lily came over to me then, and led me to the door and down below.

When we were seated, Trevor brought hot coffee for most of us. Rose and Eagle took none. Eagle still seemed distant, like he was waiting, watching, for something or someone.

I filled them all in on what happened down below and Brett chimed in now and then too, filling in his adventure, if you could call it that, when he wasn't with me.

Looking at Lily, I made the comment, "You know this, don't you? And Biton, you know him too?"

Lily smiled and told me that she saw it all but wanted to hear it from my perspective. She shared her concern regarding the confrontation between Poseidon and Proteus, and that Poseidon was supposed to remove Proteus from the picture, so to speak. She felt that his parental emotions had gotten in the way.

When she said this, the ship leaned hard to the right, almost tossing those of us sitting, out of our seats and Brett and Jordan, who were standing, did take a tumble but were okay, as a large wave hit us from the side.

Lily shouted with irritation, "Poseidon, that is enough!" and I heard from not far away, a chuckle and again, we were tossed about before everything calmed down.

"No bother," Lily said, "We will take care of Proteus in good time and Poseidon, you have done enough, and then some, for now. I suggest you mind your business and let me mind mine."

Suddenly, the skies went dark, and as we looked out the portholes, we could see the clouds swirling and the rains started to pour down on us, as Lily reluctantly said, "All right Poseidon, you win for now. I'm sorry for being insensitive. Now would you please, and I say, please, stop this nonsense. We don't have time for this."

The rain stopped and the sun came back, letting light back in from the portholes as I again heard a chuckle, and a face appeared in one of the portholes. Poseidon, beaming with pride, tapped on the window until Lily would look, and then he disappeared.

"Well now," Lily said, when he was gone, "let us continue.

It was my turn to ask questions, so I started with Rose, "How did she get well?" I asked, looking at her and since Rose was seated next to me, I reached out and squeezed her hand.

Lily, looking serious, replied, "She is here for now Princess, only because you need her. You are stronger with the people you love and who love you, around you. That is all I can say about this. Keep her close, when you can."

Before I could question this, because I didn't like the way it sounded, "For now", Lily continued to speak. "The doorway is closed. Your wings did their duty, as did the necklace and all of your special gifts."

What a minute!" I spouted, "The necklace, it was around Rose's neck when I went down to the city. I didn't even think about it until now. I didn't have it on until..." I stop to think back and realized that the necklace wasn't around my neck when I was with the dragon in my dream and when I came out of the dream, it was there around my neck.

"How?" I asked.

Lily looked to Rose and Rose had her wonderful, enthusiastic smile on her face as she said, "I was there with you. I have been since that creature injected you with its venom. I gave you the necklace when you were with her, the dragon. She told me to and when you woke, I woke too, so to speak." And Rose looked towards Lily.

Lily got up then, went over to Rose and asked her to stand. Lily lifted up Rose's shirt just enough for us to see a tattoo of a dragon. "For now, this will keep her with us. Shinar, your dragon, has powers too."

"For now?" I asked.

Rose sat back down and took my hand again, squeezed it affectionately, and said, "No worries, Princess, we can do this."

I looked back at Lily as she went and sat down and I asked, "Where is Douglas, and who is Biton to you?"

Lily explained then, "Eagle took Douglas to where he was needed, back on land with the Wolves, on their way to Pineville, and as for Biton, well let's just say that he has been around a long time and is a very special friend. He has done his duty in the underwater city, has closed the room for now and is at rest until I need him again. We all have roles to play in the future, as we did in the past and present.

"Because things changed when you were in the room, when you took your hands off the sphere, sending you to Shinar, the Dark One saw it all. Your thoughts, along with the thoughts in the sphere, were open to him for just a moment for him to see.

"The sphere opened your mind to the universe, Emilee, so that more could be revealed, but when you let go of the sphere without Biton closing the sphere down properly, the Dark One, always spying, saw but a glimpse. That glimpse was the whereabouts, of your dragon. He knew of it but didn't know where it was."

"The dragon." I said softly. "How did he know where she was?" I didn't see it."

"You were not the only mind opened in that room, Emilee. You were to see her, know where she was and go get her, but he saw, and has her now." Lily replied.

"But how do you know he has her?" I questioned.

Lily looked at Rose and Rose spoke, "I feel her too Princess, just as I felt you and was with you, even though my body was here on the ship. She, Shinar and I are connected." And Rose looked to Lily to finish.

Lily sighed, and picked up where Rose left off, "Your gifts are from very special and powerful beings. Some are fey, as Douglas and ..." She stopped then.

"You?" I said. "You are not a cat, I know this, I have seen you, but not quite."

When I said this, everyone in the room started to whisper, and I had forgotten that others were around, they were all so quiet.

It was Brett who questioned, "What do you mean, Emilee? She is a cat fey, just a pesky cat fey that thinks she knows so much."

Lily gave Brett a scowl of a look and then changed her look to delight as she stood up and said, "I guess it is time. Lily, back away, would you please."

I was so confused, as was everyone else, Lily was talking to herself. Just then, Lily turned into a cat and started to glow. The glow got larger, spreading out and away from Lily, until it was a large orb the size of the doorway that Brett and I had come through earlier. Suddenly, out of the orb came a woman, beautiful, my grandmother.

The orb disappeared and Lily turned into her cat fey form. There were two of them. Lily turned to my grandmother and said rather rudely, "Finally, this charade is over. You give me way too much responsibility, mistress. Can I be done now?"

My grandmother laughed and informed Lily that she still had work to do. That only the ones in the room could know that Lily did my grandmother's bidding.

"Emilee, my dear granddaughter" she said as she came over to me, and taking my hands in hers, continued, "You do exhaust Lily at times with your stubbornness and impatience."

She looked to Brett then and continued, "Brett, Lily is an annoying feline to those around who see her as a cat, but she is so much more."

"Annoying Feline?" Lily sneered.

"Now, now, Lily." My grandmother said, "Brett, she keeps me close, for I have many duties to attend to in other places. She carries a great load."

Angelina spoke up then, "You're the woman who came to me in my dreams, you led me to Proteus, you insisted I give Emilee away, you helped me escape to be reunited with Emilee. Are you my mother then, if you are Emilee's grandmother?"

My Grandmother went over to Angelina and putting her hands on her cheeks, kissed her forehead gently. "I have missed you so. It was one of the hardest thing I have ever had to do, giving my only daughter to strangers, even though I knew you would be safe, away from me, from him. Emilee had to be born, and be safe until now. I understand your pain."

My grandmother turned then to Jordan and continued, "And Jordan, your father is a great being, the leader of your people, the ancient ones, who were here so long ago. He knew you had a special purpose and allowed us to hide you also, from the Dark One.

He, the Dark One, found you both once, that day in your house, they were sent to kill you both, so Emilee would not be born. Luckily he hired idiots who thought it funny to leave you alive, Jordan, and therefore able to save Angelina. You had to be separated until the time came for you both to be back in Emilee's life, to help. It had to be this way."

I looked from my mother to my father, and saw the pain and anguish, the sadness that they felt. Their lives had been so difficult, the losses that they had experienced had been so harsh. My grandmother had a look of sympathy for them but I could feel her own pain, sadness and loss of the time she missed, spending with Angelina.

"What of my father and my family?" Jordan questioned. "I was not abandoned, but sent away?"

"For your protection, Jordan," my grandmother said.

"The ring, you gave me the ring to give to Emilee." Trevor shared. "It was you."

"Yes, Trevor, you played a part as well. You all have, it was written long ago. I had to ensure that it all played out the way it must. Unfortunately, Biton..." and she paused for a moment and then continued, "You are stronger, Emilee, my dear, than is good for you, at times. Biton didn't realize or hadn't foreseen that you would take your hand off the sphere, nor did I, such a small detail, but it changed the future. Now the task that you have Emilee, is more difficult, will take a bit longer and we are running out of time."

Adam chimed in then, "And what about me?"

My grandmother turned to Adam with fury in her eyes and spoke with contempt, "I will deal with you later, my good captain. You just keep all of these fey safe and when I deal with you, I may be merciful."

We were all dumfounded by her outburst and not understanding what Adam had done, Jordan came to his defense, "Wait a minute, he has been nothing but good to us all. He kept me from killing myself and..."

"Exactly!" My grandmother said, with a tone of assurance.

Everyone started talking all at once, and as I looked around the room, I saw the pain, fury and confusion filling the room. It was Rose's sweet but very piercing voice, that rose over all as she shouted, "Stop, everyone!" And they did. Everyone looked to Rose as she continued. "I don't have a lot of time, and Emilee needs me."

My grandmother turned to Rose, and Lily went over to her, turned into a cat and leaped into her arms, purring and rubbing against her cheek. Rose smiled a sheepish smile and said then, "We have to help the Princess, before its too late."

"I need to get to Pineville." I said then, with urgency in my voice. With everything that was going on, I had gotten side tracked and I needed to know if my family was safe or not.

"We don't have time my dear." My grandmother said, but I wasn't having any of that and informed her that I was not going any farther, into this, her quest for saving the humans' world and the universe, until I went to Pineville.

I spread my wings out, furious with everyone around me then. They didn't understand, that was my family in Pineville, the only family I knew for most of my life. These fey here, yes, were my family too, but in my heart, Pineville was home and they were still my family.

As I spread out my wings, my grandmother suddenly had a glow about her, and she spouted,

Tina M. Engel

"We can argue if you want, but I will win, my dear, and we don't have time for this."

It was Jordan who came over to me, put a hand on my shoulder and released his wings too. He smiled, amused, and said, as he looked to Eagle, "Would you like to join in, and Rose? I believe there is still room here for another set of wings."

I looked up into his face, as he looked down at me with silliness that was expressed in his eyes, and as his smile grew, I couldn't help but giggle.

The glow around my grandmother subsided and then Jordan and I put our wings away.

Eagle had just ignored Jordan's request, not seeming interested in the least, as to what was going on in the room, and Rose just smiled.

I looked over at Eagle and wondered just what he was thinking, as he stood there staring off into space. He glanced at me then and when our eyes met, there was a strange longing there, something I hadn't seen before in his eyes.

Before I could question Eagle as to what was bothering him, Jordan asked again, what was up with Adam and what trouble was he in for keeping him, Jordan, safe all these years.

My grandmother, looked at Adam, and answered, as Adam seemed to be a bit uncomfortable, "The future was set, decisions had been made, but now, Adam has changed it. One decision changed, no matter how slight you may think it is, will change so much."

Adam suddenly changed his attitude and stance, and shouted, "Enough of this, I have kept them all safe and done what I was told! If I made the decision to remove Jordan from the octopus's stomach, to save him, and it has changed the future some, it can only be to make it better. And how was I to know that Jordan was Emilee's father, and that the love of his life, was Angelina, Emilee's mother?!

"Now if we are to get Emilee to Pineville or wherever you want her to go next, I suggest we get this ship pointed in that direction. And if you are going to be seen hanging around, maybe you should let us know what to call you, because I am in no way planning on calling you mistress, or my lady or queeny, or whatever.

"I took my orders from another and did my part keeping Jordan alive and well, and he is more like a brother to me than you or anyone understands. He saved Emilee, and I can't see how his crime could possibly be so severe to deserve death. Besides, he was the one who saved Angelina, and in turn saved Emilee. I don't understand why I was to let him die.

"He lets me sail his waters, staying safe from harm, and in turn I do tasks for him at times. But that one order, to let Jordan die, was not something I could do."

"Poseidon?" I questioned.

Adam nodded his head but said no more.

My grandmother changed her look from irritation to sorrow as she looked from Angelina to Jordan, as they were looking at each other with longing in their eyes. "It has changed Angelina's future now, the path that she was to take.

"Angelina will not go forward and become what she was meant to be. She will stay with

Jordan, now that they have been reunited. I know she will not leave him. Her destiny has changed.

"In turn, Emilee's path has changed a bit, and will be more challenging. It will end in a different manner, but Emilee's quest to save all life, hasn't changed."

"But I don't understand?" I questioned softly. "My wings, if Jordan had died after saving me from the octopus, the tears from my mother and father? What about my wings?"

My grandmother looked a bit flustered for just a fleeting moment before standing a bit taller and confident and answered, "Your wings were to become a part of you but not the way they did. Shinar was to help your wings emerge but as one slight decision changes the future, it trickles down and changes other possibilities for the future."

My grandmother paused then for a moment and with a look of curiosity, in her eyes, as she looked at me, said in a questioning tone, "I didn't see your wings emerging this way. The tears from your mother and father are full of love and combined, they...maybe this was how it was supposed to happen, but I didn't see it. Curious."

Jordan went over to Angelina then, and taking her in his arms, they embraced and he placed a simple kiss on her lips. I hadn't seen any physical affection from them up until now, maybe they were afraid to allow their feelings to show, but now they knew as did I, that they would make it together.

But as for me, what did it mean? More challenges for me in the future? And why did my grandmother not see the future as it unfolded where my wings were concerned?

Everyone was silent then, not quite knowing what to say or do. It was a bit awkward too, Jordan looking at Adam with suspicion and Adam looking defiant.

"Well then" said my grandmother, with a tone of authority, "I guess, it is time to get Emilee to Pineville so she can see to her human family and then get back on track. I fear it will change the future, a future that didn't need to be, but when it happens, we will deal with it.

"Eagle, see to it that she gets there safely and you already know my name, you all do, Varda Elentari, but Varda is sufficient. Lily, it is time."

Varda, my grandmother, went to Angelina, hugged her genuinely and then came over to me and did the same. As she released me, she said, "I will see you soon, don't be foolish, and listen to Lily, for she is not alone. I am always watching; she speaks for me."

She turned to Brett then and cautioned, "Keep your feelings and desires under control, for she has her own to deal with and combat. You will have to be strong for both of you. Stronger now. Let us not do anything else too damning, to change the future. I can only do so much to fix the messes that you all make."

Brett opened his mouth but stopped, thinking better of it, when Varda gave a look of challenge.

Eagle then spoke, "How am I to get her there?"

Varda responded curtly, "She has wings, go with her and fly quickly. There is a doorway on the beach, which she can use to get through to her Pineville. Rose, you go with them, she still needs you."

Brett frantically spoke, "I'm going too. I'm not leaving her alone."

"Of course you are, Brett, but she will not be alone." Varda replied. "Eagle will get you there, and as for the rest of you, Adam will get you all back to port safely." And looking at Adam, she added, "Correct?"

Adam gave her a scowling look and stormed out of the room. Jordan came to me, taking me in his arms and hugging me sweetly, told me to be safe. I was his daughter, and he wasn't about to lose me now, and he headed out the door after Adam.

I turned towards my grandmother, wanting to ask if she would be there too, like in my dream but before I could, she was surrounded by the glow and then Lily walked towards it and they both were swallowed up by the light. When the light subsided, only Lily, the cat remained.

"I wasn't done!" I fumed. "I want to know about the female water fey who is helping the Dark One. Did my grandmother know she was Queen Anahita's twin sister?"

Lily just chuckled and said with slight irritation in her voice, "She knows most, but she doesn't tell me everything either so, you will have to wait until..."

"Emilee, let it go for now." Lily continued, but I knew it was Varda, my grandmother who spoke then.

Lily stormed towards the door as she said, "Well I was hoping to be done, but I guess we are still stuck with each other for a while longer. Let's get this show on the road, shall we." And Lily left the room, assuming that we would all follow.

Looking at Brett, I regretted mentioning Queen Anahita just then. For Brett, hearing about her twin and the deception that must have occurred during his time with her, must have been painful. He had fury in his eyes. He looked at me for only a moment and suggested we follow.

We did just that, followed Lily to the deck of the ship, where Adam and Jordan were having a heated discussion. As we approached them, I asked if everything was okay.

Jordan slapped Adam on the back a bit more aggressively than he should have, as he said, "It's all worked out Emilee, not to worry. This buffoon kept me alive and I am thankful for that. It's good that he doesn't always do as he is told." And he let out a boisterous laugh.

Angelina came to me then, and taking me in her arms, kissed me on the cheek and told me to be careful. Her love for me was so full, shining in her eyes, and then a few tears fell. I realized that I was crying too, and we hugged tightly. She told me that she wasn't about to lose me now and that she would be waiting for me. Angelina then went over to stand by Jordan.

Trevor was next, giving me a large bear hug, then did the typical fey parting and told me that

Adam was a good man and he would be with him until we saw each other again.

"Can we be done with this silly emotional display and get on with it, please?" Lily muttered. "Eagle, you will be carrying Brett, anyway you please."

Eagle spread his wings out and held up his hands. They turned into talons, long and sharp and he smiled an evil grin, but then laughed and Brett laughed with him.

"Emilee, you will carry me, for I don't really trust that Rose, as small as she is, could carry me safely." Lily commanded and looking at Rose, she winked.

Rose, smiled, and spreading her wings, lifted herself into the air and suggested, we all get going. Eagle scooped Brett up in his talons and I heard Brett grumble something about being careful with those sharp things as he was lifted up into the sky.

Lily jumped up into my arms and suggested we follow. I stood there for a moment, and then my wings released as if they had a mind of their own and lifted me up into the air too.

I was a bit clumsy, I might add, and almost dropped Lily. She commented that maybe she should have let Rose carry her, and I just laughed as we all followed Eagle up into the sky, towards the sun.

Chapter 16

Family!
People you love,
And who
Love you!

The air got thinner the higher we went. Suddenly, the stars were above us, but there was a barrier between us and the stars. It was a glimmering protection, keeping stars and planet separate.

We went no higher, flew just under the barrier, heading in the direction of land. It was cold and quiet up there between stars and land, but I felt calm, like this was a place I belonged.

Looking at Brett and Rose, they seemed to be handling this strange place with no problem. Brett however appeared to be a bit chilly. He had his arms wrapped around his chest and looking at me, he smiled and I heard him say, "You can warm me up later." And then smiled as he winked at me.

Rose was facing Eagle with a look of concentration on her face, not looking at anyone or anything as she flew ahead, as if in a hurry to get there.

It didn't take long before I saw land and we started to descend out of the place between the land and stars. I felt a longing to stay up there, but also to go farther, up past the barrier to the stars.

I could see the water meet the land then, the docks with ships and boats, large and small. We were still in Terrafirma, the colors all around so vivid and alive. As we got closer, there, just out of sight from the docks, was Kimberlite and Queen Anahita, standing next to a waterway, a river.

As we landed, out from behind some bushes came a wolf and as he changed into his fey self, I saw that it was Weylyn, the wolf pack leader.

They stood there waiting as we approached them, and as we did, Kimberlite came up to me and did the fey greeting and I gave him a look of annoyance. He chuckled then and gave me a hug as Queen Anahita just stood with her arms crossed over her chest, looking irritated.

Brett went over to her and her expression softened, as they gave each other a chilly embrace. I was a bit surprised and miffed, that he would even want to touch her, but then, they had been close once. I knew now that it was her, Queen Anahita or her sister, who had ended their relationship, whatever that was. It was none of my business anyway. Brett would have to deal with it at a later date, if he so chose.

I noticed Brett whispering into Queen Anahita's ear and I couldn't help myself, I wanted to know what he was saying. I pushed myself into his mind, feeling his struggle to keep me out, but then, I don't think he was struggling that hard because I was there, and heard him say, "You have some explaining to do, when this is done."

Brett stood and looked at me with annoyance across his face, but in his mind, he was chuckling a bit and said, "Can't mind your own business, can you?"

I smiled meekly as I looked down to the ground and when Weylyn spoke, I looked to him, trying to ignore Brett's stare.

"Follow me, Princess, we must hurry. I was sent to bring you to the humans' realm." And he headed back into the bushes.

As we walked between the bushes, there not far ahead was another circular glowing shape, a doorway that I hoped would take me straight to Pineville. I knew it would take too long if we had to traveled by land and underwater routes.

"Rose, you come with us but the rest of you stay here. These are orders from Douglas." Weylyn said.

Lily, turning back into her fey self, declared, "Excuse me, but I will be going too!"

"Of course, I wasn't including you. That was a given that you would be coming." Weylyn stuttered.

Brett of course, was having none of this and insisted he come too. He was not to leave me alone and would be alongside me every step of the way.

Lily walked over to Weylyn then and turning towards us replied, "Brett, don't worry, she has plenty around her to keep her safe, but the fewer bodies going into the doorway, the better. She needs you safe here, according to Varda.

"We will be back soon. It looks like you and Queen Anahita have things to discuss, anyway." As she looked towards Queen Anahita and gave a sly and snotty smirk, just like a cat.

Queen Anahita gave me a smug look which I didn't appreciate and those stupid jealous feelings came gushing back. Well what could I do but go up to Brett and taking his face in my hands, brought him down to my face and gave him a very intense, long kiss. (Was it a good idea, you ask, probably not)

I had only intended to anger Queen Anahita, but as our lips touched, the longing I had for Brett exploded, I ached for him and I knew that he felt the same. Suddenly, we were alone, no one else was there, only Brett and I. Where we were, I couldn't say, it was as if we were in a space in between dimensions, earth and sky, just the two of us. The passion was overwhelming, stronger than ever and I knew that I couldn't stop myself. I wanted Brett, every part of him, but especially his blood.

It was Brett in my mind then, telling me that we had to stop. He kept repeating over and over, that it wasn't time. I could feel his desire, his want for me, not my blood, but me. He was stronger though, than I, and I felt his hands go around my waist and pull me away, breaking our kiss. It felt like a blast of hot air hitting me as our bodies separated and we were back there on land, with everyone standing and staring.

I realized then that Lily was standing next to us and she had a hand on both of our shoulders. She had been the one to help Brett stop us from doing something that would ruin everything we had accomplished so far.

Lily just shook her head, and taking my hand, led me towards the doorway as Brett released me. As I walked past Queen Anahita, the look on her face was exactly what I wanted, the look of jealousy. I should have felt like I had won a battle, but I didn't, I felt lost, not being in Brett's arms.

Rose and Weylyn were standing in front of the doorway and disappeared into it, and we followed. As we entered, it was cold with a sound of wind whipping all around, but I felt no wind at all, it was still. The colors were that of a vibrant mural, colors everywhere, swirling all around, pulsating. Then as we took a step, we were out of it, in the forest of Pineville, behind my house.

As I looked around, I knew instantly we were in the humans' realm. It was grey and dull in color. Of course it wasn't really grey, but felt that way. After being in Terrafirma for so long, I had forgotten how different the two realms were.

I saw Douglas first. He was bent over someone, Emilee, the human Emilee. Lily released my hand and headed towards Douglas. As she did so, she started to glow and Varda separated from Lily and knelt down next to Douglas.

Weylyn was with other wolves, and they had someone backed up against a tree, Stephan.

Rose, I realized was next to me, holding my hand. I removed my hand from hers as I hurried over to the other Emilee. I looked at Stephan with contempt, and he had a smug look on his face.

I knelt down and looked at Douglas, as he said, "We got here too late. He had her on the ground. We were too late."

I looked into Douglas's eyes and saw the sadness and rage, but as he looked from me to my grandmother he said, "Varda, my dear Varda, it has been too long." And as he touched her cheek, his look softened.

"What can we do for her?" I begged, "She can't die!" and as I stood and faced Stephan, I continued, "What did you do to her? She has nothing to do with this."

Stephan started to laugh and the wolves, all growling now, moved in closer to him. Stephan threw out one of his hands then, and he held something in it. A force of wind came, knocking the wolves back a few feet, and holding the other hand up over his head, he held the dragon egg, large, gleaming and emerald green.

Varda let out a soft moan and said simply, "No."

Suddenly, tree fey came out of their trees, surrounding us all, and they were not here to protect us, I knew.

At almost the same moment, from behind one of the trees to my right came Queen Widow, as hundreds of spiders came down from thc trees.

Douglas, stood and barked, "Emilee, you, Rose and Lily, take this Emilee to safety. Hurry, she doesn't have much time!" And he headed in the direction of Stephan."

Varda, my grandmother, stood and stepped back as Lily, Rose and I lifted Emilee and before I turned to help carry her in the direction away from Stephan, Varda started to glow and I heard her yell, in a commanding voice, "Enough!" And all was still, except for Stephan, Rose, Lily and I.

Stephan laughed and lowered the hand with the dragon egg and said, "I have it and there is nothing you can do now, my lady. I am protected, a protection that you gave to him, a long time ago and now he has given it to me.

Rose, Lily and I put the human Emilee down out of harm's way, and I put my shield up around us as I listened to what was being said.

Stephan then continued, "Emilee, it is time to go. You need this creature that I hold in my hand. You can come with me now and make it easier on you and the rest, or be stubborn as I know you so well, from the past..." and he smiled an evil grin, "or more will die, the one being that pitiful human they kept alive for so many years, just waiting for the time that you would return to Terrafirma, and they would then put her back where she belonged.

"They were fools, all of them, for she was the one who held the dragon within her. You were to come back and retrieve it without harming her, but well, I didn't have that special touch that you must have, so I took it from her forcefully.

"You have the choice, my dear sweet Princess, to come with me and get this over with, or stay behind and heal her, your choice, but she will probably die anyway. You can heal her, but wake her, now that is something different. The torment that I put her through, has damaged her small, weak mind. Her mind is gone." Stephan said and held out his hand for me to come.

Varda struck out with her hand, sending a streak of light at Stephan but it shot off of what seemed to be a force field and struck a tree next to the wolves, shattering the tree. It fell on several wolves and they were buried under the rubble.

Stephan let out a boisterous laugh and said, "You have forgotten what this can do, my lady." as he held up a small glowing object.

Tina M. Engel

Varda let out a soft cry, and in a whisper replied, "I was told that it was taken away from him and destroyed. Where did you get it?"

"They are not all faithful to you. You are foolish to think they are. You may have banished him to that place, but those who took him there may not have followed all of your instructions.

"He promises protection to those who are loyal to him. He will win." Stephan said with a smug look, and then held out his hand towards me again and said, "Are you coming Princess, or are you going to make this just a bit more fun?"

I looked to my grandmother and she shook her head as if to say no, and told Stephan to go crawl back into the tree from which he came.

I knew that I needed the egg, but I also couldn't let Emilee die. I didn't know what to do, how could I do both. Suddenly, out of the doorway that was still open, flew Brett. (Well not really flew, but rushed out)

With his sword out in front, he struck out at Stephan, but the sword, as it struck the field that protected him, bounced off and out of Brett's hand, only to land a few feet from where Stephan stood.

Stephan laughed as he pushed his hand with the glowing object in Brett's direction and Brett went flying backwards, hitting the downed tree and knocking over a wolf fey who was standing in his way.

Stephan then went over to the sword, and as he picked it up, he said, "Well thank you dear brother, I have wanted this gift from you for a long time. Emilee, are you coming with me or not?"

"When hell freezes over!" I yelled, as I went to Brett's aid.

"Well that can be arranged and will be soon. I will see you soon, for I know you will come for your precious dragon, you need her..." and he stopped talking and looking at Rose, continued, "Rose, poor Rose..." and then looking towards Brett with a gleam of hate in his eyes, said, "And Brett, I do hope you come along too. I'm sure you will want this back." and he held up the sword.

At that, Stephan disappeared into the tree that he was standing in front of, the tree dropped into the ground, with a thunderous sound, and the ground shook as if an earthquake had just struck. Then the ground closed up, leaving no sign that a tree had ever been there.

As I looked around, everyone started to move again, the sky turned grey, the wind stared to howl, as did the wolves, some of them slightly wounded but others severely. I went to Brett as he got up on his feet and when I reached him, our embrace was short and sweet. I had to tend to Emilee, I knew, but needed to touch him, Brett, I needed that strength.

"Go, Emilee, and do what you can for the human, Emilee." He said as he squeezed my hand.

As I went over to her, Brett went to Douglas and Varda, who were deep in conversation, Varda not looking too happy to see Brett.

I bent down to Emilee, as Rose held one of her hands and Lily held the other. I smiled a concerned smile, as I could see the affection they both had for this human.

I wasn't sure what to do. Inspecting her body, I saw that she had a large gash in her chest, where her heart was. I placed my hand with the ring over it, and could see inside her. Emilee's heart was still there, but next to it, I realized, was where the dragons egg had been hidden, attached to her heart.

Emilee's heart was beating but very sporadic and slow. The vein that had been attached to the egg, was severed, as the egg had been ripped out of her chest. Blood was gushing from it. She was bleeding from her ears and nose and had a few scrapes and bruises starting to appear. She fought hard, I knew, not knowing why, but she had to protect something.

I had to heal her heart first, in order for her to live. I placed my hand with the ring inside her chest, and wrapped my hand around her heart. I could feel the ring get hot and my hand became warm and tingly. Soon her heart was beating with a normal rhythm and sped up to a normal human's beat. The vein that had attached the egg to her heart, shriveled up and fell off. She seemed to breathe steadier then.

I took my hand from inside her chest, and ignoring the blood that covered my hand and the surrounding area, I removed my necklace from around my neck and put it around hers. I then put my hand with the ring, over the gash and I felt it close and heal within seconds.

The stone on the ring was glowing a soft green as I felt Emilee's wounds heal. As I stared at the glowing stone, I saw Emilee in a bed, or was it me. As soon as the vision came, it was gone. The ring allowed me to see something, but I didn't understand what I was seeing.

I pushed the vision out of my mind for now, as the human Emilee was breathing normally, but her color was so pale, for she had lost a lot of blood. Too much I feared. She was human and I was fey, but I felt that the only way to keep her alive was with blood, someone's, but who's, mine, Rose's? I didn't know.

Lily touched my shoulder softly and said, "A few drops of your blood, should help, but just a few drops. We don't want her turning fey on us. That wouldn't help the human population, at this time, anyway." And she grinned that cat grin.

I bit down on my finger, just enough to make a small hole and watched the blood pool to the opening. I placed my hand over Emilee's mouth and as Lily gently opened her mouth, I placed a few drops into it and Lily lifted her chin to close her mouth again.

I felt a presence behind me and my grandmother caringly said, "That is all you can do for her now, Emilee. We must go before they come looking for her."

Still looking at the human Emilee, lying there injured, I questioned, "You said my forest friends had the egg hidden but it was in Emilee, how? I don't understand."

Varda replied, "When she took your place, before we put her back here in the humans' world, we hid it inside of her. We felt that it was a place no one would think to look."

I stood, and as I turned around, I saw Brett still talking with Douglas and Weylyn, and Rose was over tending to an injured wolf. I didn't remember Rose leaving my side. She looked over at me with an expression of sadness and I went over to help.

I tried to heal him with my ring, but he was broken so badly, his back, neck and both legs, that the ring did nothing. My ring wasn't strong enough. I didn't understand, I had healed Emilee, and she was far more injured, I thought.

"He wasn't meant to survive, Emilee. Your ring and your abilities can only do so much." Varda said, as she stood behind me, resting her hands on my shoulder, as I stood.

"I don't understand. I healed, Emilee. What do you mean, he wasn't meant to survive?" I questioned.

"It was his time, child, he was meant to go to Nirvana. It was his time and he welcomed it. There was nothing anyone could do." Varda said wearily, as two semi-injured wolves picked him up and carried him into the bushes, out of sight.

Lily came then, and stood next to Varda as Varda bent down, and placed a kiss on my forehead. She told me she had to leave, and that Douglas would take care of everything. As she stepped away from me, the glow came, and she vanished.

Lily let out a soft moan and said, "This is getting tiresome." As she looked at me with dismay.

The weather was getting rougher, thunder and lightning filled the air and the wind was causing the tree tops to bend at its will. There was noise through the trees behind me and Douglas insisted we leave the humans' realm and head to Terrafirma.

I looked at him in disbelief and back to Emilee, laying on the ground, pale and unconscious. "We can't just leave her here. She will die."

Brett came to me and took my hand, as Douglas told me that it was her parents, coming through the forest, looking for her, and we had to leave. They would take care of her and we had to get the dragon from the Dark One, before he turned her to his ways.

As I looked around, the wolves were disappearing, as were the spiders, Queen Widow and the tree fey that had been injured during the scuffle. Before Queen Widow disappeared though, she smiled and said, "Try to stay out of trouble."

Rose, Lily and Douglas all vanished, back to our realm, Terrafirma, leaving Brett and I still in the humans' dimension. Instead of leaving, I walked over to a large tree, pulling Brett behind me, since he wouldn't let go of my hand and was grumbling something about me never listening.

When we got behind the tree, I put my hand up to Brett's mouth to shush him and then peeking around the tree, watched as my mother and father, Katie and Willy, emerged from between bushes, and ran to Emilee.

Kneeling down, they inspected her and then lifting her up, Willy carried her back from where they came. Just before they disappeared though, something fell from Emilee. It was my necklace, I had forgotten that I had put it around her neck.

I heard a voice then, my grandmothers, "No loose ends left behind, my dear."

I went over and picked up the necklace, put it around my neck and just stood there, standing, staring into the forest where they had entered. I felt a lump in my throat, and tears burned my eyes. They were my parents too, my mom and dad.

I felt Brett behind me and his arms went around my waist. I turned towards him and buried my face in his chest and cried. I wanted to go to them, hug them and tell them that I was okay, but it wasn't me they were worried about, but her, their daughter Emilee, not me.

I felt such pain, a pain of not belonging. This was my home, they were my family, and being here again and seeing them, opened up all the memories that had been slowly drifting away over the past months.

"It's time to go now, Princess. He's causing great destruction now, here in the humans' world, and we must stop him before he destroys their world, and those in it.

"The grey fey that escaped from Gehenna, and disappeared as we struck out at them, were not there to hurt you or us. They were sent to this dimension, to the humans' realm to create destruction and chaos. Douglas told me that we don't have much time. I know where we need to go now but we must hurry."

I looked up into his face, full of worry and anger. The anger I knew was at himself for listening to Weylyn, telling him not to come with me through the doorway to the humans' realm, and for allowing Stephan to get hold of his sword. The worry was for Emilee, the human Emilee. I saw it in his mind. He didn't think she would survive.

Brett smiled then and bending down, kissed my forehead and told me that we needed to go. Brett, being in my mind also, continued, saying that I wasn't alone and my home was in the humans' realm as well as Terrafirma and elsewhere too.

Somehow I understood this, my home was growing, and maybe, just maybe, I wasn't just getting closer to my real home, but maybe I was there already. Maybe my home was everywhere.

Chapter 17

The fear of losing those you love,
Can paralyze you momentarily,
But don't live in that fear,
Have faith
That you will see them
Again.

Suddenly the doorway closed and Brett, looking in that direction said, "Damn!"

I looked at him and asked with curiosity, "Can't we open it again? I thought the doorways were always there. I thought all I had to do is think of Terrafirma and we would enter it. I see it all around us right now."

Brett, looking frustrated, replied, "It isn't just Terrafirma that we must enter but to get back to the beach where everyone else is waiting. We need to get to Adam's ship. And I must get my sword back before it becomes Stephan's, for good."

I didn't understand what he meant by the sword becoming Stephan's for good.

Brett seeing the confusion on my face, continued, "The sword was given to me by my father, but it had belonged to someone else before me. It was Stephan's father's sword, and has very special powers. It took time for it to accept me as its owner, but the sword has always had the imprint of Stephan's father deep inside.

"Now that Stephan has it, Stephan being his son, it is possible it will imprint on him, and if I touch it, it will burn me, will not listen to me and will be lost to me, forever. I can't let that happen.

It will make Stephan stronger and I will have a harder time protecting you from him."

"I can protect myself from that bastard," I responded strongly. "And we will get both the dragon and your sword back."

I looked around, hoping to see something that would help us get back to the ship on the other side of the continent, we were on.

Brett chuckled, gave me a squeeze and said with a silly grin, "Bastard yes, but I think you still need a little help from your friends."

Suddenly I heard, a man's voice say, "Emilee, I've waited long enough. Maybe this will get you moving?" And the ground started to rumble and Brett and I both struggled to stay upright as we were forced away from each other, by some invisible presence.

I couldn't keep my balance and fell backwards, landing on my butt and as I looked to Brett, the ground opened up beneath his feet and he disappeared, the ground closing then, and he was gone.

I shrieked Brett's name as I got to my feet, running to where he disappeared and started to dig with my hands as I screamed his name over and over.

I heard menacing laughter, all around me, and the voice commanded, "Come to me or he will die! Well he will die anyway, in time, but you can prolong his life! I am tired of waiting!"

I pounded the ground and yelled as tears fell from my eyes, "I will kill you, if you lay a hand on him, I will kill you!"

The laughter subsided slowly, and I sat down on the ground and sobbed quietly. I felt a hand on my shoulder and without thinking I removed the barrette from my hair as I twisted away from whoever was behind me, and swung my knife in front of me as I scooted away and put up my force field.

There, standing just a few feet away and looking quite shocked and a little frightened, was Tobias. "It's okay Princess Emilee, it is just I, Tobias. I won't hurt you. We're here to help. She sent us to you."

Looking around then, movement everywhere, were the trolls, all coming out from holes in the ground. Tree fey came out of their trees, different tree fey than before.

I looked back at Tobias and saw Tilly standing next to him. She came over to me, but stopped as she touched the shield and she reached out her hand to me. I dropped the shield and she came and knelt down in front of me, reached out with both arms and wrapped me in a safe embrace.

"I couldn't stop him." I sobbed. "I couldn't stop him and now Brett's gone."

Tobias said quickly, "Come Princess, she sent us to get you, to take you to safety. He has somehow blocked your friends from getting here to the humans' realm and you to them, but we were close by, are always close by to watch over her, Emilee."

I looked at him as if he were crazy, not understanding what he was saying. Then it dawned on me as I looked around, these were some of my childhood friends. Even though the troll family's home was far from here, they somehow were here too. The tree fey and others, small creatures that I realized were lizards and frogs, chipmunks and birds, in humans' eyes, but I saw them as fey, were here, and were my friends.

"Come Princess, we must hurry." Tobias implored, and he reached out to take my hand as I tried to stand.

Tilly helped also and soon all my old friends were around me, all but Eliza, my would have been sister, if I had been human.

Suddenly a tree opened up not far from where I stood, and out came another tree fey. It was Albee, but was it the real Albee or Stephan, disguised as Albee, like before?

I put my shield up around myself and Tobias and Tilly, as Albee approached us. He smiled and bowed, and then said calmly, "It is I, Princess Emilee, Albee. She sent me to you." As he looked around at the troll clan and the other fey here to help me.

"She, Varda, I can call her by her true name now that you all know who she is, sent me to help. We will go through the trees' root system to get to a place where he hasn't found a way to block, and a doorway will be there to get you to the rest of your allies. Adam will take you to Cape Matapan. That's where Stephan went, where you will get your dragon back before the Dark One turns it against you."

Tobias, not seeming to be happy to see Albee, snorted, "She sent us to retrieve and help the princess and take her through our tunnels. We were here first!"

Tina M. Engel

Albee chuckled at this and I could see that Tobias was getting even more upset. When Albee saw this, he replied, "Yes, I know Tobias, but she wanted to make sure that the tree fey and troll clan worked together. She felt that if I came also, the tree fey would cooperate more freely. As you know there are some who are working with the Dark One and my presence will ensure their cooperation."

"Who is the Dark One?" I implored. "Do you know? No one will tell me and I am getting really tired of these secrets. Everyone tells me that no one knows for sure, but surely someone does, and how do you know where I must go next, Cape Matapan?"

Albee sighed, and said, "Princess, I don't know who the Dark One is, but she does, she, Varda, knows. Right now we need to go. It isn't safe here in the humans' realm. He is changing things. Creating chaos and destruction here."

Albee was right, I knew. The wind was blowing more forcefully and as it howled through the trees, looking up, I saw the trees were full of crows, large and menacing looking, and suddenly the rain began to fall. Not just a sprinkle but a downpour.

I wanted to go to my house, Emilee's house, and make sure that the real Emilee was alright, but I knew that it wasn't a good idea at the moment. I dropped my shield and headed in the direction of the open tree, as Albee headed that way too.

When I got to the tree, I questioned again, "You didn't answer me, how do you know where Stephan went?"

"I was told by Varda, and I will be accompanying you. She believes I can help since Stephan took over my essence for a short time as he tried so desperately to get you. Varda feels that I may have a small connection to Stephan and will be able to weaken him just enough for you to retrieve Brett's sword and free Brett. She hopes anyway."

"What about the dragon?" I asked.

"That is for Varda to share. I haven't been given any more information other than what my role will be." Albee said as he turned and entered the tree.

Tobias grumbled something derogatory about tree fey always getting their way and Tilly was trying to console him. When we got to the tree and I turned around, only Tilly and Tobias were standing there. All the other fey, were gone from the humans' realm, safe in Terrafirma, I hoped.

Tobias said, "We can help too, if she would let us."

Tilly replied looking at Tobias with affection, "We are helping, Tobias, she sent us to get the princess to safety. We must trust and obey."

Tobias had a look of embarrassment on his face as he looked up at me. I knelt down, and putting my hands on his shoulders, told him that this was the third time he had rescued me and I was eternally grateful. I was in his debt and would always come if he needed me, if it was possible. I hugged him tenderly and when I moved away, he was blushing, and feeling my face warm, I knew that I was blushing too.

As I stood, the three of us entered the tree. I looked back to face the entrance, and I saw my human mother enter the clearing. She looked directly at me as the wind was thrashing around her, she trying to stay upright.

From behind a bush, not far from her, came movement and out from the bush came Eliza, the little goblin who was once a human baby, but never to be born, my human sister. She went to my mother and as my mother bent down to her, she put one arm around her waist, holding her tightly, to protect her from the angry storm that surrounded them. She looked at me and blew me a kiss, as Eliza waved.

The opening to the tree closed, as I stood there dumfounded. She saw me, and she knew I was there? I thought.

I turned to look at Albee and he was smiling a kind and understanding smile. "You have a lot of friends and family helping you. They are not all fey but they are all working together to help you." He turned then and headed down a pathway, a tunnel in the trees' root system.

We didn't walk for long before he stopped in a large opening. Albee turned and reached out to me. I took his hands in mine.

"Princess, think about where you want to be. Help me get you to the beach where Captain Adam's ship is. Think about it, put yourself there." Albee stated with a look of concentration.

I didn't quite understand what he was wanting from me. He knew where I wanted to go, where we needed to go, but not wanting to sound silly, if I asked a question that I should know the answer to, I thought of the beach where I had left the others. I thought of the wolf pack, my mother and father, Douglas, and I figured Rose and Lily were there too.

Suddenly, the area we were in started to pulse, and I felt dizzy. This feeling lasted for only a few seconds and then it stopped. There in front of us, was a portal, swirling with color.

It was Tilly who spoke first, "She did it. Princess, you are getting stronger as the days go by."

"Come", Albee said, and released my hands, turned, and headed into the portal. We all followed, and there on the other side was a tunnel.

The tunnel that we had been in had been wood, a tree root I knew, and suddenly it was dirt. Albee stopped and Tobias and Tilly came around me and took the lead, in front of Albee. I followed for a few more minutes and then I saw up in front of us, steps going up.

Tobias led, as Tilly followed, up the dirt steps and disappeared before I got to the stairway. I looked up and saw the blue sky, and just a part of the sun, shining down.

I turned to look at Albee and he just smiled, held his hand out as if telling me to go and said, "You got us here quicker than I could have."

I was dumfounded. How could we be on the other side of the country already? I climbed up and out into the sunshine, and there waiting was Lily, Rose, Angelina, Jordan, Douglas and Weylyn.

I hugged them all, but when I got to Rose, being the last one to hug, she didn't feel right. She was cold and had a strange look about her. I pulled away slightly and looking into her face, she smiled, and told me not to worry. She was fine.

She pulled away from me but still holding my hand, turned to look at Douglas, as he spoke. "We need to get back to the ship and get to Cape Matapan as soon as possible. Emilee, you can help Adam get us there faster. There is no time to lose."

Not budging, as Rose gently tried to pull me along, I spoke with a questioning tone in my voice, "What do you mean, I can help, and how did I create the doorway that got us here so fast, and for that matter, I saw Eliza with my human mother."

My head started to hurt, and everything started to spin just a bit. *I saw Brett then. He was in a cave, dark and damp. I could feel the dampness, the evil surrounding him. He was chained to the wall, but besides chains on his wrists holding them up over his head, the wall looked like it was slightly attached to him. Like fingers, wrapped around him. I saw him then, for just a moment in the rock, Kimberlite's face.*

My diamond necklace started to vibrate and the dizziness subsided. I took hold of my diamond and looking into it, saw the lava pebbles, but not Kimberlite. The pebbles seemed upset, concerned, but communicated with me that it was going to be okay, they would always be with me.

"What did you see Princess?" Douglas questioned with urgency.

"Answer my questions please, Douglas." I begged.

"Princess, you are strong, you can move faster than we can now. This is who you are, one with all, everything around you. You are still growing and learning but soon..." Douglas stopped as the ground closed up where we had entered just minutes before.

He continued then, "She can explain more later, but" and I cut him off, saying, "Varda?"

Douglas, looking a bit frustrated now, and continued, "Yes, and as for the human you call mother and the Goblin you call sister, they have been with you all along, working to keep you safe. She, your mother, Katie, has been with us from the beginning. She has known about Eliza also, but your human father knows nothing about this. Katie was the strong one, could handle the knowledge, but remember, not all humans can."

"And I can help Adam get us to Cape whatever you said, quickly?" I questioned.

"Yes!" Douglas said in a frustrated tone, "Can we please go now, if you want to save Brett from more torture and possibly death?"

As he said this, I saw the fear in his eyes. Brett after all, was like a grandson to him, the love Douglas felt for Brett was deep, and I realized that he knew what I had seen just moments ago.

"You know what I just saw, Brett in chains and the rock wall behind him, holding him captive?" I asked calmly, but wanted to scream.

"That is what you saw?" Douglas replied. "I only know he is in grave danger and the longer we wait..." Douglas paused for a moment as he looked up into the sky.

I looked to where he was staring and saw grey wisps, the fey who chose darkness over light, circling overhead, high above us, as the sky darkened.

Douglas continued then, "Brett doesn't have much time and neither do any of us, humans or fey in Terrafirma. Tobias and Tilly, you are coming with us and the rest of your clan that is here too. We will need your skills. Weylyn, you too, bring your strongest with you."

Douglas headed up to the top of a sandy mound and disappeared over it as we all followed, even Albee. It didn't take us long before we were on the docks, heading towards Adam's ship, with fey staring and pointing both at us and at the sky, as the darkness continued to creep over the entire sky.

Chapter 18

The past,
Is just that,
The past.
We need to understand it
At times,
To go forward.

As we climbed up the walkway to board the
ship, Adam and Trevor stood on deck along with
several deck hands, including the one that seemed
smitten with Rose. They were all looking up at the
menacing sky, as the wind seemed to whip across
the deck of the ship, tossing barrels around like
they were toys.

Suddenly, I heard Lily cry out softly and
mutter loudly then, "Could you give me warning
before you do this to me?" As she staggered a few
feet and my grandmother appeared beside her, a
glowing orb first, then transforming into Varda.

Varda, spending no time with Lily, looked up
into the sky and shouted as she raised her hands
into the air, "Not now! Not ever, if I can help it! Go
back to wherever you came from."

From Varda's hands came blinding lights
that filled the sky, so bright that I had to look
down. When it subsided and I could see again, I
looked up as everyone else was doing the same, and
saw that the sky was blue again, no grey wisps
could be seen, and the wind was calm.

Varda looked at me then and with firmness
in her voice said, "You can ask questions later, but
now, we must get to Cape Matapan. That is where

the cave, the opening to Hades is. Gehenna lies deep inside where he has Brett and your dragon. You need them both or you all will be lost.

"Adam, you and Emilee go to the control room and get us there quickly, I can't hold them off much longer. He's stronger now, the dragon has been hatched, and Brett's sword is beginning to transform to evil.

"I've been fooled by one, and when I find him, I will show no mercy." Varda cried, and I actually felt frightened by her anger.

"Who is he?!" I yelled, "Who can be so strong, and evil. No one seems to know, but you must. Stephan said that you gave the Dark One something, something that he gave to Stephan to help him retrieve the egg and take Brett's sword, and Brett! Who is he? I have a right to know before I go traipsing off into a cave!" I stood my ground, frustrated, frightened and angry.

Varda's look softened then, a sadness crept into her eyes and calmly she answered, as she came up to me and softly put a hand on my cheek, "Emilee, he was someone I trusted with my life a long time ago." She looked to Angelina then, my mother, and the sadness deepened.

She continued then, "I will share everything soon, I promise, but right now we must get there. Help Adam and then come down to the dining area. I will tell you all what you need to know before going to rescue your dragon and Brett."

I opened my mouth to say, (What I want to know, not just need to know), but she put a finger to my mouth and said almost in a whisper, "Please my dear, not now."

Tina M. Engel

She stepped away, and looking at Angelina she started to glow, as she turned back into an orb, sucked poor Lily into it too, and when the light dissipated, it was only Lily standing there, looking quite irritated.

"Princess," Lily grumbled, "When this is over, I am staying a cat. I may be by your side, but a cat I will stay." And at that she headed to the door that led down below, and disappeared inside.

Adam and Jordan chuckled, but Angelina seemed deep in thought, Eagle was staring off into space as if not a part of us at all, and Rose was standing by the fey she was smitten with, but he didn't seem to be aware that she was even there, next to him. I wondered why he was even allowed to be here, but then, it didn't really matter, they knew that he had been working for Poseidon, secrets were out.

I looked to Albee and he had a questioning look on his face, as if not sure what he was to do. Jordan, seeing this confusion, suggested that he, Albee, and Weylyn go with him down below. They followed him but Angelina, before heading there too, came to me and held me for a moment, kissed me on the cheek and whispered, that she loved me so.

I suddenly felt emotional and sad to let her go, as she disappeared through the doorway. Adam suggested we head to the control room and get to the island so I knew I had to put my emotions away, for now. I had no idea how I was to help Adam, I still didn't quite understand how I got us clear across the country in such a short amount of time. I knew however, that I had to get to Brett soon, I couldn't live without him.

Rose left the fey's side that she had been standing next to, and came over to me. Eagle looked at me, gave me a slight smile and turned into a bird, flew up to the top of the control room, and landed there.

Rose and I followed Adam up to the control room, and there he adjusted buttons and did whatever it was he needed to do, to get us heading in the proper direction.

Adam looked at me then, and said, "Ok, Princess, this is where we must go." And he spread out a map on a table nearby. "We are here," as he pointed to an area on the map. "and this is where we need to go."

I looked at Adam, acknowledging that I understood the point A to point B part of all this but still had no idea how I was to help get us there faster.

"And what do you want me to do?" I questioned.

Rose touched my arm softly, so soft that I almost brushed the feeling away, thinking it was just a fly, bothering me, but realized that it was Rose. Something was very wrong with Rose but I couldn't quite figure it out.

"Princess Emilee, just put your hands on the map and think about your destination, where you want to be." And she took my hands and placed them on the map, between where we were and where we needed to be.

She continued then, "She is there, your dragon. She and I can help you, Princess." Rose said as she placed her hands on mine.

I still felt confused as to how I could do this, but then, everything about what I could do these days, was confusing. I did what she asked, and again, the room started to pulse and I felt dizzy. It seemed to last a bit longer than before, but when it stopped, and as I looked out the window in front of us, there was a large circular glowing orb. I knew it was a doorway and I knew on the other side was our destination, Cape Matapan.

Adam's grin was large as he said, "Well done Princess. I wish you could be with me all the time. You would definitely make traveling quicker."

Adam sailed the ship towards the doorway. As we entered, everything got fuzzy, and dead quiet. It seemed to take several minutes and then everything cleared, and we were in the water, grey skies up above with the wind whipping around us, and an island in front of us.

Rose let go of me and began stumbling backwards and her appearance seemed to be fading. I reached out to catch her, and as I grabbed her hands, her appearance solidified.

I guided her over to a chair and asked if she was alright, but then of course, I knew otherwise. Not only was she not alright, but I was frightened as to what was wrong with her. I realized that Eagle, too, had the same appearance now and then. That of fading, becoming transparent.

Rose looked at me with a sheepish grin and said, "I'm okay, princess. You don't need to look so worried. I am with you and will be for a long time,

I promise. She told me so." Rose reached up and wrapped her arms around my neck in a loving embrace.

Adam suggested that we get down to the dining area and talk to my grandmother before we went any closer to the island, and as he opened the door, Adam yelled out for a deckhand to take over until he returned.

In came the deckhand that Rose was smitten with, and I was a bit confused and concerned since he was the one spying on us, through Rose. I gave Adam a look of concern and he informed me that it was fine. Everything was out in the open and he was a good worker. Adam told the deckhand though, not to touch anything.

As we left the control room and went down the steps, I started to feel dizzy again and...

I found myself suddenly standing, just in front of Brett, in the prison where he was being held. A pain shot through me as I felt for a moment, Stephan's thoughts, and he appeared in front of me, blocking Brett from my sight momentarily, until he moved over to my right.

I realized that Stephan had walked right through me. I wasn't there in solid form, just my thoughts, but as he came in, not knowing I was there, he was able to go through me and I felt him. I felt nauseous but was stunned by Stephan's emotions. There was resentment for Brett, and jealousy but also a tiny bit of regret for what he was about to do.

Stephan said then with a sinister laugh, "You will die at my hands brother, but not yet. I will wait until sweet Princess Emilee is here and I will let her see, just what a weak fey you are. She will be mine as soon as you are gone and the great Dark One is done with her."

Stephan held out Brett's weapon, in knife form, and continued as he pressed it to Brett's chest and slowly cut crosswise, not deep, but just enough for a small amount of blood to ooze down his stomach, "I will drain you dry, right in front of her and she will drink only from me."

What Stephan said to Brett and what I felt in Stephan's mind were different, contradictions. What I felt in his mind was remorse, mixed in with the anger and rage. There was a part of him that didn't want to do this, but the evil within him was stronger.

As I looked at Brett I could smell his blood, I could smell everything, all the odors in the prison that Brett was in, but his blood was, at that moment, all I could think about. Why Stephan thought for a moment that I would want his blood, was a mystery to me, or was it? They were brothers, after all.

I was in his mind then, or he in mine, Brett. "Leave Emilee, before he senses you. Hurry." And he looked up and as our eyes met, I knew he felt me there.

I gasped, as Stephan turned his head in my direction, looking directly at me, and suddenly I was laying on the deck of the ship with Rose and Adam beside me.

"I saw him again. Stephan is torturing him!" I cried out as I sat up.

Adam helped me to my feet as I continued, "We must hurry, and get to him. Brett knows that

Tina M. Engel

we are here. He saw me standing there in front of him."

Looking around, the deck was covered with trolls and wolves, none of them seeming happy to be on the ship, as the winds tossed us around like a toy boat. By the looks on their faces, I guessed that the trip through the doorway to get here, hadn't been a pleasant ride.

I headed to the door to go down and talk with Varda, to find out the details that I needed, to get Brett out of there before it was too late.

What frightened me the most about all of this was that even though I was fearful for Brett's safety, I was more fearful that I wouldn't get the chance to drink from Brett, taste his blood. I had smelled it and the desire, need, I felt to have his blood, was so strong, I was disgusted with myself. The thought still lingered in my mind, why would Stephan think that I would want or need his blood?

When I walked into the dining hall, only Lily, Angelina, Jordan and Albee, were there. I felt instantly angry, Varda should have been here, she had promised me an explanation.

From behind me came voices, Douglas and Varda. I turned and must have had a look of annoyance, for Varda cut off her discussion with Douglas and looking at me, said, "What? I told you I would share with you what you need to know."

I could feel my anger growing, and my body heating up. I wanted to know everything, not just what she thought I should know. I opened my mouth to speak but Varda put a hand up, and gave me a look of exasperation.

"Calm down granddaughter. It is time that you know everything," and looking over at Angelina, she continued, "and you too my daughter." Varda added.

My body cooled as Varda took my arm and led me to a table where we sat. Before my butt landed on the seat, I stated, "Brett is being tortured. I saw him again, but this time he looked at me and told me to go before Stephan felt my presence. Brett knows we are here. Tell me everything quickly so we can stop Stephan. But the blood...?" and I let that thought drift away, not continuing the sentence. It disturbed me so.

Varda asked Angelina to come sit with us too and she took both our hands in hers. "It's time for you both to know your story. I must tell it quickly. We don't have much time, so try to keep your questions to a minimum, if you can."

Varda continued, and as she told the story of our past, we, Angelina and I, were seeing it as she spoke.

"You Emilee, are not human, nor fey, as you have guessed." And Varda smiled. "You are human and fey but so much more, as am I. There are very few, who are like us, my sweet granddaughter."

Varda looked to Angelina then and with a smile of pure love, continued, "You Angelina are a part of me and him, but were chosen to carry Emilee, the chosen one. Why you were not the one that the prophesy spoke of, I cannot say. It has always been written in the stars. The one who gave me life, chooses who will continue to care for all life, in this, seventh section, in the great universe, and it is Emilee who will take my place, eventually.

"This planet that we are on, has many dimensions, Earth, Atlantis; a water world, Terrafirma, and Hades. There are other dimensions within Hades. One is called Gehenna. There are many other worlds, all of which have many dimensions on each.

"This planet, however, is the center of all in this section of the universe and therefore here on this planet, we can enter all of the other places through entrances, portholes, windows and doorways.

"Angelina, the day I banished him to Gehenna, a dimension deep in the heart of Hades, was the day I hid you from the universe. I knew that he had eyes still in Terrafirma and earth, and he suspected that I would send you elsewhere, to keep you safe.

I couldn't though, the other lands on the other plants would not have accepted you as did Terrafirma. I needed you safe until the time came for you to meet Jordan. Knowing that he didn't think you were here, I thought you were safe.

"Jordan is from a very special species of life that came to this planet and made Terrafirma their home. Jordan's ancestors came from the sky, the stars, they were the fallen, as his people called them; from the heavens, was the tale. Not welcome in their homeland due to different beliefs, they came to Terrafirma and battled with the land fey for thousands of years. They found peace eventually, and over time, joining, became one species.

Tina M. Engel

"You Emilee, are part of the sky people too, as Jordan is a descendant of one of the original sky people." Varda looked to Jordan then and said, "That is a story, in itself, for another time"

"You, Jordan, were taken from your family as a baby, and placed in the orphanage because he knew who you would become and the destiny you had. I had to protect you also. Douglas..." and Varda looked to Douglas with a look of longing, I believed, and he nodded his head. "took you to the orphanage and when it was time, you were given the idea to go and find the elders. They were waiting for you."

Jordan interrupted hotly, "You mean that the council, elders, knew what was to happen, knew all along that we would be together? Did they know that Angelina would almost die?"

"That was not the plan, Jordan. I know things, the future, to a point but if someone decides to change one detail, or makes a decision that is different from what was supposed to be, everything changes. You were all given the right to choose, make your own decisions, and in doing so, potentially changing the path that you take to reach your destination. Every life form has a destination.

"I knew that Emilee, my granddaughter would be the chosen one, like me, to keep the peace, bring life from other places together, as well as keep them apart until the time was right, starting with Earth and Terrafirma. How we would get to that place in time is always a bit sketchy and at times challenging." And Varda chuckled a bit when she said, sketchy.

Tina M. Engel

Lily let out an irritating meow, and then a cough as if trying to get up a fur ball, which brought all of our attention to her, as she said, "A bit sketchy, and challenging? It has been a hellish journey, if you ask me. Dragging me here and there, carrying you in me, as we traipsed all around that dreadful world of humans. Let's just call it what it is, shall we, my lady? Hellish!"

Varda chuckled and said in a manner that was friendly and welcoming, "We have been together long enough Lily that you don't have to call me, my lady. We have been in too tight quarters to be that politically correct, don't you think?"

Lily gave Varda a, (whatever) look, and Varda turned her attention back to Angelina and I, and continued.

"Jordan, you and Angelina were to find each other but when the council was ready, they would separate you. Your life Jordan, would have gone as planned, the way it did, up until Adam..." and Varda glared at Adam, and then continued, "decided to change your destiny by saving your life.

"I didn't realize that the one who was close to me, who was privy to things of importance, was working for the Dark One. This fey was supposed to take the artifact away from the Dark One, that gave him powers, a gift from me, but I find out now, that he still had it. Worse yet, let that traitor's son use it to get the egg and his sword."

"Wait a minute!" I interrupted sternly, "Are you saying that Stephan's father is the traitor, and Brett's sword belonged to Stephan's father before him?"

Varda pursed her lips together, anger emanating from her eyes for a moment and then continued, "Yes, Emilee, Stephan's father, Hedrick DeMill."

"Who is the Dark One then, since I am assuming that Hedrick DeMill isn't the Dark One?" I questioned.

"Hedrick was a fey that was brought to me early on, in the beginning of Terrafirma. I needed assistance from the life forms there, and because he was chosen to assist me with helping the new life forms to grow and evolve as they must, Hedrick was given the gift of longevity." Varda spat with disgust.

Angelina said then, "He will never die?"

"Oh, he will die eventually and I will see to it, but his life span was to be a greater length. He was with me, however, working for me when I was introduced to ..." And Varda paused, removed her hands from mine and Angelina's, stood and walked over to a porthole and stared out for a moment.

"Who?" I questioned with kindness in my voice, for I felt that this was difficult for my grandmother to say. "Who is the Dark One and why does he want me?"

Varda turned from the window, came over, sat down and placed her hands back on ours. "His name is Mephisto.

"Mephisto, was like me, in charge of one of the sections in the great one's universes. He was the one caring for and guiding the sixth of the seven great areas of the universe. Humans call this one that I care for, the seventh heaven.

"I was created to care for his latest creation and Mephisto was sent here to help me, I was to learn from him. We, well let's just say..."

Angelina replied, "You fell in love and that is how I came to be? He's my father?"

"And my grandfather?" I added.

Varda looked from Angelina to me and nodded her head and continued, "Yes, we did and he is. He was a good soul, loving and kind, but firm when need be. He learned how to guide without interfering or rushing the life forms on his worlds.

"But something happened. At some point, Mephisto became competitive. He wanted the life forms on his worlds to stay more advanced than the life forms in my section of the universe. I watched him deteriorate, but I was in denial for some time.

"When I was told of the prophecy, of a baby girl who would one day take my place and I would go up with the great one who created it all, as we all would, Mephisto also saw the vision of the prophecy and we both knew who it would be. Mephisto however, wanted to be the ultimate power over both sections of this great universe, and then more.

"When I learned of his evil desire and confronted him, I tried to convince him to stop what he was trying to do. He set into motion a plan to end my existence as you see me, and take over. He knew that I was with child, you Angelina, and since Emilee was to be the chosen, if he ended my existence, then he could change the future.

"Biton, one of the elders from one of Mephisto's worlds, came to me, and shared this information. For he was one of Mephisto's top aides, but Biton disagreed with Mephisto.

"Biton is a seer, telepathic. On Biton's world, they are all telepathic. The doorways to his world are closed for now. Their abilities could damage or destroy other worlds. Biton has been working with me since his change from one of Mephisto's aides to mine.

"It wasn't until a few days before you, Angelina were to be born, that Biton came to me and showed me Mephisto's plan. You see, I cannot die, like other life forms, for I am not living as others do. I was not born as other life forms are, I was created. Only the creator could remove me from existence.

"Mephisto thought he had the great one convinced that I was plotting against his plans, but then that just shows what corruption and greed can do to a soul. Mephisto was blinded by his own evil, not realizing that the great one saw all, knew all and gave me the power to put him in Hades, not destroy him as I wanted to."

Varda took a breath, such sadness in her eyes, and this gave me the opportunity to ask, "Why would he, whoever he is, not let you destroy Mephisto? This gave him the opportunity to continue what he had planned. Which is exactly what is happening now."

"He is the creator of all. There is no name for him, I say he, but only because there is no word or name that can explain. I could say, she, or it but I have called my creator, he, for so long that it is just easier.

Tina M. Engel

"I will one day stand beside him, but for now we must stop Mephisto, and Emilee, you have much to accomplish before that time. Why I was to banish him and not destroy him was not for me to question. It will all play out as it should."

"What about Jordan?" Angelina asked, "Why was Adam not to save Jordan after he had saved Emilee?" How cruel is that?"

Varda gave Angelina a meek smile and answered, "We all have a role to play in the destination of the future of all.

"I needed you, Angelina, to keep watch over Terrafirma, for it is difficult for me to come here in my true form, and Lily will have her work cut out for her watching over Emilee in the ..." Varda paused, looking at me and continued, " I am much stronger when I do not appear in a physical shape.

"Mephisto knows this, and that is why I thought for a short time that Adam was working for him, refusing to follow orders, by not letting Jordan die, and therefore changing the future, just a bit. But I know now that it was just brotherly love that stopped Adam from allowing Jordan to die. Even fey emotions get in the way of things.

"I had other plans for Angelina, but with Jordan back in her life, it has changed the future. Emilee must continue on her path, which is to stop Mephisto, but to do this, she will have to take the next step, which will be difficult for her to do.

"Now, the future being changed, I can't see yet, but will soon, how Angelina and Jordan play a role in the future. As for now, Emilee, we must get your dragon, save Brett, get Brett's sword back before Stephan turns it against good, and defeat Mephisto."

"What about Kimberlite? Where is he now? I saw him there, behind Brett in that awful prison. Is he working for Mephisto? He is a lava rock and Mephisto is deep in Hades." I asked as I removed one of my hands from under my grandmother's hand, and lifted the diamond so I could look deep within it.

"I have seen fear and embarrassment on his face on and off from the beginning of this nightmare of a journey, that you have put me on. Where is he now?" I continued.

Varda reached out and touched the diamond as I continued, "I saw Kimberlite standing behind Brett, whispering something into his ear. Brett's head hung down then, the hopelessness shown in his body."

"But where is he now?" I asked again. "He was with Queen Anahita, the last time I saw him. Do we trust either of them?

I looked up at Varda, and she said, "Only time will tell. We all have the right to choose. Kimberlite has his own path to follow, they all do."

When Varda removed her hands from mine and Angelina's, we were transported back to the dining room with everyone standing and sitting around. As Varda had spoken, Angelina and I could see it, feel everything that had happened and we could better understand the past.

But I couldn't stop thinking about Kimberlite. Was he the spy all along? And what of Eagle, his attitude, solitude and strange translucent appearance, every once in a while, since he came back to us after being injured? And Rose's odd look and behavior too. Should I be worried that they were both working for Mephisto?

Varda reached over and placing a hand on my cheek, caused me to look up into her face. She smiled and said, "My dear, time will answer those questions but now, if you are ready, I think Brett needs you and Shinar, your dragon is struggling to remember who she truly belongs too. She must touch you soon, or will be lost."

"That is another question I have!" I shouted, not meaning to shout but with everything else going on, I had forgotten about her.

Varda chuckled, sighed and then said, "Ask."

"What about the dragon, where does she fit into this and where does she come from? I haven't seen any dragons in Terrafirma, or earth for that matter. Only in stories and movies when I was a human. There was the dragon in my vision though, an evil dragon." I said.

"That is where she's from Emilee. That place. You will know of it soon, I promise, it will all make sense soon. There is more to Terrafirma than any of you know. First, you must take care of the issue in front of you." And Varda stood.

Chapter 19

Insight,
Listen!

Douglas came over to Varda and as he put his arm around her waist, she lay her head on his shoulder. Tipping her head slightly up, she looked into his eyes. She smiled a longing smile, and stood then, stepping away from him slightly, as he removed his arm from around her waist.

I saw something there, in that moment, between the two of them. I had seen it before several times but didn't think anything of it, until now. It was affection I saw in both of their faces, but what kind of affection and how strong? I knew what it was, a longing, because I felt the same for Brett.

I was deep in thought, but as I looked at Varda, she was looking at me, and she knew that I understood. She may have been in love with Mephisto a long time ago but at some point after, Douglas and Varda became close, closer than they felt they should.

"I must go now." Varda said. "There is trouble in the humans' dimension. The greyness, dark spirits, are entering your Pineville through the tree that Stephan had used to get to you. What could still possibly be in Pineville that Mephisto could want, unless, it is Pineville where he intends to start his destruction first? The fey that belongs to that tree is nowhere to be found. The tree is sick and dying so we fear that the true fey of that tree is dead.

"Douglas, see to it that Emilee gets where she needs to be, with the help of the trolls, Wolves and Albee. Jordan, you are to stay here with Adam. He will need your help to keep this ship safe and ready for departure as soon as Emilee has rescued Brett, his sword and the dragon."

Douglas nodded as Varda came to me, hugged me tightly and did the same with Angelina before going to the middle of the room. As she started to glow, an orb appeared and then she was gone, orb and all. Lily was still in a corner and looked a bit perplexed.

"Well now," Lily commented, "she has left me alone here, to take care of things without her constant nagging on how I should be handling them. This is a nice change."

"Lily!" I heard my grandmother say in an authoritative tone.

Lily looked around the room and then gave a look of annoyance as Douglas informed Lily that she would be accompanying me, as well as Rose. Lily would be in cat form. He headed out the door and we all followed, but before I left the room, Trevor called my name.

I stopped and turned around, as he came up to me. "Take this Princess, it may help." And he handed me a small flask.

I looked at him with curiosity and he continued, "It's a small amount of the drink that you needed while you were growing and strengthening. I saved the last bit, I don't know why, but something inside me, told me to do so. I don't know if it is for you or someone else, but take it."

Then I heard Varda's voice again, "Thank you Trevor, I can always count on you to remember things." And Trevor smiled, I knew that he heard her voice too.

I saw the dragon then, in my mind. Shinar, my dragon, a part of me, I was told. She was laying on the ground, and I was giving her the fluid in the flask.

Shinar is a part of me and I needed this liquid to grow. She is still growing. She must need it too, for some reason, I realized.

I gave Trevor a hug, placed the flask in a pocket in my jeans and headed out the door and up to the deck where everyone was waiting.

"Grandmother?" I said, out loud. "Are you still hanging around?"

Everyone looked at me like I was crazy but Douglas just chuckled and said, "She is always here, everywhere, but let's not worry about Varda right now. She has things to do, as do we.

"Adam is docking the ship, in a bay, and an ancient Chapel is located up on the hill nearby, with the entrance to Hades under it. Deep inside the temple is the opening to the cave which leads to Hades, and to Gehenna, where we believe that Brett is being held, as well as the sword.

"When we get to the cave, Tobias, you and half your clan will tunnel into the rock walls and floors, going ahead of Emilee and her group, to scope out any trouble that may be ahead of them.

"Lily, you get your wish, for now, and a cat you will be. You will go ahead of Emilee, quiet and sneaky, to keep watch, and share with Emilee and her group, what may be in front of them.

"Weylyn you will split up your pack, half of your pack come with me. You and the rest will go with Princess Emilee to find Brett. Where Brett is, I am sure, you will find Stephan and the sword.

"Albee, you will go with them also, hopefully you can weaken Stephan enough, and Emilee, using all the powers that you have acquired, rescue Brett, retrieve the sword and take back the relic that had given Stephan powers. Mephisto will want it back. We must not let that happen."

"What are you going to do?" I asked Douglas.

"I will take the rest of the Wolves, trolls and Rose, and find Shinar." Douglas said.

Rose looked at me and said in a panic, "I should stay with Princess Emilee, she needs me."

"Rose, Shinar needs you more. Emilee is strong without your blood now, but Shinar isn't." Douglas said, sternly.

I was taken aback by Douglas's lack of compassion, and I could see it hurt Rose's feelings, when he said that I didn't need her.

Before I could say anything, Douglas seemed to grow double in height and anger covered his face as he commanded, "Do as I say, all of you! There have been enough questions! Do as you are told or face the consequences, when this is all over!"

The ship lurched as the anchor was dropped, making a large splash and Adam came down from the control room.

Douglas calmed a bit and returned to his normal size as he pointed towards the beach, and said, "Princess, can you create an opening here on the deck of the ship that can take us to the beach on the island, just over there, below that peak?"

After opening several doorways, I figured this should be a snap, not a far distance, compared to the other doorways I had created.

Rose came over to me and took my hand in hers, and looking at Douglas, gave him a snotty glare. Lily started to laugh, and came over to me and took my other hand. Douglas just shook his head with a look of annoyance and everyone stood there staring at me, waiting.

I gazed off in the direction of land, looking at the peak which Douglas had pointed out. I could feel Rose and Lily's hands in mine and I felt strength coming from them both. I did still need them, all of them. I wasn't alone.

Then in front of me, a glowing sphere appeared. The center looked like an abalone shell, and it was swirling in a circular pattern. I had done it again. Well, I had done it with the help of my friends, family actually, yes, family.

I looked from Rose to Lily, as they still held my hand and they both had smug grins on their faces as did I, I was sure, and we all looked over at Douglas. He was glaring at first but then a softness took over and a smile appeared on his lips.

"Yes, yes, you do work well together. I suggest you remember this later on, when you all seem to be in disagreement. It will happen, I assure you." Douglas said, as he shook his head.

He bellowed then, a change in attitude, "Do you all know what you are to do when we get to the island? If not, speak now, we don't need any mistakes!"

Tina M. Engel

It was all silent as I looked around the deck at all the faces, unwavering, and determined, but I couldn't help thinking that there must be some fear hiding down deep inside of them. I felt fear but realizing this, I pushed it away, I couldn't let it affect me. Brett's life was at stake and I had to save him.

I asked then, "Is this the place where Varda sent Mephisto?"

Douglas, with a look of acceptance, answered, "Yes Princess, it is." Douglas looked over towards the island then and continued, "This may be the time, finally."

Douglas sent the wolf pack through first, to make sure it was safe for the rest of us. When a scout came back through to let us know that all was clear, we all went through one at a time, Douglas coming last.

It took Douglas a few minutes to come through and I was concerned at first, thinking that something was wrong and maybe I should go back to get him, but then he appeared.

The look on my face must have shown my concern and curiosity, and Douglas said, "The weather is getting treacherous, and the ship is struggling to stay afloat with the waves crashing over the deck. I sent them back through the doorway, to wait."

I looked at him in disbelief, as everyone started to talk at once, all seeming to be concerned. I held my hands up and shouted for all to "Shut up!", and they did.

"What are you thinking, Douglas?" I asked. "How can we get back when the ship is not here?

They won't know when we need to get back on the ship!"

Douglas just looked at me, saying nothing, just waiting, and then said, "Think Princess! The doorway is right there in front of us, yes?"

I smiled then and replied, "And the end of the doorway is on the ship."

Douglas, smiled and then shouted, as he pointed to a few of the wolves and some of the trolls, telling them that they would stay and watch over the doorway. Our lives depended on it being there, when we got back.

We followed Douglas, as he headed up a small mountain. When we reached the top, not far, I could see the Chapel.

"Come, quietly and quickly." Douglas whispered. "We don't need anyone or anything seeing us. Do they know we are here? There is a good chance they do. If not, we need to keep it that way for as long as possible.

"As soon as we reach the doorway between the chapel and Hades, they will know someone who doesn't belong has entered, trespassed and the true ruler over Hades, the Devil himself, loves newcomers."

We all followed him as he headed in the direction of the chapel, walking carefully, so as to not disturb the ground underneath our feet.

As we entered the ancient chapel, even though it hadn't been used in years, there was still a presence of others, and I knew that it was spirits that could not be seen with the naked eye, watching over the doorway, keeping evil in and those from this side, out.

Tina M. Engel

I could feel them, they knew we were here, and had been waiting a long time for me to come. I could see them then, rainbow wisps moving slowly, gliding around us, inspecting us, to make sure we were all here for the right reasons, to stop Mephisto, but also to prevent all who dwell in Gehenna, as well as Hades from escaping.

We followed Douglas down a set a rock stairs that led to a dead end, it seemed, but when Douglas put his hand to the stone wall, an opening appeared. A rush of hot air escaped and hit me in the face. I felt nauseous, the smell was that of filthy and wicked thoughts.

Douglas was next to me, suddenly, and putting a hand on my shoulder, asked, "Emilee, are you alright?"

I looked up at him and looking around at the others, I could tell they were experiencing the same thing by the looks on their faces.

"Yes." I replied, knowing that I had to be strong, not just for Brett but for all of these fey, who were helping me.

I looked towards the opening and saw the rainbow wisps blocking the entrance. Only I could see, and suddenly they moved slowly, circling the entrance, leaving an opening large enough for us to enter.

Douglas said with caution in his voice, "We can enter now." And I realized that he too, must be able to see the ancient spirits, the rainbow wisps.

Douglas continued, "Once we enter, you will not be permitted to leave without Princess Emilee or myself. Entering is easy, but leaving this place is almost impossible."

We entered the opening to a tunnel and walked single file for a few minutes, until we came to a large cavern that had several tunnels branching out from it.

Douglas asked then, after we were all in the cave, "Emilee, what do you see? What do you feel?"

I looked at him with questioning on my face, but then I shut my eyes, and taking a deep breath, I reached out to find Brett. I saw him then, chained, hanging limp.

I could feel my diamond warming, the lava pebbles upset. They felt him too, Kimberlite, I couldn't see him but felt his presence somewhere here in Hell.

I knew which direction to go to enter Gehenna and I knew which direction Douglas had to go to find Shinar. I could feel it all, the hate, the ugliness, the sadness and despair. There was regret and there was even pleasure, so many feelings, emotions, rage and even fear. There were so many dark souls, those who made bad decisions and couldn't or wouldn't work to fix things, and those who willingly and joyfully made destructive choices.

My hearts were heavy, full of sadness and pity over what I was feeling, the cries I heard, some of sorrow wanting to repent, but it was too late, but some full of fury, wanting, needing to continue their venomous ways.

I opened my eyes then, and looking around, I saw all the faces of my friends, the wolves, trolls, Albee, Douglas, Rose and Lily all watching me, waiting as if holding their breath, just waiting.

I also saw the grey wisps coming from the tunnels, swirling around all of us, but they were not the ones full of fury but the souls full of regret. The sadness that was radiating from them, was so painful, and I could see in everyone's faces that they were feeling it, and I knew that we were in trouble.

I focused on my shield and imagined it surrounding us, with the grey wisps pushed away, and as I imagined it, the grey souls were pushed to the outer edges of the cave.

There were great sighs of relief, and looks of calmness appeared across the faces of my friends. I put my finger to my lips to hush everyone, as they were all whispering to each other.

I focused on the grey wisps, dark souls, then, wanting to communicate, for I believed that they wanted to help, wanted to do something to try and achieve redemption. I shared with them the fact that they were hurting us with their sadness and despair. The best way to help would be to stay away from us and keep all the evil grey wisps away from us too, if possible.

I told them if they helped us, I would try to help them, if it was possible, to get another chance at life and start over. I repeated that I would try, but couldn't promise it would help.

I felt a pull then, like something was wanting me to go towards the opening of the tunnel that I knew was where Shinar was. As I approached, there was a darker grey wisp in the middle of the opening.

I somehow knew, it was the tree fey that belonged with the tree, in front of my house in

Pineville. He was dead, and here in hell for his acceptance to work with Stephan and Mephisto himself. He was full of shame and sorrow. I touched his mind and saw a memory, one of him watching me play as a child. I saw him, standing, leaning against his tree, smiling as I played. I felt a moment of joy and then the regret and sadness came back with a vengeance. He was one of Mephisto's spies. He was the one who told Mephisto where I was.

"We will help you child." He said, "Even if there is no hope for us now, for we made our choices and had many opportunities to fix our mistakes."

At that, they all disappeared, some into the tunnels and some into the walls until it was just my friends in the cave. I released the shield and turned to look at Douglas when he asked me what I saw.

I told Douglas and everyone else what was going on, about the grey wisps, dark souls, and that they were going to help. I pointed to the tunnel where I was sure Shinar was, and where I was to go to rescue Brett. Each tunnel was a way into Gehenna, deep into the realm of Hades.

It was Lily who spoke next, "Well shall we get this show on the road then, before those ungodly lost souls come back and cover us with their sadness and despair? How we can trust that they will help is beyond me."

I looked at Lily with a scolding scowl and she just said, "What?" Like a cat does.

I looked to Douglas then and said, "I need to find Shinar too, I must give her something and soon." And I pulled the small vial with the liquid in it, out of my pocket.

"You will give it to her, Princess, don't worry about that, but Rose will strengthen her first, enough to get her out of here." Douglas calmly said.

He continued then, "Trolls, you know what to do, burrow quietly but quickly, and Lily, do your thing."

Lily, did just that, turned into her cat form, turned away from us, lifted her tail with attitude and pranced into the cave.

The trolls went to the walls between the tunnels, disappeared as small holes appeared where they touched, and as they all vanished into the small tunnels, the openings closed back up. Before the last small troll tunnel closed, a young troll turned and gave me a large grin, waved and he was gone.

Rose came up to me and gave me a big hug, but it felt wrong. Even though she was holding me tight, and I held tighter yet, it was as if she was barely there. When I let her go, she smiled meekly, and walked over to Douglas.

"I'll take care of her, don't worry Princess." Rose said. And I wondered why it was Rose who had to tend to Shinar before I would.

I watched them disappear into the tunnel and at the last minute, before the last one entered, a wolf, I sent part of my shield in that direction with them. I could feel it encircling them all, even the trolls. It wasn't as strong as when I was in the middle of it, but I hoped it was protection enough to stop the grey wisps from sensing them.

I placed what remained of my shield around the rest of us, as we headed into the opening of the tunnel that would lead me to Brett, Stephan and maybe Kimberlite.

After walking for some time, I started to wonder how, with so many of us entering Hades, could we do this without Mephisto knowing we were here. Of course it was possible he knew. Why would he let us just prance in here and save Brett and take Shinar? I suddenly felt like this was a big mistake. What were Douglas and Varda thinking?

I felt Brett then, in my mind. He was weak but there, and not the least bit happy that I was coming to get him. I stopped walking then and put myself in Brett's mind, and suddenly, I was standing in front of him again. This time though, I was there, not just in mind but body too. Somehow I was able to go where I was thinking. But how, I didn't know.

Brett, looked at me in horror as a hand wrapped around his body and pulled him into the rock wall, chains and all, as the rocks that the chains were imbedded in, that held his hands up, crumbled.

I felt him then, behind me, and as I turned, Stephan was there so close that I could feel his breath. He had a look of anger on his face, and suddenly I was back with my group. I gasped as I started to fall back, but Weylyn was close enough to catch me in midair.

The other wolves were now in four legged form, growling and snarling as if there was danger close by. I couldn't feel Brett anymore, he wasn't here in this tunnel or this area of hell. Kimberlite, or something, took him and Stephan knew we were here. We had to leave, get out, or these fey would be hurt or worse.

I told them we had to go back, and without arguing, they followed me as we backtracked and ended up back in the cave. I went to the wall where the trolls had disappeared in and put my hands on it. I sent out a thought, strong and loud, for them to return, come back to the cave. It wasn't a suggestion, but a demand.

I backed away from the wall, stood with the rest, and strengthened my shield as much as possible. I tried to communicate with Douglas but wasn't getting anywhere, then I thought of Rose and Lily. They were closest to me, Rose, especially. So I thought of Rose, and soon could see her, feel her and I was there, in front of them.

Douglas, with a shocked look, exclaimed, "What are you doing!?"

Before I let him finish, I shouted, "Go back, you must go back. We are waiting there for you. Hurry!"

And I suddenly was back with Weylyn, Albee and the other wolves. The trolls suddenly started to appear out of holes in the walls of the cave and I combined the shield that was around them, with the shield around the rest of us.

Suddenly the tunnel that Douglas, Rose and the other wolves had gone in, crumbled, when the ground shook as if an earthquake had struck. When the dust settled the only tunnel left open was the one that lead to the chapel where we had entered.

"We must get out of here now before this entire place crumbles around us. I won't let you die." I shouted. "Go!"

We all ran towards the opening, as all around us, grey wisps, angry and vile, swirled around the shield, trying to get in. We made it to the opening of the tunnel where the ones guarding the entrance to Hades stood firm. The rainbow colors covered the opening. I went up to it and putting my hand through it, the rainbow effect dissipated and I shouted for all to get through the doorway quickly.

I sent them all up the rocky steps to the chapel and as the last one headed up, Albee stopped and turned to look at me, as I turned and went back the way we had just come. The rainbow wisps covered the entrance once more. I instructed the rainbow wisps, no one, good or evil would be permitted in until I allowed it. I was kind of liking this power that I had. Okay, not really, but I was trying to feel confident with my newly found authority.

Chapter 20

The few shall die,
So that many
Will live.

As I looked through the rainbow covered opening, I could see Albee standing there on the other side. He placed his hand on the protective cover that blocked the entrance, but as he touched it, his hand came through.

I shook my head and said "No." but he stood there waiting for me to take his hand.

"I'm coming with you Princess, it is my job to help." Albee said. "Take my hand and accept me, letting me through, or I will come without your permission and will be stuck in there, forever."

I didn't understand what he said but I had the feeling that he meant it, he would enter with or without my permission, so I reached out, took his hand and he walked through the rainbow covering.

I was angry with him for disobeying me, but there was a part of me that was happy to not be alone. "What do you mean?" I asked. "You will be stuck here if I don't allow you in."

"Those who enter after doing sinful things cannot leave, and when I allowed Stephan into my house and trusted him, even though I felt he was up to no good, it put a negative mark on me. I can and have been working towards making amends for my lack of judgment and my weakness, allowing Stephan to impersonate me, but I have not forgiven myself yet, so the negative mark remains." Albee said.

"But it wasn't your fault and you have been doing all you can to help me. Surely that is enough to set things right?" I inquired, with some frustration in my voice.

Albee replied, "Princess, until I forgive myself, it doesn't matter how much good I do in the eyes of others. If I still feel undeserving, then I am. I will see you to the end, keeping you safe or die trying. That was my vow to you when you forgave me, and I will keep my vow."

I felt frustrated and a bit angry, but the anger was not towards Albee, though, the frustration was. These fey seemed to complicate their lives way more than humans did. I felt anger towards Varda, she was the one who could fix everything, change it all if she so chose, or the one, the great one who created her. Why would he let this go on?

"What happened, why did you bring us all back here?" Albee asked.

"Something is wrong, I saw Brett being pulled into the rock and Stephan, he knows we are here, they all do, but are letting us in. Why? I can't feel Brett anymore, I can't find him in my mind but I feel Stephan and another dark presence. I must find Douglas before it's too late." I stated strongly, even though I wasn't feeling strong at the moment.

"Princess, we will find Douglas and the rest, together. I feel Stephan also, and he is feeling sure of himself. That is a weakness we can draw upon." Albee said, in a reassuring way.

I smiled and thanked him for his positive attitude and suggested we go back to the tunnel entrance that Douglas and the others had entered. Even though it had crumbled shut, there must be a way in.

The tunnel was dark and damp and I shivered just a bit as we entered. There was cold wind blowing towards us, creating an eerie sound all around. It was voices, whispers, sadness and dread, that the wind carried with it.

As we walked, the air got heavier and warmer and the sounds became cries, shrieks and sometimes laughter; an unnatural laughter. At times I could feel something touching me, hands reaching out for help but I couldn't see anything. I felt it though, the sadness, the emptiness that they all felt. I pitied them, the pain they felt was so great.

We reached the area where the tunnels had split and the one that Douglas and the others had entered was open again. The dark one knew I was here, and wanted me to go that way.

As we entered, not far ahead, the tunnel split again and I suddenly felt the living, just up ahead. But which tunnel was it coming from? I could feel the living bodies in distress and we heard it then, screams, real screams, loud voices, and chaos.

A dark grey wisp came at us. I put my shield up and it struck and disintegrated before my eyes, only to appear again in front of us. It didn't move, just hovered there. I knew it was the tree fey's spirit, from Pineville. The sadness it felt, the need to help.

"What can you do for us?" I asked, as Albee looked at me like I was crazy, talking to myself.

I ignored Albee and continued, "My friends, they are in trouble?"

I could smell it then, the smell of blood, and charred flesh. They were in trouble and I had to help. The spirit suddenly shot away, entered the tunnel to our right and disappeared. I told Albee that we had to follow it. That it would take us to the others. Albee, with a firm and confident look, headed into the tunnel and I followed, still keeping my shield around us both.

The air was getting hotter as we went and I knew that I could handle it, but Albee wouldn't be able to for long. I thought about my shield being thicker, more protection, and it worked. The air cooled somewhat in the shielded area that we were in.

As we came around a bend in the tunnel, there in front of us were my friends, allies, fighting for their lives. The grey wisps were everywhere, but it wasn't just the grey spirits. Other familiar creatures seemed to be all over Douglas, the wolves and trolls. They looked like the creatures that had been in the underground city of Bermuda, and they were piercing everyone with their long, sharp tails.

I saw Lily then, coming from around Douglas, she was scratching the creatures off of him, still in her cat form hissing like a cat out for vengeance. How she got here was beyond me.

One of the creatures jumped from the ceiling onto Lily's back, just above her tail, but it wasn't there long, for Lily, like an acrobat, did a flip in the air and grabbed the creature in her mouth and swallowed it as if it was a mouse. She then landed back on Douglas, as if she had never left, and continued to remove the venomous creatures from his body.

Rose was kneeling down, holding a troll in a protective embrace. It seemed that nothing was bothering Rose. It looked like she was singing to the troll as she held tight, but lovingly.

When a wolf, being severely wounded by these creatures, fell just a few feet from me, I extended my shield to bring him in.

Albee was horrified by what I did, because there were still those beetle-like creatures attached to the wolf. I bent down quickly before Albee could stop me and placing my hand, with the ring, on the wolf's back, the creatures vanished in a puff of smoke.

I looked up at Albee with surprise and saw that he was just as shocked. I didn't know why I did what I did, but now I knew that the ring was a good thing to have down here.

I extended my shield to the others, one at a time, and as I touched them, the creatures' disappeared. When I was done, the shield was filling the small cavern that we were in.

I went to Douglas as he leaned up against the wall, blood oozing from his temple and welts on his face and neck and I assumed other places, where the creatures stung him. As I put my hand up to heal his wounds, he smiled wearily and said, "She was wrong. She is never wrong, but he was ready for us and somehow was able to break through the shield you had put around us earlier."

I said nothing, I knew he was talking about Varda but I didn't want to think about her at the moment. Douglas stood upright then, and I knew that he was healed, this ring was a blessed gift.

I saw movement out of the corner of my eye and looking over to the opening of the tunnel where we had come in, was the tree fey spirit. Douglas looked in the same direction and asked what I was seeing.

"It's the spirit of the tree fey from Pineville. He is here in Hades, and helped us to get to you."

Don't trust it, Princess Emilee, they are not to be trusted." Douglas said with venom in his voice.

I had never heard Douglas talk with such hatred in his voice before. This place was affecting all of us in a negative way, and I had to get everyone out to safety.

I knew that Varda, my grandmother, was wrong. I had to do this on my own. My friends couldn't help me down here. The evil and hatred, sadness and remorse, was too strong and it was causing the living to feel this.

I left Douglas's side and went to my allies, one by one, to try and heal them, but some of them had damage too severe. We had lost four wolves and three trolls and if we didn't get the rest out, they wouldn't survive either.

I barked out orders then, telling the ones who could walk to help the others and I went over to Rose, who still sat with the one troll held lovingly in her arms. I bent down and knew right away the troll was dead and I saw then that it was Tilly. I felt the tears in my eyes, and placing my hands on her, I tried desperately to bring her back.

Tina M. Engel

Rose placed a hand on mine then, and said softly, "Princess, let her be, let her go. It's her time."

I looked up into Rose's sweet face as tears filled my eyes and blurred my surroundings. Rose was crying too and as she reached up and brushed some tears from my cheek, I knew what Rose was.

Rose stood then, as did I and we all carried the dead and wounded out as I kept my shield up, double thickness, around us. The tree fey's spirit led, as we followed. I trusted that he would lead us to safety even though Douglas was skeptical.

We reached the opening to the world outside and as I approached the spirit that helped, I saw him then, as he was in life. He bowed to me, thanked me for trusting him, and turned back into the dark grey wisp and disappeared into the wall.

I touched the rainbow doorway cover and it opened to let us out. As we left, one by one, some alive and injured, and some dead, the opening made a quivery sound, as each passed through it.

When one of the wolves carrying another tried to pass, the doorway wouldn't let them pass. I approached and told the wolf carrying the other, to put him down and go through. He wanted to argue, but Douglas put a hand on his shoulder and nodded, for him to obey. He did and was able to walk through.

I looked down at the wolf that had died and a grey wisp came out of his body. I felt pain and despair as it hovered over its body for a moment, then came to me, hovering just in front of my face. I knew it was waiting for me to drop my shield. I did so and could feel its fear as it disappeared into the wall.

The sadness in the tunnel was agonizing, everyone was heartbroken over the death of their friend and the fact that he had to stay here in Hades, what could he have done that was so horrible?

Had he been one of Mephisto's spies too? I wondered.

Douglas then picked up the wolf's body and placed it over to the side. Another wolf was quite agitated by this, wanting to take him with us, but Douglas explained that his friend, a member of his pack and family, would not be permitted to leave.

Douglas put his arm up towards the opening and asked everyone to continue on, and no one else was left behind. I was the last to leave, Lily just in front of me, and as she turned to look at me, she turned back into her fey self and there were tears streaking her face.

Lily had a welt on her cheek and as I approached her and reached up to touch it, to heal it, she put her hand up and stopped me, and said, "No Princess, leave it, the pain reminds me of what I just saw. I will heal on my own, just let it be." And she turned and walked through the opening and up the stairs.

When I entered the world of the living, the sun was behind dark grey clouds and the wind was howling. It would rain soon and everyone had to get back to the ship.

As I looked around, at all the fey together again, they were sharing their stories as to what had happened to each of them, their friends, and

Tina M. Engel

family and pack members. The tears and aguish was overwhelming, but when I looked over and saw Tobias with Rose and Douglas, my heart broke.

Tobias was kneeling, Tilly in his arms. I could hear the sobs coming from him over the commotion and anguish from the others. I wanted to go to him, to console him, but I knew that there was nothing I could do or say to bring her back. I also knew that he would say it was meant to be, that they were here to help me save us all.

I was angry then, angrier than I had ever been. I looked to Douglas and he knew what I was thinking, what I was about to do. I had to go back in alone, find Brett and his sword, rescue Shinar and defeat Mephisto, after dealing with Stephan. Oh, yes, I was going to deal with Stephan.

Albee came up beside me and putting his arm around my shoulder, bent down and whispered in my ear, "I am coming too. I can help with Stephan." I was still looking at Douglas as Albee said this, and Douglas, from afar, nodded a yes. He knew what Albee had just said, and insisted that Albee come.

I stood there, silently, as I watched Rose go from one fey who had lost their life, to another, and as she bent down to each, she touched them and whispered something into their ears. As she did this, suddenly, wisps came out of their bodies. They were different colors, each one an individual spirit.

When she had gone to them all, all the colors joined together and created a rainbow and then drifted up into the sky. The greyness parted for a moment to allow them to enter and then closed again, leaving us in a grey, cold place.

I knew then, that Rose was among the dead. Rose had died on the ship. She was a spirit and was here to help those who would not make it. Help them to cross over to Nirvana. Oh, she was here to help me too, I knew, but Varda brought her back to do this job.

Was it always meant to be this way? Was this Rose's destiny. Was Rose really dead? I wondered.

I knew that none of these fey were really gone. They had left their physical bodies, but now were in Nirvana, the final place that every life wants to go. But why was Rose still here? I could see her and touch her, she was solid, but different.

What had Varda done to Rose? Did the venom that sped up my change, have anything to do with Rose? Varda would answer these questions when I saw her again, my grandmother or not, I would demand answers.

I went over to Tobias. I couldn't leave without talking to him, but what could I say? As I approached and knelt down next to him, Tobias looked up, and as our eyes met, there wasn't sadness in his eyes, but pride.

I realized that he was full of pride towards Tilly, for she gave her physical life to help me save our home, and the lives of every creature out there. Oh, he was feeling the loss, and soon would feel loneliness, but he knew that they would be together someday. He could also visit her now and then in Nirvana, since all fey could go there from time to time, for a rest.

Tina M. Engel

Tobias took my hands in his and said in an uplifting voice, "She did what she had to, Princess Emilee. We all did. Tilly is watching over us all now and if she can, she will still help. Look for her color, purple. You saw it, did you not?"

I nodded my head as if to say yes. I had seen a purple wisp, a spirit, leaving Tilly's body as Rose had touched her.

"Just know, Princess, when you see the color purple, she is there with you." Tobias continued.

Tobias then let go of my hands, I stood, and he picked up Tilly as Douglas ordered everyone to gather the dead and wounded, and head back to the doorway that would send them back to the ship. Weylyn offered to carry Tilly, but Tobias kindly declined the offer. He wanted her close, for as long as possible.

Rose approached Douglas and as he bent down, Rose whispered something in his ear. When he stood back up, Douglas nodded in agreement of something, and Rose came over to me and Albee.

"I'm coming too, Princess, and don't even think about stopping me. You both need me, you and Shinar. Nothing can harm me, as you already know, so let's get this over with. Brett can't take much more and I really would like to see you heal him, instead of me sending him to Nirvana." Rose said, in a matter of fact manner, and headed back towards the Chapel.

I turned and watched the rest of the fey, looking deflated, head down the hill to the place where the sphere, the gateway back to the ship was. Why did Varda think that sending an army into Hades, to find our way into Gehenna, was going to work? I should have been thinking more clearly and questioned this. But with Brett on my mind, he was all I was thinking about.

As they disappeared from view, I turned to see Albee standing at the opening of the chapel, waiting for me. I headed in that direction as it started to rain. The sky lit up with lightning strikes, and thunder boomed loudly.

We entered the chapel and I saw Rose standing at what was once the altar. There, just above where a wall used to be, but was now crumbled, was a tapestry. It was translucent, like a vision from the past, but I could see it and was confused by the sight of Poseidon standing guard in front of a cave opening.

I stood next to Rose and she told the story, as if knowing what I was about to ask. "It was Poseidon who helped banish Mephisto to the realm of Gehenna, in Hades. The humans back then thought Poseidon a great god for saving them from the devil. You see, Mephisto was already causing havoc in the humans' realm. So they built this chapel over the doorway to Hades.

"There is a cave down the hill that you can only get to by water, which is also an entrance into Hades. Poseidon guarded that entrance, stopping any from leaving, which is what this picture shows.

"I believe Princess, that is the way we should go, through the underwater opening. He isn't expecting you to enter that way with Albee and I. He expects you to go in the same way that we did before. Your anger is great and he believes you are irrational, and will behave foolishly. This was all planed, she knew this was the only way for you to enter and succeed."

I understood then. Varda knew that we would be ambushed, that many would die, just so I would be able to trick Mephisto long enough to enter without his knowledge. The few will die, so that many will live. I still was angry and saddened, but I understood.

It was Albee who spoke next, "Princess Emilee, you must go to the cave in the water and enter from there. Rose and I will enter this way and follow the only tunnel that will be open. He will feel our presence and assume we are all together."

Rose nodded as she looked at me.

I however, started to object when I saw Brett suddenly. *He was leaning against something, but I couldn't make out what it was at first. It was many shades of green with multi colored sparkles, shimmering as a dim light struck it. As I looked around I realized that it was a dragon, Shinar, Brett and Shinar were together.*

The vision ended and I found myself kneeling. These visions seemed to take me by surprise, it would be nice if I could have some warning. I started to stand but Albee came down on his knees too and took my hand.

"Princess Emilee", Albee said, "I see him. Look."

Suddenly, another vision, *Stephan was in the room, the prison that Brett had been in. He was furious, ranting about a traitor. He was saying something about melting him down to lava, permanently. Stephan looked in my direction then and smiled an evil grin and said, "Princess, you are almost mine. They can play tricks on me all they want but in the end, he will win. He has from the first day of his existence."*

The vision ended and I knew that arguing about Rose and Albee's plan was not going to work. I had to go alone and they had to be the bait, so to speak, to keep Stephan and Mephisto thinking that I was falling into their trap.

I stood, hugged them both, gave Rose my diamond necklace and cameo, hoping that these two items which gave me power, would keep Stephan and Mephisto thinking that I was with them. Rose started to object but I reassured her that with my shield, weapon and ring, I was still completely protected.

I led them down into the underground room under the chapel. I let them both into the opening and reassured them that I would get them out somehow.

Chapter 21

Who do you trust?
Your eyes tell a different story
Than your instinct
At times.
What do you believe?

I put my shield around myself and hoped that it would stop Stephan and Mephisto from seeing me, and they would assume I was with the others. If Kimberlite was working for them, he had his eyes in that diamond and would also think that I was in the tunnel with Rose and Albee.

I reached the water and upon entering, I knew exactly where to go. There was a rocky wall where water met land, and about 30 feet down, was an opening. I entered a large tunnel, and swam for only a minute or two before I came to the end and surfaced, finding myself in a large cavern.

Looking around, I didn't see any way to continue, there were no openings in the walls to get me down to Gehenna. Looking up towards the ceiling of the cave, I spotted an opening that looked just big enough for me to fit in. I spread my wings, and instantly they lifted me up to the opening.

It was larger than it looked from down below, so I was able to land and retract my wings with ease. Looking around, I saw that I was on a landing, the top of a stone stairway that descended downward.

The walls were glowing with an eerie red light that showed me the way. I started down, walking slowly and carefully, for the steps were slippery, covered with a dark, slimy film. The further down I went, the heavier the air became, with a rancid smell.

I was feeling alone and lonely without my diamond, the lava pebbles were such company, and I realized what else they did for me. They had a calming effect on me. The feeling of loneliness was overwhelming and I had to fight to keep my mind focused on my task, telling myself that it was this place that was causing these feelings. I wondered though, should I have given the diamond to Rose, was it a mistake?

I saw movement down below me, just before a bend in the staircase. It was a purple wisp, fluttering up a few steps and then back down, and I remembered what Tobias said. It was Tilly, here to help me.

As I approached Tilly, the feelings of loneliness dissipated and I felt strong and confident again. "Tilly" I said, "I sure am happy to see you."

She headed down the stairway as soon as I had reached her, and I followed, still slowly because the goo that was covering the stairs and walls now, was a thicker mass and the smell was even more rancid than before. The red glow was still present, but with the goo covering the walls, the light was diminished, so I had to be cautious with every step.

It seemed like I was descending forever and at one point, the wall on my left disappeared and gave way to a great drop off. I looked over the edge and couldn't see the bottom, only the stairway going down and then disappearing into the darkness.

Tina M. Engel

I slipped once, and thought for sure I was going to fall over the edge into the nothingness. As I put my hand up onto the wall, I thought for sure that someone had reached out and grabbed me, pulling me back up onto the stairway. I looked up in shock but there was nothing and no one there. I remembered then, I have wings, I would have been just fine.

I decided to spread my wings and fly down to the bottom. These stairs were treacherous and the goo was getting thicker with each step.

I stepped off the edge and my wings held me there as I looked to the wall again, sure that someone or something had grabbed me. There was nothing there though.

I flew down carefully, not wanting my wings to touch the wall. I didn't know if the goo would interfere with my flying. I reached the bottom finally. It was a long way down, and there just a few feet from the bottom step, was an opening to a large tunnel, covered in a black tar substance. The red glow of the walls was gone, only the oozy goo that ran down them remained. There were ornate lanterns, however, hanging on golden hooks spaced evenly down the long corridor.

I could hear noises and realized just how quiet it had been, descending the stairway. It was voices, mumbling, whining, moaning, grumbling and suddenly, I could see faces in the walls, terror-struck, and tortured faces. The faces were those of humans and fey, and other creatures that I hadn't seen before.

Tilly was still there with me and when a grey wisp came at me, she intercepted it with amazing speed and it let out an agonizing cry and disintegrated right before my eyes.

A dark grey wisp appeared then, but didn't dart at me like the other one did. It stayed a good distance away, wary of Tilly and her determination to keep me safe. I knew then that it was the tree fey from Pineville.

"Tilly", I said, "It's okay, this is the spirit who helped us earlier. He is from Pineville and wants to help."

The dark spirit came closer and Tilly went to it and they seemed to spin slowly around each other as if checking each other out. Then they separated and both came closer to me.

I had my shield surrounding me and it was out about two feet from my body. I wanted room to move and to stop anything that might be out to get me, now that I was deep down in this pit.

The dark spirit then led the way as Tilly followed, and then I. The faces in the walls and the desperate sounds continued, and we came to several openings on both sides of the tunnel. I somehow knew that they were openings to different parts of Hades. Gehenna was the area though, where I needed to go.

I passed several dozen openings and each one had different odors and sounds. The dark spirit finally stopped at an opening and I knew it was the one. My stomach felt sick, the smells down here were suffocating at times, changing from rancid, to sickly sweet to sour and bitter. I was feeling cold and clammy.

I looked down at my hand with the ring on it. It was glowing and the green emerald color made me think of Christmas, and I smiled. I held my hand to the middle of my chest, between my two hearts and focused on healing, easing my sick stomach and after a few seconds, my body started to feel stronger, and the nauseated feeling subsided.

The dark spirit hovered just to the right of the opening, and then disappeared into the wall. I gathered, that this was as far as he was to take us. Maybe Gehenna wasn't where he wanted to go.

Tilly went in first, and as I entered the opening, the heat that was in the tunnel struck the shield that surrounded me and caused a humming sound as it bounced off. I was warm but was feeling confident that I would be fine, with or without the shield.

I started to worry about Albee and Rose, well Albee, anyway. I knew that Rose would be fine but what would the heat do to Albee? After all, he was a tree. Why did I let them come with me, I thought and worried?

Tilly's spirit stopped suddenly and then started to dart back and forth sporadically, as if in a panic. I could see a shadow coming towards me from a bend up ahead and knew that I was going to have to fight and win, if I was to save Brett and Shinar.

I opened my wings out as wide as they would go, spreading the shield to let them stretch until they touched the sides and almost touched the ceiling of the tunnel and I engulfed Tilly into the shield also. I activated my weapon and stood ready, but Tilly stayed firmly in front of me.

Kimberlite came around the corner, walking as if he belonged here. When he saw me, a look of shock and irritation covered his face.

"Princess, what are you doing here?" He bellowed as anger replaced the irritation. "You are supposed to be with Rose and Albee!"

I saw shadows behind him then, as someone or something was coming from the same direction that Kimberlite had come. Kimberlite suddenly had a look of panic, and touching the side of the wall, opened a passageway.

"Hurry Princess, get inside before they see you!" Kimberlite demanded.

I just stood there looking at him, wondering what to do. What was he doing here and why did he have Brett in captivity. He was working for Stephan and maybe even Mephisto. As I looked up ahead, I knew that whoever or whatever was coming was just about to turn the corner and would see me.

Tilly was trying to get through my shield and to the opening, so I removed it from her and she disappeared into the tunnel behind Kimberlite.

I reached the opening just as several creatures stepped into my view. I ducked into the opening before they had a chance to see me, I hoped, and Kimberlite sealed up the opening.

I turned then to face him, with anger in my eyes and my wings still slightly out. I let them out fully again and flung them forward, knocking Kimberlite up against the wall of the area that we were in. He was strong but my wings, it seemed, were stronger for now.

I held Kimberlite there, knowing that he could escape into the wall and get away, if he really wanted but he didn't move, didn't seem to want to. Looking around, I saw that we were in a smaller cave with bones scattering the floor; human bones, fey bones, animal bones, everywhere. Tilly was nowhere to be seen.

I looked back at Kimberlite and he had an irritated expression on his face as he said, "You can let go of me now Princess Emilee, if you don't mind. I did save you back there and now it seems I have to save you, Brett, Rose, Albee and that blasted dragon of yours too."

I was perplexed, what did he mean, by saving all of us? I wondered.

"Princess, please." Kimberlite implored. "Let me explain. There isn't much time. If you are here and Rose and Albee are there alone, well, this isn't good."

I let him go and my wings went back into my back, but before I could ask anything, Kimberlite said quickly, "Come, and hurry. I must get you to a safe place and then go get that blasted pixie and tree. You were supposed to be together. Your shield would have protected all three of you, until I got there to get you out."

Kimberlite headed to the side of the cave and an opening appeared. Kimberlite disappeared into it and I stood wondering if I should follow. Well of course, I had no choice but I felt irritated and confused. Did I trust Kimberlite? Of course not, but I had to follow, and trust for now.

I entered the opening and as I did, it closed up. Looking ahead, I saw Kimberlite dashing down a narrow passage way and he stopped just long enough to wave for me to follow, as a purple wisp darted past him. I did so and it seemed that we took twists and turns for several minutes.

Kimberlite stopped then, and said, "Okay Princess, I know you have a lot of questions, but for now just let me share enough to get you off my back and you can give me hell later. Well, we are already in hell..." And he laughed.

I gave Kimberlite a very sour look, and he stopped laughing, looked a bit sheepish and continued, "I know it looks like I am working for Stephan, and well, I am, kind of, but not really."

I looked at him with confusion, thinking that maybe he was crazy, the way he was talking.

He continued, "Princess, let me take you to Brett and then I will go get Rose and Albee, then get you all out of here. I will explain everything else later. Please."

"Brett, you know where he is?" I asked.

"Well, yes, I am the one who removed him from his prison and pissed off Stephan." Kimberlite said, pride across his face.

I was so confused then but said, "Please take me to Brett and explain as much as you can, as we go."

Kimberlite made another opening and held his hand out for me to enter. As I did, there in a cavern lay Shinar, with Brett leaning against her.

I turned around to face Kimberlite and he said quickly, "Sorry Princess, I can't explain anymore right now." And he disappeared into the opening and closed it up.

I went to Brett, and bending down, I placed a hand on his cheek. He lifted his head and opened his eyes slowly and looked at me.

"What took you so long?" Brett managed to whisper and a smile crossed his lips.

My eyes blurred just a bit as they filled with tears and as a tear ran down my cheek, Brett reached up with some difficulty, and brushed his finger across my cheek to wipe it away.

When his finger touched my cheek, I felt it, that wonderful zing, tingling sensation, when he touched me. I joined him in his mind, he was with me, I felt the love that he had for me and the worry, knowing that I was going to come for him.

I bent down and placed a kiss on his lips as he held my face softly in his hands. When I moved my head away slightly, I said, "You do go to the most undesirable places, for me to have to chase you down. It will take days to get this stench from my clothes."

Brett chuckled at this and then winced with pain. Humor wasn't necessarily a good thing at the moment, but then if he hadn't followed me to Pineville, thinking I needed saving, he wouldn't have gotten himself kidnaped by a crazy lunatic, and I wouldn't have had to go to hell and back to save him. Yes, a little humor and pain is required.

I placed my hand on Brett's head and let the ring do its job. He had many cuts and bruises, several broken ribs and one of his hearts had a small puncture wound. This worried me and I searched his mind to see how this happened. It was Stephan, using the sword, pushing it into Brett's flesh, slowly until it just slightly punctured his heart. He then told Brett that he looked forward to pushing it in all the way, and then doing the same to the other heart.

The anger I felt was overwhelming, and I felt ugly, feeling this way. I wanted to take all of my powers and destroy him, but not just destroy him, I wanted to make him suffer first. These feelings where not good, not healthy, no matter what Stephan had done, these thoughts where not healthy for me. This place was getting to me, causing me to lose my focus. I was here to stop Mephisto, and in doing so would be the downfall of Stephan.

Brett slept when I was done healing him. Oh he didn't want to, I could feel, but he needed to so I put the thought into his head and he fell asleep.

I looked at Shinar then, my dragon. She was laying quietly, eyes closed but I knew she was alive, for as she exhaled every once in a while, a small puff of smoke would escape from her nose. She was beautiful, the size of a large Clydesdale horse, with emerald green scales that shimmered in the light from the torches that hung on the walls.

Shinar turned her head towards me and opened her eyes slightly, I saw that they were a sky blue that glistened as she looked at me. I got up and walked over to her head, and taking out the small flask that Trevor had given me, I started to put it to her lips.

"Princess, don't do that!" Rose yelled.

I turned abruptly and fell on my butt as I did so, shocked to see Rose, Albee and Kimberlite come into the cave from yet another direction, than where I had come in.

Albee didn't look like the Albee that had left with Rose. This Albee looked like the tree fey that I had seen in my house the night that he, or I should say, Stephan tried to kidnap me the first time.

His skin was greyish, with cracks, like tree bark, his hair was long, the color of leaves in the autumn, a burnt red, hanging down his back, with some strands covering his face slightly.

I stood, as Rose came over to me and Shinar, and we embraced as if we hadn't seen each other in years. As I held Rose, looking over her shoulder, I saw Albee stumble a bit before he crumbed to the ground and sat there with an expression of emptiness in his eyes.

"Princess, you can't give that to Shinar until she and I have bonded. Albee needs you. He protected your gifts by wrapping himself around me and your gifts, as Stephan and his goons tried desperately to take them.

"The grey spirits have a physical body somehow, and they were trying to burn him as a tree would burn. Go help him while I do what needs to be done with Shinar so that you can heal her properly." Rose said in a rush.

I was perplexed by what she said, her having to bond with Shinar before I did, but Rose pushed me towards Albee and she approached Shinar. I walked backwards in Albee's direction as I watched Rose reach out both of her hands and place them on Shinar's side. Shinar suddenly had a look of relief, almost a smile, if a dragon could smile, and Rose turned the color of Shinar and seemed to dissolve right into her. Oh, I could see Rose's outline on Shinar's side, but they were one with each other.

It was Kimberlite that broke my attention from Rose and Shinar as he said, "Princess Emilee, come quick, I don't think Albee has much life left. Let Rose be."

I turned then to see Albee, laying now and the leaves that were once hair, were dead and laying around him. I knelt down and placing my hands on him, could feel the pain he was feeling. His insides were scorched and over half of his body was burned so badly, that I didn't think I could repair him.

I felt Kimberlite behind me and realized that he was putting something around my neck. It was my diamond necklace, and as soon as it fell softly to my chest, I could feel the lava pebbles inside, we were joined again. He laid my cameo pendant down on Albee's chest and then backed away.

As I looked down at the cameo, it seemed to sink into Albee's bark and suddenly, the greyish bark started turning into skin again. The cracks dissolved and clothing, though tattered and torn, appeared around the cameo. The dead leaves that were lying on the ground, crumbled and a gust of wind suddenly blew what was left of the leaves away.

Albee's hair became hair, long and grey, still knotted and slightly matted, but his color was coming back to normal, as normal as a tree fey's color could be. I removed the cameo and placed it on my shirt, as I removed my hands from Albee and he sat up.

Albee's smile was weak as he said, "Thank you Princess, although I was ready to leave this body for you, but not before giving you this."

Albee held out his hand to me and as he placed something in mine, I saw that it was a seed. I looked at him with curiosity.

"I was going to have you plant it, wherever you ended up, so that I would be with you once more. Anyway a small part of me would. Keep it safe and know that if anything happens to me, plant it, and I will be with you." Albee said, and then smiling, leaned up against a rock and shut his eyes to rest.

I stood, placed the seed into a pocket of my jeans and walked over to Shinar, as Rose seemed to reappear from her side.

"Shinar needs that fluid now, Princess." Rose said, looking drained as she sat down next to Shinar's side and placed a hand on her.

I went to Shinar's face and asked her to stick out her tongue. I wasn't sure exactly how else to get it into her mouth.

Shinar did as I asked, she lifted her head slightly and stuck out her tongue. I opened the flask and dumped the small amount of liquid onto it.

Shinar put her tongue back into her mouth and laid her head back down on the floor. I put both my hands on her face, and bent down, placing a kiss on her cheek. I placed my cheek on hers and shut my eyes, and we stayed this way for some time.

I could feel her, feel what she was feeling then, hear her thoughts, and saw what she had gone through since her hatching. The torture that Mephisto put her through.

She was still struggling inside, was Mephisto her master and should she bow to his will and bring me to him, or did she belong to me; Daughter of Angelina and Jordan, Granddaughter of Varda and ... Mephisto?

I saw him then, Mephisto, in Shinar's thoughts, but I knew then that the creature I had seen in my dream, the bug-like creature, was Mephisto. That was the Mephisto that Shinar saw too. Was that really what he looked like though? How could Varda love a hideous creature like that? Or, was this his appearance since he was banished to Gehenna, reflecting his ugly, evil nature.

Our connection was interrupted by another entering my mind, my thoughts, Brett. I opened my eyes and sitting up, turned and looked in his direction. Brett was sitting there, staring at me with a loving smile on his face.

"I didn't mean to interrupt, Emilee, I apologize, but I was curious about what was going on between the two of you. It's none of my business but well...," Brett said with a little bit of discomfort in his voice.

I stood then with a smile of understanding and as I looked around the room, Shinar and Rose resting, Albee still sleeping, and Brett looking much healthier, I turned to Kimberlite.

Brett sensed my mood change as I looked at Kimberlite. He stood up and came over to me and said quickly, but quietly, "Stay calm Princess, not all is what it seems. It never is."

Tina M. Engel

"What do you mean? He is a traitor and a liar. I could tell he wasn't who he seemed!" I fumed.

"No Princess Emilee, I'm not, and never have been. Even Brett had no idea who I really was. No one, not even Varda knew I was here, though she knows me." Kimberlite said, as he transformed before my eyes from a rock fey to a kind of fey, I had never seen before.

As I watched the transformation I was stunned, not just because Kimberlite wasn't a rock fey anymore, but this fey standing before me was like no fey I had seen so far. He was tall and thin, not too thin, well-built but not bulky, had long white hair, shimmery purple eyes and had earrings like me, with the shell-like covering on his cheeks and down his neck. He let his wings spread out and I saw they looked like mine, and he then retracted them.

"My name is Liam, and I'm like you Emilee, a keeper of peace, bringing many different groups of life beings together, to live in harmony. I did my job many ages ago and did my job well, I might add.

"I was sent here to impersonate a rock fey, not all that fun either, and befriend Stephan, to keep an eye on him while waiting for you to come.

"If Mephisto wins and conquers the humans' earth and Terrafirma, he will then be able to enter other realms, including my worlds eventually, and I can't let that happen.

"One day, your worlds, Terrafirma, earth and many others, will join with mine. You and I will help them all find peace and unity while still having different ways of living. But that will take some time, and will only happen if you can stop Mephisto."

I looked from Brett to Liam and suddenly felt exhausted. This game that I was thrown into kept changing. I was so tired of the unknown, never knowing when the rules of this game, of my existence, would change.

I looked over at Shinar then and said, without looking at Liam, "So do you have a dragon too, and a weapon like this?", as I removed the barrette from my hair and opened the dagger as I turned back to him.

Liam smiled and tapping what looked like a pin of some kind on his chest, he suddenly had a knife that resembled Brett's and it then turned into a sword. He said then, "I don't have a dragon, but I do have a flying lion." And his smile turned into a slight chuckle. "You'll meet him someday."

Rose was suddenly next to me and she said, "Who in the world is this?"

I turned to her and replied, "Kimberlite!"

Brett and Liam laughed as Rose looked quite confused, and from behind Shinar came that familiar voice, with a slight irritation in it, "Well now, surprise, surprise, but then, should I be surprised? I know you, don't I?" Lily asked.

I looked at Lily as she came around me to stand slightly in front of me, but to the side so I could still see everyone. Liam smiled and nodded slightly.

"Yes, Miss Lily, you do. You almost messed everything up one day in the caves, when you were wandering around in places that you shouldn't have been in. Luckily, my pretending to be one of

Tina M. Engel

the fey in Queen Anahita's hidden springs, worked. I was in need of shedding that blasted rock covering for a bit."

"Wait a minute" I said in a huff. "Kimberlite, I mean Liam…"

Rose cut me off saying, "Liam? Kimberlite? What?"

This time it was Albee who laughed a very weak laugh as he joined us all standing around, staring at each other. He said then, "It was you who told me to find Princess Emilee and help her when she got off the boat on Lake Erie. You were the one who assured me that the princess would forgive me and allow me to help."

"Yes, it was me. I have been busy working all angles to ensure that Emilee would succeed. Oh, don't get me wrong, Varda is in control and sees all possibilities on how this can turn out. But we needed it to turn out a certain way, with Mephisto defeated.

"Varda is very special and very powerful, but she isn't to interfere with the future. She can guide only so much, but for me, now that is a different story."

"What do you mean, as for you? Where are you from, how did you get here and why have you been working with Stephan?" I asked, feeling frustrated. And then looking at Lily, I scolded, "What are you doing here? You were supposed to go back to the ship with the others!"

Before Lily could answer, Liam spoke, "I have been in cahoots with Stephan from the beginning. Stephan was my way in, to try and get close to Mephisto, but I never saw him, and still haven't. I do know where he hides but I was not strong enough in that blasted rock disguise to break through his protective shield. It wasn't my place to face him anyway, and I didn't want him to figure out who I was. I have learned things, as we have all learned, on this adventure."

"Adventure!" I yelled, as I threw my arms up over my head with a scowl on my face.

Brett came over to me and touching my arm said, "Emilee, I didn't trust him at first either, the time Kimberlite put his arm around me, and whispered in my ear that everything was going to be alright.

"I thought he was working with Stephan also. He had the rocks holding the chains tight and around my waist. It wasn't until Kimberlite pulled me through the wall to safety and transformed into Liam that I realized my best friend wasn't who I thought he was.

"Finding out that it was Stephan who led Kimberlite to me, a long time ago, so that he could become my best friend, created even more anger and distrust. I still am a bit miffed at this fact but we must let it all go, we must defeat Mephisto and figure everything else out later."

"Princess" Liam continued, "I knew that Brett would be in trouble, that they had plans for his abduction and death, and I couldn't let that happen. You still need him in order to succeed."

"But they wouldn't have abducted him in the first place, if he had done what he was supposed to and stayed put." I said in a huff as I looked at Brett.

Tina M. Engel

I looked back at Liam and he responded with assurance, as he looked to Brett, "It was one of the futures that was a possibility, and me knowing Brett so well, and his stubbornness, I was confident that this was the future to be."

Surprisingly, Brett said nothing as he looked from Liam to me and shrugged his shoulders.

Rose then piped in, "She needs us all and you could have let us know who you really were, then maybe Tilly would still be alive and Eagle and I would..." She stopped then, suddenly looking a bit embarrassed by her outburst.

I turned to Rose and started to ask, what she meant about her and Eagle, but a voice from behind me interrupted.

"My princess." Shinar said, "It doesn't matter right now. What does matter is taking care of that evil creature before he finishes his work, turning me against you. I feel him still inside me, we have work to do."

I went over to her and put my hand on her side, and she stood then. As I still had my hand on her side, Rose came over to me, and touching her too, the three of us were joined.

"We need Albee too." Rose said, "He will be able to confuse Stephan enough, I think, for us to get to Mephisto, but you must defeat him."

"How? I asked, "No one has told me how I am supposed to stop him. I am just a..." And I stopped. What am I? I thought. I have been a nobody for so long, why do any of these fey think that I can defeat such evil?

Brett was in my mind and heard my thoughts and said, "Emilee, you have always been a somebody. You have parents who love you in both the human and Fey realms, you are a friend to all that you meet, you are good and kind, and help anyone who is in need. You have touched so many lives, even though you didn't know it."

Brett was behind me then, and put his hands on my waist. I felt the desire, the need for him then, every part of him, and I felt embarrassed since Shinar and Rose were connected to me still and felt what I felt. I removed my hand from Shinar and turned into Brett's arms, and his eyes locked onto mine instantly.

There was no time for this now. I wanted him but I had to keep my head. I could feel the strange sensation that I had experienced on the ship, when I had turned silvery white. This was what the creature from the deep did to me. It gave me extra strength, but also strengthened my desire for Brett's blood. Brett bent down and placed a kiss on my forehead, then backed away from me.

"So we all must work together to defeat Stephan, but I must face Mephisto alone." I said, "Albee, you will help Brett distract Stephan and get the sword back, but keep him alive. I want him, when this is done."

Brett looked at me with surprise, but before he could say anything I spouted, "Not that way and you know it!"

Brett started to chuckle a bit as he said, "Well I hope not."

That seemed to lessen the tension in the air, even though it wasn't really funny. Humor though, no matter how you find it, is helpful.

Tina M. Engel

"Shinar and Rose, I don't quite know your role. Shinar, you are still weak and vulnerable to him, I can feel it. I think it best if you Liam, help Rose get Shinar out of here to safety."

Shinar let out a slight roar with a bit of fire, as she said, "I am fine and should be with you! I don't want to be away from you, it frightens me, for I feel him stronger when you are not near."

I turned and put my arms around her neck, and reassured her that she would be alright. That I needed her to be safe or I wouldn't be as strong as I needed to be. She and I were united, and once he, Mephisto, was taken care of, she and I would complete the bond and figure out the next step of our future.

I turned to look at Rose then, and my thoughts went to her. What did Rose have to do with Shinar, who was she really, and was she alive, dead, or in between?

Lily spoke up then, "I am coming too, just so you know Princess Emilee. Varda may not have known about Kimberlite really being Liam, but she does now, because she and I are always connected, and she is mighty pissed. Just sayin, so I am going with you. I have no intention of facing Varda without you. We will live or die together." And Lily gave me a look of determination when she said, live or die together.

"And furthermore, she wasn't happy that you thought you would go on without me, so she sent me into Hades after you entered, to keep an eye on you but I did lose you for just a bit." Lily said with a nonchalant tone in her voice.

Feeling speechless where Lily was concerned, I turned my attention to Kimberlite, and said, "Kimberlite, I mean Liam," and I mumbled under my breath then, "This is weird." Then I continued louder, "how do I get to Mephisto? Are we in Gehenna yet? Tell me what I need to know."

Liam answered, "Princess, I am coming with you. I can get you to Mephisto and yes, we are in Gehenna. They do not know who I am, only as a rock, so that will throw them off too. Rose and Shinar should just stay here. Together, you and I Emilee, can put up a field around this cave to block anyone from knowing that it is even here. They will be safe until we come back to get them."

"But what if we don't succeed? Will they be stuck here?" I asked with uneasiness, in my voice.

Lily said in her own (whatever), attitude, "If you don't succeed, it won't matter, now will it?" And she turned into a cat and proceeded to clean herself. She looked up at me once with annoyance, and then continued.

Brett touched my arm and said calmly and with confidence, "Emilee you will, I mean we will succeed and we will come back for them. Kimberlite, or Liam, is right."

Brett then looked towards Liam and he wasn't Liam anymore, but Kimberlite. Brett shook his head and said with a bit of humor, "Ok, just stay as Kimberlite. That is who you are to me, no matter what you look like."

Kimberlite chuckled as only Kimberlite could, and it felt familiar and safe. I did need him back. I had missed him and hated the thoughts that I had about him being a spy.

Chapter 22

It may be their time,
Apart you must be,
But love never dies!

Kimberlite went over to the wall and opened a doorway leading into a tunnel. "Follow me and stay quiet."

When we were all in the tunnel, Kimberlite and I putting our shields together, created a protective cover that no eyes or creature could penetrate around the cave that Shinar and Rose where in, I hoped. Then Kimberlite closed the doorway.

We followed quietly, Lily still in her cat form, dilly dallying behind, as if not concerned in the least. I could tell that Brett and Albee were still a bit weak from their ordeals and I worried that maybe they should have stayed back there too.

Brett being in front of me, stopped walking, turned and said in a confident voice and with determination on his face, "Emilee, I am fine and there is no way I am letting you go without me."

Kimberlite chuckled from up front and said under his breathe, "Lovebirds, always seem to think that the other can't survive without them." And he shook his head, looking back at us with a large grin.

I ignored him and patted Brett's cheek, saying, "Just stay out of trouble, will you please, and do something about Miss Lily, will you." As I walked by him, letting Brett deal with Lily straggling behind.

Lily came darting past me then, and before I could say anything, she disappeared past Kimberlite, as he bellowed for her to stop. Of course, a cat never does what they are told, so she disappeared from sight and Kimberlite looked back at me with frustration.

We walked for only a few minutes when Kimberlite stopped abruptly, and before he could say anything, creatures started to come out of the walls, bug-like creatures, like the ones I saw in my dream, like Mephisto, only smaller. They were about 5 feet tall with pinchers for hands that oozed a greenish goo, and their heads were narrow with beaks and they squawked, like a bird in distress, as they came at us.

Kimberlite yelled to us, not to let their pinchers pierce our skin, for the ooze was poison and would kill us slowly, and no one would be able to heal us.

Since I had put my shield around the room that Shinar and Rose were in, I couldn't protect any of us and I had to fight like everyone else. Kimberlite had no problem knocking down and smashing these creatures, and as he did, they burst into the grey wisps and scurried away, disappearing back into the walls, but I worried about Brett, not having a weapon and Albee, being just a tree.

Silly me, for worrying. I heard Albee yell to Brett and looked over to see him throw Brett a large branch and Albee had one too, sharp as a dagger at the end and about three feet long.

As we struck these creatures, they burst into grey wisps, but they just kept coming. Kimberlite yelled for us to follow him and we moved forward, slowly, still fighting off these creatures. They were slow at striking and didn't seem very smart, and soon we left them behind.

We came to a bend in the tunnel, and as we entered the bend, there was a great doorway in front of us. The door frame was gold and the door itself was riddled with diamonds. The air was filled with grey wisps but they stayed put, not coming at us.

Suddenly, from behind several of these grey spirits, came a purple one and the dark grey one. The other grey wisps scattered then and disappeared in the walls and floor. I reassured everyone that these two spirits were good; they were Tilly and the tree fey from Pineville. They just hovered over the door.

Kimberlite told me to come up with him, and together we would open the door into Mephisto's great room, and finish this. I wasn't sure how, but I did as he suggested and he took one of my hands.

We placed our free hands on the door, and I could feel Kimberlite's powers mix with mine. He was powerful, but there was a gentleness about him and a hunger within, similar to mine. He hungered for the blood of another. I was curious then, what were we, exactly?

"Later." Kimberlite said, not in Kimberlite's voice, but Liam's. I had a hard time remembering that there really was never a Kimberlite, he was just fabricated. Liam was the true fey.

The great door shuddered as we pushed with all our might, and then suddenly, it gave way and splintered into hundreds of pieces, flying inside the room, sparing us from injury.

As we entered, there stood Stephan with the sword held out in front of him, surrounded by more of those bug-like creatures.

Stephan laughed an evil laugh as he said, "I now have you right where I want you. Did you honestly think that you were sneaking up on us? We've watched you all along, and Kimberlite, you will be punished and then serve him for all of eternity, along with the rest of you.

"Though we couldn't see what was going on in that room you were in, we knew you were all there and we will get into it when we are done with you. That dragon is his, and will do his bidding, right alongside of you Emilee, his granddaughter."

Stephan looked towards Brett then, and continued, "And my wife. I will have you and you will bear my children, as I take you for mine."

I shuddered just thinking about his filthy hands on me, and the pure hatred on Brett's face was frightening.

"You will touch her over my dead body!" Brett gushed with venom in his voice.

Stephan chuckled at this, and replied, "That is the plan."

Before I had a chance to react, Brett lunged at Stephan with only the stick that Albee had given him earlier. Without my shield to protect him I was useless to help.

Stephan raised the sword out in front of him to block the strike from Brett, and the stick was sliced in half as if it was made of clay.

Tina M. Engel

Stephan laughed as he lunged at Brett swinging the sword at the height of Brett's chest. Brett took an awkward jump backwards in time, the sword just grazed him, slicing his shirt slightly.

Brett grabbed a small table that was in the corner, which held a carafe of a liquid of some kind. He held it up in front of him just as Stephan swung the sword at Brett again, this time aiming for his head. The table cracked but stayed in tacked long enough for Brett to dodge Stephan while smashing the table on his head.

Stephan was dazed for just a few moments and then with a chuckle that sent shivers up my spine he started towards Brett again.

At that, Kimberlite's appearance diminished and there stood Liam, as he said in a comical, relaxed tone, "Now boys let's not fight over the woman. We both know where her heart lies and we really don't have time for this."

This surprised Stephan and disoriented him for just a moment, but it was long enough for Albee to weave between the bug-like creatures, and take hold of Stephan from behind. When he did this, I could see Albee's face change. He turned back into the tree type fey that had been in my house, and Stephan struggled to free himself.

Albee's arms became branches. As Stephan struggled desperately to free himself, he started to turn into the same tree looking fey, as Albee. Within seconds they were both trees, grounded there in the middle of the room. Suddenly Albee turned back into his fey self and letting go of Stephan, fell to the ground. Stephan was a tree, unmoving.

The purple wisp, Tilly and the dark grey wisp, the fey from Pineville, came rushing in with other grey spirits and circled the bug creatures, causing confusion and fear until they turned into grey wisps and scattered into the walls, leaving us alone with only Stephan, frozen in a tree.

I could see Stephan's eyes, peering out at us filled with hatred, as Brett sauntered up to him casually, with a triumphant grin and took the sword from his hand, or I should say, branch. Brett had to break the branch to get it, and did so with pleasure.

Stephan howled with pain. Sap oozed from the end of the broken branch, and I knew that, if in fey form, it would have been blood.

I went to Albee, fearing that he was dead but as I bent down to check on him, he opened his eyes and smiled meekly and said, "Well now, that wasn't as hard as I thought it would be. I wasn't sure how much of me was still left in him but it seems he wasn't done with me yet. He believed that one day he would use me again. What a fool he is."

I stood up and Brett came over to help Albee up, since he was a bit woozy. Suddenly, Tilly was standing there in her fey body, a bit transparent, but I could see her and standing beside her was the tree fey from Pineville.

I went up to him and thanked him for his help and asked him his name. He responded with shame, "I am not that fey anymore and have no name to be called. I am honored to have been able to help you, but your task is not finished yet."

As this fey looked at Tilly then, she continued, "The Dark One, you call him Mephisto is waiting for you Princess Emilee. We will come with you. I have one last task to do before I go to Nirvana, and Ian, has one more task too." She said as she pointed to the tree fey spirit.

Tilly continued, "You need something from Brett before we proceed. Shinar told me what it was. He, Mephisto shared it with her as he tried to turn her against you. I spent time with her earlier, before you rescued her. I comforted her for some time on and off, trying to keep her strong as she waited for you. You know what you need."

I looked towards Liam, and I knew that he was aware of my needs too, because I felt it within him, when we were joined.

"You took from another too, didn't you?" I asked. "Your sadness, it is because you took it all, didn't you?"

I saw in Liam's eyes a deep loss and my heart ached. The room started to shake, like an earthquake, the ground moving underneath us. Then I heard a laugh, and I knew that only I could hear him. He was waiting for me.

Brett came over to me, and taking my hands in his and looking at me with love and acceptance in his eyes, said, "Emilee, take what you need from me. I am not going anywhere, I will be with you to the end. If you need the sword take it, if you need my..." And he stopped in mid-sentence, for he knew what I needed.

Brett bent down and placed a soft kiss on my lips. Feeling his lips pressed against mine, I felt the urge, so strong, the need so alive and I wanted nothing more than to taste his blood. Our lips pressed harder as he wrapped his arms around my waist, pulling me to him.

When our lips parted but our faces still close, Brett whispered, "It's okay, Emilee, I have known this was what you needed for some time. Take as much as you need."

Tears were streaking my cheeks and Brett slipped in one more sweet kiss before turning his head to the side slightly to show his neck, where a large vessel pumped his blood.

I felt the strange sensation again, and looking down at my arms, they were white again, giving me the strength to do what I must. I could see through his skin, Brett's blood rushing through the blood vessel, and placing my mouth over it, I bit down slowly and gently.

The taste was intoxicating. It filled me with a desire I had never felt. I wanted more of Brett, not just his blood, and as far as I was concerned it was only he and I in the room. If I drained him, I would never have the rest of him, and I wanted him so desperately and I knew he wanted me.

I had the willpower, thanks to the creature's venom from the deep, somehow to stop myself. I removed my fangs from his neck as he slid down to the floor. I moved with him, holding him, so he didn't hurt himself, as my normal color returned. Liam came over to assist.

"Emilee, you need it all, to fully become who you must be, to win. There is no other way." Liam said.

I looked at Liam as I placed my hand on Brett's neck to stop the bleeding, and said, "No, I won't drain him, I won't kill him. I love him and we will be together one day. I will do what I must, but I won't end Brett's life."

A voice from the corner came then, Lily, "Kimberlite or Liam, or whoever you are, leave her alone. Emilee must chose her path, who she will save and who she will fight. Varda is very anxious to meet you, so Emilee, can we please get this over with, one way or the other."

Lily knelt down next to me, and moving my hand from Brett's neck and placing hers in its place, kissed me on the cheek and said, "It's time Princess. He waits for you." As she pointed over at the wall to our left.

I looked down at Brett. His eyes were closed, but he was breathing and I bit down on my wrist and started to place it on Brett's lips, as Liam protested.

"Emilee, you mustn't do that. This isn't the way." Liam spouted.

"Let her be!" Lily shouted.

Lily laid Brett down, and opened his mouth just enough for me to place my wrist between his lips. It didn't take long for me to feel Brett start to suck, not much, but enough to start the healing process, for his body to produce his own blood fast enough to heal him. I knew I hadn't taken enough of his blood to kill him but, he was extremely weak and I needed him strong, when we were ready to leave this place.

"Go now Princess, fight your demons, I will look after this irritating fey for you." Lily said with a frown, but then winked at me and gave me a slight shove.

I kissed her on the cheek and of course she winced and brushed off her cheek, as if I had put something unpleasant there.

I stood and walked over to the wall where Tilly and Ian waited patiently. I looked to Liam and said with a bit of impatience in my voice, "Well, I think I need Kimberlite to pave my way through this rock, maybe?"

Liam, looking quite upset still after I seemed to have broken some rule, by not draining Brett dry, turned into Kimberlite, which I preferred, and walked up to me. He put his hand on the wall and an opening appeared.

Tilly and Ian entered the opening and I turned to look at Albee, Lily, Brett and Kimberlite. I said before I entered the opening, "I prefer this look, Kimberlite, please just stay this way until we are done with this."

I turned and walked through the opening and when I did, the ground began to shake and the walls started to crumble as the opening disintegrated, separating us from the rest.

I found myself standing in a lavish entry, with a stairway going up to a balcony, both of which looked like they were made of gold. The entry was a large circular room, lined with cells, and behind the bars of the cells were fey and humans and other creatures. They were reaching out to me, moaning, crying, weeping and the agony and hopelessness on their faces caused such sadness inside of me. They may have done horrible things, but was it right to make them spend an eternity suffering so?

Tina M. Engel

Tilly and Ian seemed to glide up the stairway and I followed, wanting to get away from the unbearable sight that surrounded me.

I reached the top of the stairway, and followed Tilly and Ian to the left, as it circled halfway around the room below. There was yet another door, snow white, and as I approached it, I realized that it was made of bones that looked as though bleached by the sun, but I assumed they were bleached white by the heat of Hades itself. It was opened slightly.

I heard a voice say from behind the door, "Come in, stop wasting my time. It seems like an eternity that I have been waiting." And someone chuckled.

I pushed the door open, and standing as tall as I could and opening my wings out as far as they would spread, I walked into the room as Tilly and Ian followed.

There, standing by a cell was the same creature I had seen in my dream. He was hideous in looks and larger than I remembered. Behind the bars of the cell was Shinar. I gasped at the sight, horror and fear took hold of me, but I knew that if I didn't get myself together, all would be lost. I didn't see Rose and wondered where she was.

"My beautiful granddaughter." Mephisto said, "I have been looking forward to this day for so long, it seems."

I heard a piercing scream from the other side of the room, and looking over, there was a female fey, chained to the wall and one of the creatures was stabbing its claws into her skin.

Tina M. Engel

She looked up at me in horror and I saw that it was Queen Anahita. Then I remembered that she had a twin and supposedly had taken care of her, as she had said to Poseidon. I knew this was not Queen Anahita, but her twin sister. Queen Anahita had ended her life, sending her to this place.

When the creature pulled out its claw, the green ooze ran out of the wound, thick like molasses, and it stabbed her again. Suddenly, she let out another long horrendous shriek and turned into one of those bug-like creatures. The chains released her and the shrieking was only the sound that the bug-like creatures made.

I looked back at Mephisto, and there standing where he had been was a fey, tall and muscular, with no hair on his head. Completely bald but extremely handsome. What I found odd though, was that he looked human, no pointed ears or slanted eyes. He was human. I was shocked and knew that I had to pull myself together or I would fail, we would all be doomed.

"You look surprised, Emilee. Did my dear sweet Varda not tell you what I really was?" Mephisto asked with glee in his voice.

I just stood there, not knowing what to say, but as Shinar turned her body sideways, I got a glimpse of Rose, there on her side and then she vanished.

"How?" Was all that I managed to get out of my mouth, when suddenly Shinar opened her mouth and spewed fire in my direction. I felt heat, and then my shield was back, I had it and put it up around myself.

Tina M. Engel

Mephisto let out a chuckle, and holding a staff in his hand, pointed it at Shinar, who let out a painful cry and shrank back away from the bars.

"Stop!" I yelled and I felt my body tremble as it heated. I turned a flaming red and my shield pushed out from around me, pushing Mephisto away from the bars as my shield encircled Shinar in the prison cell.

Mephisto looked at me with some shock and amusement as he walked towards me, entering my shield. I let out a gasp as he laughed, walking towards me.

My mind was racing, I had no idea what to do. I felt my body change from lava red to silvery white, and my wings suddenly came around in front of me, whipping so hard that Mephisto was knocked to the ground and his staff went flying.

I adjusted my shield, pushing Mephisto out as he tried to stand, but keeping his staff in my shield. When I picked it up, I felt such power. I felt it combine with my powers, strengthen them, and I felt invincible. I had the feeling of greatness, I could do anything and no one could stop me. I could rule it all.

When I realized what was going on in my mind, I shuddered at the thoughts that I was having.

Mephisto brushed himself off, and said with a chuckle and tone of pride, "Yes, Emilee, it will belong to you one day, when I feel you are ready. Give it back now though, you are not strong enough to handle it, although I am a bit surprised at your strength. Varda has done well with the gifts that she has made sure you received. All in vain though, for her and the rest of this pitiful planet."

Mephisto turned and looked at Shinar then, walked over towards the cell but stopped abruptly, and I knew he ran into the shield. He took something out of his robe and held it out in front of him and an orb appeared, large enough for him to walk into. A flash of light blinded me for a moment, and when I could see again, Mephisto was standing inside the cell next to Shinar.

"You see dear Granddaughter, I have my ways too, thanks to Varda." Mephisto said.

"But you're human?" I questioned.

"I am what fey call human, but where do you think humans came from? What do the fey legends, or stories tell you, that humans appeared one day, maybe out of the sky during a light rain or from deep beneath the ocean bottom?" Mephisto laughed as if this was silly.

"Humans came from the sky, Emilee, from a galaxy far away, my galaxy, the sixth heaven. Varda was here, watching over her galaxy when humans were sent here to populate a dimension that would help this ball of dirt survive. I came here to assist her with the job of getting the young humans settled, I guess you could say. Humans where I come from are far more advanced, though.

"We put the newborn humans here, to learn and grow on their own. This was, I guess you could say an experiment. A new dimension was created and the hope was that someday, the fey from Terrafirma and the Atlantians from the water world, along with the humans from my realm, would be able to combine and live in harmony.

Then, open more doorways to other dimensions and places in Terrafirma and other galaxies, other worlds.

"Emilee, you are special, a mixture of an advanced race of humans and of course Varda, who comes from the stars. You have every type of fey blood in you.

The task that they created for you so long ago, is such a menial existence but I realized just what we could do together, rule all of it, every galaxy, every heaven and all life. We would be gods, like him. Oh, yes, I didn't want to share this power, and I tried to end your life before it ever started, but now I know, she was right, you are important to me."

"Stop! I spouted, "Stop talking! You can't convince me that what you want to do is good for anyone or anything. You are evil. Greed and need for power fills your veins. I am not like you and never will be."

Mephisto went to Shinar, and placing his hand on her head, she let out a cry of agony and then her eyes suddenly turned red. Shinar spewed fire in my direction but it only increased my energy, for the lava blood that was within me, accepted the heat.

I saw Rose for a moment, beside Shinar and then Shinar's eyes cleared again, they were her glorious sky blue eyes once more. She turned her head towards Mephisto and pelted him with fire as she reached out and scratched his face and the top of his head with her front claws causing deep gashes to appear.

I focused on the bars of the cell then, while Mephisto was temporarily distracted by the pain that Shinar inflicted, and with just a thought, the bars flew open and Shinar came to me as I slammed the bars shut again.

Mephisto laughed an eerie laugh, as if what I had done was petty and small, but when he reached to retrieve the object that had opened the doorway, which had allowed him to enter the cell in the first place, it was gone.

Rose stepped out from behind Shinar, holding an object, the one Mephisto needed to transport himself to wherever he wanted, I was guessing. This was the gift that Varda had given him years back. The one that he let Stephan use to get Shinar's egg and kidnap Brett. It was a stone, oval in shape, smooth as ice and blood red in color.

Calmly, Mephisto said, "Very good my dear, you are going to make an excellent ruler when I am done training you. Give me back my stone and staff, now. Let's stop playing. You feel the power and you want more. I see it in your eyes."

With a bit of irritation in Mephisto's voice he continued, "Come now, give it back and drop this blasted shield."

I did feel it, he was right about that. The power that surged through my body, the desire to rule and crush any who would stand in my way. It was frightening and exhilarating all at the same time. I wanted to crush him and then go back and crush Stephan, pulverize them after I made them suffer.

Tina M. Engel

It was Rose who came up to me and reaching out, said quietly, "Give me the staff, Princess, you don't want to use it. You are not like he is."

Mephisto howled at Rose, saying, "Shut up you silly little dead pixie! You are nothing to Emilee and can do nothing to stop her. I will see to it that you never leave this place. You will never see Nirvana again."

When I heard Mephisto saying that Rose was dead, I knew that I had been right, but was it my fault? I looked at Rose and seeing her sweet face, and kind smile, I handed her the staff.

It was Tilly and Ian who came to me then. Tilly held out her hand and asked for the stone. She was to take it to Varda at once. She told me that when this was all over, Ian's job was to hide the staff so that no one would ever find it again.

With my head clear now, I asked Tilly why I couldn't just destroy it, but she said it was so powerful that it would destroy this entire planet, and all dimensions that called it home.

Tilly left then as Mephisto screamed her name, as fury filled his face, and demanded that she bring the stone back to him.

I looked towards Mephisto as his hands gripped the bars and the strength that he still had without his staff and stone was incredible. He was bending the bars and there was a strange vibration radiating from his body.

As I put my hands up into the air, I could feel Brett's blood flowing through my veins. I flung my hands in Mephisto's direction, sending an invisible force towards him that pushed him away from the bars. Suddenly chains fell from the ceiling and cinched around his wrists. They pulled his wrists up so he hung slightly from the ceiling.

Mephisto, scoffed then and said in a cold manner, "Princess, you can't destroy me. You didn't drain him like you were supposed to. He was your final gift, his entire essence. You needed that to rid me of my existence. I made sure of that. He was my final gift, and I knew that her blood flowed in you too. You have the emotional weakness that she did then and still does. She should have killed me when she had the chance instead of letting someone else deal with me."

I lashed out at him, sending fire and ice, pounding him, over and over. Mephisto turned back into the bug-like creature and screeched in pain, but I kept it up. I would destroy him. Burn him and freeze him until there was nothing left but ash and ice shards, and I would sprinkle him over many worlds so that he could never come back.

I kept it up for several minutes and when I felt that he was destroyed, I stopped, feeling drained. Rose touched my shoulder and Shinar came over to my other side. I looked from one to the other, their eyes were the same, sky blue, and I knew that they were bonded. Rose would never truly die. We, the three of us, were bonded and I loved them both.

He laughed then, that sick evil chuckle, and as I turned my head to look at him, he was there, the bug-like creature, with not a scratch on him.

"I told you Granddaughter, you have to drain him if you want to destroy me, and you don't have it in you. You will let Varda down and I will

destroy all life in this universe to punish you."
Mephisto scoffed.

He was right, I couldn't destroy him without all of Brett but I couldn't, I wouldn't kill Brett. I wouldn't. Then from the doorway where I had entered earlier, came Brett, Lily, Albee and Liam.

Varda appeared, first as an orb that appeared out of thin air, and then her full presence, tall and beautiful.

"He's right, my dear." Varda said, as she walked over to the cell. Mephisto, changed back into his human form and I saw the sadness in Varda's eyes when he did so.

She came over to me then and said softly, "It is your choice Emilee, no one else can make it for you. You have all the answers inside of you."

I felt the tears welling up inside of me. I looked at Brett, and he at me, and as our eyes met, we were one again in mind, and he said. "Emilee, you must do what is best for all. I will always be with you, never fear, my blood will flow with yours, inside of you."

Brett came over to me then as I looked to Varda with a pleading expression. "Isn't there another way?"

Varda shook her head with such sadness in her eyes that I saw her for the first time, vulnerable. Understanding the pain she must have felt, walking away from the one she once loved sending him deep into Hades.

Brett reached out and took both of my hands in his. He pulled me towards him, and putting his arms round me, pulled me tightly to him, our bodies together. Brett kissed my lips softly, but the passion that I felt caused me to press even tighter, a kiss that I wanted to remember, for I knew deep down inside, that it would be for an eternity that I would hold this memory.

When we broke the kiss, everyone around was silent, looking away, wanting to give us as much privacy as possible.

Mephisto started to spout off and Varda threw her hand in his direction and his mouth suddenly was bound, but the hatred and anger in Mephisto's eyes was apparent.

I looked to Varda and wept, saying, "I can't do this, I just can't."

Brett took me away from the others, to the other side of the room and he kissed me again, soft and sweet and said, "Emilee, I have loved no other, like I love you. You will always be my Princess, even though we will be apart. I will never be far, talk to me when you need, and I will hear you and somehow help. You must do this."

I heard him say in my mind, "Your blood flows in me" and I suddenly felt it, my blood was mixing with his. What did it mean? I didn't know. I figured, that it would make his death painless. He said it again, in his mind for only me to hear and then sat down, pulling me with him.

Brett tilted his head to expose his neck and as I bent down to bite, I said softly, with the taste of salt, from my tears, "I will love you until the end of time."

I pierced his skin, and the second his blood struck my tongue, I knew I couldn't stop. This time I wouldn't. It was like we were making love, how I dreamt of that moment. Wanting him so badly.

We were not there, in the room anymore with the others, but in a place, white, all white, no one around, nothing around, just Brett and I.

It was done then. I was back in the room, Brett in my arms, and the emptiness I felt was agonizing. I laid Brett's head down softly as my tears fell quietly on his face and I placed a soft kiss on his still lips. I wanted so much for him to kiss me back. In my mind, I spoke to him, tried to find his mind, to join, but there was nothing. He was gone. He was gone.

I sat up and placed his hands across his chest and stayed there for several minutes, just looking at him. I wanted to remember every line on his face. I wanted to remember his laugh, his silly comments. I didn't want to forget a thing.

I stood then and turning around, I saw not a dry eye in the bunch, except for Mephisto. His eyes were full of hatred. Then for just a moment, there was something else I saw in them, a little fear.

I went to Varda and she took me in her arms and held me gently. She bent down and whispered in my ear, "You made choices, and the future will unfold as it should. I am proud of you and you will see, it always works out."

I stood then, stepping away from her wondering, how it could possibly work out now. Brett and I were supposed to be together, have a daughter, Katie, and live happily ever after.

I turned to Mephisto and walking over, I told Shinar and Rose to stand with me. I knew I needed them, even though Brett was my last gift. I also realized that I didn't want to destroy Mephisto, I wanted to make him live an eternity alone, totally alone.

I looked back at Varda and she had a look of acceptance. She knew what I was thinking. She knew what I was going to do.

I felt another close by, an evil, even more sinister than Mephisto or Stephan. He was watching, excitement filling him, waiting to see what I was about to do. He wanted me to feel hate, disgust and anger. These were the emotions that he fed on. He wanted me to kill Mephisto and then Stephan, with all the lust of hatred that I felt inside. I wouldn't let him win either. I wouldn't give a part of myself to him.

This vile being who ruled Hades, wanted me too, but he would not have me. I held Rose's hand and placed my hand on Shinar, thought of the opening, the exit from Hades. Behind Mephisto a portal appeared, covering the entire back wall of his cell. On the other side was the opening to the outside, the world above, with the rainbow cover.

I let go of Rose and Shinar, and placing my hands on the bars of the cell, my thoughts were, cold, freeze, and suddenly the bars where like icicles and as I squeezed them, they shattered.

"Go, all of you!" I said, "Take Mephisto and wait for me."

They all did as I asked. It was Varda who took the chains in her hands that bound Mephisto. I knew that Varda would be able to open the cover over the entrance for all to leave, and I would follow. Albee lifting Brett, carried him with gentleness and compassion. When they were all through the portal, I turned and left the room. It was time to deal with Stephan.

I entered the room where Stephan stood. A tree, a sick looking tree, was what I saw. The only thing resembling a human were his eyes, and they held nothing but hate. I could still feel the other presence, watching and waiting. He was hoping that I would kill him, and find pleasure in it. That was what he wanted, my pleasure. I knew that if I killed Stephan, I would not feel pleasure, it would not heal the pain that I held inside of me over the death of Brett. Hate would never heal my pain.

"You want to die, and you are waiting, filled with anger and a bit of relief. But that is not what I will give you, Stephan." I said with contempt and a bit of pity filling my voice.

Stephan's eyes changed from the hate and anger to fear, for he realized what I was going to do.

I spoke then, not to Stephan but to him, the other one watching, "You want me to kill Stephan, to take my rage and anger and violate what I hold dear, within me, my humanity, my belief in good and love. I feel no love for this pathetic fey, only pity, for he chose the path he took and it destroyed any goodness that may have been in him, and I know there was goodness in him at one time.

"I will not kill him and give you a part of my soul, but I will keep him like this, a tree forever, down here in your hell. I will keep a small part of my shield, my essence, wrapped around him so that no evil can kill him. He will live an eternity like this.

"You can torture him, burn him, and do as

you want, but you will never be able to kill him! I don't want him to be a spirit in this hell of yours, I want him to be alive and feel the pain every day."

I put my cameo on Stephan and it sunk into the bark so deeply that the bark covered it. This would keep him here for all eternity.

I heard Stephan cry out then, as if the cameo caused him pain, and I knew it did.

I heard him then, the one watching. He laughed a sinister laugh and said, "Well played my dear. I may not have a piece of you yet, but I will accept your gift of this pathetic creature. I have been waiting a long time to have him, one way or another. I will find a way to free him from your protection and when I do, I will see you again." He laughed again and suddenly a wall appeared in front of me, blocking my view of Stephan.

I turned and walked out of the room, up the stairs and through the portal, and as I did the portal disappeared. The opening to the chapel was waiting for me with Varda standing on the other side. I didn't look back, there was nothing there that I wanted to see. I approached the opening and then felt it, a hand touching me.

I turned to see Ian, the tree fey spirit, still in body form, holding Mephisto's staff. He smiled a genuine smile and turned back into the dark grey wisp. He changed then into a blue wisp, the color that he must have been, once upon a time. The staff was imbedded within him and I knew that he had made amends and now had a job to do, to take the staff and hide it somewhere far away, where no one would find it.

Tina M. Engel

He flew out the opening and up the stairs, and I hoped that he would find peace once more for helping us all.

Chapter 23

They are never really gone,
They are alive in your memories.
Hold them tight.
Bring them with you
As you continue to live.

My thoughts went then to Stephan's father. What of him? He was the one who betrayed Varda in the beginning, by not destroying Mephisto and giving Mephisto back the ruby stone that allowed him to travel through space. Varda had the stone now, but where was Hedrick DeMill?

I left the entrance to Hades, and followed Varda up the stone steps and out of the Chapel into the fresh air, sunshine and warmth. The dark clouds, wind and vile smell were gone. We had completed our mission. Well, almost. Stephan was dealt with, and Mephisto was captured but my job wasn't done yet.

I walked over to Mephisto as Rose and Shinar came up to me. Shinar bent down to allow me to get onto her back and Rose got on behind me. Varda handed me the chains that bound Mephisto's wrists and Shinar lifted us up into the sky.

I didn't need to say anything, for Shinar knew what we were doing and where to go. Rose wrapped her arms around my waist and I could feel her presence, her strength within me. It was the same feeling that I would get while drinking her blood, the same strength, I would receive.

We went high into the sky, beyond the clouds, higher still. The air grew colder the higher we went. I put my shield around us all and holding my diamond in my hand, I felt the lava pebbles, as they warmed the air that surrounded us.

Higher we went, until we were amongst the stars. I knew then, I was out there far enough to do what needed to be done.

Still holding the diamond, I thought of it in a larger form. The diamond was hard, unbreakable, and as I thought of it this way, the lava pebbles assisted, separating a small part of the diamond they reside in. It continued to grow as it moved down towards Mephisto, hanging by the chains around his wrists, below Shinar.

I heard Mephisto shout, "No!" As the diamond encircled him and the chains holding Mephisto were cut, he drifted slowly up to face me.

"You will not die, not today, tomorrow or the next. You will float in space, locked in this shell, alone, all alone, forever. Nothing and no one will be able to free you for you will never come into contact with another, ever again. I have made this prison you are in, invisible to all eyes. You will see those who may pass you, but they will not see you." I said, with no emotions.

"And you think that this is not evil, Granddaughter?" Mephisto spat. "You have my blood flowing though you too."

I ignored what he said, for I knew that somewhere I was being judged and if this was not the right thing to do, I would find out one day.

I shrunk my shield to remove Mephisto from inside. I raised my hand and reaching out through the shield, I touched the diamond prison, slightly, and with a flick of my wrist, I sent Mephisto out into the darkness of space, with only the specks of the starlight to keep him company, and even that, I felt he didn't deserve.

I spread my wings then and shrunk my shield just enough for me to be free of it, keeping Shinar and Rose safely protected from the cold of space, just to be sure. I didn't know if they could survive out here in the quiet, cold darkness.

I watched as Mephisto drifted away and then disappeared. Oh, I could see him, but no one else could. The stars from afar talked to me in whispers, the cold void of space kissed my cheeks softly, and my wings sparkled as the starlight from billions of stars touched them. I was one with it all, and I knew that this was home too. It was all home.

I turned to look at Shinar and Rose, and said softly, "Let's go home girls."

When we reached the ground, Shinar landed gently next to me, as I let my wings fold back where they belonged. The only one there to greet us was Varda. She was standing next to the opening that would take us back to the ship. Rose and Shinar entered as I went up to Varda, and she took me in her arms.

As she released me, I said, "It's done, he is gone forever. And Stephan is exactly where he should be, but what of Stephan's father? Where is he? We should take care of him too. He is the one who went against you, gave Mephisto back the stone that was supposed to be destroyed."

"Emilee, Hedrick DeMill has nothing left. He has lost his master and his son. He has no power and no guidance as to what to do now. He is more lost than they, I believe. Hedrick isn't a danger to anyone but himself. He knows that if he is careless and loses his life, the one ruling Hades is just waiting for him. For now, we can let Hedrick's future be decided later." Varda replied.

I wasn't sure I liked this idea and felt a bit unnerved by the fact that Mephisto was floating out in space and Stephan down in hell, not destroyed, not gone.

"Come, Emilee, the ship and all on board are waiting for us. It's time to go home." Varda said, with compassion.

We entered the opening, and as it swirled and hummed I thought of Brett, realizing that I had killed him. I had taken his life to save others. I stepped through, onto the ship as many looked on.

Angelina and Jordan were the first to greet me with hugs and relief on their faces.

"Brett, where is he?" I whispered as I looked around the deck. Angelina took my hand and led me to the door that led down below.

We got to the room that Rose was in, her physical body anyway, and as we entered, there he was, laying on a bed next to Rose. There they both lay, still, as if sleeping, but I knew the truth. Because of me, they both had to die.

I fell to my knees suddenly, weak and tired. Angelina knelt down next to me and took me in her arms and cradled me like a child. The sadness and emptiness I felt was unbearable. I wondered if this was worse than what Mephisto and Stephan were feeling at this moment.

I felt him then, just a slight presence, like a feather touching my mind softly, but I felt him,

Brett. I let out a soft sigh as I looked up at the bed he was laying on. Angelina helped me to stand and I told her that I was fine and wanted to be alone for a while with them both.

Angelina left and as I turned back to the tables, there stood Rose, next to her physical body. I went to her and we held each other. I could feel her, touch her, she looked and felt alive but there on the table next to us, was Rose, her body.

"Princess, don't despair, I am not gone. I will never be gone.", and she lay down on top of her body on the table. She opened her eyes then, and reached out and took my hand.

"Shinar, keep her close. We are with you always." And Rose closed her eyes.

I don't know why but I suddenly needed to give Rose my blood. Something inside told me to, just like with Brett. I felt him then, just slightly, I couldn't get to him, but he was there just under my consciousness.

I bit down on my finger and opening Rose's mouth just a bit, squeezed a small drop of blood on her tongue and closed her lips again.

I understood the role that she had to play. Rose was a part of what I needed to become whole, the fey that I was now. She also had to physically die in order to help the fey who lost their lives in battle, to go on, leaving their bodies to journey to Nirvana. Her role was vital and the sacrifice great.

I went to Brett then and placed a kiss on his lips and whispered, "You are there somewhere, I feel you still, different, but I feel you. You will always be with me. I don't know how I will go on, but I know I must. I wanted you beside me, and I still need you." I bent down then, laying my head on his chest, wishing desperately for a heartbeat, no matter how slight, but there was nothing. I sobbed quietly for some time until I felt a hand on my back.

I sat up and turning, there stood Lily. The sadness in her eyes showed the love that she had for them both. Lily still had the mark on her cheek, which she received down below in Hades, but it was a scar now. She was still so beautiful, inside and out.

"Come Princess, Varda wants you. We are going home." Lily said as she took my hand and led me out the door and up onto the deck.

As we reached the deck, I saw that we were docked to the pier where we had first got onto the ship, when I first met my mother, Angelina. It was time for everyone to go home.

The skies were blue, the breeze was calm, and the evil was gone, for now. The trolls came to me first, taking my hand and doing the traditional fey parting and I knelt down, hugging them all, one by one.

Tobias came to me then, as several of the trolls carried Tilly's body down the ramp and onto the docks. I knew her body was an empty vessel, but her essence still lived on. They would lay her body to rest in their home land but her spirit, her beautiful purple spirit, was free and at peace in Nirvana.

"Princess Emilee, it has been a great honor to serve you and help you to save our home, our planet and others. Our home is always your home, please remember that." Tobias said.

I let him take my hand and do his fey good bye, but I then took him in my arms and we held each other for several minutes. I didn't want to let him go. Tobias had done so much for me through this journey. He and his clan risked everything and many died doing so. He pulled away gently and with a smile filled with love and pride he turned and disappeared down the plank to the others.

The wolf pack did the same, with their fey farewell and when Weylyn came to me he said, "Princess, you have helped us all see a different way of living. We thought of the humans as a bother, not necessary for our existence, but we were wrong.

"We may not be able to interact yet with the humans, but I look forward to the day when I can make a difference, and help bring the two dimensions together.

"I will admit, we liked to push the limits, so to speak, and enter the humans' realm and cause a little mischief, but we will behave now. I promise."

I watched the trolls dig holes in the sand and disappear, leaving no trace. The wolves turned into their dog forms, let out howls that could curdle a human's blood, and disappear up over the sandy hill.

Albee was the next to approach me. He knelt down and took my hand and placed his forehead in my palm. He stood then and I did the same and we embraced. Albee and I had an interesting journey, just the two of us. It started with his tree. I thought it was he who tried to kidnap me, but of course it was really Stephan. And now here we

were. He was here to help me, and give his life, if
need be.

"Princess, when you reach your home, plant
the seed. A part of me will be there to help and
protect you, and I will be able to come if you need
me. Just call." Albee said.

He left the ship, and walked over to a tree
not far from the docks. It opened up as another
tree fey greeted him, and as he entered the tree, he
looked back, waved, and it closed.

I turned to see Jordan and Angelina, my
mother and father, together holding hands as they
watched their new friends leaving too. They were
together, finally, after being apart for so long,
thinking that the other was dead.

Jordan, was punished for something he had
never done. Such suffering he endured thinking
he had killed Angelina, an elder, all to play this
game, as they waited for me to come and hopefully
stop the destruction of humans' earth and
Terrafirma, as well as others out there that I have
yet to meet.

Angelina, lived a lie, being the wife of a fey,
Proteus, whom she loathed, just to keep me safe,
not knowing that the love of her life, my father, was
alive. They both endured such pain, but now
together, they could have a life.

And what of Proteus? Where was he, and
what was he up to now? I wondered.

Angelina and Jordan looked at me with
smiles of love and admiration, but I admired them
so much more, for the sacrifices that they suffered,
for me. They came over to me, each hugged me and

Tina M. Engel

let me know that they would be down below with Varda.

Captain Adam Banks was barking orders to the deck hands, getting the ship situated for a long stay, for Adam was saying something about his ship in the human realm, needing to be ready to set sail soon. He looked over at me and winked as he headed back up to the control room.

I hadn't seen Douglas since I had boarded the ship and assumed he was with Varda, I knew that the two of them had a special relationship, they loved each other, but how far could that relationship go, with Varda being, well, whatever she was? Could she trust and truly love and give herself to another? Her responsibility was so great, could love ever not get in the way, and cloud her judgment?

Suddenly, an eagle came flying overhead, and as it landed on deck, Eagle transformed.

"You didn't survive the battle with the goblins, did you? I asked.

Eagle went over and sat on the edge of the railing and shaking his head, replied, "My physical body was poisoned, and they took one of my hearts. There was nothing that could be done for me, but Varda needed me still, as did you and Brett, so she gave me the ability to stay in physical form temporarily.

"I was her eyes, when she needed me. I could see things at times that she couldn't, when she was spread too thin with you, Rose and Lily.

"After my physical body died, Varda took me someplace, a place known only to her and the others, Poseidon, Zeus, and Ares, and other special beings who watch over this ball of dirt that so many realms call home.

"That is where I took her, Varda, just past the sun, when she needed to stop Poseidon from interfering any farther, when he had the water beast inject you with his venom, speeding up your development and increasing your strength.

"Your wings, by the way, Princess, are beautiful and I enjoyed flying with you." And Eagle smiled a melancholy smile.

"You have to go now, don't you?" I asked sadly.

"Yes, it's time, but just know that when you take flight, I will be with you. I will always be watching over you."

"Brett?" I said, "Will you be with Brett?"

Eagle smiled and answered, "We will all be with you, never fear."

Eagle came over to me and hugged me, extended his wings and wrapped them around us in a cocoon, then released me, turning into a bird and as he flew away, he disappeared.

Lily was standing at the edge of the ship, staring out at the hustle and bustle of the fey down below, doing what they do in their everyday lives. She turned to me with sorrow in her eyes, turned into her cat form, came over to me and jumped into my arms. She stretched up, wrapping her front legs on each side on my neck, and nuzzled her wet nose against my neck and started to purr. She was tired and weary. This was what she needed at that moment.

I carried Lily down the steps to the dining area, and found Varda, Angelina, Jordan, Douglas and Liam, as Trevor poured what I assumed was coffee or some kind of steaming brew. It smelled like coffee and I had a warm sensation come over me, like a little bit of normalcy. Hot coffee, a simple drink, but normal.

Trevor came to me and handed me a mug as I put Lily down. Trevor wrapped his hands around mine as I held the mug. Trevor said nothing, just smiled and kept his hands there for a moment or two and then went into the kitchen area.

I looked at Liam and said, not meaning to be rude, but it did come out that way, "I prefer Kimberlite." As a tear escaped down my cheek.

He was suddenly Kimberlite with that teddy bear look that he would give me, and he came over and wrapped me in his arms. I sobbed quietly, and then spilling my coffee, we both stepped away as I apologized and hoped that I hadn't burned him. Of course you can't burn a rock and we both started laughing and the more I heard Kimberlite's laugh, the more I laughed and cried, loving his laughter although knowing that he really wasn't real.

"Princess, I have been this rock for so many centuries that I kind of miss it too. Talking with Varda, we both think it might be a good idea if I stay this way for a while and stick around, just in case." Liam said.

I felt the lava pebbles deep inside the diamond around my neck, vibrate, and I knew that they were happy too. Kimberlite had a family down below, who didn't know what his true identity was, and they didn't need to. He was Kimberlite to them and that was all he needed to be.

Tina M. Engel

I saw Shinar then, over in a corner, curled up and sleeping. She had been through so much. Her life since she had hatched had been horrendous, enduring torture, as Mephisto tried desperately to turn her against me and towards his evil ways.

I went to her and knelt down, placed a hand on her head gently. She didn't open her eyes, she didn't need to, for I could feel her emotions, hear her thoughts. We were one, different from Brett and I, for Shinar and I were one, joined and strangely, I felt Rose too.

I looked to Varda then and asked, as I stood and walked over to her, "What of Queen Anahita. She hasn't been around since we were in the city of Bermuda. Does she know that Brett is gone, that I killed him?" I asked, with a bit of irritation in my voice for even having to ask about her.

"She is home, in one of her underwater springs. She did her duty by Poseidon, as she was instructed to do. She will stay with her fey, for now. We all have our next tasks, to get ready to join the humans and fey, slowly. There is no time for bitterness or regrets. Anahita and Brett were never meant to be, and they knew it, she knew it, and did what she had to and will continue to do what she has to, for the good of her fey." Varda replied.

"Queen Widow and her little ones? Tiny?" I said with sadness.

"They are back in her forest, doing what spiders do. They seem to like to enter the humans' realm and scare them. What can I say?" Varda laughed.

Tina M. Engel

"What now?" I asked wearily, "Where do I go from here?"

"Home." Varda replied. "You go home."

"But, don't I have to figure out how to bring fey and humans together?" I asked, feeling confused and tired.

Varda stood and came over to me. "You have done what you needed to do, for now. Mephisto cannot harm the humans' earth or Terrafirma anymore. Stephan is no longer a danger either, and the grey spirits will still annoy the humans on earth and even in Terrafirma, but for now, we will let them be.

"Remember, there must be balance. You can't have good without evil, happy without sad, safety without fear, love without... Well you get the picture. We must have balance, for without it, we wouldn't truly understand the good and appreciate it.

"You still have work to do but for now, it's time to go home. You are needed there, but you won't be alone, I promise."

"Home, where is home?" I asked.

Before Varda answered, Angelina and Jordan came over to me. Angelina took my hands in hers and said, "We are going home now, too. We have a job to do, keeping the peace here in Terrafirma. The water fey and land fey still fight with each other and that does give the grey wisps more energy to become unruly. Now that we are together, we can, and will be a force to reckon with, if need be."

"Your home, where?" I asked.

I saw it then, as Varda put her hands on top of ours.

I was there in the wheat field, the tree in front of me with the stone castle in the distance. It was beautiful, sparkling in the sunlight. The tree was standing tall and strong, the leaves so green and the trunk had an opening, I had not seen before. I didn't feel worried though, for I knew that I would see what was inside one day.

I turned and with the breeze in my face, could smell the sea water, and I heard the waves as they crashed against the stone wall. The wheat was tall and golden, and up in the sky was the red dragon. He wasn't ferocious as before, he was beautiful, and then several more dragons joined him as they soared through the air.

I could see the pond then, midway down the steep cliff, where the waterfall entered the small pond, where I had seen Brett disappear, back in one of my visions. Was he there waiting for me? I wondered.

I was back in the room, on the ship, my hands still in Angelina's.

"Where is this place, it is your home and mine? Is Brett there too, waiting for me? Is he alive somehow?" I asked in a hurried manner.

Angelina looked to Varda, and Varda replied, "It is home to many and you will be there one day, when it is time. Angelina and Jordan will be there and will watch over Terrafirma and earth from there, for now. The future is open wide, Emilee. But you must rest now. It's time to sleep and go home."

I didn't understand what she was talking about. Angelina wrapped me in her arms and kissed my cheek and reassured me that we would be together one day, as did Jordan. I didn't want to let them go. It felt like I had just found them, they were my parents, well my fey parents, but I had human parents too and I missed them terribly.

Angelina and Jordan left the room as Varda took my hand and led me out the door and Shinar, awake now, followed. We went down the hallway and entered my room.

"It's time to sleep now Emilee." Varda said, as she walked me to the bed, and I laid down. Shinar came over, and laying down on the floor beside me, she rested her head on my shoulder. Lily jumped up on the bed and curled up next to me, purring softly in my ear.

I started to speak, to ask, why I had to sleep if I was to go home, wherever that was, but Varda waved her hand over me and I suddenly felt sleepy. I couldn't keep my eyes open and then, darkness.

Chapter 24

Home,
Family!
Reality
Or
Dream?

"Brett!" I yelled as I sat up in bed. Looking around, I was in a hospital room, with a hospital gown on. I had an IV in my arm and a small oxygen tube just under my nose. I removed the oxygen tube as the door opened and in came a nurse, a human nurse.

Looking around, seeing the dull drab room, I realized I was back in the humans' realm. The door opened again as the nurse started to fuss over me, trying to put the oxygen back under my nose as I protested. It was my parents, Katie and Willy.

"Emilee" my mom said as she came to my side. "You're awake, oh my god, you're awake."

"Young lady, put this back under your nose this instant." The nurse, insisted.

I pushed her hand away, feeling confused and angry as my father, Willy grumbled, "Leave her alone, will you. She's awake and doesn't want that blasted tube in her nose."

I stopped fussing as I looked at my dad, his gruffness was so familiar and I started to cry. I was back home. Home?

"Where am I?" I pleaded as I looked at my mom. "What happened? Why am I back here?"

Tina M. Engel

"It's alright Emilee, you're alright now, you're awake." My mom said, as she bent down and hugged me, a bit too tight.

"We were so worried" she continued, as she let me go and sat down on the bed, next to me.

"Do you remember anything?" my mom asked, with a strange twinkle in her eyes.

I looked around the room again. There were flowers, sunflowers in vases situated around the room, music playing softly, my favorite; country, and cards, open and standing up on the windowsill and a table that was next to my bed.

Looking outside, it looked like spring. The flowering trees were in full bloom; beautiful, and some trees with leaves not quite mature. But somehow, they were not as beautiful as in Terrafirma.

"Remember what? And why am I in the hospital?" I asked, not wanting to say too much, remembering that she had known who I really was, supposedly.

"Emilee" my dad started, "you were in an accident several months ago. There was an explosion, your house was on fire, pieces of debris everywhere. We couldn't find you around the house and the firemen couldn't get into the house to look for you. We thought we had lost you."

He took a breath as a tear rolled down his cheek and he wiped it off quickly before continuing. "We heard chaos and great commotion in the forest behind your house and went to investigate.

"You were there, unconscious, bruised and scraped up, but other than that you were fine. We were not sure why you were in the forest, some

Tina M. Engel

wondered if you were blown from the house all the way out there, but we don't really know. They didn't know why you wouldn't wake up.

"Your scrapes and bruises healed but you wouldn't wake up. You've been here in this blasted nursing home, not a hospital, ever since. They didn't know what else to do for you."

"Do you remember anything?" my mom asked again.

I couldn't very well tell them that I hadn't been here, but was in Terrafirma, a fey realm attached to earth, and that I was really a fey princess, out to save our world and many others. They would lock me up.

But my mom, does she know? I wondered.

I shook my head, still trying to grasp what was happening. "Take this out of my arm please." I begged as I lifted the arm with the IV in it.

The nurse looked worried as my dad grumbled again, "Do it! She is awake now."

"We should get the doctor first." The nurse said timidly. I gathered my dad made her nervous. He gave her a stern look and she removed the IV.

I got up as my mom helped me, saying, "I don't think you should be getting up, you're weak." But I continued to rise and she assisted then.

When I stood, the room started to spin just a bit, and I heard my grandmother, Varda say, "Take it slow, child, you have plenty of time to adjust."

I gasped as I heard her, and hoped that when the room stopped spinning, I would be back in Terrafirma with Varda.

I was still in the room, in the nursing home, with my human mom and dad. I took small steps, heading over to a mirror. I wanted to see what I looked like. I was after all a middle aged woman, when I left here and an 18 year old fey when I left Terrafirma.

When I got to the mirror, I was shocked at what I saw. It was me, human Emilee, but I looked younger, much younger. My hair was long and wavy, not a grey hair in sight and my face appeared smoother, less wrinkles, of course I didn't have many before anyway, but I was younger.

My mom said, with a bit of concern in her voice, "When we found you and they cleaned you up, you seemed to have, well how do I say it, you looked younger. The doctors think that the trauma you experienced, either in the house before the explosion, or out in the forest, changed you somehow.

"Usually it will age a person, causing hair to turn completely grey, but with you, it did the opposite. They ran every test they could think to run. You were healthy, and if they were to guess your age, if not knowing, they would have guessed late twenties."

"What happened?" I asked again.

"They said it was a natural gas explosion under your house. Funny though, it also ignited the tree out front and all that is left of it is a burnt stump." My dad said, with a concerned and baffled expression on his face.

He continued, "And how you got all the way out in the forest, we still don't quite understand."

I touched my cheeks, strange, just skin, and my ears, no earrings on them. I was Emilee, fey Emilee but as a human, different than before but they, my parents didn't see me differently, only younger.

My mom, standing behind me smiled, gathered my hair in her hands and bringing it back to lay down my back, kissed me on the cheek and said, "Everything is fine, you are right where you need to be."

Suddenly the door opened and in came a man in a doctor's coat. "Well now Emilee, it looks like you came back to us. You had us all convinced that you were out there, somewhere else, living a totally different life." He said as he laughed. "Come now, back to bed so I can take a look at you, and everyone, out until I'm done."

Dad started to object but I assured him that it was okay so that there wouldn't be any confrontation. I wanted this checkup over with and to go home. But where was home? It sounded like my home was gone, destroyed, as well as the tree. The tree that started it all.

Mom and dad left, but not until mom gave me a tight hug, again, and dad just brushed my cheek with his hand and smiled, saying, "We've missed that sweet smile." And I gave him a grin.

The doctor checked me out, listened to my heart, and that gave me a bit of a scare, but he didn't seem to hear anything other than what a human's heart would sound like. He asked me questions about what I remembered last and I couldn't tell him the truth, so I racked my brain, trying to remember what life was like before the craziness started.

I told him that it was the beginning of spring, and there was a storm coming and customers were stocking up with groceries and necessities, as did I. I told him about my visit with my mom and dad, having lunch, napping, playing scrabble and dinner, before I went home. Of course then the fun began.

"When did my house explode, when did this happen?" I asked.

The doctor didn't answer right away, as he got up and went over to the window. "That is the last thing you remember, Emilee?" And he paused, waiting for me to answer. I assumed he was waiting for me to continue, but I had nothing else to say.

"It happened mid-fall. You have no memories at all after your visit with your parents last spring?" The doctor asked, trying to act calm, but I could see he was concerned.

I shook my head, knowing that it wasn't me, here after my visit with my parents, but the other Emilee, and she had the memories, not me. But then, I was here now, not her. Where was she, or am I her and just had a very strange and bad dream, or nightmare, more like it? But it wasn't all bad. Brett, I loved him, he was real, they all were.

The doctor came over to me then and patted me on the head as if I were a child, and said calmly, "No worries Emilee, short term amnesia can be common during times of trauma. I'm sure you will remember more, as the days go on."

The doctor let my parents back into the room and was happy to inform my parents as well as me, that I seemed fine. He wasn't going to worry about my short term memory loss and tried to be optimistic, for my parents' sake.

Tina M. Engel

He wanted me to stay in the nursing home for a few more days, while my body got used to solid food again, since I had been on a liquid diet for so long. He also wanted to run a few tests just to make sure that my body was taking in the nutrients properly, so he said.

I started to fuss, but it did no good, for everyone was in agreement. Mom let me know that my room upstairs was ready for me and we had so much catching up to do.

We had a new neighbor across the street who had been doing some house repairs for them, since dad was getting too old to do some of the more strenuous work. They had taken in a boarder, also, to help with bills. Mom was excited for me to meet her, she felt that we would get along well.

When I was alone, I got back up and went back to the mirror. Looking at myself, I was still shocked. How could I be human again but look like I did in the fey's realm and no one seems to notice? And the human Emilee, were we one and the same? Two different Emilees, one in each Realm, but were we really just one?

The food I must admit, was not real tasty but I ate, even though I had not much of an appetite for this human food. It was tasteless and drab. I roamed the halls when I could, wanting to regain my strength. It was an odd feeling, being weak when I had been so strong.

I spent time with the elderly patients and it seemed that my touch, did something for them and they for me, for with every visit, every physical touch, my strength seemed to increase, as did the light in their eyes, brighten.

I longed for the nights, however, for that was when I could see him, Brett. He was there, just out of reach, but there. Sometimes even during the days, if I shut my eyes, and was very still, I could feel him. Silly I know, but I believed that I could.

They kept me there, in that blasted, (as my dad would say), nursing home for a week until finally the day came, that the doctor released me. I was excited but also frightened. I would be going back to my childhood home, next door to my home that didn't exist anymore. I would sleep in the bed that I slept in as a child and look out the window at what was left of the tree, just a charred stick.

I wondered, more often as days went by, could it have all been just a dream? Was I not special, at all? I was different though, than before this all began, before I met Brett and he took me on an incredible journey, an adventure that tested me beyond my wildest imagination. I was not just different in looks, but in the way I viewed the world, every speck of dirt, every living creature, was a truly amazing miracle.

Tina M. Engel

Chapter 25

Friends from the past,
They are never far away,
Always close, tucked safely
In your memories.

We pulled up to my parents' house and I could see where my house had once stood, was now an empty lot. They had removed what had been left standing, just the fireplace chimney still stood, and a concrete slab that was once a floor, and the partial basement, which I assumed was there, even though I couldn't see it.

I relived for a moment, the terror I had experienced in that space, not just the beginning of my adventure with Brett, but my life with Stephan, for it had all been a lie and I viewed it differently now. It was my mom who brought me back, asking if I was alright.

"Yes", I said, "just tired all of a sudden." As I tried to smile and act like I was okay even though I didn't feel it at that moment.

As I got out of the car, on the side next to the sidewalk, I heard someone call from across the street, "Hello, Katie and Willy."

My mom helped me out, and looking up, responded, "Hi" as she waved.

I turned to see who she was waving to and as I did, the sight I saw nearly knocked me off my feet.

"Brett" I whispered, and had to hold onto the car, because I thought I was going to fall. The world seemed to be spinning.

Tina M. Engel

My mom grabbed hold of me and said, "Emilee, are you alright? What did you say, dear?" As I pulled myself together.

I looked down at the ground. It was solid and I was awake, just tired, I decided. A shadow appeared at my feet then, and I looked up as my mom introduced the neighbor from across the street. She said, "Emilee, this is Brett. He lives in the house over there." As she pointed.

It was Brett, my Brett, only in human form. I couldn't talk, I just stared. It seemed like an eternity that we just stared at each other.

My mom finally said, with worry in her voice, "Emilee, honey, are you okay?

I looked at my mom, smiled and then looked back at Brett. It couldn't be him, I was just hallucinating, but no, it looked like Brett.

"Brett?" I said, more in question than statement.

Brett reached out his hand and I put mine in his as he said, "Emilee, it's so nice to finally meet you. I have heard so much about you over the last few weeks, since I moved in. Your parents are great, helping me to feel welcome. I know how happy they are to have you home."

As he was saying this, and I had to really focus to understand what he was saying, I felt it, very slight, a vibration, an electrical current attaching us together. He felt it too, I was sure, for he looked from our hands to my face several times as he spoke.

"Home?" I said, with more a questioning tone than a statement.

Tina M. Engel

"Brett?" I said again, and he just smiled, that same silly grin that I so loved, as he took his hand from mine. The feeling ended, but the look of curiosity on Brett's face remained.

"Brett" my mom said, "I think we need to get her into the house. How about you come over for dinner tonight? At least let us feed you in payment for your hard work, over at Emilee's house."

"I'd love that Mrs. Stevens. After the last meal you fed me, I look forward to another wonderful meal, and getting to know Emilee better." Brett said, as he smiled at me and continued, "It was nice meeting you Emilee and I look forward to tonight."

I still didn't quite know what to say so I just smiled as mom led me towards the house and dad got out my bags.

The door suddenly flew open and out ran a young woman, who bounded down the steps, to stand in front of me.

"Rose!" I exclaimed.

Everyone looked at me then and my mom asked, "Do you know each other?"

Rose looked at me funny and shook her head side to side. I immediately said, "No, but you told me about her and called her Rose. That is her name, isn't it?" Even though they had never told me her name.

Rose smiled that same wonderful sweet smile as she said, "Yes." And gave me a hug, and said with humor in her voice, "I'm so glad you're home. I need someone young around so maybe your parents will stop fussing over me so much."

Tina M. Engel

My head was spinning, my heart was racing and suddenly there was movement on the porch, a black cat, with a patch of white over one eye, came out from under a chair.

"Lily?" was all I said, before it all went black.

I woke, but I kept my eyes closed for some time, just lying there, wherever I was. I could feel the soft, warm sheets, several blankets on top, and smelling the air, I knew it was my old room. I was sure, but still wondered, had I seen what I thought I saw? Were Brett, Rose and Lily, here in the human's world but looking very much human? Well, Lily a cat, a real cat?

I opened my eyes slowly, and yes, I was in my room, in my old bed, under the covers and the warmth of the bed and aroma in the air, was truly amazing. I tucked the blanket up tighter under my chin and took a deep, long breath. The scent of an old house, my childhood home was welcoming and ordinary. Nothing strange was here as I looked around, no odd sounds.

Maybe I had just been seeing things. Maybe the man across the street isn't Brett at all, and the girl staying here isn't Rose, and my dad hates cats, it must be a neighbor's.

Suddenly something pounced on the foot of the bed and I felt, whatever it was, creeping up towards me. I sucked in a large breath, told myself to stop being a chicken, after all, look at what I had just endured for months, and I lifted my head to see what was there to greet me or hurt me.

"Lily." I whispered, as I sat up, and she crawled into my lap.

Tina M. Engel

I sat frozen at first, not believing what I was seeing, but then I reached out slowly and patted her head. She started to purr and rub her face against my stomach for a minute or two and then, having had enough, she meandered down to the end of the bed, walked around in circles a few times and then laid down and started to clean herself.

"Lily." I said again, "is it really you?"

She looked up at me with a sparkle in her eyes and went back to cleaning herself.

"Please Lily" I pleaded, if it's you, please talk to me. I don't know if I'm losing my mind. Talk to me if you can."

Again Lily looked at me, but this time with a smile on her face, if a cat could smile, that is. She got up, jumped off the bed and as the door opened, and Rose peeked her head in, Lily ran out.

"Emilee, is it alright if I come in? I heard you talking as I was walking by your door and figured that mangy cat, somehow got in. She does show up in the strangest places at times." Rose said, as she entered the room.

I smiled and waved Rose in, as I leaned against the headboard. Rose left the door open a bit, and came over to sit in a chair next to the bed.

"I hope it wasn't me that caused you to faint, but that silly cat, who is so annoying." Rose started.

I chuckled at this, it was so Rose, to talk about Lily in that manner, but then, they can't really be them, now can they? I thought.

"Rose? That is your name?" I asked sheepishly, not wanting to sound silly.

"Yes, it is." Rose said with pride.

Tina M. Engel

"The cat's name is Lily?" I continued.

With a curious look on her face, Rose answered, "Yes."

And the man across the street? Is Brett?" I finished.

Rose, with a look of uncertainty said, "Yes."

I didn't say anything else. Wasn't sure what to say. I felt confused and foolish. They were here, all three of them but Rose didn't seem to know me, I didn't think.

Do I start talking about Terrafirma and realize that she is my Rose, or freak her out and have her go to mom and dad and then be committed?

But then, I thought that mom knew, maybe. I still hadn't had the nerve to ask her. Would she admit to knowing all along what I was, or would she know nothing about Terrafirma and me being a princess, and then have me committed to a home for the insane?

"Are you alright, Emilee?" Asked Rose.

I smiled and decided it wasn't a good time to discuss Terrafirma. Either I was crazy or she really didn't remember who she was or...or what?

"Yes, I'm fine, I just wanted to make sure I was remembering names. Since I don't seem to remember the last months before the accident or the accident itself, I was just checking." I said with a confident tone.

I saw it then, a necklace around Rose's neck, on a silver chain. It was an emerald green dragon. I took a calm breath before I asked, "Your dragon, I mean necklace?" I stated uncomfortably. "It's beautiful."

Tina M. Engel

Rose, stroked it as if petting an animal and smiled, saying, "Yes, a dragon, isn't it beautiful? She keeps me company, I think it's a good luck charm. Someone gave it to me..." Then Rose got quiet with a questioning expression and mumbled, "But I can't remember who, but they said to keep it safe."

The door opened then and in came mom with a tray that held two steaming mugs of something and a plate that held her famous chocolate chip cookies. I could tell by the smell, before she set it on the bed next to me.

"Oh good, you're awake." Mom said with glee. "I was hoping you would be, and are you feeling better?"

I smiled and nodded as she continued, "I wasn't sure if I should call the doctor, but Brett carried you upstairs for us and we decided to just let you rest."

At the sound of mom saying, Brett, my heart pounded a bit harder and my mind wandered away from the questioning of the dragon necklace that Rose had around her neck.

Mom was still talking but I wasn't hearing anything she was saying. My mind was back in the underworld, as I was draining Brett of his life force. The sadness and emptiness that I felt, came rushing back.

It was Rose who brought me back to the present, as she put her hand on my hand. I turned and looked at her and then back down at the dragon, as she questioned, "Emilee, are you okay?"

Her sweet, concerned look was tender and full of kindness. I looked up at mom and she had a look of worry, also.

"Oh, I'm fine, I guess I am just a bit overwhelmed with the lack of memory and all."

I lifted one of the mugs and putting it to my mouth, I found that it was hot chocolate with whipped cream on top. I took a sip and pulling the mug away, knew that I had a whipped cream mustache, like I used to have as a child.

Mom giggled as I licked my upper lip and then took the napkin that was laying on the tray and wiped off the rest. Rose smiled as she lifted the other mug and did the same.

"This is great mom, thanks, and yes, I am fine. Rose and I are getting to know each other and I think she will be good for me." I realized how that sounded, so continued, "Not that you and dad aren't good for me, but having someone younger around may help me remember."

That still didn't come out right and I stammered a bit before mom laughed and stopped me from making a bigger fool out of myself and said, "That's okay, Emilee, I know how you meant it. Your dad and I think the same way. We feel like Rose was sent to us just at the right time.

"We were feeling hopeless that you wouldn't come back to us, and when Rose came, her positive attitude about you and just everything, really helped us to hang on. She kept telling us that you would wake up soon, she just knew it."

I looked at Rose and saw a twinkle in her eyes, as if there somewhere was a light that I saw, but she didn't know was there.

"And Brett and Lily?" I inquired, nonchalantly.

Mom chuckled as she sat down on the other side of the bed. "Well", she started, as Rose and I took another sip of the hot chocolate. "It was the funniest thing. They all showed up on the same day, at the same time.

"Rose had answered our ad to rent the room across the hall, so we knew that she was coming on a certain day. But it was Brett who dropped her off."

I looked to Rose and she was grinning from ear to ear, and took over telling the story. "Yes, I got off the bus and was pulling my suitcase along the sidewalk, when it opened up, spilling my stuff everywhere. I was horrified, I might add." Rose said.

"Suddenly a moving van pulled up next to me and from around it came a man, Brett. He helped me gather up my things and asked where I was going. He offered me a ride and what a surprise when we realized that I was going to be living across the street from him.

"Brett was renting the house across the street. He was so nice and it's funny, I felt like I had met him at some time, somewhere, but just couldn't remember where, and he said the same thing."

Mom cut in then, to continue this strange story, "Yes, Brett pulled up as I was outside getting the mail. They came over, Brett bringing Rose's bag, and they both introduced themselves.

"I was facing his moving truck and saw that he was towing a pickup truck, and there sitting up on a box in the back of the truck, was a cat. I commented that I saw he had a cat, and Brett and Rose both looked where I was looking.

"No? Brett had said with a questioning tone, as the cat jumped down and came over to us. She brushed up against me and then headed to the porch and sat at the door as if waiting for me to let her in."

"And you did?" I asked, surprised. "Dad doesn't like cats and especially in the house." I said.

Mom laughed and continued, "Well, we left her out on the porch overnight, giving her some water, and the next morning she was still here. I went to the store that day to get some cat food and well, funny thing, when I got back, your dad was sitting in his porch chair with the cat on his lap. She became his cat, so to speak, but Rose here, now that's a different story."

We both looked at Rose as she wrinkled her nose. "She is trouble, I can tell. That cat just barged in like she owned the place, went right to your room and made herself at home. Just look at the end of your bed, all covered with her black hair and she constantly hisses at me whenever she walks by me."

Just then, up on the bed jumped Lily and she did just that, hissed at Rose as she came up to me. I put my mug down on the tray as Lily crawled into my lap and stared at me.

I noticed then that she had a scar on her cheek, which her long whiskers covered slightly. She put her front paws up around my neck, and putting her face just under my hair, she rubbed her nose against my neck and started to purr.

Tina M. Engel

I looked at Rose; she had a disgusted look on her face and mom just smiled and laughed, saying, "Well, I think Lily is good for the family."

"Lily?" I asked, "Who named her?"

"She has a name tag, and it says Lily. That's all though, no address or phone number. We put an ad in the paper but no one has called, so I guess we are her family now." Mom said with content in her voice.

Mom continued then as she got up off the bed. "Time for me to think about dinner. Are you feeling up to coming downstairs, or do you want dinner in bed."

Rose spoke before I could answer, "Oh, can I help again, Katie?" and mom smiled and nodded her head, accepting the help.

"Let me rest a bit and take a bath, then I'll be down." I answered with a smile, as mom and Rose headed out the door.

Before Rose left, she turned and said, "Lily, you should leave her alone. Do you want me to take her out of your room, Emilee?"

I smiled and told Rose that it was fine that Lily was here, and that I would be down in a bit. Rose didn't seem too happy about it but shut the door quietly as I looked down at Lily. She had moved down and was sitting next to me then, just looking at me.

"Well, Lily", I said, "Do you know more than you are letting on? After all, you can't talk in this form and I do believe that Rose has no memory of Terrafirma or…" and I stopped talking as Lily's eyes widened just a bit, when I said Terrafirma.

Tina M. Engel

"You do know something, don't you?" I asked.

Lily went down to the foot of my bed then, and turning around a few times, and kneading the blanket, she curled up and shut her eyes.

"Fine, Lily, be that way for now, but there is something going on and I'm going to find out what." I said, then looking up at the ceiling, I said, "Grandmother, Varda, I know you are watching. You told me it was time to go home, but this wasn't what I thought you meant. Why am I here and what am I supposed to do here?"

I waited for a few minutes, not really expecting to hear a voice, my grandmother's, to be exact, but then, I was hoping I would. I looked back at Lily and she was staring at me and then, letting out a quiet meow, she lay her head back down and shut her eyes.

I got up, went over to the window, and looked over at the house that Brett was living in. I wondered, why they were here, why was I here? Brett and Rose had died and supposedly went to Nirvana, supposedly, but they were here.

From around the side of the house, came Brett, carrying a tool box as he crossed the street to our house. He looked up at my window and seeing me, smiled, waved and then headed up the stairs and into the house.

I decided that I would go soak in the tub before heading downstairs for conversation and food. The ache I felt in my heart was so great, seeing Brett, that wonderful, familiar smile on his face, and knowing that he didn't know me. I wanted him to hold me, tell me that everything was going to be alright. I wanted him to tell me what I was supposed to do now, why I was back here in the human realm, back as Emilee Stevens, only I wasn't her anymore. I was me, a fey princess, only to be locked away again, in a human body.

As I crawled into the bathtub, the water was soothing as it covered my entire body. Just my head was exposed to the air. I could feel the water soaking into every pore, as if my body was drinking it in. I'm human though, I thought. Why would I feel this way? I wondered then if I could breathe underwater. Did I dare try?

I slowly lowered my head down until I was completely submersed. Did I dare take a deep breathe, let the water fill my lungs? What would happen, would I be able to breathe or would I drowned?

I heard her voice then, Varda, calm but demanding "Not now Emilee, stop being so stubborn and just let it be, let it all be. They need you!"

I jolted up out of the water as I sucked in a gulp of air, but wasn't quite out of the water yet, so inhaled some water also. It burned as I coughed, choked and gagged, throwing up slightly.

"Okay", I said, after several minutes of thinking I was going to die. "I'm not in my fey body, I get it Grandmother, but what is going on?"

Of course there was no answer, why would there be. She didn't need to answer, for she stopped me from killing myself and I was where she wanted me, for the time being.

I laid back down in the water and just let it take me, soak into me, soothe my very soul. My eyes were shut and I could see a rainbow just under my eyelids. I just let it be, didn't try to figure it out, just let it be.

I opened my eyes when a knock came at the door. It was Rose's voice, asking if I was okay and that dinner would be ready soon.

I reassured her that I was fine and would be out soon. As I lay there looking up at the ceiling, I noticed in the corner, a spider in a web. I watched it for a few minutes, and then decided, what the hell, talk to it.

"Hello there." I said, and chuckled to myself. "Are you Tiny?" I asked.

The spider suddenly moved, coming down the wall and stopping just a few feet from the rim of the tub. I laid there motionless, hoping that it wasn't thinking of taking a swim. I still wasn't fond of spiders, even though I had befriended many hundreds, along with the Queen of all spiders, Queen Widow.

When it didn't move anymore, up or down, I continued, "Well maybe I can take that as a yes? Are you all here, in the human's world, to watch over me?"

The spider came down then and planted itself on the rim of the tub and just looked at me. I knew it was looking at me and I felt confident that it was Tiny.

"Well if you are Tiny, I must inform you that my mother dislikes spiders a great deal, so it may be a good idea for you to flee this bathroom while you can, and head outdoors. You'll be safe out there." I said, with a hint of humor, in my voice.

Tina M. Engel

The spider did just that. It crawled up to the ceiling again, and there in the corner was a small hole into which it disappeared.

"Alright then." I said, as I stood and stepped out of the tub. "This is going to be very interesting. Who else is hanging around?" I wondered.

I dressed and headed out of the bathroom. As I shut the door and turned to go into my room, I ran into Brett, as he was coming down the stairs which led to the attic room. He was carrying boards, and the boards came down first, which was what I almost ran into.

When he saw me standing there, just inches from the boards, and I let out a small cry of shock when I dodged the wood, it surprised him too.

"Are you alright, Emilee?" He started, "I didn't see you. I didn't hit you, did I?"

Brett had the same look, the same fright on his face, which he would get when he was concerned. My whole body ached just then, it was Brett, somewhere in there, I just knew it.

"No." I said in a whisper, my voice didn't seem to want to come out. I swallowed hard as I saw the concern on his face deepen.

"I cleared my throat and said louder and with more confidence, pushing the pain down deep, away for now, "I'm fine, I've had lots of practice dodging things that come at me lately." And I laughed slightly.

Brett stood there with a dumfounded look, and I remembered that he had no idea what I was talking about, as far as he was concerned, I had been in a coma for months.

"Really?" He commented, "In your dream world?"

I chuckled at that statement and said, as I shook my head and gave a little smirk, "You wouldn't believe me if I told you." And then under my breath, I mumbled, "But I wish you would."

"Well give it a try, you never know. I have seen and heard some of the oddest things in my life." And then he got a queer look on his face and mumbled, which I heard, "I think."

We looked at each other then, for a few moments not quite knowing what to say, but Brett wasn't unsure for long and said as he pointed up the attic stairwell, "Spiders."

I looked at him with confusion and he started to laugh.

"Oh, there was some damage to the roof a while back, during a wind storm, just before you woke up. It caused a small hole. Spiders were getting in, and well, you know how much your mom hates spiders, so I repaired it from the inside, and will fix the outside tomorrow." He said in a triumphant tone. "We don't want those creepy crawly things in the house, as she says." And he gave that comical smile that I so loved.

Mom called up from the bottom of the stairs that it was dinner time and Brett being the gentleman that he was, held out his hand for me to go first.

I pointed to the piece of wood he was carrying with an, are you sure, look on my face, and he gave me a quirky smile and pretended to swing it my way.

Tina M. Engel

"No worries, princess, you are in good hands, I'll protect you." He said, and then chuckled.

I looked at him, I'm sure, with cautiousness on my face, "Princess?" I questioned.

Brett chuckled and said, "Well, I do believe you are the princess of this castle, since your mom and dad are the king and queen of their home, are they not?" And he laughed a silly laugh, held out his hand again and I headed down the stairs.

We had a nice dinner with Rose, Brett and Lily, all sitting in the dining room, Lily on my lap, which I found curious but didn't fight it. It felt normal. Not the normal from human Emilee's past, but from Princess Emilee's past.

Mom and dad seemed so happy that I was home and having so many other's at the table. I remembered then that they had two other children, who had died in the beginning of their tiny lives, a boy Ragnar and girl, Eliza. Maybe Brett and Rose were filling a void in the house with their presence, and mom and dad were happy they were here.

Rose and Brett would say odd things at times, things they would say as fey, and it would catch me off guard. Brett called me princess a few more times and my dad would laugh and inform him then in a gruff voice that he was right, I was his princess.

Rose mumbled about Lily sitting on my lap, and that she should be outside. Called her a trouble maker and filthy, a few times too, but Lily just lay there on my lap ignoring her and just enjoyed being close.

Chapter 26

Be patient,
When the time is right,
It will be.

The next few weeks went by quickly, nothing unusual, and I regained my strength one day at a time. I took walks through the woods behind the house, short ones at first, but with every day they grew longer.

Mom wouldn't let me go alone, Rose always accompanied me and Lily always tagged along. I asked a lot of questions of Rose about her past, but never got many answers. She came into town on the bus from the east coast, but when I inquired from where, she seemed to change the subject.

I asked her about her family, and she informed me sadly that she had none, friends, just a few casual. When Rose did talk about the past, it was strange, she would have a queer look on her face, as if she was surprised to be remembering it.

Rose and I became close friends, more like sisters and as for Lily, well, she was Lily. She might not talk to me but I always knew what she was thinking.

Brett worked at the lumber yard there in Pineville, and in his spare time was always doing work on either his house or mom and dad's. He came over for dinner every Wednesday and Sunday, even though mom invited him every day. Brett would tell her that he didn't want to become a bother and he would give me a wink.

Tina M. Engel

I would walk next to my old house, or what was left of it, to get to the woods, and could see the hole that held the stairwell down to the basement, and wondered what I would find there if I entered.

I tried to head in that direction several times, but Rose took my arm gently each time, and informed me that it wasn't safe. Mom had given strict instructions not to enter, or let anyone else go down there. Brett had been down there a few times, helping Dad get some of my things that had survived the strange blast, but it wasn't safe.

I went out to the burnt tree trunk that once housed the fey, Ian, just a few days after I came home. There lying next to the tree, was a seed. Remembering the seed that Albee had given me, I wondered if this could be it. I placed it in a groove that was on the top of the burnt out stump, and filled it in with some dirt. Maybe he would grow. I would go to the trunk and touch it daily as I headed out for my walk, inspecting it.

As the weeks went on, my pull to go down in the basement increased, as did my need to go into the woods and sit by the stream with my feet soaking. Rose would talk to the plants and bugs, and at one time a spider on a tree caught her eye. She went over and let it crawl on her. I shivered at this and she giggled, that wonderful Rose giggle.

Rose told me about the spider that was living in her bedroom, and I knew it was Tiny.

"You had better not let mom find it in there or it will be a dead spider. She doesn't like them in the house." I said, with a bit of humor, but also concern.

"Oh, I know and so does she. Tiny, that's what I named her. Not sure why, but it just seemed to fit, even though she isn't tiny at all." Rose said with a grin, and continued, "Tiny seems to know when Katie is coming in, and she scurries up to the ceiling and hides behind the curtain."

That same day, as I lay down in the grassy area, a shadow came over me. I looked up, and watched an eagle, large and graceful, circle over the tree line and then land in a tree right over me. Oh, he was high up in the tree, but I could see him and he seemed to be watching me. After a while he flew away, but every day after that, he was there, as if waiting for me. It was Eagle, my Eagle, I just knew. They were all coming to me, waiting, watching, but why?

One day when checking on the seed I had planted, there in the top of the burnt out stump, was life. A very tiny bud, sticking out of the dirt. I talked to it for a few minutes while waiting for Rose, and then every day after, I would talk to it as it seemed to grow rapidly.

Every time I saw Brett, he took my breath away, and caused sweaty palms. At times when he would call me princess or give me that silly grin, I thought for just a moment that it was him, that he remembered who he really was, but then, nothing.

Brett and I spent time together, alone, when he was fixing things around the house. I would sit and watch and he didn't seem to mind. It became routine, so to speak. I asked him questions about his past but never got any answers. He was a mystery and he liked it that way.

Tina M. Engel

Brett remarked often that he should go with me sometime on my walk in the woods, to see just what it was that I was so drawn to. I always told him I would love that, but he was always too busy when it was time to go for my little adventures in the woods.

I asked Brett about my house, and the basement, what it was like, what he saw and if he would take me down there, but his answer was always, "It's too dangerous and your mom would kill me, if I took you down there."

At times I would sit in the kitchen with mom as she cooked, or out in the garden, helping her prune plants, water them, dig just to dig, and she always talked to each plant. I wanted to question her about Terrafirma and what she knew, but never quite knew how to start.

I brought up the subject of my brother and sister, before me, and with a twinkle in her eyes, she sat down in the grass and shared memories of her pregnancies, her feelings and her sadness.

When asked about her pregnancy with me and my birth, she gave me a queer look, looked up at the sky then and shared that story. I had been born, premature, and lucky to have survived. My mom had been walking in the forest, 8 months pregnant, when she went into labor. The pain was excruciating and she couldn't get back to the house. A woman came to my mom and I was delivered right there in the forest.

Mom looked at me then and said, "It was all written in the stars. She held you for a moment, gave you a kiss on the forehead and whispered a story in my ear, before Willy came crashing

Tina M. Engel

through the brush. When he got to me, she was gone."

Mom smiled then and with a look of knowing in her eyes, she said again, "It was written in the stars."

Several months passed, and after dinner one night, with a beautiful full moon, Brett asked me if I would like to take a walk. He was feeling restless, as he put it, not sure why, and thought a walk would do him some good. I was thrilled that he asked, and I said, yes, of course.

I wanted to go into the woods, but Brett being Brett, still protective, thought the woods would be too dangerous at night. I teased him a bit, trying to get him to change his mind, but to no avail. He stood firm, saying that he was protecting me.

As we headed down the front steps towards the tree, Brett stopped and had a questioning look on his face as he faced the tree. "What are you feeding this tree?" He asked with humor in his voice. "It is growing at an unbelievable rate."

I just smiled and shrugged my shoulders and said, "I just talk to it daily and give it water. It is just happy to be alive, I guess."

We continued to walk down the sidewalk, past the lot where my house once stood and as we walked by, out of the corner of my eye, I saw a flash. Turning quickly as I stopped, I saw a glowing mist rising from the basement opening.

Brett stopped a few feet in front of me and turned to see what I was looking at. The glowing mist vanished, but I knew I saw it, and I was sure that it was time I entered the basement. I felt that it was time.

"What's wrong, Emilee?" Brett asked, as he stood next to me looking in the direction that I was looking.

I didn't say anything at first, but looked from Brett's face to the area where I saw the mist. Then I asked, "Did you see that? A strange mist was drifting out of the basement. We should go and check it out, don't you think?"

Brett chuckled and with a smirk, said, "You will say anything to get down in that basement. What is it that you think you will find down there anyway? I have cleaned everything out. I promise."

I gave him a pondering look and whispered, "The past." But decided to drop it then. I didn't want to spoil the evening, the moon was so beautiful and the air, cool, with just a slight breeze that would tousle my hair just a bit.

Brett just stared at me as he waited for my answer. The breeze drifted across my face and blew a strand of hair across my eyes. He reached out and brushed it away, tucking it behind my ear. The touch of his finger as he did this, caused a slight zing, like static electricity when you touch someone after rubbing your stocking feet in the carpet. We both had stunned looks on our faces, he felt it too.

He started to pull his hand away, as he said, "I'm so sorry. That was sure strange, there must be electricity in the air tonight." As he laughed slightly.

Tina M. Engel

I put my hand up to stop him from moving his hand. "You felt it too, didn't you? It's still there." I said, and then immediately felt foolish, and figured I just ruined our walk.

Brett lowered his hand, but as he did, he turned his hand and held mine as we lowered them. His smile was sweet, but his eyes had an intense gaze as he looked at me.

"I feel a lot of things when I'm around you princess." Brett said, as he started to bend down and I just knew he was going to kiss me.

Suddenly something ran between us, and as we looked away from each other a few feet in front of us, was Lily, looking at us with disgust.

Brett let go of my hand and said, casually, "Still want to take that walk with me?" As he held his hand out in front of us. "I think Lily is going to be our chaperone." And Brett let out a nervous laugh.

We walked around the neighborhood and up a hill, where we had an amazing view of the moon as it rose in the sky. The stars were out, and I felt like we were a part of them. We sat on a bench, and Lily, well, she was right in between us, acting all smug and sassy. It was alright though, it all felt right.

Brett reached behind and put his arm around my shoulders quietly and even though I knew that Lily was aware, she didn't let on that she knew. She just looked at me, gave me a sly wink and settled herself down and proceeded to purr.

We had stayed out later that I realized, and when we got home, Mom and Dad were in the living room with looks of curiosity. It was Rose, however who had no problem scolding us as she came down the stairs.

"Where have you two been? We have been worried sick!" Rose scolded. Looking at Brett then she continued, "You know that Emilee is still getting her strength back, and the cold air isn't good for her!"

Brett suddenly had a look of embarrassment but it quickly turned to a matter of fact attitude, as he said, "The air is cool but not cold, and I think that the fresh air is good for her. After all, you take her into the woods every day, and she comes out looking healthier each time. I think the fresh air gave her nice rosy cheeks, tonight. Besides, Miss Lily here decided to join us and kept us out of trouble."

Mom and Dad started to laugh, as Rose just huffed and insisted that I turn in for the night. She came over to me, took my hand and led me upstairs with the intent on helping me.

I heard them all laughing as we climbed the stairs, and looking back at Brett, he had a quirky smile as he said, "Sleep well Princess."

When I reached my room, I informed Rose, as kindly as I could, that I didn't need any help. The look on her face changed my mind quickly, for I remembered then, the sadness in Rose's eyes when I said that to her in Terrafirma. When I didn't need her blood anymore. It was the same sadness.

I let her draw my bath, for I was a bit chilly but reassured her that I could bathe myself and get myself into bed. She insisted that she pull my bedding down for me and I agreed. I told her

Tina M. Engel

goodnight as I shut the bathroom door and just smiled. I didn't ever want to hurt Rose. She was so special to me.

I didn't soak for long because I was suddenly exhausted. Maybe Rose was right, I was still regaining my strength, but I had been feeling well for weeks now. I got out of the tub and walked over to the mirror, but before I brushed the moisture off, I thought I saw a figure standing behind me, a man. I turned quickly but there was no one there.

Turning back, taking my hand and swiping the mirror once, there behind me was the same glowing mist. I stood there, still, watching as it hovered over the bathtub. I knew it wasn't steam from the bath, though if I told anyone about it, they would say that was what I saw.

When I turned back around, it was gone but I was certain that I saw it and a man, I saw a man. Something was about to happen. What, I didn't know, but I was sure it had to do with Terrafirma. Something was happening and I knew I had better be ready.

I crawled into bed and shut off the light. The moon was so bright, I think brighter than it should have been. I got back up and looked out the window. The moon was directly above Brett's house and it had a subtle, but strange beam of light that descended to Brett's house.

Brett had the curtains drawn, but I could see movement in the living room, so I knew that he was still awake. I saw the curtains open a bit and there was Brett's face looking up at my window. Though it was dark in my room, and there was no way he could see me looking at him, he waved, shut the curtains and the lights went out.

I looked back up at the moon and saw it had a blue tint to it. I looked over at the tree stump and remembered Albee, or Stephan I should say, and shuddered, remembering the figure in my bathroom, just a bit ago. I crawled into bed and as I closed my eyes, I whispered, "Grandmother, I'm ready."

Tina M. Engel

Chapter 27

Listen closely
To your dreams.
They tell a story
You must hear.

I felt warmth on my face and as I opened my eyes, the sun blinded me momentarily, until I put my hands up to block it. I wasn't in my bed anymore.

I sat up and discovered that I was there again, in that place, where the wheat field meets the ocean, with the tree in the middle. I was sitting on the landing however, half way down the pathway, from wheat field above to ocean below. My feet were dangling in the pond and the small waterfall was just to my right. This was where Brett had disappeared, as a hand had reached out and he took it, walking into the waterfall.

My feet were motionless, and the pond was suddenly still, as if the water from the falls had stopped moving. It was as if the water was a mirror and I could see the world around me. I saw the waterfall and there stood Brett, a hand came out of the falls and then there she was, or I should say, there I was, standing before him.

It was my hand that had reached out, it was me. I was fey, looking as I remembered. Brett took my hand and we walked into the water.

Ripples in the water stopped the vision, and I stood and turned around, watching the waterfall and wondering what was behind it. It was me who Brett entered the waterfall with, not Queen

Tina M. Engel

Anahita as I had assumed. Why, I didn't know, but I always thought it was her, taking him away from me.

I started to go towards the falls, planning on going in to see what was behind, when I heard her voice, Varda. "It's not time yet, Emilee." And I looked up to see her standing at the ridge, watching me.

She reached out her hand and continued, "Come, Emilee, it's almost time."

I walked up the narrow path to greet her and she embraced me with such love that I started to cry. The warmth and safety I felt in her arms was so empowering that I didn't want her to let go. The pain and emptiness I had felt since the day I woke in the humans' realm vanished the moment she held me.

Varda released me, but holding my hand, we walked through the wheat field to the edge of the cliff, where ocean met land, and just stood for a few minutes letting the salty ocean breeze fill our lungs.

"Brett is alive, but how?" Was all I could think to say at that moment.

She didn't turn to look at me, we both continued to stare out to sea as if waiting for something to come.

"Yes, he is, Emilee. You changed the way it was supposed to go. Your choices changed the future." Varda said calmly.

"I don't understand, if you knew how the future was supposed to be, why did you not stop me, and direct me to do what I was supposed to do." I said with confusion in my voice.

"You still don't understand, dear granddaughter, I can see what is to be, I watch over many worlds, realms, dimensions and do what I can to help all life grow and become. But I cannot interfere as I may want to. At times I wish I could.

"With every choice one makes, it sets the future on a certain path. Each choice changes that path of existence.

"You chose not to kill Mephisto, but to send him into the abyss of space to live eternity in silence, alone. You chose not to kill Stephan, but to turn him to wood, a tree of all things, stuck in Hades as a punishment. And the one thing that I didn't foresee, was you giving Brett your blood.

"You see Emilee, the dreams you have been having, were visions of what the future could be, all depending on your decisions, choices that you made. If you had followed Mephisto, become Stephan's wife, the vision of this place, destroyed, dark and desolate would have resulted. Your choices, put you here, now."

"Am I really here, or is this just another vision of the future, depending on what I do tomorrow or the next day or the next? You sent me back to the humans' world!" I said angrily.

"You are here, but in a dream state. Your body is there", and she reached out her arm and pointed towards the roaring ocean.

I saw myself in my room, in bed, asleep with the moonlight striking my face, softly, shining through the window. I assumed I was asleep and dreaming.

"This is a dream then." I stated.

Tina M. Engel

"No, Emilee, this is real, the only way I could get to you."

"Brett, he's alive then? I didn't kill him?" I asked in haste.

"He is alive, your blood saved him, but in doing what you did, keeping him alive, as well as Stephan and Mephisto, you have changed the future." Varda said with sadness in her eyes.

"If Brett is alive, then why did you send me back to the humans' world, and make Brett and Rose human too. Why are we not back in Terrafirma? Brett and I were supposed to be together and have a baby, Katie." I paused then for a moment and then continued, "I named her after my human mother." And I smiled at that thought.

"If I had drained Brett dry, killed him, then that future would not have happened. Can it still?" I asked.

"Varda smiled and answered, "With every decision you make, your future changes. I sent Brett, Rose, Lily..."

I interrupted Varda then and said, "Eagle, Tiny the spider and even Albee's seed, to plant."

"Yes, Emilee, I sent them all to keep watch over you. He still watches you from afar. He, Mephisto, has his eyes everywhere. They can't get to him, but they want to. If they can get you, they believe you can bring him back. The moment you chose to give Brett your blood, I foresaw this future."

"But Brett, Rose and Lily don't know who they are. They don't remember. Lily, she does though, doesn't she? And Tiny and Eagle, they do!"

Tina M. Engel

"Yes granddaughter, they do but Brett and Rose were weak, and going through the transformation from fey to human, took its toll on them. Their memories are there down deep but they need someone to remind them." Varda said as she looked at me, smiling.

"Rose, she died, the creature that poisoned me, it somehow killed her, I thought." I said, feeling confused. "And Shinar and Rose are connected and the three of us share a bond. I don't understand."

"Rose was brought to you, because her blood was what you needed to survive in Terrafirma while your body changed from human to who you really are. I needed the same thing when I was trying to survive in the world of Terrafirma. You see, Emilee, I'm not a fey, as you know, nor are you totally.

"Rose is a pixie, but not just any pixie, for it was planned that she would be here for you when you came. Rose was given something special at birth, a drop of dragon's milk, from the dragon that laid your egg. Shinar would need Rose to survive, as you would need Rose's blood to help with your change.

I needed the same, only not dragon's milk, for I don't have a dragon, I have Lily." And Varda laughed.

"Lily was my connection to Terrafirma and the humans' earth, but I have other connections that I need in order to go to the other realms that I watch over.

"Oh, I don't have a dragon or I should say, am not connected to one, but if I need, they do

come. You however, where given the gift, one dragon to be a part of you, and Rose, who was the one to join you both.

"When Poseidon decided to speed up your transformation and cause your strength to develop before it was time, that threw off your needs, and caused a disconnect between you and Rose. The poison not only spread through your veins, but also Rose's. It wasn't really poison to you but was for Rose.

"She couldn't die, I couldn't let that happen, so I did intervene, and slowed down the poison, allowing Rose to still be, as you saw her. She had a job to do, to complete your bonding with Shinar. Rose's essence was not lost and would never have been, for her spirit had joined with Shinar, they had become one.

"When you gave Rose a drop of your blood, however, it reversed the damage to her physical body, and brought her spirit back into her body. She is still connected to you both, Shinar and you, as it was meant to be.

"As for Poseidon, he has been warned not to interfere again and the same goes for Queen Anahita. Their meddling caused quite a bit of trouble."

The sound of her name, Anahita, sent fury through my body. And I asked, "What of her, was she with us or against?"

Varda smiled and said, "Let the jealousy go, Emilee. They were never meant to be."

"But..." I started, and Varda gave me a scolding glare, and then smiling again, I knew that it didn't matter. Brett and Queen Anahita's bond,

Tina M. Engel

whatever it was, was gone, especially after we found out she was working for Poseidon. Queen Anahita did her duty by Poseidon but did she also have ulterior motives? I believed she did.

I asked, "Why did you send me back to earth to portray the human Emilee? Where is she? Or are we one and the same?"

"I had to hide you temporarily, until I could determine the danger, assess what the future might entail now that you changed things. After sending your companions to keep watch over you, I closed the entranceway between Terrafirma and earth. Fey cannot see humans even if they wanted to.

"There are doorways, however between the two dimensions, which can be crossed from one realm to the other, only if one knows where to look. I couldn't separate the two worlds, completely.

"Before Brett was sent to earth in human form, he was shown where the doorways were hidden. He was told where he would be going, as was Rose. They understood that their memories would be temporarily blocked and that it was up to you, to help them remember."

I interrupted Varda then, "And if I can't help them remember?

"Then you will all live your lives as humans and the future will happen as it may. Will Stephan escape Hades and find a doorway back to earth and find you? Will Mephisto's followers find a way to release him?" Varda said in a matter of fact tone, and shrugged.

Tina M. Engel

"What am I supposed to do? I have sent them both away, and I have no intention of freeing them, even if I do get captured." I said.

Varda took my hand and said, "Come, it's time you see."

We walked to the tree and an opening appeared. I looked at Varda and she smiled and said, "This is where I see all. If this tree is destroyed, then all is lost in the worlds that I take care of. I will go back to where I came from and start over, with other worlds, dimensions. We will let this section of the universe be as it will, and destroy itself from the inside out.

We walked into the doorway then, and I was amazed at what I saw. This tree, this beautiful tree, wasn't a tree at all. It was a room, like the one that Brett and I were in when we met Biton. It was white, sterile white, but all around the room, there were portals to different worlds.

I could see Earth, but it wasn't dull and dreary, as I thought, the colors were that of fall, a forest was where the doorway was. The leaves on the trees were reds, yellows, oranges and browns. A stream meandered through the forest. It was my forest, Pineville.

Then yet another, Terrafirma. The doorway entered a village, one I hadn't seen before and another, a water world, Atlantis, maybe? There were many more, like pictures hanging on the wall, but there was movement in each one, as if a movie.

"This is where I watch over all." Varda said. "Mephisto must not be released, for if he comes here, and he does know how to get here, remember, *he was once like me, he will have it all, and I will have to walk away."*

"What is under the waterfall, Grandmother?" I asked. "Why did I see what I saw, me taking Brett's hand? It was me!"

"That is the future I see for you and for Terrafirma, Earth, Atlantis and the other realms that are joined here. That is a special place, but only if that future becomes.

"You must stop them from releasing Stephan and Mephisto. Your journey continues, humans and fey, must come together and find a way to live in peace and acceptance of each other, to work together to combat the evil that lurks in the dark spaces of all worlds. The Atlantians and other realms will join you, but only when Terrafirma and earth are in harmony with each other.

"It is time to awaken Brett and Rose's memories. Time to find a doorway back to Terrafirma."

"But Emilee? The real Emilee, if I leave here, will she come back or is she gone?" I asked.

"The human Emilee, died. Her wounds that Stephan inflicted, were too great, even with your healing. Your healing powers kept her body alive long enough for me to put you back here. You share the body that she had, and her spirit lives on, in the Goblins' village. Eliza and Ragnar came and took her home the moment I put you here." Varda explained.

"If I leave and go to Terrafirma, then Emilee disappears, as well as Brett, Rose and Lily? What will my parents think? How can I do that to them?" I questioned wearily.

Tina M. Engel

"There is one thing I can do, temporarily. I can freeze the human's earth time, make it stand still. But only temporarily. If you succeed and bring humans and fey together, then, your parents will know you as who you truly are, a mixture of all, human, fey, plant, animals, water, stars, soil, and air. You are all, Emilee."

Varda held her hand out then towards the opening of the tree and we walked out. As I turned to look at the tree, the doorway closed and it was just the magnificent tree that had been in my visions from day one of this incredible journey that I was on.

"It's time, Emilee. They are getting stronger. It is time."

Tina M. Engel

Chapter 28

> *The ending is*
> *The beginning,*
> *The beginning is*
> *The end.*

I woke in my bed, in my human room. Lily was sitting at the end of my bed, looking at me. I got up and went over to the mirror to see what I looked like. I still looked human, but inside, I felt different, stronger. I put my hands on my chest, and there were two heart beats.

"It's time Lily." I said, and she jumped off the bed and went to the door, sat down and waited for me.

I got dressed and called Brett. I told him that I was going into the basement of my house and I needed his help. I hung up then, that was all I needed to say. I knew he would rush over, he was protective that way.

I opened the door and Lily headed down the stairs. I knew where she was going. I went into Rose's room, and upon waking her, I asked her to get dressed and come with me. I had something to show her.

As we headed downstairs and to the front door, Lily was there waiting. "What Lily, can't you open doors yet?" I questioned with a giggle and Rose looked at me queerly.

"Where are we going?" Rose asked, as I headed out the door, after grabbing a flashlight from the desk, which sat next to the door.

Before I closed the door, I saw a silhouette of a person, standing in the doorway to the kitchen. It was my mom, and as she stepped out from the darkness, a smile on her lips, she nodded her head, knowing where I was going. She knew it all. I turned and closed the door quietly.

I bounded down the stairs, Lily racing ahead, and seeing Brett running across the street to stop me, I ran and reached the top of the basement stairs, just before him.

"Emilee, stop, this isn't safe! What are you thinking?" Brett said, out of breath.

"I have to show you something. Trust me, it's worth it." I said as I pointed the flashlight down the stairs into the dark.

As I got to the bottom step, and shined the light around the small room, there didn't seem to be much there. I walked to the middle of the room as Brett and Rose followed, Lily already there, sitting on top of a large boulder.

Brett stammered, "Where did that rock come from?"

I just smiled, for I suspected it was Kimberlite, here to guide us back into Terrafirma, and I was sure he wasn't at all happy that Lily was sitting on him.

"Please, sit and let me explain why you are here." I said as I walked over to the large rock. There sitting on top, next to Lily, was my diamond necklace, earrings, and barrette. My cameo was still in Hades, with Stephan, I hoped.

"Emilee", Brett said, "it isn't safe down here. We need to go!"

I turned, and looking at both their frightened faces, I didn't quite know how to start or what to say. I just knew that I had to help them remember.

"It's alright, Brett, there isn't anything down here that can hurt us. Please sit down on those boxes. Please, trust me." I begged.

I saw something in Brett's face then, trust, and a spark in his eyes. As Rose started to complain, Brett said, "Okay, Rose, let's hear what she has to say."

Rose looked at Brett in disbelief but they both sat down.

As I started to put on my necklace, earrings, and barrette, I said, "Have you ever wondered what was out there just beyond your sight? You can see it but just not quite. You see a movement just out of the corner of your eye, but when you turn to look, it's gone. Well I have a story to tell, and what a story it is. I hope that you can believe, it means the worlds to me."

And as I put my earrings into my ears, a portal opened up behind me and...

Tina M. Engel

He grins evilly as he watches from afar. He drifts in the blackness of the galaxy, encased in a shell of diamond as he watches her explain. As an unnatural giggle escapes his lips he whispers, "Granddaughter, it's time to come home."

His pain is deep, so deep. The torture from the one who rules Hades is endless. But the pain from him, doesn't compare to the pain of losing the woman he wants, and to his brother at that, and knowing that his brother still lives. But there is another pain, so deep that he doesn't recognize it; the loss of innocence, kindness, love and compassion that his mother had tried to teach him, so many years ago. As the tears fall on the wooden tomb encasing him, the area around the cameo softens and the cameo falls to the floor.

Tina M. Engel

There's a tree in my yard,

So big and so strong.

It's old,

It's twisted,

It's gnarly,

It looks sad!

It's been cut,

It's been broken,

But it still stands!

There's a tree in my yard

It's seen so much in its life,

Being a home for so many.

Been through all the storms

Still standing tall.

Does it feel pain?

Does it feel pity?

Does it want to cry?

Still growing to the sky,

There's a tree in my yard,

So big and so strong.

Tina M. Engel

Please feel free to check out my Facebook site

www.facebook.com/tinascorner3

https://www.amazon.com/Tina-M-Engel/e/B01C277GVY

Tina M. Engel was born in Seattle Washington in 1960. Her father served in the Navy, so they lived in many places, in the United States, both East and West coast. Her parents grew up in Ellensburg Washington, which is where Tina raised her two daughters, with the help of her family as well as the community. She worked in the food service/retail business while raising her girls but discovered the love of putting her day dreams down on paper, at a later time in her life. Tina's philosophy: Life's a journey, keep dreaming, reach for the stars and keep the laughter alive!